DEMCO

THE CROSSED SABRES

★

GILBERT MORRIS

BETHANY HOUSE PUBLISHERS
MINNEAPOLIS, MINNESOTA 55438

Published by Bethany House Publishers
A Ministry of Bethany Fellowship, Inc.
6820 Auto Club Road, Minneapolis, Minnesota 55438

Printed in the United States of America

Library of Congress Cataloging-in-Publication Data

Morris, Gilbert.
    The crossed sabres / Gilbert Morris.
        p.   cm. — (The House of Winslow ; bk. 13)
     1. Frontier and pioneer life—West (U.S.)—Fiction. 2. Indians of
North America—Wars—1866–1895—Fiction. I. Title. II. Series:
Morris, Gilbert. House of Winslow ; bk. 13.
PS3563.08742C75   1993
813'.54—dc20   92–21190
ISBN 1–55661–309–1 :   CIP

There are many dark things in this world, but sometimes a man or woman will come into my life who radiates light. This light is always a reflection of the true light, the Lord Jesus Christ.

This book is dedicated to a man who shared that light with me—James Ferguson.

THE HOUSE OF WINSLOW SERIES

★ ★ ★ ★

GILBERT MORRIS spent ten years as a pastor before becoming Professor of English at Ouachita Baptist University in Arkansas and earning a Ph.D. at the University of Arkansas. During the summers of 1984 and 1985 he did postgraduate work at the University of London and is presently the Chairman of General Education at a Christian college in Louisiana. A prolific writer, he has had over 25 scholarly articles and 200 poems published in various periodicals, and over the past years has had more than 20 novels published. His family includes three grown children, and he and his wife live in Baton Rouge, Louisiana.

CONTENTS

PART FOUR
THE FIERY TRIAL

THE HOUSE OF WINSLOW

★ ★ ★ ★

THE
<u>HOUSE OF WINSLOW</u>

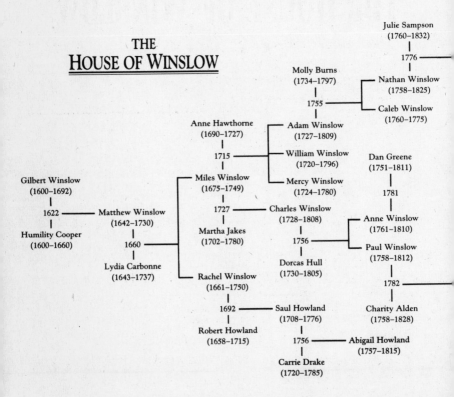

Julie Sampson
(1760–1832)

1776

Molly Burns
(1734–1797)

Nathan Winslow
(1758–1825)

1755

Caleb Winslow
(1760–1775)

Anne Hawthorne
(1690–1727)

Adam Winslow
(1727–1809)

1715

William Winslow
(1720–1796)

Miles Winslow
(1675–1749)

Mercy Winslow
(1724–1780)

Dan Greene
(1751–1811)

Gilbert Winslow
(1600–1692)

1727

Charles Winslow
(1728–1808)

1781

1622

Matthew Winslow
(1642–1730)

Martha Jakes
(1702–1780)

Anne Winslow
(1761–1810)

Humility Cooper
(1600–1660)

1756

1660

Paul Winslow
(1758–1812)

Dorcas Hull
(1730–1805)

Lydia Carbonne
(1643–1737)

1782

Rachel Winslow
(1661–1750)

Charity Alden
(1758–1828)

1692

Saul Howland
(1708–1776)

Robert Howland
(1658–1715)

1756

Abigail Howland
(1757–1815)

Carrie Drake
(1720–1785)

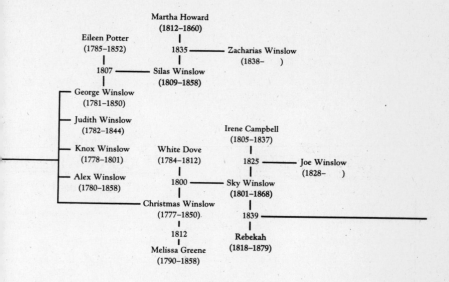

Martha Howard
(1812–1860)

Eileen Potter
(1785–1852)

1835 ———— Zacharias Winslow
(1838–   )

1807 ———— Silas Winslow
(1809–1858)

George Winslow
(1781–1850)

Judith Winslow
(1782–1844)

Irene Campbell
(1805–1837)

Knox Winslow
(1778–1801)

White Dove
(1784–1812)

1825 ———— Joe Winslow
(1828–   )

Alex Winslow
(1780–1858)

1800 ———— Sky Winslow
(1801–1868)

Christmas Winslow
(1777–1850)

1839 ————————————

1812

Rebekah
(1818–1879)

Melissa Greene
(1790–1858)

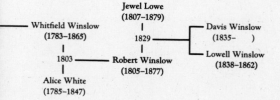

Jewel Lowe
(1807–1879)

Whitfield Winslow
(1783–1865)

Davis Winslow
(1835–   )

1829 ————

1803 ———— Robert Winslow
(1805–1877)

Lowell Winslow
(1838–1862)

Alice White
(1785–1847)

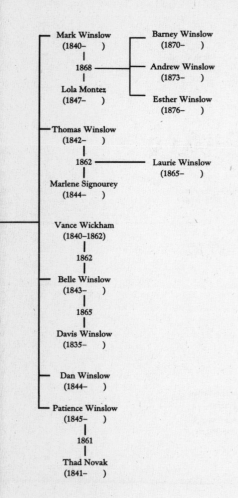

Mark Winslow
(1840–   )

1868

Lola Montez
(1847–   )

Barney Winslow
(1870–   )

Andrew Winslow
(1873–   )

Esther Winslow
(1876–   )

Thomas Winslow
(1842–   )

1862

Marlene Signourey
(1844–   )

Laurie Winslow
(1865–   )

Vance Wickham
(1840–1862)

1862

Belle Winslow
(1843–   )

1865

Davis Winslow
(1835–   )

Dan Winslow
(1844–   )

Patience Winslow
(1845–   )

1861

Thad Novak
(1841–   )

THE
HOUSE OF WINSLOW
(continued)

PART ONE

THE RIVALS

★ ★ ★ ★

CHAPTER ONE

AN END TO EVERYTHING

★ ★ ★ ★

Many families in the South lost everything in the Civil War—including their sons, fathers, and brothers. Some families lost all the men in that tragic conflict.

Sky Winslow and his wife Rebekah had three sons and two sons-in-law fighting in Confederate gray. Except for Vance Wickman, Belle's husband, all came out of the war alive—a miracle in their judgment, for which they never forgot to give thanks.

Most people remembered the night of April 13 as the beginning of the Civil War, but Tom Winslow always remembered the date as the night he first kissed Marlene Signourey. He maneuvered the beautiful young creole girl off the ballroom floor at Belle Maison and into the moonlit garden at exactly five minutes before midnight.

"But, Tom," Marlene Signourey protested, "we mustn't leave the party!" She was not a tall girl, no more than average height, but held herself so erectly that she seemed so. The black dress she wore was adorned with tiny fragments of silver that glittered as they caught the rays of the moon, and a large solitary diamond at her throat refracted that same light as she turned to him. She had the blackest of hair and a pair of black eyes to match—eyes that could glitter with anger, or warm a man if she chose to do so. And she chose to smile at Tom Winslow, for he was tall, handsome, and rich.

Now he laughed at her, his white teeth gleaming against his tanned face. "If I don't keep you hidden from Spence, he'll run off with you to New York," he said.

"Oh, Tom, he's not going to kidnap me!" Marlene protested with a smile. Her lips were small, but full, tempting to a man—as she well knew. Now she pursed them, adding, "I think you are the kidnapper, taking me away from the ball like this!"

"I haven't had a moment alone with you for days," Tom insisted. "Every time I turn around some fellow is in my way."

"And I must go back home in a week," Marlene sighed. She said no more, but with an intensely feminine gesture threw her head back and parted her lips. "I will miss you, Tom!"

Her skin was like translucent ivory in the moonlight, and the fragrance of her perfume came to him. Without thinking, Tom reached out and drew her into his arms. She did not protest, but lifted her lips, and when she leaned against him, the hungers in him grew rife. Her lips were soft and yielding, yet firm, and the touch of them brought a roughness to his caresses. Her arms went around his neck, and she urged him closer for a time, seeming to savour his kiss—and then she pulled away, her lips sliding from his— "Tom—we mustn't!"

"Why not?" he demanded, reaching for her again.

She had the ability to draw a man, yet at the same time keep him at a distance. He had seen her use this on other young men, and now it was his turn. She put her hand on his chest, holding him away—yet there was a light of invitation in her dark eyes as she whispered, "A girl has to be careful, Tom. Most men will take liberties."

"You think I'm that kind of a man?"

She smiled then, and removed her hand. "No," she said, shaking her head. Then she put her hand on his cheek, whispering, "You're too exciting for me, Tom—I don't trust myself with you!"

Winslow quickly kissed her again, but the kiss was never finished, for the door to the garden burst open with a clatter. The sound jarred them, so that they at once stepped back, and when Tom glanced in that direction, he was half angered to see Spencer Grayson approach. He didn't close the door, and the light from the ballroom framed him, a big, solid man with yellow hair and blue eyes.

Tom glared at him, saying at once, "Spence, you've got rotten manners!"

Grayson grinned broadly, then shook his head. "I always did, Tom. You never complained before."

"You never were such a pest to me before!" Spencer Grayson was Tom's best friend, but he spoke the simple truth. Since Marlene had come to visit, Grayson had become a fixture at Belle Maison, Tom's home, always on the scene. He had done this before, and Tom had enjoyed his company. But both of them knew that the creole girl had put a strain on their friendship.

"Didn't mean to intrude," Grayson said easily, "but I thought you'd like to hear the news."

Both Tom and Marlene were now conscious that something was happening, for cheers were coming from the guests. "Has the war started?" Marlene asked quickly, her eyes wide with apprehension.

"Yes. Fort Sumter was fired on last night," Grayson nodded. He sobered then, his handsome face chiseled in the moonlight. He was a cheerful man, but now that was gone. "I'll be leaving soon. Got to get out before I get arrested for treason."

"Don't be a fool, Spence," Tom said abruptly. "Nobody's going to arrest you."

"Don't be too sure, Tom. I've been getting some pretty hard looks from some of your fire-eating friends out there." A taut smile touched Grayson's full lips, and there was a cynical light in his eyes as he added, "You and I will probably be shooting at each other pretty soon, Tom. Have you thought about that?"

Winslow met the man's gaze, thinking of the good times they'd had together. They had practically grown up together, for though Grayson's family lived in New York, they owned a plantation not ten miles from the Winslow place. The two youngsters had roamed the hills, hunting together, and later, had experimented with liquor and flirted with girls together. Without willing it, Tom thought of a time in Richmond when Grayson had stepped aside, giving him first choice with a young brunette they'd both been interested in.

"I guess we've all thought about things like that, Spence," Tom said slowly, hating the idea. He knew that Spence would never fight for the South, for though he'd grown up in Virginia—

at least partly so—his family was of the North. They had spent endless hours arguing about the political quarrels, about slavery—but neither man could change. They were both products of their blood, and Tom knew that what Spencer said about their shooting at each other was a real possibility.

Marlene looked at them as they faced each other, then said quickly, "Oh, don't talk about things like that!" Taking an arm of each man, she said, "Come on, let's go back inside and see what's happening."

As they allowed themselves to be led away, Spence looked down at Marlene's hand on his arm, then to her other hand that was resting lightly on the arm of Tom Winslow. His eyes lifted and he met Tom's gaze. They knew each other very well, and the same thought that came to his own mind, Grayson saw in Winslow's expression.

She'll have to choose, they were both thinking. *Sooner or later— she'll have to decide between us.*

But neither man spoke, and they passed into the ballroom where they were at once surrounded by young men and women bright-eyed with excitement.

★　★　★　★

War came to Richmond like a whirlwind. Schools were broken up and knots of excited men gathered at every street corner. Every patriotic citizen had his house ablaze with a thousand lights, and the dark ones were *marked*. The non-illuminators were dubbed "Yankees," "Abolitionists," and "Black Republicans," and were virtually ostracized. Churches were full on Saturday as women met to ply the needle, cutting out clothes for the soldiers, indulging in talk about the vile usurpers from the North. Snatches of song improvised for the emergency—"Maryland, My Maryland," "John Brown's Body," "There's Life in the Old Land Yet" were sung, and a favorite was written for the times:

> I want to be a soldier,
> And with the soldiers stand,
> A knapsack on my shoulder,
> And a musket in my hand;
> And there beside Jeff Davis,
> So glorious and so brave,

I'll whip the cussed Yankee
And drive him to his grave.

And while the grown-ups were about their business, the
younger rebels were keeping their patriotism warm by *playing*
"Yank" and "Reb" in mock battles. So fervent did these battles
become that there were frequently cuts and bruises to show for
them.

Hatred for the North swelled, and the fire-eating element,
made up largely of country editors, preachers, lawyers, and pol-
iticians-on-the-make, was the most vocal and eloquent. Recrim-
ination and name-calling in private conversation, in public meetings, in editorial columns, from professor's desk and country
pulpit, produced a tide of emotion in those days. An overseer
on a plantation forty miles below New Orleans wrote in his journal:

> This day is sat a part By presedent Jeffereson Davis for
> fasting & prayer owing to the Deplorable condishion ower
> Southern country is In My Prayer Sincerely to God is that
> Every Black Republican in the Hole combined whorl Either
> man woman o chile that is opposed to negro slavery as it
> existed in the Southern confederacy shal be trubled with pes-
> tilents & calamitys of all Kinds & Dragout the Balance of there
> existence in misray Degradation with scarsely food & ray-
> ment enughf to keep sole & Body togeather and O God I pray
> the to Direct a bullet or a bayonet to pirce the Hart of every
> northern soldier that invades the southern Soile & after the
> Body has Rendered up its Traterish Sole gave it a trators re-
> ward a Birth In the Lake of Fire & and Brimstone my honest
> convicksion is that Every man woman & and chile that has
> give aide to the abolishionist are fit Subjects for Hell I all so
> ask the to aide the Sothern Confedercy in mantaining Ower
> rites & establishing the confederate Government Believing in
> this case the prares from the wicked will prevaileth much
> Amen.

Spencer Grayson had found this sample of Southern fire-
eating printed in the Charleston *Mercury*, and had brought it on
his latest visit to Belle Maison. The family had sat down to the
evening meal, and were halfway finished when they heard the

22

sound of a horse coming at a dead run. Sky Winslow glanced out the mullioned windows, then grinned at Tom, saying, "Your friend Spence is here, Tom." He was a smiling man of sixty, with strength in his face and upright figure. He was one-fourth Indian, and that heritage was revealed by his olive skin and high cheek bones. "I may have to ask him to pay rent if he stays around here much longer."

Patience Winslow giggled. At the age of sixteen she was not the beauty that her sister Belle was, and there was an impish streak of humor in her. "Funny how fond Spence has gotten of you lately, isn't it, Tom?"

Tom colored, turned to her and said, "Pet, you keep quiet!" He had been teased about the competition for Marlene Signourey that had heated up between Spence and himself. It had been a joke at first, for the two had often competed for the favors of the local girls. But this was different, as both of them had sensed. The beautiful young creole had gotten into the blood of both men, and though his family didn't realize it yet, Tom was determined to marry her.

Belle was smiling at Tom, for she enjoyed the rivalry. At the age of eighteen, she was considered by most to be the most beautiful girl in the area. In her bright red taffeta dress, she made Pet look like a dowdy sparrow, and even Marlene could not match her for beauty. Now her eyes were bright with mischief, and she asked innocently, "Marlene, isn't Spence taking you to Richmond for the President's reception tonight?"

"Yes, he is," Marlene nodded. She was wearing a purple dress, one which only a woman with her spectacular coloring would dare to wear.

Tom flushed, saying, "I thought I was taking you."

"Oh, I forgot, Tom," Marlene said. "But we can all go together."

"Spence will *love* that," Mark Winslow grinned. He was, at twenty-one, the oldest of the Winslow boys. Winking at Dan, his seventeen-year-old brother, he added, "He's our token Yankee, so we've got to be charitable, don't we?"

Spence came in just in time to hear the last remark, and grinned broadly. He was looking fresh, his cheeks glowing and his eyes bright. Waving a paper, he took the seat that Sky offered, and said, "Let me read you a sample of good old southern charity."

"What's that paper?" Sky asked.

"The Charleston *Mercury*," Spence answered. "It's part of a journal written by an overseer from a plantation near New Orleans. Listen to this—"

He read the crude account of the overseer, then laughed with just a trace of malice, adding, "Now *there's* Christian charity for you!"

"Come on, Spence," Mark protested. "You can't judge the South by one illiterate overseer."

"That's right!" Tom nodded. "Have you read any of the northern newspapers? They're calling out for blood."

Sky listened as the argument ran around the table, and finally said, "Let's eat our meal. I've heard enough war talk for a time."

This was his way, they all understood, of taking the pressure from their guest, and Tom was glad of it. After the meal, he got to Marlene as fast as he could, saying, "Why are you letting Spence take you to the reception?"

"Oh, Tom, don't be angry!" Marlene pouted attractively, patted his cheek, then whispered, "Afterward, you can bring me home. I'll tell Spence it's too far for him."

"All right."

Marlene avoided his attempt to kiss her, laughed and ran away to her room. She spent the next hour getting ready, with Pet coming to "help" her. As she dressed, Marlene listened with amusement to the young girl's patter. Finally Pet asked, "Which one do you like best, Tom or Spence?"

"Oh, I like them both," Marlene smiled as she worked carefully at plucking her eyebrows.

"But you must like one of them best!"

"Why, I don't like to say. They're both fine young men, aren't they? But you probably think Tom is the nicest."

"Well, sure!" Pet nodded emphatically. Then she frowned and pondered a thought that came to her. "Which one would you rather marry?"

Marlene laughed at the girl, saying, "They'd both make good husbands, wouldn't they?"

"But Spence will be going back to New York, Marlene. Everyone says he'll join the Yankee army. You wouldn't marry a Yankee, would you?" She pronounced the word *Yankee* with distaste, and Marlene smiled at her.

"He has a fine family, Pet. Very rich."

"Well, we're rich, too," Pet stated with indignation.

Marlene finished her eyebrows, then came to slip into her hoop. "Help me with this, Pet," she said. The two of them worked at the dress, and only when Marlene was examining herself in the mirror, did she answer. "Yes, your family is well-off, Pet, but have you thought that you might lose it all—if the South loses the war?"

Pet stared at the young woman as if she had uttered a vile obscenity. "That's crazy!" she protested. "How could we lose? Everybody knows that one of our men can whip six Yankees!" She was disturbed by the conversation, and could not find a way to express what was going on in her mind. Finally she said defiantly, "Anyway, getting married is more than money!" With that she flounced out of the room, and Marlene laughed softly under her breath.

Finally she gave herself one more inspection, then nodded, pleased with her appearance. She left the room and found Spence downstairs waiting for her. "Come along, we'll be late," he said, then winked at Tom who was standing with his back to the wall. "Don't wait up for us, Old Boy," he said cheerfully.

When they were in the buggy headed for town, Marlene chided him, "You shouldn't have made fun of Tom like that, Spence."

"Do him good," Grayson laughed. "He needs a little humility."

"I told him he could take me home after the reception—"

"That'll be the day, sweetheart!" Spence grinned. He reached out and pulled her close beside him with a strong arm. "Tom's my best friend—but not where you're concerned!"

They arrived at Richmond to find the city packed. Spence parked the buggy at a livery stable and they had to practically push their way through the throngs to get to the center of the city. When they got to the square, Spence said, "Let's go up on the balcony of that hotel. This is too uncomfortable."

He led her through the lobby, bribed a grinning bellboy to let them use the balcony, and stood there looking down on the square. It was late afternoon, and the air was hot, but that in no way discouraged the crowds below. There was a holiday atmosphere about the affair, as though beginning a war were no more than beginning a hunting season.

They arrived just in time to witness the presentation of a battle flag to a new company that was being formed. This was a common practice, the flag usually being made by one having a heart interest in one of the volunteers. When the flag was completed, there was a presentation, usually at a dress parade, a banquet, a religious assembly, or a mass meeting especially for the ceremony. In most instances oratory flew high, and as Miss Idelea Collens offered the colors on a bunting-draped stand, Spence and Marlene got a full sampling of it:

"Receive then, from your mothers and sisters, from those whose affections greet you, these colors woven by our feeble but reliant hands; and when this bright flag shall float before you on the battlefield, let it not only inspire you with brave and patriotic ambition of a soldier aspiring to his own and his country's honor and glory, but also may it be a sign that cherished loves appeal to you to save them from a fanatical and heartless foe!"

Spence laughed softly, saying in Marlene's ear, "What nonsense!"

"Oh, Spence, be quiet! She means it!" Marlene allowed herself to lean against him, saying, "Look, that sergeant is going to receive the flag."

A color-sergeant had advanced with his corporals to receive the flag, and his response was high-flying indeed: "Ladies, with high-beating hearts and pulses throbbing with emotion, we receive from your hands this beautiful flag, the proud emblem of our young republic. To those who may return from the field of battle bearing this flag in triumph, though perhaps tattered and torn, this incident will always prove a cheering recollection. And to him whose fate it may be to die a soldier's death, this moment brought before his fading view will recall your kind and sympathetic word, he will bless you as his spirit takes its aerial flight. May the God of battles look down upon us as we register a soldier's vow that no stain will ever be found upon thy sacred folds, save the blood of those who attack thee or those who fall in thy defense. Comrades you have heard the pledge, may it ever guide and guard you on the tented field! Let its bright folds inspire you with new strength, nerve your arms, and steel your hearts to deeds of strength and valor!"

A wild yell of exultation rose from the crowd, and since every eye was on the platform, Spence took the occasion to draw Marlene close. She protested, "Oh, Spence—!" but when he released her, she was flustered, and pushed him away, saying, "You're awful, Spencer Grayson!"

"No, I'm just in love with you," he said, and tried to embrace her again, but she pulled away, an arch look in her dark eyes.

"I didn't come here to be kissed by you in full view of all Richmond," she pouted.

"Well, we'll just have to find a better place," he answered, and then they left the balcony and went to supper. He had made reservations at the Elliot, the finest hotel in Richmond, and it was well he did, for every table was taken. During the meal he kept her entertained—something he did well, for he had made a study of pleasing women. He was one of the finest-looking men in the room, his handsome features and tall stature drawing admiring glances from many of the ladies. The reception didn't begin for an hour, so they drank more wine than was proper, and by the time they arrived, Marlene was a little unsteady.

But she recovered quickly, and soon they were moving about, noting that the cream of the newly birthed Confederacy was gathered under the roof. The new president, Jefferson Davis, was a tall Mississippian with austere features, but his wife, Varina, was a beauty!

For over three hours the pair enjoyed the music, managing to slip outside to a convenient garden while the speeches were being made. Finally, Marlene said, "Spence, I've got to get back to Belle Maison."

"You sure you want Tom to take you home?" he asked.

"Yes, it's too long a trip for you."

"All right. I'll go find him. You wait here." He disappeared into the crowd, and Marlene waited until he returned. "He decided not to come," Spence reported. "His brothers came, but they said Tom stayed home to pout. Now, you've got to let me take you home."

She smiled, but was put out with Tom. "Well, if he doesn't care any more than that—"

They left the hotel, walked to the stable and were soon on their way back to Belle Maison. Marlene had had too much to drink, and giggled a good deal. When they got to the house, Spence pulled the buggy to a halt, and for some time they sat in the wagon, laughing and being foolish. He kissed her more than once, but finally she said, "No more, young man! I don't trust either one of us tonight!"

He protested, but when she insisted, he got down and helped her out. The house was dark, and he said as they approached the porch, "They've probably locked you out."

A voice spoke so unexpectedly that both Spence and Marlene started.

"No, the door's not locked."

Tom had been standing in the shadows, and now he came forward. The moonlight revealed the anger on his face, and he said at once, "It's late Marlene. Go to bed."

Spence had a wicked temper, and Tom's sudden appearance caused it to flare. "You get tired of spying on us?"

"Go back to town, Spence. You've had too much to drink."

"I'll go when I get ready!"

"Do as you please then," Tom said shortly. He had gone to town, but it had been an unhappy decision. He had tormented himself with the sight of Spence dancing with Marlene, and then had discovered that they had left. He knew that Spence had devised some way of getting Marlene to let him drive her home. Ordinarily he would have laughed at such a thing, but he was too much in love with Marlene to do that. He had left at once, taken a short cut and arrived at Belle Maison filled with anger. He felt betrayed and wanted to avoid a scene.

But he had a temper of his own, and answered wickedly, "Spence, get in the buggy before I do something I'll regret." He stepped forward and took Marlene's arm, but as he turned, Spence's fist caught him on the neck, and he staggered to the side. At once he was caught by a blow on his cheekbone that drove him to the ground, and he rolled once, then came to his feet. Given his choice, he might have tried to talk to Grayson— but he had no chance, for the other man was driving at him, striking out with all his strength.

Tom slipped the punch, knocking it aside with his arm, and caught Spence with a terrific right hand high on the head. It stopped the other man as suddenly as if he had run into a piling, and as Spence's eyes went blank, Tom dropped his hands, saying, "Let's stop this foolishness—" But he was stopped when a blow caught him in the mouth. He tasted the salty tang of blood, and then was forced to fight back as Grayson came at him like an animal.

The two of them threw blows that struck and drew blood, and Tom was driven across the grass by Grayson's superior weight. He caught one glimpse of Marlene, her hand over her lips and her eyes bright, but then he saw no more. Grayson was taller and stronger, and at first he drove Tom with his powerful blows. Finally, when Tom refused to go down, Spence began to huff, drawing up great gasps of air. Tom stayed away, and the power of his blows began to tell.

Both men were bloody, and Tom knew that his body would be bruised for days where Spence had hammered on his ribs. But there was a blind anger in him that matched that in Spence, and the two of them struck again and again. But it couldn't last, and finally Tom caught Spence with a hard right hand just over the eyebrow. Tom felt his hand collapse and knew he'd broken a bone, but it was the end of the fight, for Grayson went down and lay absolutely still save for his chest that rose and fell rapidly.

"Get in the house!" Tom commanded Marlene, and after one wild look at his bloody face, she wheeled and ran away. Tom stood there, gasping for breath, aware of the pain that was beginning to run along his body.

Standing there looking down at Spence, he knew nothing could ever be the same between them. And sorrow for all the good times that could never come again with this man was a keen blade of regret in him. Finally Spence opened his eyes, and when they focused, Tom got such a look of hatred that he hardly recognized the man.

Grayson got to his feet painfully, then without a word, turned and walked to the buggy. Tom tried to call out, but knew it was hopeless. He had seen Spence like this before, harsh and unforgiving, but never had felt the weight of his anger personally. He watched helplessly as the man got into the buggy, after several unsuccessful tries, then drove off without a single word or look. Then he turned and went into the house, and as he tended to his own hurts, he realized that something had gone out of his life forever. The war and all it implied had worn upon him; now the loss of his best friend weighed heavily on Tom Winslow, and he felt sad that this day marked the end of all things.

CHAPTER TWO

THE FIRES OF WAR

★ ★ ★ ★

Fort Sumter's smoke-stained flag drooped from a broken flag-staff as ninety exhausted men marched out to their ships, drums beating and colors flying. They were angry, hungry, and tired men, but their backs were straight as they marched.

General Beauregard, wearing a hussar sword with a gilded hilt—the gilded metal of the guard twisted into lovelocks and roses—watched them go. Pierre Gustave Toutant Beauregard with his dark, handsome face, posed there, feeling the thrill of victory.

But the fall of Fort Sumter was like a stone falling into a still pond, the ripples spreading over North and South.

In Washington, Abraham Lincoln waited, pacing up and down the White House halls in nightshirt and carpet slippers. He had been called many names, including an ape and a buffoon. The crude small-time politician, a comparative failure at forty, was thrust into the presidency by a series of almost comical political events. His cabinet included Seward and Chase, who hated each other, each believing he should be president instead of Lincoln. When one of Lincoln's aides protested against the disrespect these men showed toward Lincoln, the president smiled, saying, "When I was a boy, if I had just one pumpkin to bump in a sack, it was hard to carry, but if you could get two pumpkins, one in each end of the sack, it balanced things up. Seward and Chase will do for my pair of pumpkins."

In the North, Abraham Lincoln grew tired and discouraged as he faced a task no man could survive. Often he wondered about Jefferson Davis, the president of the Confederacy. He said once, "Davis was born only forty miles from my own birthplace. He got the start of me in age and raising. I guess if you set out to pick one of us two for president, you'd pick him, nine times out of ten."

In the South, Jefferson Davis was as tired as Lincoln. He looked much like John Calhoun, stern and austere. He was brilliant, but his brittle temper and caustic manner prevented him from drawing men to him. His cabinet included Judah B. Benjamin, the dapper Jew; Toombs, the tall, restless Georgian, as fine to look at as a young bull—and as hard to manage; Alex Stephens, vice-president, called "The Pale Star of the Confederacy"; and Mallory, Regan, and Walker.

Neither nation was prepared for war, and for months there was a frantic scurry to put together armies. The Northern newspapers, published by Horace Greeley, tried to force Lincoln into action by running the headline *ON TO RICHMOND!*

Throughout the country the fall of Fort Sumter was felt, and its ripple effect quickly reached Belle Maison and the house of Winslow. It was all Sky and his wife, Rebekah, could do to keep their boys from joining the army immediately. Dan and Tom were persuaded to stay out of it only with great difficulty, but they could do nothing with Mark, who enlisted as soon as Seth Barton had organized the Richmond Blades.

It was not a bad time for Tom, despite the unsettled affairs of the country. Marlene had gone back to New Orleans after Tom's fight with Spence, but had returned a month later for a prolonged stay. Her mother, a widow of fifty years, accompanied her, and the two were fortunate enough to find a small frame house just outside of Richmond. They made a place for themselves in the higher realms of the social world in the city and showed no inclination to return to New Orleans. This delighted Tom, who immediately resumed his courtship with Marlene.

Spence Grayson, to everyone's surprise, did not return to his home in New York at the outbreak of the war. At his father's request, Spence had stayed in Virginia to sell off their holdings, which were considerable. Though he was an alien in a strange land, he was not treated badly, as were others who lacked his wealth and his ability with a dueling pistol. Even the aristocracy of the Confederacy, whom he met at the home of the Chesnuts, treated him with formal courtesy.

Spence's relationship with Tom, however, had changed, partly because the Northerner continued his pursuit of Marlene Signourey.

Their first meeting after the brutal fight occurred at a banquet. Tom had known it would happen and had sought out Spence at once. Extending his hand, he said, "Sorry, Spence." Grayson had taken it quickly, nodded and replied, "Let's forget it, Tom."

But Tom Winslow knew that it would never be forgotten, no matter how many times they smiled and shook hands. There was a hard light in Spence's eyes that had not been there before, and Tom knew something had died that night they had fought in the darkness at Belle Maison.

Marlene met both of them with smiles, attended the theater with Spence and went to Belle Maison often, spending much time with Belle Winslow. The two young women were the same age, and drew the young soldiers like flies. At every ball—and there were many in the days preceding the first battle at Manassas—Tom found himself thrown into Spence's company often, for the aristocratic society of Richmond was not large.

The beginning of July, it became obvious to everyone that the first great battle of the war was edging closer. Most of Tom's friends had joined the Richmond Blades, where his brother Mark was an officer, so wherever Tom went the conversation was all strategy and battles and arms. He felt left out, and though no one belittled him—as they had some others—Tom felt left behind.

This sense of isolation only compounded one Friday when a review of the army was to take place. As he watched Mark dress in his uniform, noting the excitement and eagerness that swept him, Tom's desire to be a part of it became even stronger.

Dan, too, was affected. At breakfast that day, he begged once again for permission to enlist, but both parents were adamant.

"I'll be left out!" Dan moaned. "It'll all be over before I can join the rest!"

Sky's lips tightened as he answered bleakly, "That's your least worry, Dan. This thing won't be settled by one battle."

Later as they drove to the parade ground, Sky asked, "What are you going to do with that young woman, Tom?"

The question startled Tom, for his father rarely addressed such intimate affairs. He had brought his sons and daughters up to be independent, and though he was always available to them, he refused to meddle in their personal affairs.

"Why, I guess I'm going to try to marry her," Tom blurted out. Encouraged by his father's interest, he said, "It's what I've wanted to do, but I'm not sure if she'll have me."

Sky looked out across the rolling hills, noting the gap the carriage would pass through. He was thinking of the day when a band of Sioux might be on the other side, for the years had not taken away all his caution. Now he smiled at his own fancies, but sobered as he turned to glance at his son. He loved this tall, dark son of his, though it was difficult for him to put it into words. The men of his world rarely spoke about such things, considering it to be a weakness. But now he wanted to put his arm around his son's broad shoulders, to take away some of the burden that had come to him.

"Well, she might not," Sky said finally, speaking slowly. "Women are hard to figure out. But if she did, it's not the best time in the world to begin a family."

"No, I guess not." Tom sat there swaying with the motion of the carriage, thinking of his father's statement. Finally he said, "I guess it wasn't much better when you and mother got married. It was pretty wild in those days, wasn't it?"

"Wild enough," Sky mused; his eyes, blue as the sky overhead, were serious. "Always an Indian or two around to put an arrow in your liver. Not as bad as your grandfather had it, though. He lived on the verge of trouble all his life." He thought of his father, Christmas Winslow, born at Valley Forge during that terrible winter when Washington's ragged Continentals froze and starved. Washington himself had come by to see the new baby and to congratulate the father, Nathan Winslow.

"Well, sir," Tom said after waiting for several minutes with no response, "I guess there's no way to be safe, is there? A man can't hide in a hole."

"No, he can't. And no man can make a decision for another one, either." Sky stared at the hills, then turned his face toward Tom, a smile on his lips. "Whatever you do, son, stick with it. That's what counts. Any man can start something—but the real test comes when you're facing difficulty." He uttered a quiet chuckle. "I'm not much good at giving advice, am I, Tom? But you've got good blood in you. If you make a mistake and get floored, why, get up, wipe the blood off and go at it again."

Tom stared at his father, filled with a sudden knowledge that this man loved him, though he could not put it into words. He felt a lump in his throat, waited until it went away, then said, "I'm joining the Blades, sir."

Sky nodded. "Thought you might be. Dan, he'll be right behind you. Can't sit on a young fellow for long, not one with any spirit. Your mother and I will be praying for all three of you boys."

They spoke no more of the matter, but when they got out of the carriage, Tom put his hand out awkwardly, saying, "I—I appreciate it, sir, your talking to me like this." Then he whirled around and walked away rapidly.

Rebekah, who had come in another carriage with the rest of the family, came to stand beside Sky. "He's joining up, isn't he?"

"Yes."

She was a strong woman, this wife of Sky Winslow. There were no tears in her eyes, but she put her hand on his arm for support, whispering, "We'll have to lean on each other—and on God." Then she made herself smile, turning to say, "Hurry up, Pet! We want to get a good place to watch the parade."

Pet had been talking to Thad Novak, a young man who had been taken in by the Winslows. "Thad and Dan and I are going to walk around before the parade starts," she called out, and led the young man off.

Sky laughed. "Ever since she nursed that young man back to health, she acts as if he belongs to her! Well, come along, let's see what we've got in the way of an army."

"I'm going to find Mark," Tom said. When he saw him, Tom blurted out, "I'm joining the Blades. I just told Father."

Mark bit his lip nervously, then asked, "What did he say?"

"It was all right. Said that Dan would be in this thing before it's over."

Mark shook his head. "He's too young. We'll have to try to keep him out."

"We won't have any luck," Tom remarked. "I guess all us Winslows are too stubborn."

"It seems so. Well, be at camp in the morning and we'll sign you up."

"All right."

Tom left the parade ground and moved through the crowd until he found Marlene and her mother, seated in cane-bottomed chairs placed along the edge of the wide grounds.

"Hello, Thomas," Mrs. Signourey greeted cheerily when Tom approached. "We've been expecting you."

Tom's face broke into a smile. He liked Marlene's mother. "How'd you get the good seats?"

"Spence got them for us somehow," Mrs. Signourey shrugged. "He's gone to get some lemonade."

He groaned inwardly at the news. "Sure," he nodded. "I'm going to find my folks. Will I see you after the review, Marlene?"

"Why, of course!" She seemed surprised that he had asked. "You're coming to our house for a little snack. Come and bring Mother and me home."

"All right."

Tom left, and taking a place far across the field he watched as Spence returned with a pitcher and glasses. From his vantage point, Tom had to admit the three made a pretty picture in the crowd.

The review was impressive, and Tom gave careful attention to the Richmond Blades. Shelby Lee, the nephew of General Robert E. Lee, was their captain and had trained them well. As they marched across the field with precision, Tom wished he were in their ranks.

President Davis and several other prominent statesmen spoke afterward—all presenting much the same: If the South were to win, everyone would have to give his best. There was a performance by the military band, and for a final flourish, Jeb Stuart's cavalry rode down the field, first in perfect order, then in a wild sabre-brandishing charge spiced with high yelping cries.

The crowd rose to its feet, screaming approval, and Tom

found himself stirred along with them.

Why not do it now? The thought came to him suddenly, and he knew he could never be content unless he joined the army. Without hesitation he shoved his way through the crowd until he found Captain Shelby Lee. "Captain Lee," he said at once, "I've got to talk to you."

"Why, certainly, Mr. Winslow. What can I do for you?"

"I want to join the Blades—right away!"

Surprised, he asked, "Have you talked with your father about this?"

"Yes. He agrees, sir, and I'd like to enlist at once."

Lee smiled at Tom's urgency. "Well, I think that can be arranged. Come along and you can fill out the papers now." As they made their way to the office, Lee said, "I'm pleased to have you, of course, and your brother will be happy as well. But you won't get much training, I'm afraid. It looks as though we may be moving out in a week."

"I'll be happy to be going with you, sir," Tom replied.

He was given a hurried physical, then filled out several papers. "You are now a private in the Richmond Blades, Third Virginia Infantry," Captain Lee said. "Glad to have you."

Tom walked away, dazed by what he had done. He had always been a little impulsive, but this thing had exploded in his face. Yet he felt the excitement build up in him and could hardly keep still as he pictured his new life. But—tomorrow! How could he tell his mother?

And Marlene? The possibility of losing her hit him. *I'll be off in a war—and Spence will be here. And I know what he'll be doing!*

The thought disturbed him as he hurried to get one of his family's carriages and pick up Marlene and her mother. When they arrived at the Signourey home, he was dismayed to discover that at least thirty people were there for the "little" snack the two had planned. Spence was among them, and it was apparent that he had no intention of leaving early.

Tom endured the meal and the rest of the evening, but it was after ten before the crowd thinned out.

Knowing that Spence would be the last to leave, Tom followed Marlene into the kitchen when he saw her in the doorway.

He caught her hand, ignoring her gasp of surprise, and rushed her out into the back garden.

"Tom! I can't leave!" Marlene protested. "My guests—!"

"Come on," Tom interrupted. "I need to talk to you, and I can't do it here!" He tugged at her hand, pulling her around a hedge that bordered the small house, to a lane that led into a grove of small trees. When they reached the grove, he stopped and turned to face her.

"I couldn't stand any more people," he said, then added, "You look so beautiful!"

"Why—Tom!" she exclaimed, surprised at his compliment. He had paid her few compliments, and coming so abruptly, she wondered what produced it. "You ought to say such things more often," she smiled.

"Like Spence?" Tom asked, and immediately regretted it. "I wish I could say such things to you. And I'll learn."

"Are you going to take lessons?" Marlene laughed at him. "Don't let me hear of you finding another woman to practice on!"

"Why would I do that when I have you?" She made an enticing picture, and he put his arms around her. She didn't resist, but after they kissed, she asked, "You're behaving very strangely. What is it, Tom?"

He lifted her hand to his lips and kissed it. "Two things, Marlene. I'm leaving tomorrow. I joined the Blades today."

"Oh, Tom—!"

He pressed his fingers over her lips, muffling her voice. "The other thing is more important." He dropped his hand from her lips and said simply, "Marlene, you know how I feel. I love you. Will you marry me?"

"Why, Tom! This is all so—so wild! I can't make a decision so quickly." She had expected his proposal for some time, but this caught her off guard.

He drew her close, whispering, "It will have to be quick, because the Company will be leaving soon. I wish I'd asked you earlier, but I was afraid you'd turn me down. Could we be engaged? We'll have time, and as soon as I get leave, you can set the date."

Marlene was moved by the proposal, for she was a young

woman of quick emotions. She wanted to marry, and Tom Winslow had been on her mind for a long time. He had everything, including looks and money. And he would be in the Blades! She envisioned herself walking under the swords of the officers, wearing her white dress, and it pleased her.

"Yes, Tom, we can be engaged," she whispered, wrapping her arms around his neck as he pulled her into his arms. As he kissed her, she had some disturbing thoughts about Spence, but brushed them away. Finally she pulled away, saying, "Come along! We've got to tell Mother!"

And Spence, Tom thought but did not speak the words. When they broke the news, everyone in the room was looking at Marlene—everyone except Spence, Tom noted. Then Spence's gaze shifted between Tom and Marlene. There was a blankness in his stare when he looked at Tom, but he came at once, knowing that others were watching for his reaction.

"Congratulations, Tom," he said evenly, a smile on his lips. "I confess you to be the better man."

"Thanks, Spence," Tom replied. "I was lucky."

★　★　★　★

But the wedding was postponed. Bloody Manassas came, and Tom fought with the Blades through the worst of it. Then the Third Virginia was sent to the Valley. The months moved by, and only once did Tom return to Richmond—only to find that Marlene had returned to New Orleans.

"Her grandmother is very ill," Belle told him when he arrived at Belle Maison. "Her mother's mother, that is. They had to leave two weeks ago. I'm sorry, Tom. Marlene longs to see you." She hesitated for a moment. "Have you heard about Spence?"

"No, what about him?"

"He's a lieutenant in the Yankee army—on General Butler's staff."

"Well, I don't guess we'll be shooting at each other, then."

"But Butler's going to try to take New Orleans—with the help of the Yankee navy." She almost added, *And if New Orleans falls, Marlene will be there with Spence!* But she caught herself, saying only, "Take care of yourself, Tom."

Time dragged on, and in April 1862, two admirals, Porter and

Farragut, ran the batteries at New Orleans, forcing the city to surrender on the twenty-fifth.

Meanwhile, Spence was fighting in the Union Army, for General McClelland had brought a huge army by boat to overwhelm Richmond. The Battle of the Seven Days cost both sides dearly, and when McClelland finally retreated—partly as a result of Stonewall Jackson's Valley Campaign—both armies were exhausted.

The Richmond Blades were worn thin, and were ordered to Richmond to refit and rest up. When they reached the city, Tom got leave and went at once to Belle Maison. He pulled up in front of the house, and to his shock, instead of being greeted by his mother, it was Marlene who came running down the path to throw herself into his arms, crying, "Tom! Tom—!"

Confused and bewildered, he held her, and finally she kissed him. "Tom, I thought I'd lost *you!*"

"Marlene, how long have you been here? I thought you were in New Orleans."

"My grandmother died, Tom—and then my mother." Tears welled into her eyes, and she sobbed wildly. "I was so afraid, and then I came here—"

"Don't cry, sweetheart," he soothed. "I'm here now."

"Tom, will we be married right away?"

"All right. Sunday, in the church," he said, a warmth of great joy filling him. "By George, I thought I'd lost you!"

They were married the following Sunday, Sky insisting on paying for everything. A glorious two-week honeymoon was spent in a small village on the coast away from the war. There Tom experienced such happiness he had only dreamed of. Marlene clung to him with a fierce desire.

The days sped by, and on their way back to Richmond, Tom finally asked, "Have you heard from Spence?"

She was startled by the question, then said in a strange, dead tone, "Didn't you know, Tom? He was killed in action."

The words hit him like a sledge hammer. He put his arm around Marlene, thinking of the good days with the big blond man. Finally he said quietly, "I'll miss him."

"So will I," Marlene whispered, and then he saw a single tear run down her cheek.

CHAPTER THREE

THE WRONG MAN

★   ★   ★   ★

From the firing of the first shot at Fort Sumter, both North and South knew there was no turning back. The struggle was not like other wars, for after the last guns were fired in foreign wars, the troops could pack up and return home. This was a *civil war*—a war within a family, brother against brother. In some respects it was like a lovers' quarrel, in that once the actual fighting is done, the lovers must become reconciled. The North and the South would have to learn to live together after the shooting and the tumult faded.

But during the years from the first bloody battle at Manassas all the way to the bitter end at Appomattox, there was little time to think of what would come *after* the war. For despite the heavy advantages of the North in men and arms, it took everything both sides could muster simply to keep going forward.

The North seemed to have the best of it, for they possessed all the great material factors. These advantages, important from the beginning, became more significant as the conflict continued and the superior economy of the North became geared for war production. They had a larger manpower reservoir from which to draw men, for there were 23 states still in the Union with a population of 22 million. There were only 11 Confederate states with a population of about 9 million, of whom 3.5 million were slaves.

In industrial production, the North had an even greater advantage, for Southern industry in areas necessary for conducting a war was almost nonexistent. In the first year of the war, Northern factories converted to war production; but throughout the struggle, the South had to rely on Europe for its arsenal.

In addition to industrial superiority, the North had a transportation system superior in every respect to that of the South. The North had, for example, 20,000 miles of railroads, while the Confederacy, which comprised at least as large a land area, had only 10,000 miles. As the war continued the Confederate railroad system steadily deteriorated, and by the last year and a half of the struggle it had almost collapsed.

But all this did not mean that the South had no chance to win the war. For one thing, it was fighting a defensive war on its own land and had the advantage of familiarity with the territory. It was fighting for its very existence, while the Northern public was far less united in support of the war. All throughout the war the North's will to continue the war wavered, and at any point the struggle might have been called off.

But all of this was theory during the war, and Tom Winslow and others in the Blades thought little about the pros and cons. As the years rolled by, and names such as Shiloh, Antietam, and Gettysburg became a part of the language, the men in gray moved from one bloody battlefield to another. Their ranks grew thin, for when a man fell, there was no replacement.

Slowly the Army of Northern Virginia was driven back by Grant, whose troops suffered terrible losses. Finally in September of 1864, Lee's army was entrenched at Petersburg, which everyone knew was the last stand of the Southern Confederacy. If Petersburg fell, the Federals could march into Richmond at will.

The Third Virginia formed part of Lee's line, and Tom and the other tattered veterans settled down to trench warfare. It was a grubby life, wallowing in mud with moccasins slithering around in a man's boots; but to lift a head above the trench was to invite sudden death at the hands of the Federal sharpshooters. At the beginning of the month the supply of corn was exhausted, and hunger stalked the trenches. Wade Hampton brought temporary relief by a daring raid behind the Union lines with 4,000 cavalry, capturing 2,400 head of cattle and 300 troopers.

Tom had risen to sergeant, and when he scrambled back to headquarters after a summons, he found Mark waiting for him, a smile on Mark's face. "Keep your head down, Tom," he said. "The Yanks have been lobbing shells over this morning."

"You hear anything from home?" Tom asked. He had heard nothing from Marlene in months, and the strain showed on his lean face.

"Got a letter from the folks," Mark nodded, pulling an envelope from his pocket. "It's for both of us." He watched while Tom opened it with unsteady hands, knowing that it would bring him no peace. *Blast that woman,* he thought savagely. *The least she could do is write!* He had watched Tom deteriorate since his marriage, but had been helpless to do anything. At first, he remembered, Marlene had written regularly, but then the letters slowed, and finally stopped altogether. Tom had been home only twice in the last two years, and both times he had returned with a spirit dulled by his visit.

Tom looked up, his face empty. "Sounds like things are bad at home." He didn't mention Marlene, but Mark knew what he was thinking.

"Look, Tom," Mark said, "Colonel Lee wants to give some of the men leaves. Usually an aide gets that little plum, but Shelby owes me a favor. I talked to him and he agreed. You'll leave tomorrow at dawn."

Excitement flared in Tom's eyes. "How long can I have, Mark?"

"Depends on how soon we go into action, but I think you can count on at least a week."

Tom smiled, then looked down to hide the expression on his face. "Thanks, Mark."

"Sure. When you see the folks, don't tell them how bad things are. Now, we've just got a Christmas present from Wade Hampton." He explained about the raid, adding, "Get over to the quartermaster for your share of the beef."

Tom moved quickly, arguing the sergeant in charge of distributing the beef out of a larger share than he first offered. He put the quarter of beef, still dripping with blood, into a sack, then made his way back to the trenches. The first man he saw was Lieutenant Thad Novak, and he grinned, saying, "Christmas gift, Lieutenant!"

Novak, a dark young man who'd gotten a brevet promotion from General Lee for his bravery at Antietam, stared at the sack. "Tom, that's not something to *eat*, is it?" Novak continued staring as Tom shook the meat out of the sack, then said, "Thank you, Jesus!"

"Well, sure, but I guess General Hampton was the instrument of the Lord this time." Mark explained about the raid, and then Novak called out, "Dooley—come out here."

At his call, a short, undersized soldier popped up, ran across the opening, dodging like a jackrabbit when musket balls made miniature geysers in the mud. He threw himself headfirst into the trench where the two men stood, and after wiping the mud from his eyes, saw the meat.

"Well, I wish to my never!" he exclaimed in a high-pitched voice. "I do believe I smell something to eat!" Scrambling to his feet, he grabbed the beef. "You fellers get the table set, and put out the best silver. I'll have this little darlin' cooked 'fore you can git done!"

As Dooley scurried away to begin cooking, Tom said, "Just talked to Mark. I'm going to Richmond as a courier."

Novak gave Tom a quick glance, for he was well aware of Tom's marital problems. But he said only, "Tell Pet I'm fine. And give my best to all the folks."

"Sure, Thad." Tom hesitated, then added, "Lots of our fellows have gone home and haven't come back."

"That's right," Novak said evenly. He had a face that was Slavic, with a pair of dark eyes and stiff black hair. He had come to Belle Maison right before the war broke out, a fugitive from the North. He had been taken in by the Winslows, and in a most unlikely scenario had fallen in love with Patience and she with him. Even more unlikely was the truth that had emerged, that he was a distant relative of the Winslows. Now he was a part of the family, and a fine soldier. He was fond of Tom and wanted to help, but there was little anyone could do about another man's marriage.

Tom lifted his gaze to meet that of Novak, and the pain was evident to the lieutenant. "Thad, you and Pet get along so well. Why can't Marlene and I make it? What little time we've had together has been pretty bad." He bit his lip, then shook his head, despondency in every line of his lean body. "She wants something from me that I just can't seem to give her."

Thad Novak was a quiet-spoken young man, not given to sermonizing. Yet looking at the misery in his brother-in-law's eyes, he felt a strong urge to say something that had long been in him. "Tom, when Pet and I got married, neither of us knew anything—I mean *nothing*! I'd never even seen a happy marriage until I got here and saw your parents. What I did, Tom, was look at them—and I think that's the best advice I can give you. You know what I'm talking about, I guess. They're both fine Christians, and they learned somewhere along the line to put God first—even before each other. Your father told me about that before Pet and I got married. He said if I put her first, I'd likely lose her. But if I put God first, I'd have God *and her*."

Tom shook his head slowly. "I've never known God, Thad. It's not my folks' fault. They've always taught all of us to go to church and to pray. But somehow—it's never been real to me." His lips twisted and he added, "Nor to Marlene. We never talk about such things."

"Maybe it's time you did," Thad suggested gently. "Go talk to your parents, Tom. Get Christ in your own life—and then you can think about Marlene and your marriage."

Tom nodded, but there was no hope in his expression. The next morning after he left for Richmond, Thad spoke to Mark about it. "He's hurting real bad, Mark. If something doesn't change, he's liable not to make it."

Mark knew what he meant, for both of them had seen men lose their drive—which often led to their deaths—when their wives left them. "I know, Thad. I put a letter to Father in with other letters. Maybe he can help Tom. But I don't know about Marlene. She's never been happy at Belle Maison. Seems like she's always wanted something else, but I don't know what."

Thad hesitated, then asked cautiously, "Mark, have you ever thought that Tom married the wrong woman?"

Mark chewed his lower lip, then nodded. "Yes, I've thought

about it, but there's nothing to be done, Thad."

"Except to pray." Thad thought of his own wife and the warm love they shared. "A man's never complete unless he has a good woman."

★　★　★　★

Richmond looked little like the city Tom had last seen. The men and women who walked its streets wore haggard faces and clothing that was patched. There was an air of despondency that hung over the place, and after Tom delivered his leather bag filled with dispatches to the adjutant, he was glad to ride out toward the open country.

But an early fall had stripped the leaves from the trees, leaving the limbs bare and the sparse grass dead and brown. It was a stark countryside, and the few travelers he passed gave him no more than a slight nod. The small number of horses and mules he saw were lank skeletons, for all the cream of the stock had long ago been sent to the army.

He turned off the main road, anxious to see Belle Maison, and when it came into view, he kicked his mount into a fast trot, the best the animal could manage. The sight of the white columns that spanned the front of the house brought a light into his eyes, and he pulled the jaded horse up, throwing the reins down and running toward the house.

"Anybody here?" he called as he took the steps two at a time. The front door flew open, and his mother met him halfway with outstretched arms. He caught her to him, holding her thin frame. He noticed she'd lost weight, and when she released her grip and moved back, he saw that the times had brought lines into her face.

"Tom—why didn't you write us?"

"Guess I'm the mailman, Mother," he grinned. Then he looked over her shoulder and saw Marlene standing at the top of the stairs. He released his mother, ran up the steps, and put his arms out. She was as beautiful as ever, though paler than he remembered. He could only call her name over and over as he held her hair against his face.

She didn't speak, so finally he loosened his grip and leaned back to look into her face. Her black eyes were wide and there was an air of vulnerability about her that he could not quite understand. "It's good to see you, Tom," she said quietly. "Can you stay long?"

"No, I only have a few days," he replied. He wanted to crush her in a wild embrace and kiss her, but the knowledge that his mother was watching made him refrain. "You look well, more beautiful than ever."

She smiled briefly. "Come along. You must be hungry."

Rebekah had remained still, giving the pair their moment of privacy, but something about their restraint brought a shadow into her eyes. She shook it off, saying, "You two visit. Pet and I'll have something ready soon."

She went back into the house, meeting Pet, who had seen Tom from an upstairs window. "Mother—it's Tom, isn't it?" she asked, and would have gone into the library where the pair had gone.

"Give them a minute, Pet," Rebekah urged. "He only has a little time. We can get the news from him later about Mark and Thad."

Pet gave her a quick look, for she was a very discerning young woman. "What's wrong, Mother? It's not something about Thad, is it?"

"Oh no, Pet!" Rebekah said quickly. "If there'd been anything wrong with the boys, Tom would have told us at once. It's just—"

Pet saw that her mother was struggling with something, and she thought she knew what it was. "Did Marlene seem glad to see him?"

"Not as glad as I'd have liked."

Pet glanced toward the library. "She's not talked about him for weeks. What's wrong between them?"

"I don't know, Pet," Rebekah said. "I've tried to talk to her, to give her a chance to tell me what the problem is. But she's shut up to me, refuses to even speak of trouble." She lifted a hand to her brow, seeming to brush away the thoughts that came to her, then said with a shake of her head, "Come now, we've got to make his visit as nice as we can. Let's put out the best we have."

"I'll go out to kill Fed," Pet said with a determined nod. "He's the only chicken we got that'll feed us all."

Rebekah smiled slightly. "He'll be giving his life for a good cause. I'll get the dumplings started." The two women plunged ahead with their preparations, and when it was all on the table, Pet said, "I'll go call them for supper." She ran down the hall to the stairs, ran halfway up, and called out, "Tom! Tom! You and Marlene better come and get supper! Hurry up, because I can eat it all!"

She stood waiting with a smile, for Tom had always been a favorite of hers. She heard the door to the bedroom open, then close, and then Tom came around the landing and she ran up to greet him. "Tom!" she cried and threw herself into his arms. She held him fiercely, the tears rising despite her determination to keep them back.

"Well, now—" Tom said, holding her tightly, then pulling her back and kissing her on the cheek. He held her at arms' length, studied her, and shook his head. "I wish ol' Thad were here. He'd do a better job of kissing you than I can."

He put his arm around her and started down the stairs. Pet looked back, asking, "Isn't Marlene coming?"

"Oh, she'll be along soon. Said not to wait supper for her."

"Oh." Pet said no more, but saw that his face was set and that the smile on his lips didn't reach his eyes. *Something's wrong*, she thought, but said only, "Of course. Now, come on and let me introduce you to Fed."

"Fed? Who's that?"

He found out as they sat down to the table, for his sister waved a hand toward the huge platter of fried chicken. "This is Fed," she grinned. "His full name was Southern Confederacy, but that was too much of a mouthful, so we just shortened it to 'Fed.' "

Tom laughed. "Well, give me one of his drumsticks. He's about to join up with the Third Virginia!"

The meal was excellent—Fed, biscuits, baked potatoes, sweet potato pie, and a bubbling dish of blackberry cobbler, all washed down with sweet milk. Both women noticed that Tom ate little despite his gaunt face and lanky form. He kept looking toward the door, and finally said, "Marlene wasn't feeling too well."

"There's been some kind of fever going around," Rebekah replied quickly. "I expect she's got a touch of it." Then she changed the subject. "I wish your father had been here. He'll be sick when he hears he missed you."

"Tell us about Thad and Mark," Pet said, and for the next hour Tom spoke of the two, giving every detail he could think of. After a while he said, "I'm talked dry! You two tell me what's been going on here. When I get back those two will drive me crazy wanting to know everything. And you'd better get your letters written for me to take back."

The evening ended early. "I'd better go see about Marlene," Tom said, "and I'm pretty tired, so I guess I'll just go to bed."

"Yes, and sleep late tomorrow," Rebekah suggested. She kissed him good-night and gave him a quick hug. Pet got her kiss, then Tom left and the two women began to clear the tables, helped by Dulcie and one of the other house servants. When that was done, they sat down in the kitchen, speaking of the things Tom had said, but both of them were troubled.

Finally Pet said, "Mother, isn't there something we can do?"

"Sometimes we can help people," Rebekah said slowly. "But unless a person wants help, there's not a blessed thing to do!"

Upstairs, Tom Winslow was having the hardest time of his life. Marlene was standing with her back to the wall, her eyes cold as she said, "Don't put your hands on me—not ever again!"

When he and Marlene went to the bedroom that afternoon, Tom had been so hungry for her touch that he had made love to her at once. So frantic had he been that he was only vaguely aware of her protests, but afterward she had turned from him, crying bitterly and refusing to speak to him. He had stood there, white and shaken, unable to get her to say a word. Finally he had gone down and gotten through the meal, but all the time he was hoping that when he returned, she would be different.

But she had been even more adamant, and now he cried, "Marlene, what in the world is *wrong*?"

She gave him a stony look and finally said wearily, "I wish I'd never met you!"

"I thought you loved me!"

"I thought so too—at first. But I hate this place!"

Tom stared at her, stunned and confused. "Honey, we don't have to stay here. After the war we can go anywhere you say."

"After the war!" Marlene cried. "When that happens, I'll be

far from here!" She moved toward the door, edging around him as if he were a dangerous animal. When she opened the door, she paused and gave him a look he never forgot. "Forget about me, Tom. I'm not for you!"

She closed the door—and for the next two days she smiled in public, but once the bedroom door shut, she refused to speak. Tom slept on the floor for two nights, and on the third morning, he saddled his horse. He kissed his mother and Pet goodbye, then turned to Marlene.

"Goodbye, Tom," she said, offering her cheek. "Be careful."

"All right." Swinging onto the saddle, he rode away, looking back only once. His mother and Pet waved, but his wife stood like a statue.

And that was the last time he saw her until the war was over . . .

★   ★   ★   ★

When Tom stacked his musket at Appomattox on Sunday, April 9, 1865, he was one of the 7 left alive out of the 120 men who had enlisted in Company A in 1861. He joined his brothers, Mark and Dan, his brother-in-law Thad Novak and his friend Dooley Young, and the five walked back to Virginia. None of them had much to say, for the last months of the war had drained them.

It took a long time to get back to Richmond, and when they arrived, the sight of the city stunned them. Even after the horrors they had seen, it was unbelievable what the war had done to the proud city—nothing but gutted streets and skeletons of buildings remained.

"I hope the Yanks didn't burn the house," Thad muttered, voicing the others' thoughts.

Dooley left them to go to his own home, and the four men continued on. When they finally turned off the main road, there stood the house! With a cry of joy they broke into a run across the green grass.

As they neared the house, Sky, Rebekah, and Pet flung the door open and rushed to meet them, followed by some of the faithful blacks, mostly aged ones, who had not left.

Immediately Tom noted that Marlene was not among them.

He had not heard from her, and the cautious letters he received from his mother and Pet hinted that she had been unsettled—especially after she discovered she was expecting a baby. The news that he was to be a father had been exciting, thinking that a child might renew his relationship with Marlene. But as time went on and she had not written, hope had dulled.

"Where's Marlene?" he asked.

Rebekah pulled him aside as the others went inside. "Tom, she's not here."

"Not here? Where is she?"

Rebekah felt the pain in her son as though it were her own. She had prayed for guidance in telling him about his wife, but there was no easy way.

"She left here four months ago. We haven't heard a word from her."

"But . . . what about the baby?" Tom said hoarsely. "She can't be alone!"

"Tom," his mother said gently, "she's . . . not alone." He stared at her uncomprehendingly, and Rebekah forced herself to go on. "Your father did everything he could to trace her, but all he could find out was that she left on the train . . . with a man. A couple, the woman fitting Marlene's description, got as far as New Orleans."

Speechless and stunned, Tom tried to gather his thoughts together. Finally he said, "I'm going to find her. If she doesn't want me, that's up to her. But the child will be mine!"

"I thought you would," Rebekah nodded. "But remember, Tom, it'll be her child, too. Don't do anything foolish."

The agony in his heart registered in his eyes as he groaned, "What could I do more foolish than what I've already done?"

The next two months he spent recuperating, getting his strength back. He hadn't realized how utterly spent he was—emotionally and physically. He said little, listened a great deal, and as he grew stronger he began doing tasks around the place.

During that time, he watched Pet and Thad, happy for them, but saddened to know that the love they had would never come to him. His sister Belle, who had been so filled with bitterness when her husband had been killed at Antietam, had found happiness with Davis Winslow, a distant relative. Tom liked his new brother-in-law, and was happy when Belle's father-in-law, a wealthy man, financed the rebuilding of the plantation. He'd been worried about his parents, and was grateful that they were being cared for.

Mark, he saw, was restless, and knew that his older brother would never be satisfied to stay at Belle Maison. Nor would Dan. He had already told the family he was going to Texas. Though the war had not killed the brothers, it had somehow shattered the ties.

The day arrived when Tom was ready to leave. In his heart he knew he would not see his brothers for a long time—perhaps for good. He bade them goodbye and then turned to his folks.

"Come back if you can, Tom. We'll be here," his father said, forcing some money into his son's hand as he left.

"Yes, sir, I will."

He boarded the train for New Orleans and began his search for Marlene. It was a cold trail, for her parents were dead, and he could locate no other relatives, but he continued his pursuit. For weeks he walked the streets, sometimes approaching strangers to ask if they had seen the woman whose picture he carried. Most of them looked at him with compassion but could give him no information.

By now his money was running low, and just as he was convinced that he was on the wrong trail, he got a lead.

Tom had become acquainted with the owner of Mack's Cafe, and one June evening as he stopped in for supper, Mack waved him to one side, saying excitedly, "Tom, I think maybe I got something on your wife!"

Mack's Cafe was not fancy, but the food was good and cheap. Mack himself was a thickset Irishman, red-faced and pugnacious. He'd felt sorry for Tom, having had a daughter run away under similar circumstances. He'd kept a copy of the picture of Marlene that Tom had made, asking people from time to time if they'd seen the woman.

"What is it?"

"Well, a guy comes in here sometimes—not too often. He works in one of them big charity hospitals, St. Joseph's. He came in tonight, and I showed him your wife's picture. Bless my mother's memory if he didn't say she's in the hospital, about to have a baby!"

"Mack, was he *sure*?"

"Swore on his daddy's wooden leg," Mack said, his eyes shining. "He said there wasn't no two ways about it. Said you could come and see for yourself. He couldn't remember her name, but it wasn't Winslow. But they can't have too many women about to have babies, can they? You can check them all!"

"How do I get there, Mack?" Tom got directions and ran out the door. He had no money to spare for a street car, so he walked all the way, finding the hospital with no trouble. When he entered, he asked the black-robed woman in charge, "Can you help me? I'm looking for a woman who's about to have a baby."

"We'll need more information," said the nun. "Let me get the director."

A slight man with thick glasses named Father Matthew approached Tom and listened carefully, asked a few questions, then said, "You can see her, but . . ."

Tom noted the hesitation and asked the priest, "What's wrong?"

"Well . . . she's having difficulty. It's a hard delivery, Mr. Winslow."

Tom sensed there was more. "Is she . . . going to live?"

The question troubled the priest. He took off his glasses, breathed on them, then polished them. When he had settled them on his nose, he said quietly, "Our doctor doesn't think so, but God is always able."

"Can I see her now?"

"Certainly."

When Father Matthew admitted him to the room and stepped outside, Tom walked to the bed. A doctor with a large pale face and a heavy beard was leaning over the patient.

"Who are you?" he said as Tom drew near.

Tom looked down, shocked at what he saw. Marlene's face looked like a skeleton, and pain had drained her of every grace. "I'm her husband," he answered hoarsely.

"She's very ill, I'm afraid," the doctor said. He hesitated, then added, "Stay with her. Call if she wakes up."

Tom nodded, numb with grief. He stared at his wife, unable to believe what he saw. It was not supposed to be like this, he thought. The shocks of the war had never produced in him anything like the fear that rose within.

Then she opened her eyes.

"Marlene? It's me, Tom."

She stared at him out of hollow eyes, seeming not to recognize him. Then she said distinctly, "You shouldn't have come."

"I had to come, Marlene!"

"No." Then pain began to twist her swollen body. When the pain subsided, she gasped out, "I never loved you, Tom. It was always Spence!"

No! his mind cried, but he knew it was true.

She went on. "I was all right—until I heard that he was alive—"

"Alive? He was killed in the war!"

"No—taken prisoner!" she gasped. "He wrote me—and we kept on writing."

Suddenly the truth hit Tom. "Spence Grayson. He's the man you came here with?"

"Yes!" Then she began to scream.

The door burst open. The doctor took one look and said, "You'd better wait outside!"

Five hours later, Marlene died. Before she went, the doctor sent for him.

She looked up, eyes hooded with shadow, and said again, "I never loved you, Tom—it was always Spence—"

A sense of utter emptiness filled him, and he turned away.

A nurse nearby, holding a small bundle, stopped him. "This is your daughter, sir," she said.

Tom halted, then looked down at the baby as the face turned red and eyes squinted shut, ready to give forth a sharp cry of protest.

"Will you be leaving her with us, Mr. Winslow?"

Tom turned to find Father Matthew, who had come to stand beside him.

He reached out and took the little one from the nurse, tucking his finger inside his daughter's tiny fist, and his heart was comforted by the tug of her hand on his. She was his. She would receive his love.

"No, Father Matthew," he whispered. "No, she'll be going with me!"

CHAPTER FOUR

LAURIE

★ ★ ★ ★

Ten years had passed since Mark Winslow had worn a Confederate uniform, yet he still bore a military stance about himself as he stepped off the train and walked toward the ticket office. The pungent odor of woodsmoke from the engine filled the air, and the Wyoming sun burned so brightly he had to squint.

A stubby man with a ruddy complexion glanced up as Mark entered the one-room station. "Help you?"

"Can I rent a horse or a buggy to get to Fort Sanders?"

"Sho'ly. Brand's Stable, right across from the hotel."

"Thanks."

Winslow made his way along the dusty path that led away from the station to a group of weather-beaten buildings scattered across the rolling hills adjacent to the tracks. The stable was no more than a single barn, the paint long ago stripped bare by the sun and the winds. Four horses nibbled at the fresh sprigs of emerald grass pushing through the rocky corral floor. Leaning back against the barn on a cane-bottomed chair sat a man in faded overalls and a cavalry forage cap. Next to him squatted a boy of ten or so. The pair looked so alike it was comical, but Mark repressed a smile, saying, "I need to rent a horse."

"Shore, Cap'n," the man nodded, getting up and closing the

knife he had been cleaning his nails with. "Got a nice mare. Goin' to the fort?"

"That's right." Mark took a drink from the well nearby as the hostler threw a saddle on a long-legged bay. He noticed the boy watching him covertly, and he smiled, asking in a tone he would have used to another man, "The hunting any good around here?"

The boy's lips parted in a gap-toothed grin. "Not bad." He hesitated, then added nonchalantly, "I got me a ten-point buck a few days ago."

"Ten point? Why, that's a good buck. Hard shot?"

"Naw. Ain't hard when you get the hang of it."

Mark grinned and turned to take the reins of the mare. He swung up onto the saddle and was almost jolted off as the horse pitched, trying to do just that. He tightened his grip and pulled her head up, liking her spirit. "Lively thing, isn't she?"

"Figured you could handle her," the hostler said. He squinted in the sun, looking up at Mark. "I know you, don't I?"

"Name's Winslow," Mark replied. "I work for the Union Pacific." He held the horse's head up, leaned over and patted her neck. When he looked up he said, "I don't think I remember you."

"Prob'ly not," the man smiled. "I was one of the hooligans you throwed in the pokey the night you and Dooley Young cleaned up the town. My name's Wiley Hopper." He pulled off his hat and touched a faint scar on his forehead. "Guess you left your calling card on me that night."

Mark was instantly alert, his eyes narrowing. He had met men before whom he'd had trouble with when he was assistant superintendent of construction for the UP. At that time it had been a wild, rough town, and his main job of keeping order along the tracks hadn't been easy, sometimes needing to use fists and guns freely. But the hostler didn't seem to be hostile. "Sorry about that," Mark said. "It was a pretty tough town in those days."

"Shore. Things ain't the same now, Mr. Winslow."

Winslow returned his smile. "Well, that's a good thing. Glad to see you again, Hopper. I'll be back tomorrow in time to catch the 3:15." He nodded to the boy. "Wish I had time to have you take me out after a buck, young fellow." Then he touched his heels to the flanks of the mare, and she shot out of the lot as if she were in a race.

As Mark rode away, the boy asked, "He really the one who gave you that gash, Pa?"

Hopper sobered as the memory of that wild night came back to him. He'd been part of a bunch hired by the saloon owners to handle Winslow, to put him out of business. There'd been enough of them, he thought, remembering how they'd caught Winslow off guard, coming at him out of an alley as he walked the streets. He'd had one man with him, and they'd both gone down, but somehow the two had gotten to their feet. He remembered the cold blue flash of Winslow's eyes as he'd pulled his gun and begun slashing right and left, sending men to the dirt. There had been enough men to handle him, but Winslow would not go down; and the last thing Hopper remembered was the flash of those eyes as the barrel of a .44 crashed into his head.

"Yep, that's the hairpin, all right, Judd."

"Aw, he looks like a dude!" the boy protested. "Bet he couldn't do it now!"

Hopper shook his head. "Well, let's don't give him no reason, okay? He still looks pretty tough to me, even if he does wear fine duds. He's a vice-president of the Union Pacific now. Guess he don't have to wrestle around with tough fellows like us no more." He took one more look at the disappearing horseman, then sat down and pulled his knife from his pocket. "Let's go after another buck next Saturday, Judd." But as he opened his knife, he thought, *He looks about as ringy as he did when he cleaned up every hell-on-wheels from Omaha to Ogden!*

★   ★   ★   ★

The trail that led to the fort ran dogleg fashion up and down and around little folds of the earth, past an occasional house, past Indians riding head down and indifferent, their toes pointed outward, their shoulders stooped. He covered the five miles until he came to a highland upon which the fort sat, austere and blunt as it rose from the rolling plain. Passing through the gates after a casual inspection by a private, he rode to the largest of several frame buildings formed in the shape of an L. He dismounted, tied the mare firmly to the hitching post, and entered the adjutant's office. He was greeted warmly by a large man wearing the insignia of a major. "Well, Mark, what wind blows you out here?"

"Hello, Phil," Mark smiled. "Came out to see if Martha's keeping you in line." Phil Delaney and his wife Martha were good friends of Mark's, visiting when he traveled the road of the Union or when the Delaneys came to New York on rare occasions.

"You didn't bring Lola with you?"

"Not this time. She said to tell you she's going to be put out if you and Martha don't come to stay with us this year."

"We were talking about that the other day. I think we can swing it. Come on into my office." The two men moved to the small room furnished with a battered desk, a table, and two chairs. They sat and talked for a time about families; then Major Delaney asked, "Did you come out to see Tom?"

"That's right. Is he here?"

"Yes. Just got back last week from a three-month trip up to Powder River. Don't see how he does it, Mark!" Delaney shook his head, adding, "He's sure a moving man. Never likes to stay put."

"How's Laurie?"

"Oh, well enough, I suppose but . . ." Delaney hesitated as though troubled. He was not a man who spoke his mind lightly, and to give himself time to think, he got up and pulled an olla from where it hung on the wall by a thong. He poured two glasses of water, pushed one toward Mark, then hung up the jug and sat down again. Mark said nothing as the major sipped the tepid water, well aware of Delaney's habits.

"Well, Mark, I'm worried about Laurie," he said finally. "I think a lot of Tom, and he does his best for her—but the life he leads, it's not for a ten-year-old girl."

Mark nodded. "Lola and I have often said the same thing." He took a sip of the water, his mind flickering over the life his brother had led since his wife died. At first Tom had tried to settle down at Belle Maison, but he seemed to live under a cloud of restlessness. When Laurie was a mere child, no more than four years old, he had moved to New Mexico and taken over a small ranch, but remained there for less than a year. He had returned to Belle Maison to visit Mark and Lola, bringing Laurie with him, and they had made an offer to raise the girl. Tom had been adamant, not wanting to give her up. So Mark had used his influence to get a place for his brother with the Office of Indian Affairs. That had not been a good solution, however, as far as the rest of the family were concerned. But Tom was pleased with it, and for the past six years had moved all over the northern plains, meeting with the leaders of the tribes, then bringing recommendations on his findings. There was no man who knew the country or the Indians better.

When possible, he had taken Laurie with him; otherwise he boarded her for short terms with various friends. To Mark and Lola it seemed that Laurie had prospered, at least in a physical way, but they were worried about her future.

"Phil, I want Tom to settle down. Lola and I hoped he'd marry again, but he hasn't. I want Laurie to have some sort of permanence in her life."

Delaney nodded. "That's what Martha and I have said. We offered to take the child, but Tom's very possessive." He lifted his hand to stroke his Dundreary whiskers, then said slowly, "Guess I'd be the same in his shoes. She's all he has, Mark." Then he asked, "What's on your mind?"

"There's going to be trouble with the Indians, Phil. You know that better than I do. That expedition Custer led into the Black Hills is going to set it off, I think."

"Bound to!" Delaney exclaimed. "We gave that country to the Sioux by treaty."

"We've never kept a treaty with them, and they know we never will," Mark said. "And all that talk about our troops going in to find a site for a new fort was pretty raw!"

In 1873, General Sheridan concluded that a more strategically located post was needed to discourage the Indians from raiding the Nebraska settlements and travel routes to the south. This new fort would fall somewhere in the vicinity of the Black Hills. These invitingly wooded mountains sprawled over the western portion of the Great Sioux Reservation, remote, mysterious, and not well known to the outside world. The Sioux treasured the Black Hills as their "Meat Pack," rich in game with sheltered valleys and abundant firewood, ideal for winter camping. Drawn by these resources, they had seized the hills from the Kiowas almost a century earlier and had jealously guarded them against whites and other Indians ever since.

But though Sheridan's proposal to send a troop to find a site for a fort was backed by President Grant and General Sherman, friends of the Indians felt that the operation was a violation of the Treaty of 1868, which barred whites from the Great Sioux Reservation. Both Sherman and Grant scoffed at such a notion, claiming that the government had a right and an obligation to establish a military post on any site—for the protection of the people, they insisted.

The real purpose of the invasion of the Black Hills, however, was not to find a site for a military fort but to obtain its rich resources. The Black Hills offered the last great mining frontier of the West. For almost half a century rumors of gold in the Black Hills had periodically tantalized the nation, but the region remained unexplored, the haunt of Indians who turned aside all comers.

The Treaty of 1868 infuriated Dakotans, for it unmistakably confirmed the Black Hills as Indian domain, therefore barred to all white settlers and even travelers. The "abominable compact with the marauding bands," as a Yankton paper put it, did not dampen enthusiasm for opening the hills. On the contrary, impoverishing thousands, the Panic of 1873 kindled new ardor. "As the Christian looks forward with hope and faith to that land of pure delight," rhapsodized the *Bismarck Tribune*, "so the miner looks forward to the Black Hills, a region of fabulous wealth, where the hills repose on beds of gold and the rocks are studded with precious metal."

Nurtured by such seductive visions, when Custer took the Seventh Cavalry into the Black Hills on July 2, 1874, two mining experts, William McKay and Horatio Nelson Ross, went along. And it was a matter of course that these two men would find traces of gold, just as it was certain that their reports would leak out.

Mark shook his head in disgust, thinking of the shoddy behavior of the government. "The Sioux know what's coming. And they'll fight this time."

"I believe they will," Delaney agreed. Then he asked, "But what's all this got to do with Tom and Laurie?"

"Phil, you now how Sherman hates Indians. Says the only good Indian he ever saw was a dead one. Well, Grant's told him to 'clean up the Indian problem'—and you know exactly how Sherman will understand that!"

"Kill them off!"

"Exactly. Sherman has watched Nelson Miles destroy the tribes of the southern plains, and now he wants Phil Sheridan to do the same in the north." Mark hesitated, then said, "Don't spread this around, Phil. I got it from a high official on my promise to keep it to myself."

"Certainly!" Delaney nodded. "But I still don't see what all this has to do with Tom and Laurie."

"Sherman will use the best Indian fighters we have, and that means Custer. He's a household name and has always been successful in fighting Indians. His brother Tom is a good friend of mine, Phil. I saw him last month and he told me that Custer wants to put together the best group of scouts ever assembled. He wanted to know if I knew anybody who'd be a candidate for the job—heading up the scouts. And I told him about my brother Tom."

"Well, he knows more about Indians—and about that country around the Black Hills—than anybody else. But that's just a short-term affair, isn't it?"

"Maybe not. Custer wants the scouts to be under military authority—which means the leader will have to be a soldier."

A startled expression crossed Delaney's face. "Tom would join the army?"

"That's what I'd like to see," Mark nodded. "He'd join as a sergeant, but if he did well, Custer's brother told me it would be no problem to get him a commission. What do you think, Phil?"

Delaney stroked his luxurious whiskers, sipped his water, then nodded. "It would be good. Tom always liked the army, you know. Bad as that time was, he liked it. And he'd be a good officer. We need men who know the Indians." He drummed the desk with his fingers, thinking hard. "Think he'll do it?"

"He's a pretty stubborn fellow," Mark mused. "But if I can make him see that it'd be good for Laurie, I think he might." He got to his feet, asking, "Where'll I find him, Phil?"

"Probably working on his house. It's half a mile down the south road—back in a grove of cottonwoods on the right." He rose and accompanied his visitor outside. As Mark wheeled the mare and rode toward the gate, Delaney called out, "Come by and tell me how it comes out."

★　★　★　★

Laurie was the first to see the rider turn off the road. She had been playing a game beside the small brook in the shade of the cottonwoods—a game she often indulged in when alone. All her games were played alone, made up from her own imaginative head. Sometimes watching her from afar, her father had seen her people her small area with fictitious characters and act out their parts one by one in pantomime.

She wore a boy's shirt and a pair of tan overalls tucked into small boots. Her black hair, hanging in two braids between her shoulders, and her shiny gray eyes and tanned face were a foreshadow of her mother's graphic beauty.

"Daddy, someone's coming," she called out to her father, who was working behind the house.

At her announcement Tom Winslow came around the corner with a hammer in his hand. He took one look at the rider, tossed the hammer down, and joined Laurie as he said, "That's your Uncle Mark. Come for your birthday, I expect."

Her face brightened with a smile, for her uncle was a favorite. "Aw, c'mon!" she said. "I'll bet he's forgot."

Mark pulled the mare up and dropped to the ground, his face alight with joy at seeing her. "Well, I ran you down! Come here, you gorgeous creature, and give an old man a kiss!" As she came to him, half shyly, he caught Laurie up, kissed her cheek, put her down, then holding her hand, said, "Tie this mare up, Tom. I'm busy with my niece."

"Good to see you, Mark," Tom said, taking the reins and tying the horse to an iron ring driven into one of the cottonwoods. "Come on in and cut the dust."

The house was a plain structure with no pretensions to elegance. The men sat down at the table while Laurie busied herself making tea. Mark watched her, thinking how she had grown in the past year. "You get prettier every time I see you, Laurie," he smiled, taking the cup from her. "Hate to think what you'll do to all the young fellows in a few years."

"Oh, bosh!" Laurie exclaimed, color rising to her cheeks. "Who cares about them?"

"Why, Laurie," Tom said, giving Mark a sly wink, "I thought you told me that Leroy Blevins was a good-looking young fellow!"

Laurie made a face at him, then drew up a chair, prepared to listen. As the two men spoke of family, Mark bringing them up-to-date on the latest news from his own family and from Belle Maison in Virginia, she sat there quietly. She wasn't much for talking. Silence was a habit she had acquired from Tom and from being alone so much. That and the way she had of judging people came from him, as her vivid imagination and the growing beauty had come from her mother.

Finally Mark said, "Well, that's all the news from home, I guess."

Tom knew his brother very well. "This isn't just a visit, is it, Mark?"

"Why, no, Tom, it isn't." Mark leaned back in his chair, trying to find the best way to present what was on his mind. He studied his brother for a moment. Mark was thirty-four, Tom two years younger, but they looked much alike. Both had the dark good looks of the Winslow men, black hair and eyes, the same English nose. They were lean and muscular, Tom more so, for he ran every ounce of fat off on his constant travels through the desert, while Mark was forced to spend much of his time at a desk.

"I ran into something you might be interested in, Tom," Mark remarked, then related the encounter he'd had with Tom Custer as simply as he could, including the invitation to join the Seventh Cavalry. When he had finished, he said, "When Tom Custer told me about the need, I thought it was something you should hear about." He didn't need to say anymore, for he knew Tom would think it over.

"Now, to the important thing—" Reaching into his inside pocket, he pulled out a small package wrapped in plain brown paper and tied with a piece of string. Handing it to Laurie, he smiled. "Happy birthday, Laurie."

"Oh, Uncle Mark!" she exclaimed, her eyes like diamonds. "My birthday's not for three days!"

"I know that, but I'm here now. Let's just pretend, okay?"

Laurie glanced at her father, then took off the string. Both men were watching her glowing face as she removed the paper and then opened the small box inside. Tom did not look at the gift, but kept his eyes on his daughter's face, thinking suddenly of how much she looked like her mother. He watched as her eyes opened wide with pleasure, then she cried out, "Oh, Uncle Mark—how pretty!"

She took the gold necklace with the single large pearl from the box, held it to her neck for them to admire. "Not as pretty as you," Mark smiled, "but Lola said it was perfect for you."

"And earrings, too!" Laurie squealed, putting the necklace on the table carefully. She held them to her ears, demanding, "Daddy, can I wear them today?"

Mark and Tom laughed at her, Mark saying, "I think the earrings are for when you get older—but I don't see any reason why you can't wear them when you're alone, do you, Tom?"

"Not a bit," Tom smiled. "Things are made to be enjoyed, not shoved back in a drawer someplace." Then he added, "No sense saying you shouldn't have done it. You and that stubborn wife of yours are determined to spoil Laurie."

"We'd like to do more, Tom. She's a fine youngster."

The rest of the day Mark spent with Laurie, taking her for a ride. She had her own horse, and rode loose and straight in the deep saddle, unconscious of the horse, yet balanced to anticipate any sudden swing. Her father, Mark realized, had taught her this—that trouble was something she should always be prepared for.

They rode into the small town for supper, wolfing down the steaming hot potatoes and steak as Laurie bubbled over with things she'd been doing, asking questions about Lola and Belle Maison and New York. It was so good to see Uncle Mark again! Afterward they walked around the town, then rode slowly back to the house. Laurie brought quilts outside and they all stretched flat, admiring the stars spangling the velvet black skies. The men talked about the past, of the war, and friends who were still at Gettysburg and Shiloh. Finally Laurie, despite heroic efforts, went to sleep—wearing her necklace and earrings.

The silence of the low-lying hills surrounded them, broken only by the mournful cry of a coyote. Mark lay there, enjoying the sensation. He was an outdoor man by nature, and he hated the part of his job that kept him in the city and inside four walls. *Maybe Tom's got the right idea*, he thought. *This is better than anything I've had lately.* But he knew he had his own life, which wouldn't do for Tom or Dan in the least. Both of them were born for something wilder than he himself, so he felt only a fleeting sense of regret as he thought of their freedom.

"I'm going to join the Seventh," Tom said abruptly. He sat up and stared at Mark. "You knew I would, didn't you?"

"Well, I hoped you would." Mark sat up, carefully moving Laurie's head, which had been resting on his arm. "You were the best soldier of any of us, Tom. I had the rank, but I can remember quite a few times when you got us out of hot water. I think some men are soldiers by nature. Others learn and they try. For you, it'd be a good life. Not as free as what you've been doing—but better for Laurie. No matter where the Seventh goes, there'll be a school of some kind. And there'll be people for her to tie to—you, too."

Tom nodded. "In that, I guess you're right, Mark." He felt embarrassed, but said quickly, "Think you'll ever get your kid brother raised?"

"I don't believe I'm up to such a task!" Mark rejoined. "You'll be a general, and I'll be a worn-out old railroad man!" He looked at Tom with affection. "Come back to New York with me for a visit before you enlist. There's time for that—and for a trip to see Mom, too. She'll be glad to hear about this."

"All right."

The two sat there talking quietly, both sensing the deep affection that lay between them. Finally they rose and went inside, Tom picking up Laurie, who protested, "I'm not asleep!" He put her on the bed and stood there looking down at her face bathed in the argent moonlight. She looked so much like Marlene. With a sigh he tucked the covers around her, kissed her cheek, and went outside. He looked up at the stars, his mind awhirl as he thought about the future. What did it hold for him? For Laurie?

CHAPTER FIVE

BEFORE THE WEDDING

★ ★ ★ ★

"You're going to wear that wedding dress out, Faith!"

Susan DeForest smiled across the room at the girl standing before the oval full-length mirror peering at herself. Susan herself was rather a plain girl of twenty, and it was a tribute to her generous spirit that she could feel such a depth of affection for one who so outshone her. They had been friends since childhood, growing up together in St. Louis, or the outskirts of it, attending the same church, the same school, and enduring the fearful anxieties of adolescence.

Now, with both of them at the age of twenty, they had crossed safely over those dangerous shoals, and despite their differences, they had remained fast friends.

"Oh, Susan," Faith cried out, pulling at the bodice of the dress, "this thing *still* doesn't fit! I might as well wear a pair of overalls!"

Susan, well-accustomed to Faith's excesses, smiled. "I think I can find a pair of my father's somewhere. That would give Carl quite a shock, wouldn't it? Marching down the aisle and finding you in a pair of greasy overalls!"

Faith gave Susan a startled look, then broke into a giggle. "Wouldn't it, though?" She turned back to examine herself critically, seeing a young woman five feet five in height with a rounded figure and beautiful carriage—shoulders well back, trim waist, and shapely limbs and upper body. The face that stared back at her was not beautiful, but pretty in a lively way. Gray eyes that had a steady look at most times, but could gleam when the humor that ran just beneath the surface broke out. Beautiful auburn hair, with traces of gold, made a natural cascade of curls down her back. Fair skin showed a few scattered freckles across the high cheekbones. Her nose was short and slightly tilted upward, which added to a piquant expression, and her teeth were perfect as she smiled at herself.

"I hope Carl will be as pretty as I am for the wedding," she said solemnly, then laughed at her own foolishness. "But he's better looking than I am to begin with."

Susan got up and came to pull the back of the white satin dress together at the nape. "Yes, he is, but nobody looks at the groom at the wedding," she smiled. "Let me take a stitch here."

As she worked on the dress, Faith rambled on about the wedding and the plans for leaving St. Louis. Susan listened, but at the same time thought of the bundle of paradoxes that came together in Faith Jamison. She was, Susan had often thought, like two individuals. Not that she was unsteady or unreliable, but Faith was a complicated girl in many ways. She was highly competent and methodical—yet there was a streak in her that came close to rebellion, or at least a tendency to be impulsive.

That trait, Susan feared, had gotten her friend engaged to Carl Vandiver. When Faith had first come running in to tell her that Carl had asked her to marry him, and that she had accepted, something about the match had bothered Susan. She had said little, for Faith was euphoric, to say the least; but during the engagement period, it had become more apparent that the two were not alike. Carl was a handsome man of twenty-five, the son of a wealthy factory owner. He was a fun-loving man, one who treasured the finer things of life—meaning the expensive things—and his decision to go to the mission field had displeased his parents greatly. They wanted him to be a minister, for they were devout in their religious duties, but they wanted to keep him in the city, pastor of a large church, or a leader in their denomination. Carl's decision to marry a young woman from a lower social level and go with her as a mission volunteer to the Indians of the far West had been a terrible strain on their family.

But Faith, despite her usual level-headed approach to things, seemed oblivious to the problem. She had never before been serious about a man, and her total dedication to marriage with Carl prevented Susan from saying much about the difficulties she would face. Now as she took the tiny stitches in the fine material of the wedding dress, Susan found herself wishing she'd tried harder. But it was too late now, for the wedding was at three o'clock the next day.

Leaning forward, she bit the thread, tied it off, then stood back to examine it with a critical eye. "That's better," she announced, satisfied with the result.

"Oh, Susan, I'm so excited!" Faith said, her eyes almost snapping with bright glints. "Just think, tomorrow I'll be Mrs. Carl Vandiver!"

"I'll miss you," Susan said. She was a thoughtful girl, not given to expressions of her emotions, but the knowledge that the two of them would be parted was now very real. "I'll never see you again, Faith," she said, shaking her head slightly.

"Oh, don't be silly!" Faith came to her friend at once, putting her arms around her. That was another of the paradoxes to this girl. One moment she could be totally immersed in herself; the next, forget herself completely and become immersed in the needs of others. "Why, there are trains that run all the way to Dakota now. Carl and I'll be coming back every other year, and you've already promised to come and have a long visit with us."

"I suppose, but it won't be the same," Susan said. Then she forced herself to smile. "What am I thinking of, carrying on like this? We had to grow up, didn't we? Now, let's go over all the things that will probably go wrong at the wedding tomorrow."

Faith, glad to see her friend smile, began to talk rapidly about the ceremony. The rest of the afternoon the two women spent going over the details until Mrs. Jamison knocked on the door and entered, saying, "Faith, Reverend Thomas is here. He wants to see you."

"Oh, dear!" Faith moaned. "I can't see him in my wedding dress!"

She began to strip off the dress so quickly that her mother

cried, "Don't tear the dress, Faith. Reverend Thomas will wait."
She and Susan managed to get the dress off, handling it carefully.
As Faith threw on a blue dress, Mrs. Jamison stroked the wedding dress, her eyes thoughtful. She was an attractive woman
of thirty-seven, a widow who had lost her husband at Gettysburg. "This hasn't been worn since my wedding day."

"You must have been a gorgeous bride, Mrs. Jamison," Susan
said. "It's a beautiful dress."

"My father had it made for me in Chicago. I thought it was
the most wonderful dress in the world."

"It *is!*" Faith nodded, slipping into a pair of tan shoes. She
got to her feet, then said, "Come with me, both of you. I'm so
excited I can't think straight. Reverend Thomas might not let me
go to the mission field if he sees how silly I am."

The three women went downstairs, where Reverend James
Thomas rose to greet them. "Hello, ladies," he said, smiling. He
was a tall, rotund man of sixty, with a beautiful shock of pure
white hair and a pair of sharp black eyes. "Well, is the bride
ready?"

Faith took his hand, smiled up at him, saying, "Yes! But if I
go blank, you may have to prompt me during the ceremony,
Reverend."

"My theory about all weddings is simple," the minister said.
"If something can go wrong, it will. However, when it's over—
no matter how many things go wrong—you and Carl *will* be
married."

"Come along, Susan," Mrs. Jamison said. "Let's fix tea while
these two go over the ceremony."

When the pair had left, Faith and Reverend Thomas sat down
on the horsehide sofa, Faith bubbling over with excitement. The
minister let her run on, but finally said, "Faith, I'm not worried
about the ceremony, but there is something that—well, I've felt
we should talk about it."

Faith looked at him, curious. "Is something wrong with the
appointment, Reverend Thomas?"

"No—not really wrong," the minister said slowly. He was a
dignified man, experienced and capable, able to handle any of
the thousand details that came over his desk. He was head of
the newly organized Department of Missions for his denomi-

nation, and took great satisfaction in the work. He had been Faith's pastor for years, and when she had announced that God had called her to work with the Indians of the far West, he had been delighted.

Now he looked uncertain, a manner rare for him. Faith began to feel a vague fear building up within her, and when he spoke, she listened with apprehension.

"Preaching the gospel to the Sioux people," Thomas said carefully, "is a difficult matter. They are different from us in almost every way, Faith."

"But the gospel is the same for everyone, isn't it?"

"Yes, of course, but the *presentation* of the gospel differs. Here in St. Louis, even in the worst areas, those we talk to about Jesus have heard of Him. But not so with the Indians. They live in a whole different world, have worshiped idols for centuries." He shrugged and went on. "I've been a preacher for forty years, Faith, but I'd be almost useless in their world."

Faith stared at him, not certain where he was headed. "Are you saying I'm not fitted to be a missionary?"

"Oh no!" Reverend Thomas lifted his eyes, startled. "Certainly not, my dear!" He was distressed and leaned forward to put his hand over hers in a reassuring gesture. "I was speaking in general terms. All of us on the board think of you as one of the bright stars in our little firmament. No question at all of your calling or of your capability."

"Then what *is* troubling you, Reverend Thomas?"

"Well, to be frank with you, Faith, some of the board are not certain that your fiance is ready for the work in the West."

"But Carl is far more able than I am!"

"Perhaps, in some ways." Thomas braced himself. He had been sent by the board to do a difficult task because he was a good friend of the Jamisons, but he saw rough going ahead. "Carl is bright and active, and there's no question of his Christian walk. But some of the board feel that he would not function well in such a—a *rough* situation."

Faith was close to anger, but knew that this man was her friend. "Is that what *you* think, Reverend Thomas?"

Her question, direct and blunt, brought a grimace to Thomas's lips, but he was an honest man. "In all candor, Faith, I do think there's some doubt of Carl's call to this work."

"I see." Faith sat there, her mind whirling, but she made an effort to suppress the apprehension rising in her. "Why have you waited so long to speak about this? We're getting married tomorrow, and we have our train tickets for the trip."

"We have had several interviews with Carl, as is customary with all our volunteers. Over the past few months, as a matter of fact, I have talked with him myself several times."

"I didn't know that!"

"He didn't tell you?" Thomas lifted his eyebrows, obviously surprised. "But he has spoken to you of his doubts, I'm sure."

Faith blinked, taken off guard by the question. "Why—in some ways I'm sure we all feel some doubt. It's such a big step, and Carl feels a little inadequate. I feel the same way," she said, lifting her head with a touch of defiance. But even as she spoke, she was thinking back, remembering how Carl had shown more uncertainty as the time to leave grew near.

Reverend Thomas let the silence run on, reading Faith's thoughts. He was genuinely fond of the young woman, but he never felt as certain of Carl Vandiver's commitment as he would have liked. He wished to do nothing to hurt Faith, yet he knew that the worst tragedy of all would be for the young couple to get on the field, and *then* discover that they could not handle the problem.

At that point, Mrs. Jamison and Susan entered with tea and a pound cake, so Reverend Thomas departed, saying only, "I'll be available if you and Carl wish to speak with me this evening." He hesitated, then added, "There are many ways to serve the Lord, Faith. Even Paul had to change his plans more than once. Perhaps you two would find it possible to serve the cause of the gospel here in the East. At any rate, talk it over with Carl."

"Yes, I'll do that—but we must go to the Indians." Here Reverend Thomas was aware of another of the paradoxes in the young woman—which consisted of a soft gentleness that was backed by a stubborn determination. Her lower lip lost its softness, growing firm, and her back grew straighter as she looked at him.

"Yes—well, we'll pray about it, of course—"

After the door closed behind him, Faith stood in the middle

of the room, unconscious of the sound of the voices of her mother and Susan humming in the next room. The grandfather clock ticked solemnly, then the half-hour note struck, sending a brassy signal throughout the house. It seemed to touch her, for she blinked, then turned and walked in to join the two women.

"Mother, I'm going out for a little while," she announced.

Mrs. Jamison looked up with surprise. "Going out? Where to?"

"I have to see Carl."

Susan started slightly, for she saw that Faith was disturbed. "Would you like me to go with you?"

"No, thank you, Susan." With this brief word she put on a coat and left the house.

"She's upset, isn't she?" Susan said. "It must have been something Reverend Thomas said."

Mrs. Jamison was staring at the door, her eyes troubled. She had a long, sobering thought, but said only, "I suppose she's just anxious about the ceremony. She'll be fine when it's over."

★　★　★　★

As Faith stepped off the streetcar, she was so lost in thought that the harsh clanging of the bell startled her. She blinked her eyes, then moved along the tree-lined street, which was flanked by rows of large two-story brownstone houses. Dusk was falling and the sunset dropping behind the artificial horizon of expensive homes was a deep scarlet.

The Vandiver house was on the corner, occupying a double lot, so that the structure itself was not crowded, but bordered by a garden with a black iron fence surrounding it. Unconsciously Faith ran her hand across the tips of the blunt spear-like spikes of the uprights, then turned and moved up the walk. She climbed the steps mechanically, gave the heavy brass knocker a series of three raps, then stood back to wait.

For two hours she had walked the streets, not seeing much of the neighborhoods she passed through, for her mind was occupied with what Reverend Thomas had told her. She was a highly imaginative young woman, and sometimes given to letting herself probe at things, going beyond spoken words into possibilities. All the while she had walked the streets, she had pulled up memories of her times with Carl, the times they had talked about going to the Indians with the gospel. And slowly it had come to her that she had always been the instigator of those talks. Carl had been interested in the West, but then most people were. The papers were full of stories about the cavalry and its never-ending battles with the tribes; and novel after novel had flowed from the press, dealing with the "noble savage," as the Indians were called.

But now she was beginning to realize that all the excitement about going to the Indians, of organizing a mission and sharing Jesus with them, had been carried along by her enthusiasm. Carl had listened, a smile on his face, calling her his "fiery evangelist," but he had not shown the same fervor.

He's just not as vocal as I am about things, Faith told herself. *When he gets there, it will be different.*

The door opened, and Opal, Mrs. Vandiver's maid, smiled at her. "Why, Miss Jamison! Come in—I didn't know you were coming here."

"Hello, Opal," Faith said, feeling awkward and a little foolish. "Is Mrs. Vandiver at home?"

"Oh, I'm sorry she's not!" Opal said. "She and Mr. Vandiver went out to dinner. But Mr. Carl is here. You come into the parlor and I'll get him."

Faith followed the maid to the parlor, then stood there, her nervousness growing as she waited. When Carl entered the room, a look of surprise on his face, she felt even more foolish. "Why, Faith," he smiled, coming to take her hands. "Is something wrong?" He was a slight man, below average height and small boned. He had a smooth, pale face, with a mustache over rather thin lips, and his eyes were a flat blue.

"Oh no," Faith said hurriedly. "I—just wanted to see you."

He took her hands and raised them to his lips. "Isn't that supposed to be bad luck or something? I mean, the groom isn't supposed to see the bride before the ceremony, is he?"

Faith shook her head. "That's just on the day of the wedding."

"Good. Do come and sit down. May I get you some tea?"

"No, thank you, Carl." She sat down and began to speak of some aspect of the ceremony, all the while wondering how to approach the real subject. He was a thoughtful man, not given to outbursts of passionate expression; but many times she had wished that he were more demonstrative. Being a strong woman and perhaps even self-willed, she had longed for a husband who would be strong enough to help her overcome those traits. Though she had never admitted it, Carl had been a disappointment to her in that area, but she had thought that, too, would change when they were married.

Finally, a streak of impatience with her own thoughts rose in her, and she said, "Carl, Reverend Thomas came by to see me this afternoon."

"Oh? Something about the ceremony?"

"No. He was disturbed about something rather serious." Faith bit her lower lip nervously, then shook her shoulders. "He implied that the committee isn't fully convinced you're qualified for work among the Indians. I told him, of course, that was nonsense."

Vandiver straightened as she spoke, and she saw that the statement had struck him forcibly. Thinking that he was angry, she ran on quickly, "It's foolish, isn't it? But we can go to them— or just to Reverend Thomas. He said we could call on him tonight if we wished. Then you can give him some assurance that we'll both be fine on the field."

Faith leaned forward, waiting for him to answer, but he seemed to be silenced by her words. Finally he licked his lips, then said, "Faith, I wish it were that simple."

"Why, it *is* simple, Carl! You just haven't been aggressive enough when talking to the committee!"

"No, I'm afraid it's more than that." Vandiver lifted his gaze to meet hers. "I'm afraid, my dear, that Thomas is right." He saw Faith open her mouth to protest and held up his hand, saying quickly, "Hear me out, Faith." He got up and began to pace back and forth.

Faith noted his face, tense and flushed, and she knew what he was about to say would not be pleasant.

"I love you very much," he said, coming back to sit beside her. Taking her hand, he shook his head, adding, "Make no mistake about that. I want to marry you. I think you love me, too, so we can have a good marriage. And we can serve God in a great way—"

When Carl broke off, Faith stared at him, then perceived what he was leaving unsaid. "But not among the Indians, is that what you're trying to tell me, Carl?"

"I—I'm afraid it is," he said quietly. He was not a man who could handle bad scenes easily, preferring to let them slide away. But he knew this was one time he couldn't avoid it, so he went on as steadily as he could.

"You've felt the call of God to go to the Indians very strongly. But I've not felt it. Oh, I know I've gone along with it—but I see now that I was intrigued by the romance of the thing—going west among the cowboys and the soldiers. But if you'll think back, Faith, you'll remember that never did I show any real certainty that God was moving in that direction with my life."

"Why didn't you tell me you felt that way?"

He avoided her eyes, alarmed by the pain in her voice. "Why, I was certain that God would give me that sort of call. If He'd given you a call, and if we were to be married—it seemed that all I had to do was wait, and I'd know it was right." He hesitated, then added, "But it hasn't worked that way, and I believe my other thought was the right one."

"What other thought?"

"That you—and I—were not hearing God correctly." He allowed a pleading note to touch his voice, and spoke more quickly. "We can serve God in many ways, Faith. If I became a leader in our denomination, with you beside me, we could do so much! Why, we could raise enough money to send a hundred missionaries to the West! Don't you see that?"

But if he had thought to win her by this strategy, he was not successful, for her voice was brittle as she said, "God didn't call me to raise money, Carl. He's calling me to give my life to those who don't know Jesus."

Carl tried for a long time to reason with her, protesting that he loved her and they would be happy. But Faith said almost nothing, except when she rose to leave.

She faced him squarely and asked, "Carl, are you saying that you are not going to the mission?"

He swallowed, but nodded. "It would be a tragedy, Faith. I want to serve God, but I'm convinced that I can do more by staying here."

She took off her engagement ring and extended it. He gasped, "But, Faith—we can't call the wedding off! I love you—and it's all arranged!"

Faith smiled wryly. "Goodbye, Carl. I wish you well. But I must obey God."

She turned and walked out into the dusky night. Only a thin scarlet line of the sun's last light remained. As she headed down the street, the line faded, leaving the streets dark, with only the orange dots of the streetlamps to give illumination.

She felt totally empty and spent, the future blank—a dark pathway without even a glimmer of light. The click of her heels against the pavement sent dull echoes through the air as she made her way along the row of brownstones. Then the hot tears began to stream down her cheeks. Almost fiercely, she wiped them away with the back of her hand, pulled her shoulders back, and looked up into the ebony sky. "I'll go wherever you want me to go, God," she whispered, "but please don't ever leave me!"

She waited. The heavens seemed silent. Then something inside her began to grow, driving out the pain and fear that had engulfed her. All hesitancy was gone. And as she continued on toward home, the cloud of heaviness lifted and Faith *knew* she would never be alone again.

PART TWO

THE SCOUT

★ ★ ★ ★

CHAPTER SIX

TRIP TO FORT LINCOLN

★　★　★　★

The wood-burning train with its five passenger coaches made its way steadily across the desert's empty horizon, a gusty wind boiling against the car sides. The air scouring down the aisle laid its raw edge on the passengers. The locomotive was cracking at forty miles an hour through a condensed night. The tracks beneath the car chattered a little, and Faith felt the sudden bite of a curve. She stared out into the blackness until the sky broke with the faint light of dawn. The train paused briefly at an obscure station, the lights inside the small building making a yellow reflection on the handful of passengers, their faces obscure as they stumbled off the train.

Later as the morning light filled the car, Faith's eyes turned to trace the faces of her fellow passengers. Several were soldiers, all privates except one—a tall lieutenant, who kept himself aloof from the rough banter of the others. He gave Faith a careful look, then turned his attention to the horizon. The other travelers were women—one of them obviously the wife of a thickset man wearing overalls and the mother of the three small children she tried to restrain from running up and down the aisle. The other woman was about Faith's age, she judged. Her face was hard and her manners forward, smiling boldly at the soldiers, one of them responding by sitting beside her. The conductor came down the aisle, gazed disapprovingly at the couple, but said nothing.

One man dressed in buckskin caught Faith's eye. He sat alone, his face hidden behind a bushy beard, and once when a band of antelope rushed up from a coulee, he threw open his window, yanked a rifle from the rack over his head and pumped seven quick shots toward the herd, then slammed the window down again.

Faith expected the conductor to protest, but he only grinned at the man. "You'd better shoot straighter than that, Buck, or the Piutes will lift your hair!" He moved on down the aisle to the next car, and when he opened the door, the wind, now losing its chill, and the loud, rhythmic sound of the wheels clacking over the joints of the rails swept through the car.

Later the sun rose higher, and as the car warmed up, men popped the windows open, allowing not only a rush of air but a constant haze of fine cinders to settle on everything, including the passengers. Faith struggled with her window, but it was jammed. The lieutenant uncoiled his long body and came to her aid. "Allow me to help you, miss," he said, taking a firm hold on the window handles and yanking it with such force that it struck the top with a thud.

"Thank you," Faith murmured, then asked, "Are you going to Fort Lincoln?"

"Not this trip," he answered. "Is that where you're headed?"

"Yes. To work in a mission for the Indians."

He seemed to find that amusing and drawled, "Well, I hope you convert the whole Sioux nation." His lips curved in a sardonic grin, and he moved back to his seat.

Later the conductor started a fire in the iron stove at one end of the car and made a huge pot of black coffee. The car grew thick with cigarette smoke. *Good thing some of this will be sucked out the open windows,* Faith thought. She got to her feet and made her way to the small toilet, timidly aware of the eyes following her. When she emerged, she got a cup from the stack provided. The bottom was ringed with a dark brown stain, so she rinsed the cup with some water from the water can, then held it out to the conductor for the coffee. When she was again seated, she took a sip and grimaced at the strong brew—strong enough to float a track bolt, she decided. But she sipped it slowly as she watched the country unroll across the prairie.

Throughout the long day, she got off only once, when the train made a short stop at a small town. She bought a sack lunch sold by a one-legged man in a Civil War uniform, then walked around until boarding the train again. The ride was monotonous, and she found herself dozing from time to time.

She read a little from the small Bible she carried in her purse, but the motion of the train made that difficult. From time to time her thoughts returned to her last days in St. Louis—which had been quite unpleasant.

Carl had been gentle—at first—but finally had grown bitter. "You're not being sensible, Faith!" he had said, his cheeks flushed with irritation. "If you loved me, you'd stay here. A wife is supposed to be with her husband."

"I'm not your wife," she'd replied, "and I must do what God has called me to do."

Everyone, including her family, agreed she was making a terrible mistake. The mission board felt the same, and it was apparent they were not going to support her. "A single woman can't go to the mission field, Miss Jamison," the chairman insisted. "It's a world of men, and you'd be without protection."

But to Faith's surprise, Reverend Thomas had come to her rescue. He'd talked with her several times, and at the final meeting of the board had simply overpowered the rest of the members—including the chairman. "God has called Miss Jamison to take His gospel to the savages," he'd said firmly. "I am convinced of it, and it will not do for our board to fight against God!"

So she had packed her clothing, her books, the small supply of tracts, and had ignored all pleas to remain. It had been difficult, especially parting from her mother, and Faith was able to leave her only because she would be going to live with Faith's brother, Sherman, in Hannibal. He and his wife and three children had been begging her to move there. She would be happy, Faith knew, for the love they all had for one another was beautiful. So, secure in that knowledge, Faith said goodbye without regrets.

Throughout the long afternoon she dozed off and on until the conductor tapped her on the shoulder. "Curtisville, miss. Time to get off."

The train ground to a halt, and Faith stepped off. To her surprise, the town had no shape. It was simply a cluster of six or seven buildings scattered on the prairie at the eastern edge of Dakota. Now, at the day's end, they looked gaunt and hard-angled in the fading light.

Faith was accustomed to crowds and buildings. This stark contrast, the utter emptiness, left her almost dizzy as she looked around. The town was set in a dusty space, buildings running outward in all directions, giving no indication where the earth ended and the sky began. There were no trees, no hills, nothing to relieve the eye; nothing but gray soil and patches of short brown grass turned crisp and now ready to fade when the winter frost touched it.

She stood on the platform—alone. Not only had nobody met the train, but the utter desolation of the place hit her with force as she faced the mute buildings where yellow lamplight shone faintly through the windows. Then she turned and saw a man and a small girl who had evidently gotten out of the rear car. He spoke to the child, and the two approached Faith. "I guess we're all going over to the hotel," he said. "If you'll pick out your light luggage, I'll come back for the rest later."

"Thank you," Faith said. He was tall and in his early thirties, she judged, with black hair and a wedge-shaped face. He wore a light brown suit, a white shirt, and a low-crowned brown hat with a broad brim. He moved lightly, picked up the suitcase she indicated, and led the way down a winding pathway toward the buildings.

It had been hot all day, but as darkness fell, the air grew brittle. Winter lay just over the hills, which would soon feel the touch of a killing frost, shriveling the grass in one night.

The hotel had one door and a set of windows. A single rail-road tie served as the doorstep. The man opened the door and nodded to Faith, permitting her to enter first. A narrow hall and a steep stairway led to the second floor. The hotel keeper looked up, a man so fat he was spilling out of his clothes. "Together?" he asked in a raspy tenor voice.

"Two rooms," the man said.

"You can take room eight," he nodded to Faith. "And you can have room four," he said to the man. "Sign here." When she had signed, she was close enough to see the man's writing: Thomas Winslow. He hesitated, then added: Richmond, Virginia. She saw him glance down at the register and knew that he was reading her name.

"Breakfast at four," the clerk said indifferently. "The stage leaves at four-thirty." He tossed a key to each of them, and sat down heavily, picking up a newspaper.

The three of them moved toward the stairs, and Winslow stepped aside to let Faith go first, then the girl. When Faith reached her room, she unlocked the door, and he entered with her luggage. "I'll go get the rest." He paused slightly, adding, "My name is Tom Winslow. This is my daughter, Laurie."

"I'm Faith Jamison." She smiled at the girl, whose solemn gray eyes watched her carefully. "I wish I knew how to make braids like yours, Laurie," she said. "I could never learn to do it."

The man grinned. "I'll get your luggage."

After they left, Faith wondered where his wife was and what he did for a living. He certainly had been kind to her. She stood by the window looking at the fading light. The sun soon dipped behind the horizon, clothing the land with a dark curtain. With it came the sense of aloneness, uncertainty. But God had sent her on this mission. She would trust Him. Bringing her thoughts back, she hurriedly washed the fine coating of dust and cinders from her face, brushed her hair, every stroke reminding her of the strain of the journey, and was ready when she heard the knock announcing Winslow's return with her baggage. "I brought your trunk and the rest of the bags to the hotel. I left them downstairs, unless you want some of it." He hesitated, then asked, "Would you care to join Laurie and me for supper?"

"That would be nice."

She accompanied the pair to the dining room, where they sat at a long table already occupied by four men, who were just finishing their meal and left with a nod to the new customers. The menu was sparse—eggs, steak, and apple pie. The steak was tough and the eggs hard. But they were all so hungry they devoured the food quickly. After the meal, Winslow drank coffee, while Faith and Laurie sipped at the warm milk.

Faith said, "I've never ridden on a stagecoach. I suppose it's much rougher than the train?"

Laurie looked up, a mustache of white milk on her upper lip. "Sure is! It'll wear your bottom out in a hurry if you ain't used to it!"

Tom Winslow saw Faith flinch, and said gently, "Laurie, I don't think it's polite to mention a lady's bottom in public."

Laurie looked surprised. "Why not?"

"A rule somebody made up."

The youngster's obvious contempt for such foolishness made Faith smile. The relationship between the father and daughter was intriguing—more like adult to adult. The girl had obviously been brought up "by hand," as Faith's grandmother would have called it. She had an easy way with her father, not disrespectful, but open and frank. There was little about the girl that was feminine. Her clothing was obviously designed for a boy, and she had few feminine mannerisms that a young girl would ordinarily have.

"Guess we'll get to bed," Winslow said, rising to his feet. "Four o'clock is fairly early, and it'll be a rough trip. Good-night, Miss Jamison."

"Good-night." Faith lingered for a time, but there was nothing to see, no one to talk to, so she soon retired to her room. Stripping off her dusty clothing, she sponged off in the tepid water, put on the thinnest nightgown she had, and lay down on the lumpy mattress. Sleep came quickly, and it seemed as if she had only closed her eyes when a knock at the door startled her awake. "Breakfast in ten minutes!"

She dressed quickly and hurried downstairs. Winslow and Laurie were seated at the table, along with three men. She nodded to the pair, then ate the breakfast of bacon, hot cakes, fried potatoes, and bitter coffee—or tried to. The food was heavy and greasy, so she consumed very little. Winslow and his daughter had already finished and were outside by the waiting stage. When she emerged, Winslow said, "I put your luggage aboard." Holding out his hand, he helped her into the coach, then nodded to the girl, who scrambled inside and sat down beside a window opposite Faith. Her father climbed aboard and sat beside Laurie; then the other three passengers, heeding a warning call from the driver, came out of the hotel and got inside, one of them beside Winslow and the other, a large man, on the seat with Faith. The third man, tall and lean, crawled up to sit with the driver.

The driver spoke to the horses, and the stage moved out of the yard with a lurch. They lumbered across the baked earth, turned sharply around the corner of the hotel, then picked up speed, the coach wheels lifting and dripping an acrid dust. The coach swayed and shuddered as it struck deeper depressions, shaking the passengers jammed together on the two seats. The rolling of the coach sent the huge man roughly against Faith. He grunted an apology, but the seat was so narrow, he couldn't prevent the jostling.

The scenery at first was interesting to Faith, but as time dragged on, the day grew warm. The four horses went at a walk, at a run, at a walk, each change of pace producing its agreeable break and its new discomforts. By ten o'clock the dust had rolled inside the coach, laying its fine film on everything as the heat shot up. At noon the coach drew up before a small drab building in a yard littered with tin cans and empty bottles. Faith got out of the coach slowly, stiff from the ride, and after a quick dinner, climbed back in with everyone else for the second half of the day's journey.

The heavy man joined the driver and the other passenger this time, so Faith was a little more comfortable. "Would you like to sit with me, Laurie?" she asked the girl. "There's a little more room here."

"No thank you." The answer was polite, but firm. *She won't get too far away from her father*, Faith thought. *Those two are very close*.

By late afternoon the heat was almost unbearable, the dust like a screen through which the passengers viewed one another. Their faces grew oil-slick, the mixture of sweat and dust making small rivulets down their dirty faces. The smell of the coach grew rank with the odors of bodies, and Faith grew faint from the discomfort.

At last the driver's voice called out, "Whoa up!" and the stage stopped abruptly. The driver got down and called, "Night stop." Faith let the others get out first, and was grateful for Winslow's hand as she stepped down. Her legs, numb by now, betrayed her, and she fell against him as her feet touched the ground. For one moment she held him; then embarrassed, she stepped away.

This station was worse than the hotel where they'd stopped the previous night. Two-storied and square, it was hard for her to picture any structure more graceless. They walked into the long front room and were met by a taciturn man with three days' growth of whiskers and a fetid smell. "Only got one room left," he muttered.

Winslow stared at him, but Faith said, "Laurie, maybe you wouldn't mind sharing it with me, just for one night."

Laurie looked up at her father, who nodded. "Yes, ma'am, that'll be fine." Then she asked, "Where will you sleep, Daddy?"

"Curl up in the coach, I guess."

They went up rickety stairs that moaned and creaked under their weight. The room was the worst Faith had ever seen. The ceiling was thrown together with rough lumber whose edges never quite lay together. A single window with a green discolored roller shade provided the only ventilation. A small lamp and a wash basin and pitcher sat on a table made of fragments of wood. Above that a blemished mirror hung askew. The bed was a four-poster made of solid mahogany, strangely out of place in the rough room, and on it lay lumpy quilts and two pillows without slips.

Faith bent over to stare closely at the blankets, then peeled them back to study the mattress. "At least I don't see any bedbugs," she announced.

"A rough place," Winslow muttered.

"Yes, but the only place. It'll be all right for one night, won't it, Laurie?"

"Guess so."

"Laurie," Winslow said, "you wash up and we'll eat."

Depressed by its ugliness, he left the room and walked outside. He found the pump, took off his shirt and shook the dust out of it, then plunged his head under the rush of cool water, savoring it as it sluiced over his chest and back. After washing up, he sat on the steps and watched as riders came in, tied their horses to the hitching rail, and entered the place. Something troubled him, and he went to the stage, climbed into the boot and found his valise. He removed a gun belt with a Navy .44 in a worn holster, fastened it around his waist, then moved back to the hotel.

89

When Faith came down the stairs with Laurie, she saw the gun, but made no comment. The dinner triangle set up a series of raucous hammering sounds, and they went into the dining room. At one of the tables three women were seated. Heavily made up and speaking shrilly, they uttered harsh, jarring laughter at the remarks from men at the table. Winslow pulled out a chair for Faith at the far end of a long table, placed Laurie next to her, then seated himself between them and the others.

The meal was brief, for the others at the table soon finished and moved out of the dining room into the saloon across the hall.

When the meal was finished, Faith asked, "Could we walk for a while?"

"Sure," he nodded, and seemed relieved to get outside. The stars shone brightly, and a sickle moon, turned butter yellow by the haze in the air, lay low in the sky.

They walked far enough down the road so the sounds of the tinny piano and the raucous laughter from the saloon faded. The quiet flowed over the darkened desert, formless and mysterious.

"Do you live in the West?" Faith asked.

"Yes," he answered, then added, "My home was in Virginia—but we've been out here for quite a while."

"It's new to me," Faith murmured. Peering into the darkness, she said, "It's a bigger world than I'm used to. Back home you can't see for the buildings and the hills. Here, during the day, I think you must be able to see a hundred miles!"

He smiled in the moonlight. "Makes a person feel sort of small, doesn't it?"

"Very small." She looked up at the stars, adding, "They seem so close!"

As she watched, a falling star traced a silver line across the velvet blackness, and Winslow said, "Make a wish, Laurie."

The girl looked up at him. "Will it really come true?"

"Well, I guess sometimes wishes come true—not too often."

Faith realized he was teaching the girl something. Perhaps not to expect too much. Maybe not to trust in stars, but to lean on her own efforts. She thought of her own childhood, how she'd been at Laurie's age, and felt a trace of pity for her. *She needs a woman. She seems sturdy, but I'll bet she gets afraid at times.*

They continued walking, about half a mile. Winslow told about a bear hunt he'd gone on, and Laurie asked questions. How big was the bear? Were you afraid when he came at you?

Finally they walked back, and when they got to the door of the room, Winslow stooped over and kissed the girl. "Good-night," he said, and moved away as though he had shown too much affection in front of an outsider.

When they were inside the room, Faith put on a nightgown, but Laurie seemed shy. "You know what?" Faith said, understanding the girl's embarrassment. "I've got an extra nightgown. Why don't you wear it tonight? It's too big for you, but it'll be like playing dress-up."

Laurie asked curiously, "Did you play that when you were a little girl?"

"Of course! Now, let me find that gown—"

While Laurie put on the gown, Faith brought out her Bible and sat beside the light. "I always read a little before I go to bed, Laurie. Do you mind?"

"No."

"Maybe I can read out loud this time?" Faith asked, and when Laurie nodded, she turned to the gospel of John and read the fourth chapter. As she read the story of the woman at the well in Sychar, Laurie watched her with careful eyes. After Faith finished, she said, "Was the woman bad?"

"Well, she'd had a very hard life, Laurie."

"But Jesus didn't care about that?"

"He cared, but He knew she wanted to be a better woman than she had been."

Laurie studied the Bible, then lifted her gray eyes. "How did Jesus know that? He'd never met her before, had He?"

"No, but Jesus knows all of us. And He loves us all very much."

Faith waited, hoping that the girl would open up to her, but there was a puzzled look in her eyes. She lay there silently for a few moments, then said, "Good-night."

"Good-night, Laurie," Faith returned. She put the Bible on the table, blew out the light, and lay there wondering about Laurie and her daddy. She slept fitfully, for the noise from the saloon came through the floor, and she could make out some of the profane speech clearly. *A bad thing for a child to hear* was her last thought before she fell asleep—except for, *I wonder where her mother is?*

When she awoke the next morning, Faith found Laurie gone. Rising at once, she dressed, packed her case, then went downstairs. Laurie was sitting with her father in the dining room, and she had a small smile—her first—for Faith. The three ate the rough food, then hurried outside to get on board the coach.

A very tall thin man was standing on the porch, his back to the wall, and he gave Faith a careful look as she came to the coach. She was startled when he took her arm, thinking at first it was Tom Winslow. But Winslow was loading the suitcases into the boot, his back turned. Faith tried to pull away, but the man merely grinned, saying, "Sweetheart, you look plumb sweet this morning. How about you and me sit together on this here stage?"

He had a razor-thin face, a sharp nose, and hazel eyes that ran over her boldly. Faith said a little breathlessly, "Please let me go!" But he ignored her, his lips curving up into a pleased smile. There was cruelty in his face, and when the driver said, "Cut that out!" the man gave no heed. Slipping his arm around her waist, he said, "Lem'me help you into the stage. We got to get acquainted."

"Let the lady go."

The man looked over his shoulder, an insolent expression on his face, but when he saw Winslow standing there, his eyes grew watchful. He released his grip on Faith, then turned to face the other. "We're doin' right well without your help," he said harshly. He let his fingers brush the cedar handle of the gun he wore low on his hip. There was a threat in his voice and a menace in his posture. Sensing trouble, a man behind Winslow took one look, then scurried out of the way.

Faith had never been close to a violent situation, but she knew that she was in one now. The man who had touched her was stiff, his hand poised over his gun; and though Winslow seemed almost at ease, there was danger in him, she knew.

"Friend, you can take the next stage," Winslow said, his voice soft, almost musical, on the morning air. "There's no room for you on this trip."

The man stiffened, cursed; then his hand was on the handle

of his gun—but he stopped abruptly, for the .44 at Winslow's side appeared in his hand. His hand had been little more than a blur to Faith as he had drawn and leveled the gun at the other. Now he said, "Driver, I guess we're ready." He moved forward, took the gun from the other man, who stood as if frozen in place, then said, "All aboard."

Faith got on, then Laurie and the other passengers. Winslow stepped in, took a seat, then said to the man who was staring at him with pure hatred, "I'll drop your gun down the road a piece."

The driver spoke to the horses, and the stage pulled away. The men who sat in the stage watched covertly as Winslow tossed the gun out the window, and Faith noted that Laurie's face was so pale that her freckles stood out. Her own breath was coming in short bursts, and she clasped her hands together to conceal their trembling.

This was a different world, as foreign to her own as if it had been China or the South Pole. She had read of the violence of the West, but it had all been so academic, words on paper. Now she realized that only by the closest margin had the crisis passed, that if things had differed in just one minor detail, Winslow might be lying in the dust bleeding his life out—either he or the other man. She studied him as he looked out the window, somehow shocked that he showed not the least effect of the encounter. He sat totally relaxed as he moved with the rolling of the coach.

Finally he looked down at Laurie. "You all right?"

"Yes," she answered, but put her hand in his for a moment and leaned toward him on the seat, her eyes fixed on his face.

CHAPTER SEVEN

FORT ABRAHAM LINCOLN

★ ★ ★ ★

Once again the morning began in freshness, in bright cleansing light. Then the coolness went away and the heat, the dust, and the monotony began. Just before noon, Faith saw a faint line of smudges against the horizon, small up-and-down streaks rising against the flatness of the prairie. The horses, smelling their destination, picked up their ears and then their pace, and soon the coach moved into the main street of Fargo, flanked by raw-boarded houses.

The coach groaned to a halt in front of a depot shed standing beside a single railroad track.

"We're just in time," Tom murmured, nodding toward the east where a smudge of train smoke was barely visible. "I'll get your things." He found her luggage, piled it on the ground, and they waited as the train grew larger, whistling hoarsely to warn the town. The steaming locomotive rolled in, and the townsmen ambled out of the businesses to watch. It was a break from the monotony of the day to see this line of steel, which was a thin strand that joined this far-off outpost to the busy world of the East.

"I can't get over how lonely this land is," Faith murmured, running her eyes over the horizon.

He leaned closer to catch her words, noting the smoothness

of her complexion. "Not a place for people who like crowds."

She glanced at him quickly, for there seemed to be some sort of warning in his words, but there was no hint of anything in his face.

The bell clanged steadily and great gusts of steam geysered, scaring a team of horses tied to a rail thirty feet from the track. They reared and neighed in terror, and the teamster had to saw on the reins until they grew calmer. The two baggage cars and five coaches jerked to a stop, the conductor appeared on the steps, calling out, "Fargo—twenty minutes for lunch!"

"Better get something to take with us," Tom said. "These trains don't keep much of a schedule." He dug into his pocket, produced some bills and gave one of them to Laurie. "You want to scoot over and get three of those lunches, Laurie?"

The girl took the money, nodded, and moved over to where a young boy was selling sack lunches. Tom got the luggage on board, then Faith and Laurie came to the high step of the coach and he helped them on. "Can I have a seat by the window, Daddy?" Laurie asked. He nodded and she took the seat facing forward. Tom sat down across from her, saying, "You'd better not ride backward, Miss Jamison. Makes some people feel queasy."

Soon the train gave a convulsive jerk as the brakes were released, and after a first hard *chuff* a preliminary quiver went over the car, and the train moved forward, gradually gaining speed. One man who had been speaking with another just in front of them gave a startled cry, leaped to his feet and made a run down the aisle. They watched as he leaped off the train and fell sprawling in the dust. He got up, shaking his fists at some of the spectators who were laughing at his predicament. The man made a run at them and struck a tall man with his fist. Then the crowd shifted, blocking the passengers' view.

Faith smiled ruefully at Winslow. "Now," she said, "we'll never know who won the fight. It's like losing a book you're only half finished with."

"I did that once," Laurie piped up. "Remember, Daddy? The book about the little girl who got lost—the book that got left when we moved from Fort Ruby?"

He shook his head, saying, "Can't remember."

She said impatiently, "You got it for me for my birthday. *The Old Curiosity Shop*—that was the name of it." She sighed deeply, regret seeping across her countenance. "I liked that book *so* much!"

Faith smiled, got to her feet, and made her way toward the end of the car. She waited until the conductor came through, then said, "Would it be possible for me to get at one of my suitcases? I need something out of it."

"Why, sure, miss!" he agreed, and took her on a rather adventurous journey to the baggage car. The wind whipped at her hair and her clothing as they passed over the couplings, and it gave her a quick thrill of fright when she looked down to where the heavy wheels ground against the rails. When they got to the car, he helped her find the bag she sought, then waited while she opened it. When she arose, he said, "I'll go back with you. Can't afford to lose a pretty lady like you." He was old enough to feel concern for her, but young enough to have a sly look in his dark blue eyes.

They made their way back to her car, and she smiled and said, "Thank you so much."

Going back to where Winslow and Laurie were watching the flat land speed by, she took her seat and handed a book to the girl. "Is this the book you lost, Laurie?" she asked.

Laurie turned around quickly and took the book. It had a dark green cover, the insides well worn with dog-eared pages, but when Laurie opened the cover and saw the first illustration, she cried out, "Daddy, look—there's Little Nell!" When she looked up at Faith, her eyes were shining and her lips parted with pleasure. She started to say something, then shyness overcame her, and she could only mumble, "Thank you." She ran her hand over the cover, almost lovingly, and said without looking up, "I'll read it now, before we get to Bismarck."

"No need for that, Laurie," Faith assured her. "It's your book. I'm glad for someone to have it who likes it as much as I do."

"Really?" Laurie exclaimed, a smile lighting up her face, making her look quite different. "Is it all right, Daddy?"

Tom Winslow looked across at Laurie, pleased at the scene. "Of course, Laurie." He tried to bring good things into his daughter's life, but sometimes it was difficult. Many times he worried about the nature of the life he had given her, knowing that she was missing many things. More than once he had almost made the decision to let Mark have her to raise. The thought of marriage had come to him, of course, but he had never found a woman who fit his situation.

At once, the girl opened the book and began reading, and Tom grinned. "You won't get any conversation out of her now, Miss Jamison. When she gets her nose into a book, it takes a charge of dynamite to shake her loose."

"I was the same way," Faith said. She looked down at the girl beside her, adding, "Perhaps I have some more books she might like. I'll look when we get to Bismarck."

"That's handsome of you," Tom replied. He thought of offering to pay for the book, but realized instinctively that such an action would be out of place. "I should have gotten her the book long ago." He hesitated, then added, "Her mother died when she was born." He started to say more, but his lips clamped shut, and he turned to stare out the window.

He must have loved his wife very much, Faith thought. *He can't even bear to speak of her after ten years.*

All day the land flowed by as Faith watched out the window, fascinated by the enormity of the spaces that stretched out, seemingly endless. The coaches stretched taut in their couplings and slammed together when the engine abated speed. Cinders pelted the windows, and smoke streamed back the length of the train. A rare siding appeared from time to time, and sometimes a yellow section shanty stood lonely in the sun. Antelope bands appeared, flowing over the broken land in a water-smooth motion, a beautiful sight that pleased Faith greatly. Later she fell asleep until she was awakened as the conductor cried, "Bismarck!"

"Quick trip," Winslow nodded. As he rose to his feet and stretched his muscles, Faith noted the town's gray out-sheds and slovenly shanties; then the train stopped and she got to her feet. When they stepped outside, he collected her baggage and said, "Is anyone meeting you?"

"Yes," she replied, looking around. A man and a woman were coming toward her. "I think they may be the ones."

Winslow watched as the couple approached and asked,

"Miss Jamison?" It seemed odd to him that she would be met by strangers, but as was his custom, he didn't pry. He got his bags, gave the smaller one to Laurie, and looked up as Faith drew near.

"You've been very kind," she said. "Thank you for all your trouble."

Winslow took his hat off, saying, "Glad to be of help." He wanted to say more, but couldn't find the right words. *Been with Indians so much I can't even talk to my own people*, he mused, irritated at the thought.

"Miss Jamison," Laurie said quickly, "thank you for the book. I'll never lose this one."

Faith smiled, then impulsively gave the girl a hug. "I'll think of you, Laurie."

A quick stab of regret ran through Winslow. *Laurie needs a woman*, he thought, and he said quickly, "If you'll be here in Bismarck, perhaps we can see you again. We'll be living at Fort Abraham Lincoln."

Faith's expression changed, and she exclaimed, "Why, how nice! Perhaps you'll let Laurie come and stay with me sometime." She gave the girl a warm smile, adding, "We could read lots of books together, couldn't we?"

"I'd like that," Laurie said, her eyes glowing.

Faith turned to the couple, who had drawn off to one side, watching with interest. "This is Reverend Willis Crenshaw and his wife," she said, then nodded toward the Winslows. "And this is Mr. Winslow and his daughter Laurie. They were very helpful to me on the trip."

Willis Crenshaw was a slight, wiry man of fifty with a smooth, pale face. There was something about his manners that proclaimed his calling, not at all displeasing, however. His eyes were warm and brown behind small rimless glasses, and his voice was deep and resonant. "Happy to meet you, sir," he nodded. "Are you staying in Bismarck?"

"I'll be joining the Seventh Cavalry, Reverend," Tom said, and his statement drew a surprised glance from Faith.

"Indeed? A fine body of men, and General Custer has my full admiration. You must come and visit our church, Mr. Winslow. It's small, but we feel it's a fine one for all of that."

"Thank you, Reverend Crenshaw," Winslow nodded, picking up his bags. "Let's go Laurie."

"Have you known Mr. Winslow long, Miss Jamison?" Mrs. Crenshaw asked. She was a plain woman, appearing to be somewhat older than her husband, perhaps because she looked emaciated and sickly.

"Oh no. We met on the trip."

Mrs. Crenshaw frowned, but she said only, "You must be exhausted. Come along, Pastor, let's take Miss Jamison to the house."

"Yes, indeed," Crenshaw nodded, and scurried off to get Faith's luggage into the buggy. When they were on the way to the parsonage, he commented, "We were expecting a married couple for the work here, Miss Jamison. It's difficult for a single woman." Then he saw from her expression that he had said the wrong thing. "Well, you'll find the work here difficult, but rewarding." Faith listened as he spoke cheerfully about the new addition on the church building that he was planning.

After watching the Crenshaws take off in the direction of the town, Winslow asked the agent, "How far to Fort Lincoln?"

"Four miles." He nodded toward an elderly man carrying a sack of mail out to a wagon. "Ride along with Jed there if you'd like. Tell him I said it'd be all right."

"I appreciate it." He turned, picked up the bags, and when he and Laurie got to the wagon, said, "The agent told us we might ride with you to the fort."

"Sure. Put your stuff in the back." Winslow dumped the bags in the bed of the wagon, helped Laurie to the seat, then joined her. As the wagon moved briskly along, the harness chains made a little melody. They passed along a crooked road that ran toward a high plateau upon which sat a group of houses. Beyond that lay bottom lands reaching to the Missouri River. "There's the fort," the driver mentioned, waving his hand toward a bluff on the opposite shore.

The wagon eased down to the deck of a river steamer, once glamorous but now dilapidated. As soon as the wagon was aboard, the engines began to send a shuddering through the ship; and when they were halfway across, the current caught the ship and Winslow thought the captain had lost control. The driver, however, showed no concern, but merely spat an amber stream of tobacco juice into the muddy waters. When the ship nosed into the slip, the driver released his brakes, whipped his team into a run, and went up the grade to the top of the bluff.

"There she is," he announced.

Winslow got his first glimpse of Fort Abraham Lincoln, which occupied a broad level plain between the river and the slope. Like most frontier forts, it was not fortified. Instead, it had groups of buildings arranged with military precision around a parade ground. Officers' row, a line of seven frame houses, edged the parade ground on the west at the base of the plateau. Facing the officers' line from the east side of the parade ground were three barracks for enlisted men, with some attached buildings, probably for kitchens and mess halls. Completing the rectangle on the north and south were other buildings, which Winslow accurately guessed to be the structures needed for any installation—commissary and quartermaster storehouses, adjutant's office, guardhouse, and hospital. Beyond the barracks Winslow saw the stables and other crude buildings, mostly for the laundresses and their soldier husbands.

The driver passed by the guardhouse post, saying, "Commissary," and was waved in.

"Do you know where the adjutant's office might be?"

"Down there at the end of them buildings."

"Thanks for the ride." Winslow picked up his suitcase, gave the lighter one to Laurie, and the two of them walked down the wooden walk. It was late afternoon, and the sun was dropping below the ridge to the west of the fort.

When they reached the adjutant's office, they would have turned in, but at that moment a tall man with a fine bearded face stepped out. He was wearing a dress helmet with a plume and a sabre. Pausing abruptly, he asked, "Can I help you?"

"We'll wait until after retreat," Winslow said.

"All right." The officer continued on, leaving the pair to watch the daily ceremony. Five cavalry companies filed out from the stables to the parade ground, the commands of the officers crisp on the afternoon air. Horsemen trotted briskly, lifting quick puffs of dust from the hard parade ground. One by one, the five companies came into regimental front, each company mounted on horses of matched color, each company's guidon colorfully waving from the pole affixed in the socket of the guidon corporal's stirrup. For a moment the regiment remained still, each trooper sitting erect in his saddle.

The adjutant wheeled his horse and came to a halt before the commanding officer, whom Winslow recognized at once as George Armstrong Custer. General Custer's face was known to most people in America; in fact, he'd become a living legend, his name a household word. Though he was the poorest scholar of his West Point class of 1861, he had been promoted to major general at the age of twenty-five, the youngest in either army, achieving this distinction by his love of bold action and wild charges into the guns of the enemy. He loved the spotlight, and would do anything to attract attention.

Now he saluted the adjutant, spoke a brief word, and the band burst into a brisk march. The officers of the regiment rode slowly front and center, formed a rank, and moved toward the commanding officer, who received their salutes. Then the band stepped out and marched down the front of the regiment, wheeled and marched back. There was a moment of silence, then the massed buglers sounded retreat as the flag was lowered from the pole. When it was in the hands of the trooper waiting to receive it, Custer's voice rent the air, "Pass in review!"

The first sergeants wheeled, calling sharp commands, and the band broke into another march. The regiment passed before the commanding officer; then at the end of the parade ground, each company pulled away toward its own stable.

As the ceremony ended, one of the officers broke away from the others and came toward the walk. "Tom Winslow!" he called. Winslow turned as the slight officer strode toward him. "I'm Captain Thomas Custer, the general's younger brother. We've been expecting you," he said, extending his hand to Tom. His restless eyes turned toward Laurie. "This must be your daughter." He shook hands and smiled at the girl. "You'll be staying with a very nice lady tonight—Mrs. Jennings." He searched the rim of the parade ground, then said, "There she is. Come along."

The woman was about twenty-five, Winslow judged. She had dark blue eyes, brown hair, and an attractive round face. "Mrs. Jennings, this is Mr. Tom Winslow and his daughter Laurie. This is Mrs. Eileen Jennings."

Winslow pulled off his hat and acknowledged the introduction. "I hope we're not putting you out, Mrs. Jennings?"

"Not at all." Her voice was precise and she looked at the girl rather than at him. "Laurie, let me take you to the house. Then your father can join us later for supper."

Laurie raised her eyes to her father, who smiled and nodded. "Thank you," she said softly to the lady. As the two walked away, Tom heard Mrs. Jennings asking Laurie about her journey, and Laurie's response. "I met a lady who gave me a book. . . ."

Winslow turned to Captain Custer. "I appreciate your finding someone, sir," he said. "Is she one of the officer's wives?"

"Her husband, Frank, was killed by the Sioux six months ago," Custer said briefly. "She has no family, so she's stayed on here. Fine woman," he commented, then added rather obliquely, "Not interested in men—not yet, anyway." Then he nodded, saying, "Let's go talk."

"Fine."

The two men entered a small office just off the back of one of the buildings. "I share this with Weir and Moylan, but they use it a lot more than I do." He waved to one of the chairs, then pulled a bottle of whiskey from a cabinet fastened to the wall. Without asking, he filled two glasses and placed one in front of Winslow. He fell into one of the chairs, drained his glass, and gave a convulsive shudder. Then he grinned at Winslow. "Winslow, I'm glad you're here. Going to be a big show, and you'll be right in the middle of it."

"Well, thanks, sir," Winslow answered. He twirled the glass gently, observing the swirls it made on the worn desk.

"Call me Tom," Custer said. From what he knew about Winslow, he was not a person who revealed much about himself.

Winslow glanced up, his black eyes calm and watchful. "What's happening? Is the pot really going to boil over this time?"

"No other way it can go," Custer shrugged. "Settlers are pouring into the Black Hills, the Sioux will attack them, and we'll be sent in to drive the Sioux away."

"Pretty tough on the Sioux," Winslow murmured.

"Sure, but it's coming no matter what anybody says. The same old story, I guess. The weak get pushed aside by the strong."

That was as close to the truth as anyone was likely to get, Winslow knew. And it had been going on in America since the days of the firstcomers on the *Mayflower*. The eastern tribes had been the first, fighting a retreat step-by-step until they were either decimated or vanquished to the West. Now with the Civil War over, the expanding population of the East was pushing relentlessly across the country.

"Is there any plan for paying the Sioux for their land?" he asked finally.

"I don't know," Tom Custer answered. "I think they'll be moved to another location."

What Custer didn't know was that a scenario for launching a full-scale war against the Indians was already formed. Indian Inspector Erwin C. Watkins had submitted a report on the "wild and hostile bands" in the territory. His report condemned the entire Indian Nation, concluding: "The true policy, in my judgment, is to send troops against them in the winter, the sooner the better, and *whip* them into subjection." His report, of course, perfectly reflected military views, perhaps the first time in history that the military and the Indian Bureau had agreed. This only occurred because Watkins was a straw man, inexperienced in his post, ignorant of his subject, and owed his position to Generals Sheridan and Crook.

Custer continued speaking of the conflict with the Sioux as though it were a settled affair, and Winslow listened carefully. If Tom Custer, in the confidence of the general, was so certain, there was little doubt. As Custer talked about the strategy necessary to defeat the Sioux, Winslow thought of leaving, for his sympathy lay with the Indians, who only wanted to be left alone. But he had already gone over that option. Finally he asked, "You've got plenty of scouts, Tom. Why another one?"

"You won't be just another scout," Custer responded. He hesitated, then said in a confidential tone, "Not everyone agrees on this thing. You were in the Confederate Army, but I reckon that bunch had their problems with command, same as we do." He poured another drink, downed it, then plunged ahead. "Blast it, Tom, my brother's the best Indian fighter in America, but some of our own officers won't give him their loyalty."

"The general is a man who evokes strong feelings, Tom. Men

either love him or hate him. It'd be odd, in my view, if he did command the loyalty of all his men."

"You're right, of course—but when we take the field, the general won't be able to depend on some of the officers. Oh, I don't mean they'd disobey his orders, but he's got to have the best information available on the movement of the Sioux. And we can get that only from our scouts. But all of them are civilians."

"They're loyal to Custer, though."

"Sure, but an Indian doesn't think like a white man. We need a man like you, who's a scout *and* a soldier. Somebody to be right there. Out with the scouts, but able to weigh their reports. The Crows are so scared of the Sioux; if they see ten of them, they'll report five hundred!"

After about an hour, Custer said, "Too late to enlist you tonight. Let your daughter stay with Mrs. Jennings. I'll find you a bunk someplace."

"All right."

As they made their way toward Officers' Row, Custer asked, "What about Laurie? Be pretty lonesome for her around here with you out scouting."

"Is there a school on the post?"

"No, but there's one in Bismarck. That'd be the thing to do. Maybe you could find a place to board her with some of the townspeople."

"No, I'd rather have my own place."

"All right. I think one of the houses down by Suds Row is vacant."

"Doesn't have to be fancy. Laurie and I have roughed it before."

Custer gave a curious glance. "Eileen's a handsome woman," he remarked. "I tried to catch her attention. Maybe you'll have better luck."

"She's the widow of an officer," Winslow said briefly. "She wouldn't be interested in an enlisted man."

Custer laughed. "A woman's a woman, Tom."

CHAPTER EIGHT

AN OLD ACQUAINTANCE

★　★　★　★

Eileen Jennings took a white tablecloth from the side compartment of an ancient buffet, and as she spread it over the table, a memory from the past stabbed at her, causing her to pause and stare at the cloth. It was a fine piece of work, Irish linen, thick and smooth, given to her by her grandmother as a wedding present.

It was Frank's favorite tablecloth, she thought, and then the memory of that last supper with him the night before he'd ridden out on his last patrol came back as sharp and clear as a photograph. She could even remember the meal—all his favorite foods: roast beef very rare, sweet potatoes, green beans and biscuits. He'd been very handsome that night, his face cheerful, white teeth gleaming and eyes happy. They'd eaten, and he'd joked about leaving her alone. *Hate to leave a good-looking woman like you alone with all these dandies around!* She'd smiled at him, teasing him. He'd held her with such a passionate hunger that night, she'd returned his ardor freely.

Now, holding the cloth, her mouth went dry as she thought of her last sight of him, seated on his black charger, proud and handsome as any man in the army leading his company off on a routine mission.

She'd never seen him again, for he'd been so mutilated by

the Indians that his coffin hadn't been opened.

That had been six months ago, and she'd never shed a tear, at least in public, except for that first time, when they brought him back wrapped in a piece of canvas tied across a mule. Now, feeling the texture of the cloth, it all came back, and it wasn't until the girl spoke that Mrs. Jennings pulled herself quickly away from her thoughts.

"What did you say, Laurie?"

The girl was standing in front of the stove with the hinged door open, peering in. When she turned to question Eileen, her face was flushed with the heat of the wood stove. "Are they ready, Mrs. Jennings? I can't tell."

"Let me see—and I think you might call me Miss Eileen." She looked at the biscuits, then stood up. "Maybe another ten minutes. Why don't you set the table while I work on the food? Here's the cloth, and the dishes are in the buffet." She watched as the girl happily spread the tablecloth, then carefully put the dishes on its snow-white surface. She handled each piece of the fine china carefully, then placed the silverware beside the plates. When she was through, she looked up, asking, "Is that all right?"

"Just fine, Laurie." The girl came to watch her finish the supper preparations, and Eileen asked, "Where did you and your father live before you came here?"

"Well, we came from Wyoming, but we weren't there too long."

"Did you hate to move away and leave all your friends?"

The answer was slow in coming. Finally Laurie said, "There weren't too many children there."

"Well, there are a few here on the post, about your age. Most of them go to school in Bismarck. I'm sure you'll make friends quickly." The child, she thought, was too solemn, and she decided that it was because she had not been with other children very much. Tom Custer had told her that Laurie's father had moved among the tribes for several years, but hadn't said much about Laurie.

She told Laurie what little she knew about the school, but was thinking that her own loneliness was worse than Laurie's. *At least she's got her father!* The thought leaped into her mind, and she shook it off as self-pity—yet it was true that she had nobody.

Her own parents had died in a cholera epidemic, and what distant relatives she had in the East were not close. Frank had been her world, and though she'd had an invitation from his parents to join them in Chicago, she'd graciously rejected it. She'd met them only twice, and even if they were very nice, they were strangers to her.

She'd been aware that some of the men on the post were interested in her—like Tom Custer, a lady's man by popular rumor, who would have been drawn to any woman. Then there was Captain Nelson Leighton, who had been Frank's friend as well as hers for two years, and Eileen knew that sooner or later he would come with his offer. He was a widower, a quiet man of forty with two children he was trying to rear. There would be security for her in Nels, she knew, but something in her rebelled against such a businesslike solution to her problem.

"Here comes Daddy!" Laurie cried. She had been looking out the window and ran out the door. Eileen watched as the two met, noting how he smiled at her and put his arm around her shoulder while they walked to the house.

As they came in, he saw Eileen smiling at them, and he pulled away at once, self-conscious. Eileen said, "You're just in time, Mr. Winslow. If you and Laurie would like to wash up, I'll have it ready."

"Sounds good," Tom said, and went to the table out on the porch and washed his face and hands, listening as Laurie told him about helping with the meal. They went back inside and took the places Eileen indicated, but he waited until she was seated before sitting down himself.

"Would you carve that chicken, Mr. Winslow? I never could handle that too well."

Winslow took the carving knife and fork, saying, "My first name is Tom. I'd feel better if you'd call me that."

"Yes, and I'm Eileen." She watched as he skillfully cut thin slices from the baked chicken, adding, "I always start by trying to do that, but finally just hack it off in chunks!"

They pitched into the meal, which in addition to baked chicken consisted of boiled potatoes, pinto beans, fried squash, and biscuits. The latter came under special attention. Tom tasted one judiciously, then exclaimed, "By heavens, these are *good*! You didn't make these yourself, Laurie?"

"Miss Eileen watched and told me how, but I mixed them up and everything!"

"Well I'll be eternally confounded!" Winslow shook his head in disbelief. "I'll never cook another biscuit again as long as I live! Not with a biscuit-shooter like you in the house!"

The pleasure in Laurie's eyes pleased him, and he finally said, "I guess I'll have to brag about the other cook. This is a fine meal, Eileen."

She grew slightly flustered, saying, "Oh, anyone can cook when there's someone to cook for." Then she caught the quizzical look in Tom's dark eyes and was afraid that he'd interpret the statement as a plea for pity. She asked quickly, "I understand you're enlisting in the Seventh?"

He nodded, and explained how he'd decided to begin a new career. He said nothing about Laurie, but when he finished, she asked, "You'll be gone on scouts quite often, then?"

"Yes. And on patrols with the units sent out by the general."

Something changed in her eyes, he noted, and afterward learned that she could not bear to be around when a company was sent out. He ventured a guess that it had something to do with the death of her husband, but said only, "I'll be home more than I have been in a long time. The job with the Indian Bureau kept me on the move most of the time." He reached over and gripped Laurie's shining crown, squeezing it and giving it an affectionate shake. "Never liked to go off and leave my girl."

Laurie gave him a sober look and asked, "Will you be fighting with the soldiers, Daddy?"

Winslow nodded slowly, and when he answered it was as honest as he could make it. "Sometimes. I'll be a soldier, and that's what soldiers are for."

Laurie said no more, but they both saw that she was worried. Eileen, wishing to break the mood, said, "I have dessert." She rose and came back with a large apple pie, placing it in the center of the table. "I made this yesterday. If I eat it all myself I'll be fat as a pig."

The pie was good, so good that Tom ate two pieces. Finally he refused a third, saying with a chagrined laugh, "You're probably thinking I'm the world's biggest glutton as it is. Maybe I'll have a chance at it again."

He insisted on helping with the dishes, while Laurie sat all folded up on a chair reading *The Old Curiosity Shop*. As they talked, Eileen had another painful memory, for the sight of Winslow in his shirtsleeves drying dishes was all too familiar—except it had been a different man. Afterward, she said, "It's early. Would you like to walk around the post?"

"Fine. Want to go with us, Laurie?"

"No thank you. I'd rather read."

The post was quiet and a full moon was lifting over the river. The sound of singing and a banjo came to them faintly from the barracks, the plunking of the instrument clear on the still air.

"I hope your new career works out well, Tom," Eileen said. "It's a hard life, not as adventurous as the novels make it sound."

"I had plenty of adventure during the war," he remarked. "I'm not a young man looking for romance."

She was puzzled by him, and intrigued as most women would have been. He was a fine-looking man, and knew that sooner or later she'd find out about his marriage. Most men married after losing a wife—especially those with children to raise.

He must have had a very happy marriage, she thought as they walked along, *or perhaps a very unhappy one.*

They stopped at the edge of the parade ground and looked down on the river, catching the little leaping waves touched with silver light. Far off, the lights of Bismarck gleamed, and from far away came the mournful cry of a night bird.

He had been thinking about her comment and finally said, "I don't need any more adventure or romance, Eileen. I do need some kind of order in my life."

"For Laurie?"

"Yes." He turned to face her and was caught by the curve of her cheek, smooth and clean, in the warm moonlight. She was not tall, but straight and well-formed, slender but filled out with mature curves. "I've got to settle down. I could take a desk job with my brother, but it would just about kill me." He turned to look at the barracks, listening to the faint sound of the singing, then said thoughtfully, "I think the last time I had any kind of peace was when I was in the army."

"The Confederate Army?"

"Yes. Maybe I'm one of those men who just wants to be told what to do."

"I doubt that, Tom. But the army isn't exactly the profession I'd pick for stability. Especially not with the trouble that's coming."

He thought of that, then nodded. "You're right, of course. If I had any character whatsoever, I'd ignore my own desires and do what's best for Laurie."

She saw how deeply the problem had etched itself on his mind, and it made her say, "That might not work out very well. If a man gives up being what he is, he changes. I always wanted my husband to leave the army, to do something safer. It took him away from me. But I had enough sense to know that he would have been miserable in another job. He loved the army, and I resigned myself to it." Then she turned away from him, saying, "And it killed him—just as I always feared it would!"

Winslow felt awkward. He needed to say something, but dreaded to utter one of those empty phrases people use when trying to comfort one who has had a loss.

Finally she turned to him. "Sorry, Tom. I don't usually let it get the best of me—not in public, at least."

He fell into step with her, and they walked around the ground, she speaking of the post and the officers. He listened with interest, for as soon as he took the oath, those men would be in charge of his world. He was surprised that she had such positive feelings, for without gossiping, she spoke of the strengths and weaknesses of the group. Even for Custer, she had both praise and rebuke. "He's a masterful man, Tom," she said thoughtfully. "Whatever it is that men have that makes other men follow them, General Custer has a lot of it. But his men don't love him, as soldiers sometimes love their leaders. Like men loved General Lee."

"Some men can make men love them. But not Custer, you say?"

"No. He cares nothing for the men of his command. He's one of the worst martinets in the army, Tom. He hands out severe punishment to any man who breaks one of his rules—yet he himself violates the orders of his superiors."

"That's bad," Tom commented.

"Yes, I think so. You'll find out what sort of a commander he is. My husband had no respect for his military judgment. Frank always said Custer had no concept of strategy, that he just threw all his men against the enemy in a wild charge."

"That may have worked in the war at times. It won't work against the Sioux."

Then they were at the house, and she said, "Come in for coffee."

"No, I'll say good-night." He paused, took off his hat and stood there, a tall shape against the darkness. "This has been a fine evening. I can't thank you enough for taking care of Laurie."

"Let her come to me sometimes, Tom. I do get a little lonesome."

"Of course." He waited until she sent Laurie out, then bent to kiss his daughter. Good-night. I'll see you tomorrow."

"Good-night, Daddy." Her small arms held tightly to his neck, and she released him only with reluctance. He knew that she was worried. She had no one but him, and it was inevitable that she would fear losing him.

"We'll get us a house right away," he said, stroking her head. "You can make biscuits and I'll eat them. We'll have a fine time." He kissed her again, giving her a squeeze, then turned and walked down the walk toward the barracks.

He looked up the first sergeant of A Company, a weathered veteran named Hines, who had been told by Tom Custer to expect him. "Take that bunk there," Tom was told, and he went to it at once. Some of the soldiers were playing cards, and a few looked at him curiously, but no one said a word. He undressed and lay on the bunk thinking of the day, wondering if he'd made the right choice. He hated the uncertainty he felt. Unaccustomed to sleeping with eighty men in a room, he slept poorly and was glad when Hines called out before dawn, "All right, roll out of them bunks!"

After breakfast with A Company, Winslow waited for an hour, then walked toward the adjutant's office. He entered and found Tom Custer talking with Cooke, the lieutenant he'd met the day before. "The general wants to see you before you take the oath," Custer nodded, and led the way across the parade ground to the line of officers' houses. The Custers lived in the middle of the row of seven, in a roomy two-story house with an inviting veranda. They were met at the front door by a petite woman. "This is Mr. Winslow," Tom Custer said. "The general wants to speak with him."

"He's in the study, Tom."

The captain led the way. Custer was sitting at a table littered with books and papers, but jumped to his feet to greet the men. "Mr. Winslow? Glad to see you. Tom, I told Weir you'd see him about that trip to the Yellowstone." Then he waited until the captain left. Turning to Winslow he invited him to sit down. He himself paced the floor restlessly as he talked, filled with energy that almost crackled. Tom had seen his photographs, but the art of photography was young, requiring the subject to remain absolutely still. Custer looked rather ugly in most of these, but in person he was quite different. His long golden hair fell over his collar, and the sweeping tawny dragoon's mustache sharpened the bony nose and accented the depth of eye sockets. There was a hungry look about him, a hawkish air that was intensified by the driving quality of his rapid speech.

"You've come with high recommendations, Winslow," he nodded, his light blue eyes fastened on his guest. "I believe my brother has told you what I need?"

"Yes, General."

"Can you do it?" Custer demanded abruptly. "If you can't, say so now. After we're in the field, it'll be too late for me to replace you."

"General, I know the country and I know Indians. I was a soldier in the Confederate Army for almost five years, so I know what discipline is. That part of the job I can do." Winslow gave Custer the full impact of his gaze, emphasizing his words by speaking slowly. "But I have to tell you that I think the whole thing is a mistake."

"In what way?" Custer demanded.

"We've made a treaty with the Sioux. If the government wants the Black Hills, they should pay a fair price for it."

"True. That should have been done," Custer said, studying Winslow more carefully. "I have said so many times. But it will not be done. The decision was not mine, but the responsibility is. Now, can you give me your full loyalty, knowing that you will be in battle against the Sioux?"

"Yes, sir, I can."

Custer waited, but seemed pleased at the brevity of Winslow's reply. "Very well, I think you'll do. Now, tell me about the Black Hills, about the Sioux. Be specific and accurate."

For the next half hour Winslow reported what he knew of the people and the geography of the country. Finally Custer nodded. "Fine! Very fine, Winslow. Go get yourself sworn in. You'll have the rank of sergeant, as my brother told you. If you do well, you'll be breveted as a second lieutenant."

"Thank you, General." Tom rose and returned to the adjutant's office. He was impressed by Custer and hopeful that in the days to come he himself would prove to be of value to the Seventh.

Lieutenant Cooke was expecting him, and when Winslow told him that he passed muster with the commanding officer, the big officer swore him in. "You are now a sergeant in the Seventh Cavalry, attached to A Company," Cooke said. He scribbled out a note and handed it to Winslow. "Sergeant Hines will show you around and get you outfitted."

Winslow found Sergeant Hines working in his office. "I'm assigned to A Company, Sergeant," he said, handing him the note.

Hines stared at it hard, then looked up. "A sergeant, is it? That'll not go well with the men, Winslow." But he rose and led the way to a room at the end of the building marked ORDERLY ROOM. "Granger, give this man an outfit."

Winslow carried his supplies to the barracks and laid them out on the table: underwear, socks, field boots and garrison shoes, blue pants and blue blouse and two blue wool shirts, campaign hat, forage cap and dress helmet with plume, sabre and sabre sling, carbine with its sling, Colt revolver, Springfield carbine, ammunition, cartridge belt, canteen mess outfit, entrenching tools, saddlebags, housewife kit, bridle, lariat and hobbles and picket pin, a razor, a silvered mirror, a bar of soap, a comb, two blankets, a straw tick, a box of shoe polish and a dauber, an overcoat, a rubber poncho with a hole through the center, a pair of wool gloves, a bacon can, currycomb and brush, a pair of collar ornaments with crossed sabres, the regimental number seven above and the troop letter below and a set of sergeant's stripes.

After inspecting his outfit, Tom said to Hines, who had just come out of his office, "I need to find someplace for my little girl."

Hines nodded. "There's a vacant shack on Suds Row. Not much, but it could be made livable. You can take that."

"I'll look at it," Winslow replied. "Be back for my things as soon as I can."

"You'd better speak to Captain Moylan," Hines said. "It's different having a sergeant living out of the barracks, but I'll see that you get the house."

"I'll be coming in and out with the scouts at odd hours," Winslow said. "This way I won't be waking the men up."

After getting directions to the house, he left the barracks and headed for Suds Row. Two women were washing clothes outside, and when he asked about the house, one of them pointed to a small structure at the end of the line. When he left, the woman grinned broadly at the other, saying, "Ain't he a dandy feller, Maude? What'd you do if he came tapping at your door some night when Al was out with the troop on a patrol?" The other giggled knowingly.

Coming back from inspecting the shack, Tom stopped by the women. "My name's Winslow. I'm going to need some help getting that place in shape for my daughter," he said. "Be glad to pay whatever it would cost to get the job done."

"Oh, we'll take care of it," the woman called Maude piped up. "Have it clean as a pin by late afternoon." The two women watched him head back toward the main part of the fort, then fell to speculating about the new addition to the Seventh.

Winslow was aware of their interest, but it came as no surprise. An army post was a small world, and any addition was certain to become the object of intense curiosity. He would have to prove himself with the company, and that would not be done with words.

He found Eileen and Laurie outside and gave them his news. "I need to go to Bismarck and pick up some things for the cabin," he said. "But first I've got to get a wagon to bring them back."

"Oh, that's no problem," Eileen said at once. "The quartermaster lets me borrow one whenever I go to town. Perhaps I can help you with the curtains and things?"

"It'd be a kindness," Tom said, flashing a smile.

The three of them spent the day in Bismarck, picking out furniture and other things needed for a house. They visited the few stores there, taking time out at noon to eat at a restaurant. Afterward, they drove back to the fort.

Winslow was pleased to discover that the two women had done an excellent job of cleaning the house. It was not large, only two rooms, the larger used for cooking, eating, and everything else except sleeping. The bedroom was reserved for Laurie. She was delighted with the small bed they'd found, so while Winslow put up the stove and arranged the outer room, she and Eileen worked on the smaller room and made the place look as cozy as they could.

Finally at five, Winslow said, "Time to eat. Tonight, I'm the cook." He made pancakes, bacon, and some fried potatoes. They laughed a good deal at his efforts, but he said, "It's my last hurrah, so eat and don't make fun of the cook!"

Afterward, he and Laurie walked Eileen back to her house. They were laughing over something Laurie had said when suddenly Winslow halted as abruptly as if he'd slammed into a post.

"What's wrong, Tom?" Eileen asked.

Winslow's face had grown hard, all traces of gentleness gone. He was staring at an officer who had come out of Custer's house.

"That's Lieutenant Grayson," Eileen said. "Do you know him?"

Spencer Grayson was coming toward them, engrossed in conversation with a second lieutenant. He was smiling at something the other had said when he saw Winslow. The smile disappeared, replaced by a blank stare.

"Hello, gentlemen," Eileen said and started to introduce Winslow, but he whirled and walked away, with Laurie running after him.

"Well, what's that about?" the lieutenant with Grayson asked in surprise. "Who was that, Eileen?"

"His name is Tom Winslow," she answered, watching the pair disappear. Then she looked at Grayson. "Do you know him, Spence?"

Grayson nodded slowly, "Yes, I know him." Then he turned

and walked away without another word, anger in the set of his shoulders.

"Well, the gentlemen are acquainted," the lieutenant remarked. "But I don't think they like each other."

Eileen moved on to her house. The scene mystified her, but she knew intuitively neither man would discuss it. She had seen the rash anger wash across Tom's face, a side of him she would never have suspected.

Winslow himself walked away from the encounter in white rage, forgetting Laurie, but snapped out of it when she asked, "Daddy . . . is something wrong?"

Winslow took a deep breath, forced himself to smile, and said quietly, "No, Laurie, nothing's wrong."

But after Laurie went to bed, he stood outside, staring across the space that separated Suds Row from the Officers' Row. He had been excited about his new position, convinced that he had done the right thing. Now he knew that nothing would be right—not as long as Spence Grayson was on the earth!

CHAPTER NINE

A LEAP OF FAITH

★ ★ ★ ★

On Wednesday morning, Faith awoke with a strong determination to find a place of her own. She had gone to bed wondering if there was an area of pride in her that needed to be mortified. For hours she had wrestled with her own spirit and God without resolving the matter, but when she awakened, she found her confusion replaced by certainty.

As she dressed and brushed her hair, she thought of the events of the past few days. She lived with the Crenshaws in a comfortable white frame house with three bedrooms, and because the couple had no children, there was plenty of room for guests. Reverend Crenshaw had taken it for granted that Faith would stay with them, but from the beginning she had sensed that Mrs. Crenshaw was not too happy about the arrangement. It was not that she openly opposed the matter, for she was agreeable—outwardly.

Faith had had her first hint of the problem on Monday when Ada Crenshaw was asked to visit one of the church members who was ill. Mr. Crenshaw was gone, so as she left, she said to Faith, "Pastor Crenshaw will be back this afternoon. You can tell him I'll be home by four o'clock."

"Of course. And I'd like to do some of the cleaning, Mrs. Crenshaw."

"Oh, it's all taken care of, Miss Jamison." As she uttered those words, a frown creased her forehead as if something unpleasant had occurred to her, but she said only, "You didn't come all the way to Dakota to clean houses. I suggest you spend the afternoon with God."

The manner in which the woman had spoken was distinctively unpleasant—at least to Faith. Not that what she said was wrong, but her tone carried a rebuke, as if Faith were so far from Christian maturity that she needed to repent or go back East.

But Faith had merely agreed. "That's always a good thing to do, isn't it?"

However, she had not taken the woman's suggestion, but had wandered the streets of Bismarck, stopping to visit several of the businessmen she had met at church the previous day. They were surprised to see her, but pleased, especially Nick Owens, chairman of the missions committee, a man about thirty, who owned a large hardware store. He had left his assistant in charge of the store while Owens himself escorted her around town, introducing her to many of the other merchants.

"I'm glad you did this, Miss Jamison," he said when they returned to his store. "We'll get support for the work from some of the men you met today." He was happily married, with two children, but had not lost his ability to appreciate a fine-looking woman. Faith's auburn hair was glossy in the afternoon sunlight, and the pearl-gray dress with white lace trim made her look charming. There was so much zest and enthusiasm about her, Owens decided, that most men would take a second look.

"Thank you for taking me around," Faith smiled, and thrust her hand out like a man. "I'm anxious to get to the mission. So far the only Indians I've seen have been the ones here in town."

"Well, they're a strange people," Owens nodded. "Very spiritual people."

Faith looked at him with surprise. "You mean the ones who are Christians?"

"No, I don't mean that," he said, and tried to explain it to her, his homely face serious. "White people sort of put God in a box. When they need Him, they open the lid and invite God to come out. When they don't need Him—at least when they *think* they don't—they keep the lid on, never giving Him much thought."

"What an odd way to put it!"

"It's true enough, isn't it?" he shrugged. "But you won't find it that way with the Indians. They live in a world that is full of gods. None of them the true God, of course, but the Indians don't know that. They're very conscious that the gods are there—and I don't mean in a box. Their gods are in a tree, in the bear they kill—so much so that they pray to the bear before they kill him, asking his pardon."

"Is that actually true, Mr. Owens?"

"Oh, sure. You'll find this out for yourself, Miss Jamison. You won't have any trouble convincing the Indians there's a God. They know that better than most white people. The trouble comes when you present Jesus Christ to them as the *only* true God."

Faith was deeply interested in what the merchant was saying—so interested that she was totally unaware of the glances they were getting as they stood in front of his store. She had that habit, or ability, as it were, to shut everything out of her mind except the thing at hand.

"I never thought of that," she admitted. "I suppose they want to see some sort of evidence that Jesus is strong—stronger than their gods?"

He laughed. "You're pretty sharp, Miss Jamison—or should I call you Reverend Jamison?"

"Please *don't*!" Faith exclaimed. "I like first names best, so let's make it Faith and Nick—at least when we're alone."

Owens was surprised and pleased. "That's the way I like it," he admitted, "but a man is never sure what a woman thinks."

"Just try to forget I'm a woman, Nick," Faith urged. "The Scripture says in Christ there's neither male nor female."

Owens shook his head. "That may be fine theology, Faith, but it won't work here in the West. Too many woman-hungry men. You'll discover that soon enough, if you haven't already. Show your face at the fort and there'll be gallant young officers right at your heels!"

Faith laughed at his warning. "Then I'd better stay away from them, Nick."

"They won't let you do that."

Faith had left him, pleased with her day. When she arrived

at the parsonage, the pastor was there. As she entered the house, he came out of the study, asking, "Sister, do you know where Mrs. Crenshaw is?"

"Oh, she went over to a family named Judson. Mrs. Judson's sick and she needed someone to take care of the children."

"Perhaps I'd better go myself."

"Your wife said she'd be home by four."

"Oh? Well, in that case I can catch up on my work."

He returned to his study, and Faith changed clothes, then went to the kitchen. She hesitated, but decided to start the evening meal anyway. Mrs. Crenshaw had mentioned what she intended to prepare, so Faith plunged in. As she went about the kitchen, she sang to herself, happy and content. She felt a new sense of freedom and realized that it was because she had cast off old ties—the past was behind her, but the future, hard as it might be, was a challenge that stirred her.

Four o'clock came, but no Mrs. Crenshaw. Faith kept the food warm, but at five, she went to the study. "Pastor," she said, "the meal is ready. Should I put it in the oven and wait for Mrs. Crenshaw?"

Crenshaw pulled out his large gold watch, studied it, then said, "She'll probably be home soon. We may as well go ahead." Rising from his chair, he walked with her to the dining room, and ten minutes later they began the meal.

It was a pleasant time as he shared about the work among the Indians. Faith told him of her visit to town, of meeting the businessmen, and then what Nick Owens had said about the Indians. Crenshaw was a good listener, and his attitude encouraged Faith to speak more openly than she had with Owens. The time went by so fast that both of them were startled when Ada Crenshaw walked in. Neither of them had heard the front door close, so engrossed were they in conversation. "Why, Ada—" Mr. Crenshaw said, rising to his feet and pulling a chair out for her.

He seemed rattled, Faith noticed. Her eyes flashed to Ada's frowning countenance. *Why, she's jealous of her husband!* she thought, astonished at the very idea. But she quickly discovered she was not mistaken, for after a most unpleasant half hour, Mr. Crenshaw fled to his study, flushed and embarrassed at his wife's actions. He had tried to converse with her, but she only nibbled at the food and gave him short, cryptic answers.

"Miss Jamison," Ada said when the study door closed, "I don't want to seem critical, but do you think your behavior is wise?"

"My behavior, Mrs. Crenshaw?"

Mrs. Crenshaw drew her thin frame up stiffly, her lips compressed so tightly that her words seemed to escape only with difficulty. "You're very young and inexperienced in the work, Miss Jamison, but you must learn to observe certain . . . formalities."

"I—I'm afraid I don't understand."

"Then I must speak plainly. What if one of our church members had come to this house and found you and Pastor Crenshaw alone?"

Faith stared at her, dismayed. "Why, surely there's been nothing—"

"Ah, but there is!" Ada Crenshaw cut in, her eyes hardening. "The Scripture enjoins us to avoid the *appearance* of evil." Her lips curved down at the corners, and she shook her head with distaste. "I must say I am surprised at my husband's lack of discernment, but he's a very simple man."

Which means he doesn't know how to keep designing women like me from snatching him away from his wife, Faith thought. Anger rose in her at the accusation, but then she felt pity for Willis Crenshaw. The poor man was in for a tough time, she realized. "I'm very sorry, Mrs. Crenshaw," she murmured. "In the future, I'll be more careful."

After that incident Ada Crenshaw never gave her husband any opportunity to be alone with the new missionary. She went with them to meet with the mission board, and in the house Mrs. Crenshaw never took her eyes off either of them. Meals were a torment, for Faith had to analyze every comment before she spoke, lest she offend the woman. The situation had become unbearable to Faith. The pastor, too, was going through a private hell of his own, which was evident by his harried expression and nervous manners.

★ ★ ★ ★

Faith brought her mind back to the present, gave her hair one last vigorous stroke, and walked out of her bedroom. With a serene expression, she went straight to the breakfast table. She waited until the meal was finished; then over coffee, she said in a casual manner, "I've decided it would be more convenient if I lived close to the school, perhaps in the same building."

"Why, that would *never* do!" Crenshaw exclaimed. "The station is in an isolated location, has no conveniences, and the building itself is not fit to live in."

"I don't mind that."

Mrs. Crenshaw fixed her steely gaze on Faith. "It's not a thing a woman should do. Reputation is everything, and people would talk."

Faith looked at her, curious. "People will always talk, won't they? The important thing is the work, and if I live as a Christian woman should, anything contrary would just be gossip."

"That may be so," Crenshaw said, "and it may also be true that you're not afraid of hardship; but the fact is, Miss Jamison, it wouldn't be safe for you. This isn't St. Louis, you know. The men around here are rough—very crude. A single woman living in an isolated location would be a temptation for them."

Faith listened to their arguments—or to Mr. Crenshaw's, at least, for after her first remark, Ada appeared to give up. Finally, Faith said, "I feel very strongly about this, Pastor Crenshaw. I don't want to be stubborn or rebellious to authority, but it's something that the Lord seems to be telling me to do." She smiled and added, "Let me try it for a few days. If it doesn't work out, we'll find another way."

Crenshaw argued against the idea, but discovered that Faith was not to be moved. He finally gave up, saying, "Very well, it'll be as you say."

"Thank you, Pastor," Faith said. "I'll have my things ready in an hour. Could you take me to the mission this morning?"

"Well, I suppose so," the minister said, but after glancing at his wife, said hastily, "But I remember that Brother Owens said he'd like to go. He mentioned he'd like to take a couple of his clerks out there and give the place a good cleaning."

Poor man, Faith thought, for it was obvious that he was in bondage to his wife. So it was with great relief when Faith saw

Owens drive up. He and the pastor loaded her things in the wagon, and when they were secure, Faith said to Mrs. Crenshaw, "I so much appreciate your hospitality. You'll be coming out to visit me when I get settled, I hope?"

"Why, certainly!" Mrs. Crenshaw gave her husband an uncertain look, then nodded, "Yes, we'll both come." She hesitated for a moment. "Be *very* careful, sister—and if you need help, just call on us."

As they drove away, Owens gave her a half-concealed smile. "Glad to be leaving?" He saw that she was startled by his question, then shrugged his shoulders. He was a plain man, but highly intelligent and had known the Crenshaws for a long time. "Ada's a fine woman," he remarked casually. "But she's not too secure where her husband is concerned." When Faith turned to him with a question in her eyes, he added quickly, "Didn't mean that the way it sounded. Pastor Crenshaw's not a man to look at another woman, no more than I am. But Ada just can't believe that she's got a man who'll care only for her. She was late marrying, you know—over thirty. She thought she was fated to be a spinster."

Faith realized Owens was presenting Ada's side, and she appreciated that. It revealed a man of great compassion. "I'm glad you told me, Nick. It helps to understand better." Her face broke into a smile, and she touched his arm, saying, "You wait and see! She'll learn to trust her husband to me before I'm through!"

Owens looked at her approvingly. "I'll bet you'll do it. You're a clever woman, Faith—and a stubborn one, too. You'll need some of that to make this school work."

The morning air was clear and sharp as they drove along the narrow road, rutted and weathered and lined by scrub pine. They crossed a creek, which Owens informed her got too deep to cross during rainy seasons, except at a ford three miles south of the road. The road meandered aimlessly across the land, now dodging into the jaws of a small canyon that led between the jutting brows of twin hills, then circling around a towering butte. Finally Owen said, "There it is."

Hmm, Faith thought. *Not very impressive.* The barn-like structure, with missing boards here and there, had weathered to a silvery gray. Next to it stood a small shack with a door and two windows in the front. Behind the barn a makeshift corral of sharpened stakes had been put up. The place looked abandoned, but Faith was undaunted. "Oh, this will be fine, Nick!" she said.

He had been expecting a different reaction. "Pretty poor doin's." He shook his head. "Going to take a lot of work. I've hired two men to come and put things right. They'll start in the morning."

"Come on," she said, jumping excitedly to the ground. "Let's see if the roof of the house leaks." She ran ahead while he tied the team to a fence post driven into the ground for that purpose. "The roof looks tight, Nick," she said when he stepped inside. "We can put my things in here."

"Not yet. You can't stay here until we get the place fixed up," he replied, shaking his head. "I didn't know it was in such bad shape." He looked around morosely, noting the trash of empty cans and bottles, the stovepipe hanging sloppily over the big-bellied heating stove, spilling soot everywhere, and the broken glass on the floor. "Got to get new glass in all the windows," he commented, then walking around the room and passing into the other room, added, "Take at least two or three days to get this cleaned up."

"Send the men in the morning," Faith suggested. "I'm staying here tonight. Is there a well?"

"Yeah. Fortunately it's a pretty good one," he admitted. "That's the best thing about the place. Only trouble is that everyone knows it. The hunters and Indians use it a lot."

"Good!" she nodded. "I'll get a chance to preach to them."

Owens scratched his head and stared at her, then smiled. He was not an impressive man, but he was solid, a person who knew quality in man, woman, horse, or dog. Finally he said, "Let's go back to town. You'll have to pick out your furniture, get groceries, get lumber ordered for desks and stuff for the school. You've got to have a horse and wagon, too, and a whole list of things to get this thing started. Tomorrow you can come back with the carpenters. They can stay until the job's done. They'll bring some blankets and sleep in the barn, but you'll have to cook for them. How's that sound?"

Faith smiled. "I may be stubborn, Nick, but I'm not unreasonable. I'll do just as you say. All right?"

Fully expecting an argument, he was taken off guard by her compliance. "You are a dangerous female, Faith!" he stated. "Know how to get your own way, don't you? And then turn right around and make a man feel good about lettin' you have it." He laughed, slapped his hat on, and said, "Let's get back to town before you get any more ideas!"

★ ★ ★ ★

"Get your house fixed and your daughter settled; then you can get started with the scouts," Captain Moylan said. Moylan, a stocky man with a broad, plain face and a heavy sandy-colored mustache guarding his upper lip, was captain of A Company. He was known for being tough, but he was fair and understanding since he had children of his own. "We'll see that she gets a ride to school and back, Sergeant. But who's going to look after her when you're on patrol?"

"Mrs. Jennings offered to help," Tom replied. "I'll see if I can hire some woman to stay with her when I'm out."

"Be a good thing for Eileen," Moylan nodded. "She gets lonesome. The girl will be company for her."

Winslow borrowed the wagon from the quartermaster in Eileen's name and drove across the river to town. He was sober, even gloomy, for since he'd seen Spence Grayson, his whole world had shifted. Old angers he thought long dead had come alive, making him keep a tight rein on his words. Only when Laurie had asked, "Are you mad at me, Daddy?" did he grasp what the sight of the man was doing to him.

As he drove down the dusty street and pulled up in front of Owens' hardware store, the sight of Faith Jamison coming out with a heavy box helped him shrug off his mood.

"Let me get that," he said, taking the box. "In the wagon there?"

"Yes." She watched as he placed it in the wagon, then smiled at him. "It's good to see you, Tom. How's Laurie?"

"Fine. We've got a house." His lean face lightened with a smile as he added, "It's good for Laurie. She's turning out to be a real housekeeper." His eyes flitted from the wagon back to her. "Looks like you're buying the store out."

She explained her new situation, her face flushed with excitement. "I'd like to start tonight, but Mr. Owens made me come back and wait until tomorrow."

"Good idea," he said. "Where are you staying tonight?"

"Why, I'm not sure." She had been so busy with her shopping that the idea of a bed for the night had not occurred to her. "I suppose I could go back and stay one more night with the pastor and his wife."

He caught a tone in her voice that told him she didn't really want to do that. "Come and stay with Laurie," he said. "We can have supper, and Laurie would like it." He hesitated, then added, "So would I."

"But it wouldn't look good, Tom."

"Why, I didn't mean—!" He grew red with embarrassment and said quickly with some awkwardness, "I'll stay at the barracks, of course. Just thought it would be good for Laurie to have all the women friends she can."

She was amused at his embarrassment and said, "I think it's a wonderful idea. I have some books picked out for her, and this way I can take them myself."

He made his own purchases, then helped her load the wagon with more packages. Finally, Nick Owens said, "Miss Faith, that wagon won't hold any more. I'll get the lumber on another one, and you go get a good night's rest. Be here at dawn, and I'll ride out with you."

"Thank you, Nick," Faith said. "I'll be here."

She got the books for Laurie and a small case, then let Tom assist her into his wagon. The night air had turned cool. "Winter's coming soon," Tom said. "Be sure you have plenty of wood cut. This weather can be a hungry wolf sometimes." He admired her covertly, taking in her high color and the brightness of her eyes. At the same time, he was afraid of his impulses, for he had built such an impenetrable wall around himself as far as women were concerned that he wasn't sure how he should act.

When they arrived at Tom's place, Laurie came bursting out of the house. She hugged her father and greeted Faith warmly. "Miss Eileen let me make most of the supper, Daddy!" she cried, then asked, "Are you going to eat with us, Miss Faith?"

"She sure is," Tom nodded. "And she's going to spend the night with you. I'll have to go to the barracks, so you two can talk about books all night."

Eileen had watched them from the window and met them as they stepped inside.

"This is the new missionary, Faith Jamison," Tom said. "And this is Mrs. Jennings."

The two women spoke, each with some restraint. It was a delicate situation, for Eileen had no idea what Tom's relationship with the attractive young woman was, nor did Faith know why the woman was in his house.

But Laurie broke the ice, getting them all to the table as soon as possible. And when they sat down, Tom said, "I wish you'd bless the food, Faith. I do a sorry job of it."

Faith asked a brief blessing, then was generous with her praise of the meal as they began to eat. "This roast is so good!" she exclaimed. "Better than I'll get from now on. Unless you'll come and help me cook sometimes, Laurie?"

Tom saw the curiosity on Eileen's face and explained that Faith had come to Dakota to open a school for Indians. Neither Tom nor Faith missed the slight hardening of Eileen's face at that information, but it was obvious she was not impressed. Tom thought, *She probably hates Indians for killing her husband.* He changed the subject immediately, and the rest of the time went very well. After they were finished, Eileen rose and said, "I must leave as soon as the dishes are done."

"You've done enough," Tom smiled. "I can't thank you enough, Eileen. But don't run away so soon—"

Eileen shook her head, and after saying good-night to them, she gave Laurie a hug. "I'll see you tomorrow, dear," she said, then turned to Tom. "If you get called out, please leave Laurie with me."

"That'll be a help," he said warmly. "I'll see you tomorrow." When she was gone, he said, "Now, you two can look at books, and I'll do the dishes."

Laurie was enthralled over the books that Faith had brought, asking her one question after another. Tom watched them as he cleaned up the kitchen. He was happy for Laurie. When he finally came to sit down beside them, Laurie showed him the books, going over all the pictures as one by one Tom exclaimed over them. After a while he said to Faith, "I'll have to find a way of making this right with you. Maybe I can do some work on your school."

"Oh, I loved doing this! But if you really want to help, tell me about the Indians."

"What about them?"

"What they're like. What I should do to reach them. What I should be aware of. There must be mannerisms we have that would offend them, customs I'd never think of."

That was the beginning, and for the next two hours, Winslow talked. Laurie read for a while, then came over to sit beside him, looking up at him as he talked. He had a vast knowledge of Indians and respected them. Faith said little, but soaked up his words, storing them up for future reference.

Finally he rose, with an embarrassed laugh. "Never talked so much in my life! Getting to be a regular bore."

"No," Faith countered, coming to stand beside him. "It's been so helpful, Tom. I can tell that you love the Indians—many people don't." She hesitated, then asked, "Tom, I . . . don't like to ask for help, but I know so little. I'm willing enough, but there'll be times when I won't have the least idea of what to do. If you'd just . . ."

When she hesitated, Tom said, "Be happy to do what I can. The school is a good idea, but some of the tribe will be against it. I know one or two of the leaders. Maybe I can put in a word for you."

He was surprised to see tears in her eyes, and even if she turned away so he wouldn't notice, saying nothing, he understood her a little better. She was a courageous woman, but she was being thrown into a world so different from the one she'd known that she was somewhat apprehensive. The sudden glimpse of vulnerability he'd seen made him say, "Faith, you can do it. These people are going to be hurt. They need to see someone who cares for them—someone with a white skin. I can't think of anyone who'd do better at it than you. You don't know the language, but if you love them and are kind to them that's a language we all understand."

Faith brushed the tears away, then turned to face him. "Thanks, Tom. I . . . I needed to hear that."

He kissed Laurie, who had been listening to them, and said, "I'll see you in the morning." Then he nodded to Faith. "I'll be here early to take you to Bismarck. Laurie, you can go, too."

When the door closed, Laurie said, "I saw you crying." She came closer and said shyly, "I didn't know grown-ups cried."

"Sometimes they do, Laurie."

Laurie hesitated, then put her arm around Faith's waist. "It'll be all right. My daddy will help you!"

"And will you help me, too, Laurie?"

"Me? Why, what could I do?"

"You could ask Jesus to keep me safe from harm."

Laurie looked at her wide-eyed. "But—I don't know how to talk to Jesus!"

Faith gave her a warm hug. "Then maybe I can teach you how to do that, Laurie."

CHAPTER TEN

"Nothing Ever Dies"

★ ★ ★ ★

Lieutenant Charles Varnum looked less like a soldier than any other officer of the Seventh, but Tom Winslow soon discovered that beneath the deceptive appearance lurked a tough, hard fighting man. When Winslow walked into Varnum's office early Friday morning, the man before him resembled an unsuccessful banker or a Boston shoe clerk. A fussy-looking individual, thin and pale, with a high balding forehead and a carefully trimmed mustache overlapping his lips.

The steely look in the officer's brown eyes reminded Winslow of Sergeant Hines' words: *He don't look like much, but he's tougher'n whang leather. He knows something about Indians, too, which this outfit is gonna need pretty soon.*

"Sergeant Winslow reporting, Lieutenant," Tom said, giving a precise salute.

Varnum returned the salute. "You're new?"

"Yes, sir. Enlisted last Monday."

A smile tugged at Varnum's thin lips. "Rapid promotion," he commented, then added, "You're to work with the Ree scouts, I'm told. Captain Custer mentioned you." He studied Winslow carefully. "Have you had prior service, Sergeant?"

"Yes, sir. Five years of the Civil War—on the losing side."

Varnum's eyes gleamed with humor. "We'll try to see that

you're on the winning side this time. I believe Captain Custer said you'd been working with the Indians. Speak any of their languages?"

"Sioux pretty well. Some Crow and a little Cheyenne."

"That'll be a help!" Varnum exclaimed. "Well, the scouts are probably over at the stables. Let's go."

As they walked along the parade ground toward the stables, Varnum filled him in on the scouts. "We've got two fine white scouts, Lonesome Charlie Reynolds—he's General Custer's favorite—and Mitch Bouyer. Two others, Herendeen and Girard, are used part of the time. All are civilians, of course. You'll be the only soldier represented."

"What about the Indians?"

"All Crows. They hate the Sioux so bad they don't feel it's a betrayal to try to crush them. All of the Ree tribe. They can move about better than any white man, but their information isn't always accurate. General Custer doesn't trust them as much as I do. Bloody Knife is their leader. He's a good one. Doesn't blow up his report of ten Sioux into two hundred the way some of the others do."

They turned toward the large barns used to hold forage, and Varnum nodded. "Looks as if they're getting ready to pull out over there. You can meet the men and get some kind of a feel about them, but don't make this trip."

The scouts stopped talking and turned to face the two men. "Hello, Charlie—Mitch," Varnum greeted. "Got someone for you to meet—the man we talked about."

Lonesome Charlie Reynolds was stoop-shouldered, short and stocky, with restless gray eyes. He surveyed the new man silently. Winslow learned later that Reynolds was a man of few words, soft-spoken, and quiet to a fault.

Mitch Bouyer was somewhat taller than Reynolds—a spare man with moody brown eyes and a large nose. He was dressed in a faded brown suit and wore a broad-brimmed hat pulled low over his brow. His thin lips opened in a slight smile. "Hello, Tom. Kind of pulled your picket, ain't you?"

"Guess so, Mitch," Winslow smiled. "Good to see you."

"You two have met?" Varnum asked, surprised.

"Sure have, Lieutenant," Bouyer nodded. "Winslow here

pulled my bacon out of the fire down south. I got crossways with a Cheyenne war party and was about to give up when Tom here come along. Saved my scalp, I reckon."

Varnum was pleased. "Well, that's fine. You can help Sergeant Winslow get settled. You're going out today?"

"Taking a little trip over to Wolf Canyon." It was Reynolds who spoke this time. "Heard that Gall was in those parts. Like to know about it if he is."

"Lieutenant, I may as well ride along, part of the way, at least," Winslow offered. He wanted to talk to Bouyer and to get better acquainted with Reynolds and the Ree.

"Of course," Varnum agreed. "Report to me when you return."

He turned and walked away, and Bouyer chuckled deep in his throat. "Another old acquaintance of yours here, Winslow."

He gestured toward the small group of Ree Indians, and Winslow smiled. Walking over to the group he nodded to a tall, heavy Indian. "Hello, my friend Yellow Face," he said in the Sioux language. "It is good to see my brother again."

The Indian nodded. "You are in this place," he answered. "But you will not put your friend Yellow Face in the jail this time!"

"No, I don't think so."

Winslow had gone into an Indian camp to rescue a pair of Mexican teamsters captured by the band of Yellow Face, and when the big Indian had tried to stop him, Tom had been forced to knock him out with the butt of his revolver and put him in jail for the night. "My brother is much wiser now than to drink the firewater that eats the brain."

A laugh went up from the Indians around Yellow Face, and Mitch Bouyer inserted, "Ain't got no more sense now than he did then, Tom!"

Yellow Face grinned.

Winslow met the rest of the Indian scouts, one of them Bloody Knife, whom he rode beside as the group left. This was, according to Varnum, the Indian the general trusted the most, so Tom wanted to find out what he was made of.

Bloody Knife was better looking than most of the Ree Winslow had met—smooth aquiline nose, small ears and mouth, superbly cut lips. But there was a curl in his mouth that indicated he was a scornful man, which proved to be true, as Winslow learned later. The Indian was impertinent toward whites and even ridiculed Custer's marksmanship. Instead of being offended by the latter, Custer was amused and made him a court jester.

He seemed amiable enough, however, and spoke freely with Winslow as they rode along. Tom learned that the Indian was half Sioux, a fact the Ree seemed to hate. Bloody Knife was well aware that the Sioux hated him more than the rest of the Indian scouts, the full-blood Ree, and this pleased him greatly.

"What will the Sioux do, Bloody Knife?" Winslow asked.

"They will fight," Bloody Knife nodded, his lips drawn into a scowl. "They are gathering now, and they will be many when all are come. More than any gathering of the people!"

More for a test than for information, Winslow said, "But there are many old enemies among the people. The Sioux and the Crow have killed each other for many years. They hate one another greatly."

Bloody Knife shot Winslow a brittle look. "They hate each other—but they hate the white eyes more!" Those cryptic words Tom would never forget.

All day the small band rode through the broken country, keeping their eyes peeled for any trouble. At noon, the Ree were sent in another direction so more terrain could be covered. As Winslow watched them go, he repeated to the two men what Bloody Knife had said.

"He's not wrong about that," Bouyer nodded emphatically. "Me and Charlie have tried to tell Custer the same thing, but he's a stubborn man."

The three rode along for a time, and then Winslow said, "I'm heading back. Just wanted to get acquainted."

"Keep your scalp on tight, Tom," Bouyer grinned, and when Winslow was out of earshot, Mitch turned to Charlie. "What you think of him?"

Lonesome Charlie Reynolds was chary with his praise. "Knows how to keep his mouth shut, and that is good. But can he scout?"

"Good as you or me, Charlie."

Reynolds snorted. "Let's not be giving the man too much credit, Mitch. If he's half as good as either one of us, he's an angel!"

"You'll see," Mitch nodded confidently.

★　★　★　★

Winslow had left the scouts purposefully, having an errand on his mind. He rode south, following the snaky windings of a dry riverbed, crossed over and let his horse pick the pace. The country was broken by raw outcroppings of rocks, and he deliberately kept away from them out of habit. As he rode along, his eyes moved restlessly from point to point. He was not expecting trouble, but he had lived with danger so long that it was second nature for him to look for it, to expect it even when there seemed to be no danger. Many of his friends had died because they had let their guard down, and he wasn't taking any chances.

Like the Indians, he was one with the land. The circling of three buzzards far off to his left sent a tiny message to his brain, as did the explosive burst of speed that propelled a large rabbit out of a thicket. Most men would have watched the rabbit, but Winslow watched the thicket, knowing that *something* had triggered the wild run of the animal. When a coyote came plunging after the rabbit, Winslow's mind registered the fact, and his eyes moved on. Every movement of tree, bush, cloud of dust, or animal was within the realm of his interest, and he was well aware of the three Indians who came from behind a low-lying hill before they appeared.

They stopped their horses and waited for him. Two of them were armed with bows and arrows; the other one carried a repeating Spencer.

Tom drew to a halt, lifted his hand upward, and spoke to them in their language. "Have my brothers had good hunting?"

The Indian with the rifle gave him a closer inspection. "How does the pony soldier know my speech?"

"I have spent many years in this country. Tall Antelope is my blood brother."

This information brought a definite change in the three, and the one with the rifle nodded. "We hunt the antelope." Then he spoke to his two companions, and the three of them wheeled their ponies and headed west without another word.

If I'd met them at another time—or if I didn't speak Sioux, it might have had a different ending, he thought. He moved on, storing the incident in his memory. Someday he might meet one of these three again, and he wanted to have this experience to call on. It was this careful attention to details that had enabled him to survive as long as he had, and he was aware that if he let his guard down for one brief moment, he could well become one of those bleached skeletons that dotted the land.

At four o'clock he saw what he was seeking, now just a dim smudge on the horizon. Soon it grew larger, becoming a barn and a house. He noted the horses penned in the corral and heard the sharp blows of hammers. He had asked Nick Owens how to find the place, and the businessman had given him instructions, but had not asked the question that was in his eyes: *Why are you looking for a mission?* Tom had said, "I told Miss Jamison I'd try to stop by. I know some of their Sioux language and a few of the chiefs in the area." The answer had satisfied Owens to a point, and he'd expressed his thanks for any help Winslow could give the missionary.

He pulled his horse up to the watering trough, let him drink a little, then tied him to a post, and walked into the barn. Two men were busy putting up partitions, while Faith did the cleaning up. She was wearing an old dress, with her hair tied up in a bandanna. When she did glance up, she was startled, not recognizing him at first.

"I didn't hear you ride up," she smiled. "Are you on duty?"

"Not now. Came to see what I could do."

"Well, these two know their business; they're very good carpenters," she said, turning to the men. They didn't cease working, but had their eyes on Winslow. "I'll go fix supper," she said. "You two must be starved."

"Could do with a bite," one of them nodded, a tall, lanky man with red hair and bushy whiskers. "Just give us a call, sister."

"Is that what they call you—sister?" Winslow asked as they left the barn and headed toward the house.

"They do call me that," she nodded. "Sometimes they call me reverend. I think they get kind of confused. Guess I don't know what I am exactly."

As he followed her inside the house, he saw that she was indeed a tidy woman. The rooms were neat, and the air smelled clean, with a mixture of putty, soap, and disinfectant. He noted the small table and four chairs, the cook stove, and the new pipe, and through the door he could see a bed with a pink counterpane.

"You've been busy," he observed. "It looks nice."

"Nick Owens brought some men from the church," she nodded. "They did most of it. Now, would you rather have bacon and eggs—or eggs and bacon?"

"Whichever's the quickest." He saw the woodbox was nearly empty, so he left to work on the pile of logs dumped to the side of the house. The wood was dry, and the dust smelled good as he bucksawed a log into short lengths, then picked up an axe and split the cylinders into quarters. When he finished the log, he carried the sticks in and filled the woodbox.

"Would you go call the men?" she asked. "It's all ready."

The four of them dug right in. Not only had she made bacon and eggs but also sawmill gravy, biscuits, and a pot of pinto beans, which she had prepared earlier. When the men finally slowed down, she brought a deep dish to the table and removed the cover. "Peach cobbler!" the tall carpenter groaned. "If you'd told me about this, I wouldn't have made such a hog of myself. Well, a man's got to eat it or he ain't no man atall!"

The shorter man had not said ten words, but he smiled when Faith gave him the remains of the cobbler as they left. "Don't go to bed hungry, Roger," she said.

Tom leaned back in the chair, sipping his coffee from time to time, apparently at ease. "Where'd you learn to cook?" he asked as she washed the dishes. He had offered to help, but she had refused.

"Oh, my mother taught me." She finished the last dish, took off her apron, and moved to the window. "It's so quiet out there!" she said finally. "Let's go for a walk."

"All right."

The night was dark, for it was that time just before the moon and stars came out. As they wandered down the path, she spoke of her gratefulness for all the help she'd received, her lilting voice conveying the happiness she felt.

"I want to start having services of some kind," she said. "But how would I get the Indians to come?"

He smiled. "They know you're here, Faith."

"But—I haven't seen a single person except the men who've worked on the mission!"

"They're looking you over. Trying to figure you out. They're pretty careful."

"Like you, Tom?" she asked. The question popped out impulsively.

He gave her a sudden glance, wondering about the question. "Well, I guess so. I've lived with them so long, I guess I'm like them in some of their ways."

She considered that, wanting to understand him. He was an enigma to her. "I guess you might as well know the worst thing about me, Tom."

He was amused at her remark. "You drink on the sly?"

"Oh, worse than that!" she laughed.

When she said no more, he took her arm and pulled her around. "Well, don't leave a man hanging! What's the worst thing about you?"

"I meddle."

"Well," he grinned, "I guess that's part of being a woman, isn't it?"

"No, I mean I can't let people run their own lives." She grew more serious, and was acutely aware that he had not released her arm. Not only that, she was a young woman alone with one of the most attractive men she'd ever met—and she was telling him her faults! *You'll run him off like a scared rabbit!* she thought, but plunged ahead.

"Tom, we haven't known each other very long. But you were so kind to me on the trip here. And I've grown fond of Laurie."

"She likes you too," he said soberly. "I joined the army to have some kind of stability." Then he asked, "Is that your meddling?"

"No." She hesitated, debating whether she should forego the question that had been troubling her for days. Then she said quietly, "Laurie told me how angry you became when you saw Lieutenant Grayson. Why do you dislike him so much?" She could see that her query had hit a nerve, and said quickly, "Well,

I told you I was prone to meddle. I have no right to ask—but Laurie said you changed so abruptly after you saw him. You became harsh, and it frightened her. I think that's why I asked. If I'm nosy, it's because I don't know any other way to go about it."

Winslow dropped his hand, and she thought he was going to walk away angrily. Instead, he stared out over the desert, seeming to hear something. Then he brought his eyes back to her. It was so dark she could not see his face plainly, but his voice gave him away, for it was tense, not his easy, casual tone.

"It goes back a long way, Faith. I don't think it'd do any good for me to talk about it."

"All right, Tom."

She moved away from him, and he followed her. They said nothing for a time; then he said with a trace of anxiety, "I hope you're not angry."

"Why, of course not!" This time it was she who reached out, touching his arm lightly. "I just hate to see you hurt . . . because when you're affected, Laurie is, too."

"In that, you're right." He let the silence run on. Finally he said slowly, "We had trouble once. I thought it was all gone, forgotten. But as soon as I saw him, it all came back, worse than ever." He hesitated, then added, "Nothing ever dies."

"I don't believe that," Faith countered. "I have a scar on my wrist. When I was ten years old I ripped it open on a barbed wire fence. It hurt worse than anything I'd ever known." She held her wrist up and peered at it by the faint light of the moon that had risen. "See? It's still there, the scar."

"What are you trying to tell me?"

"That the pain is gone, Tom. Only the scar is there. I know I was hurt once, a long time ago. I still can *remember* the pain. But it has nothing to do with me now!"

They walked the rest of the way back to the house in silence. When they came to the door, Faith could see by the light of the lamp that his wound was still raw. His face was torn at its re-membrance.

"I guess that's true of a cut on the arm, Faith . . . but other kinds of hurts are different."

"Tom . . . you have to learn how to forgive," she whispered.

"Unforgiveness is like a dreadful disease, eating away on your spirit. It makes you bitter and you forget how to love. And when that happens, you're dead inside."

Winslow listened to her, and for a moment, she felt he was going to speak, which was what she so badly wanted. If he would only *talk* about it, something might happen!

But he shook his head. "I know that's the way you feel about it. My mother says the same. Fine people, my family, Christian to the bone. All my people have been Christians." He struggled to put his thoughts into words, then finally gave up. "Whatever it takes to do that, Faith, I don't have it in me. Thanks for the supper."

He moved away so quickly she could not stop him; even if she ran after him, it would be hopeless. He was in a prison of his own making, and nothing she could say would change it.

He'll have to be broken, she thought, standing there alone in the darkness. *Whatever happened between the two men must have been terrible—and it's still terrible, for it's killing Tom!*

She went inside and shut the door, locking it firmly, then read for an hour. She went to bed, despondent over the scene, and when she woke up the next morning, her first thought was of Tom. *He's got to make things right with that officer!*

She dressed, got a fire going, and made breakfast. But when she opened the door and stepped out on the porch, blind panic hit her—her front yard was lined with Indians!

"They came to say 'welcome to the neighborhood.' "

Faith whirled at the voice. There stood Tom, leaning against the house, his rifle held carelessly in one hand. He nodded to one of the Indians. "This is Running Bear, chief in these parts."

I must not be afraid!

Faith took a deep breath, smiled at the silent Indians, and said, "I am glad to see you all."

Not a twitch in any of the bronze faces!

"Will you have something to eat?"

Tom said a few words in a guttural language, and when he finished, he laughed. "They say, 'Thank you, yes.' I hope you've got enough grub." He saw the startled look on her face, then said, "I'll help with the cooking. After that you can preach at them a little bit. I'll do my best to interpret."

"Do they understand any English at all?"

"Yes, but most of them won't admit it. Come on, let's get to work."

Three hours later, Faith dropped her weary frame onto a chair. Her hair hung over her brow, her legs were trembling. They had fed every one of the Indians, and then the chief had said, "You preach now!"

Winslow had almost laughed at her expression, but encouraged her. "They expect it, Faith. Do your best. I'll try to get it across—but make it simple!"

She had spoken for only ten minutes, telling them she wanted to teach their children and to have a worship service. "Jesus Christ, the great Spirit who made all things, loves you and has sent me to tell you of His love. . . ."

Now it was over, and she was astonished at how the effort had exhausted her. She turned to see Winslow watching her with an odd expression on his face.

"I don't think I made one bit of sense!" she said, her face flushed. "They think I'm crazy, I expect."

He got to his feet and came to stand beside her. "You did fine. You'll get your school, all right. Indians are curious, and they'll send the kids just so they can have an excuse to hang around. But you can't feed the whole tribe."

"Tom, how did you happen to be there? When they came, I mean?" He shook his head, and then she knew. "If you hadn't been here, they might have—have done some bad things."

"Well, I had a long talk with Running Bear. He's only a sub-chief. I did the big chief a favor once, and now Running Bear knows if any of his people harm you or the mission, he's in hot water. His chief is called Red Needle. I won't ask you to guess why they call him that, but I can tell you he's one fellow nobody likes to offend. So I think you'll be all right."

He moved toward the door, pulling his hat down, but her voice caught him. "Tom . . . thank you!"

He nodded. "Call on me if you need help, Faith."

Then he was gone. She walked out on the porch to watch him until his horse disappeared around a tall butte. All day she worked steadily, thinking about Tom and Spence Grayson. Somehow there was a potent danger in that situation—and neither she nor anyone else could do anything to change it.

CHAPTER ELEVEN

SOME THINGS A MAN CAN'T DO

★ ★ ★ ★

For two weeks Tom Winslow immersed himself in the life he had chosen. Although he was detached from A Company, he spent as much time as possible with the troop, getting to know the men and the officers. The routine and discipline of army life brought back his days in the Confederate Army, and he soon discovered how much he had missed the comradeship of men. There was a pleasure in becoming part of the group, and as the days passed he realized that he had needed acceptance from men like himself.

They were a tough group, the Seventh, and the enlisted men of A Company did not roll out a red carpet for any man. Every new addition was on trial as the men waited to see if the rookie could pull his weight. The test they chose would prove it. It was not a formalized initiation, but in the violent world they inhabited, the soldiers had to know if the man on their right and their left could be trusted. And when the bullets started flying, it was too late for such tests; therefore, there were other ways to test a man's mettle.

Winslow was targeted for such a test more than most, due to his rapid promotion. Most men endured years of hard work for the right to wear the sergeant's stripes, but the fact that Tom's was a special assignment made no difference to the men of A

Company. He had joined them; now they needed to know if he had the backbone they needed to see in their noncoms.

Corporal Babe O'Hara, a red-faced, battle-scarred hulking Irishman with beefy shoulders, made it his business to put the new sergeant of A Company to the test. He had, he thought, a legitimate grievance, for he had expected his third stripe for a year. And the sight of a rookie without a day's service being promoted over his head brought his ready temper to a boil. O'Hara was not highly intelligent, but he was crafty, and he knew he had to be careful. He understood that if he destroyed Winslow with his huge fists, he himself could lose his place, so he would wait for the right opportunity.

Winslow was aware of the big man's dislike and the reason for it; therefore, it came as no shock to him when he had to face the challenge—though he was caught off guard by the way it happened. O'Hara had slyly maneuvered a situation that would force Tom to fight. It came during a patrol. Among the group going out was Yellow Face, who could come and go pretty much as he pleased. Babe O'Hara had decided to make him his instrument leading to a row with Winslow.

The first day of the patrol, they stopped for a night camp by a small stream Captain Algernon Smith had chosen. While the food was being prepared, some of the men made the campsite safe by beating along the earth to rout out any rattlesnakes. After supper, Winslow rolled into his blanket, his head on the saddle, and listened for a time to the murmuring around him. The creek made a soft gurgling sound that brought sleep quickly, but he was conscious of many memories of bivouacs in the past as he lay there. He thought, too, of Marlene and the brief time they had spent together. Inevitably this led to thoughts of Spence Grayson, and bitterness, like gall, welled up in him. After tossing about, weariness finally overtook him, and he slept.

On scout patrol there were no trumpet calls. Men simply awoke and sat up to put on their hats, blouses, and boots; fires sprang up, rich yellow in the half light; then breakfast was served.

O'Hara saw Captain Smith eat early, mount his horse, and leave, saying, "Sergeant, I'll take a look at that ridge. When the troop's ready, bring the men over there to meet me."

"Yes, sir," Winslow nodded, and when Smith moved out of the camp, Tom went for his own breakfast.

O'Hara had noted the manner in which Winslow treated the Ree scouts, especially Yellow Face. As soon as the captain was out of the camp, O'Hara rose and moved to where the large Ree was standing beside the campfire waiting for his breakfast. Quickly, the corporal glanced around and saw that none of the men were watching. Then he spun around and drove his fist into the face of the unsuspecting Indian, and as Yellow Face was shoved to the ground, O'Hara began to curse the man.

Tom Winslow whirled and saw Yellow Face jump to his feet, only to be knocked down again by the corporal's fists. Tom dropped his tin plate, sprang toward O'Hara, and caught the man's arm, spinning him around. O'Hara never stopped but sent a hard fist into Winslow's chest, knocking him backward. "Keep your hands off me, Winslow!" he yelled. "Your pet Indian gave me a shove—which I'll take from no man—including you!"

By now the men had gathered in a circle around O'Hara and Tom, their eyes bright with anticipation. He got to his feet knowing that if he didn't whip the big Irishman, he would be laughed out of the troop, and no man would pay any attention to his stripes. They moved in close, the faint light of the rising sun catching their eyes. Winslow saw the lust for violence and the greed for raw action. As individuals, they were good men with stamina and courage and kindness, but now they were a pack, and the smell of the pack was on them, making their faces all alike—hollow-eyed with expectation, mouths partly open, and eyes glittering in the half-light.

"All right, Babe," Winslow nodded. "Too bad you chose this time to try me out." He slipped out of his blouse, adding, "It'll be a long ride for you after I teach you a lesson."

Babe grinned, winked at his comrades. "A lesson, is it? I'm not a good pupil, Winslow—" He waited no longer but lunged forward, throwing a long left that would have destroyed Winslow if it had landed, but it missed as Winslow moved his head to one side. The force of the blow threw O'Hara off balance, and Winslow followed it with a punch to the temple with a short, chopping right hand. O'Hara's eyes glazed and his jaw dropped, but he was an old veteran, so when Winslow stepped in, he threw his arms around him and hung on until his head cleared.

Winslow whirled around, finally managing to throw the big man away, but when he stepped in to finish the corporal off, O'Hara caught him flush in the mouth with a driving right hand. The blow was shattering, shaking him down to his toes, so that O'Hara's roar of triumph seemed faint and far away. Desperately he roused himself to fend off the blows from O'Hara's big fists till his head cleared. He was driven to the ground by a hard left hand, but when he got to his feet, he saw that O'Hara was breathing hard; and for the next few minutes he merely moved around, blocking blows and making no attempt to fight the tiring corporal.

Angered by his failure to finish Winslow, the big Irishman paused, glared at the man across from him, and wheezed out, "What—are you—some kind of dancer?" Then when one of the troopers taunted O'Hara, he turned his head to answer. It was the opportunity Winslow was looking for. He threw his hardest blow, every ounce of his weight behind an uppercut that caught O'Hara flush on the jaw. The blow made a distinct click, and O'Hara dropped to the ground like a rock.

"He's out!" Leo Dempsey exclaimed, then peered at Winslow with a grin. "Guess you learned how someplace, Sarge."

Winslow saw the smiles of the men and knew they approved. He had been admitted to the lodge. He waited until O'Hara's eyes fluttered, then stooped and helped him to his feet. "You're a tough fellow, Babe," he said.

O'Hara weaved slightly, his eyes confused, but when he came to himself, he asked curiously, "Was I out?"

"Dead out," Dempsey grinned. "Sleeping like a baby!"

Silence fell over the group, for O'Hara had been the bully of the regiment, never bested in a rough and tumble. Some men grow bitter when they lose, and if the Irishman chose to take it that way, it would be unpleasant. But O'Hara grinned and put his meaty hand out. "You win, Bucko," he said. "You can wear the stripes."

Winslow took the hand and grinned in return. "My head feels as if you hit me with a sledge hammer, Babe. I'd just as soon not do this every day."

But it was over, and when Captain Smith saw the bruised

faces of the two men, he smiled but said nothing. Later when he got back to the fort, he said to Tom Custer, "Winslow licked Babe O'Hara. Some doubt in my mind about how that would come about—but he's been admitted to the club."

As the morning wore on, a bleak chill lay in the still air, its thin edge cutting the faces of the troopers. Sunrise broke tawny in the east, and the sleazy fog lying on the earth vanished. All this was familiar country, and the ride was just one more scout detail flung out daily to keep an eye on the Sioux. East of the river the Indians lived in sulky peace, sitting in motionless shapes along the sidewalks of Bismarck. But west of the river they rode as they pleased, made haughty and insolent by the memory of the many evils done them by white people, made proud by the recollection of their vanishing freedom, made war-like by nature.

The troop ran across many trails, some old and some new, and from time to time passed traveling parties of Sioux. One of them was a large string of ponies and riders and travois. "Fifty lodges in that group," Smith said to Winslow. They watched the Indians as they moved west through and over and around the depressions and hummocks of the land. The line passed, but some of the warriors returned to stare at the troop, then rode away with a yell of defiance.

"Feeling pretty tough," Smith observed. He shifted his gaze to Winslow. "How do you feel about the scouts, Sergeant?"

"Better than I feel about the general's opinion of the Indians as fighters."

"So?"

"I read an article by General Custer in an eastern newspaper. He said that the Seventh could whip any collection of Indians in the West."

"You don't believe that?"

"No, sir." Winslow eased his weight in the saddle, watching the horizon. "Custer won his promotion to general in the Civil War by cavalry charges. But charging Indians isn't like charging us Rebels. We would stay put and meet force with force. The Indians think that's stupid."

Smith nodded slightly. "In that, Sergeant, you're probably correct. They ride around like ghosts, and we make enough noise to wake the dead. We'll never take them by surprise." He was an excellent officer, this Algernon Smith, a hard man, but with a keen knowledge of men. A dozen years of soldiering had formed him into a good soldier who knew the difference between caution and daring. Now he seemed to be brooding. Finally he said, "When spring comes, the Seventh will be ordered out for a campaign. We'll do what we're told, which will be to subjugate the Indians." He looked at Tom, saying, "We'll all be depending on you and the scouts a great deal, Sergeant Winslow. Don't let us down!"

★ ★ ★ ★

The encounter with Babe O'Hara left Winslow with sore ribs and a purple bruise high on his left cheekbone, yet there was an ease inside of him, and the men joked with him freely—always a good sign.

When he returned from the patrol at dusk two days later, he immediately reported to Major Marcus Reno, Custer's second in command. Reno was a stocky, rumpled figure, round and sallow of face with black hair pressed close to his skull, and round recessed eyes, darkly circled. He listened to Winslow's report, then asked, "What do the Ree say, Sergeant?"

"A big build-up coming, sir," Winslow answered. "They hear that Gall and Crazy Horse will make up their differences. Rain-in-the-Face, too, and when you get chiefs like that to thinking alike, it's trouble."

Reno shook his head thoughtfully. "I've tried to tell the general we're in for a big fight, but he thinks the only trouble we'll have is getting the Indians pinned down for a fight. And he's got some reason for thinking that, I suppose. We've spent a lot of effort chasing the bands across the desert, just to have them melt away before we can throw out troops at them. Like fighting smoke." He waved his hand, saying, "We'll keep sending the patrols out, but it's wearing us down. I think we'll find out more by sending out individuals—Reynolds, Bouyer and you—and the Ree scouts, of course."

"I agree with you, Major," Winslow nodded. "When a troop goes out, they're watched every step of the way, but a single man can hide himself and do a lot of seeing."

"I'll talk to Lieutenant Varnum," Reno said. He was a slow-moving man, and Winslow had the impression that he functioned well under controlled circumstances, but not under pressure. "I think we'll follow that procedure. You'll be on your own, Sergeant. Do whatever scouting you feel is good, and keep me posted at all times—especially if you see any heavy concentration of hostiles."

"Yes, sir." Winslow saluted and left the office. He took his horse to the corral, rubbed him down, and saw that he was grained. Then he headed for Suds Row. The sun in the west half blinded him, and he kept his forage cap pulled low over his brow to shade his eyes. He was tired and so occupied in his mind with plans for future scouts that he paid no heed to the figure coming around the corner of the building to his left.

"Winslow!"

The sound of the man's voice ran across Tom Winslow's nerves like the rasp of metal on metal. He halted abruptly, turned and saw Spence Grayson advance. He had no control over the emotion that exploded in the pit of his stomach, but did remember somehow that he was in uniform and saluted.

Grayson stopped and began to curse Winslow, his eyes pulled into slits by the heat of his anger. He had changed little over the years, Winslow noted, and was still trim and handsome.

"Get yourself transferred out of this fort, Winslow," he snapped, "or I'll break you!"

Winslow stood stock-still, knowing that he was on the razor's edge of destroying himself, for he longed to throw himself against the man and destroy Grayson's handsome face. Tom had often known violence, but even when he had fought the Yankees, there had been nothing like this—a blind rage that longed to destroy. Finally he took a deep breath and said in a controlled voice, "I didn't know you were here, but I won't be leaving."

"You'll leave!" Grayson growled. "I won't have you in this fort!"

"Are you afraid I'll spoil your reputation?"

Grayson ignored the taunt, saying, "You're an enlisted man, Winslow. How long do you think you'd last making an accusation against an officer? Custer would have you in the stockade for the rest of your life—or worse—if you lifted your hand to me. That would get you shot."

Winslow listened, but was thinking how little of the rottenness in the man's spirit was revealed in his face. He looked every inch a soldier, and was brave enough, but his deliberate betrayal of his best friend, his callous treatment of Marlene, abandoning her when she was in such dire need—these didn't show. He made a gallant figure, his smooth good looks attractive to women, Winslow well remembered. Nor had it been just Marlene. There had been other women also before her—and afterward as well, he had no doubt.

They stood in full view of the men passing by, and Winslow made his choice. "I'm here to stay, Lieutenant Grayson. You will do your best to ruin me, but I warn you, do a good job of it." He could not help one barbed statement about the past. "I'll be a little harder to get rid of than a sick woman."

Grayson's face tensed, but he made no reply. Turning his back, he stalked away, and Winslow found that his hands were trembling from the effort to control himself. He forced himself to walk slowly along the path, and by the time he got to Eileen's house, where he had left Laurie, he had himself under control. Not inwardly, for he knew that the cold rage that he kept pressed down was not going away; however, when he knocked on the door and Laurie answered it, she would not see any signs of the terrible strain.

"Daddy!" she squealed and threw herself into his arms. Her own arms tightened around his neck as she clung to him, and when he finally put her down, she took his hand and pulled him inside. "Miss Eileen! He's here!"

"Hello, Tom," Eileen said, entering the room. "You must have an instinct. You always come when the food is ready." She looked cool and clean and fresh to Winslow after the heat of the desert.

Holding to Laurie's hand, Winslow moved into the room, saying, "The mark of an old soldier—always knows where the chow line is."

"I'll get the food on the table while you wash up," Eileen said. "Go with him, Laurie, and make sure he does a good job—check behind his ears, too!"

Laughter followed the two as Laurie excitedly pulled her dad down the hall to the sink. Dousing his hands and face in the water, he sluiced away the accumulation of dust and dirt of the day. As he washed, Laurie talked as fast as she could, which gave Winslow more time to control his feelings after his encounter with Grayson. When they were seated at the table, Tom cast his eyes over the meal and commented, "Better than the cold sandwich I'd planned on, Eileen. Laurie, don't get your hand too close to me—I'm so hungry I might bite it by mistake."

They began to eat, and Eileen asked, "Did you have a good scout, Tom?" She and Laurie listened as he related some of the details, but it was Laurie who asked, "Daddy, why is your face all bruised? Did you get thrown off your horse?"

Feeling Eileen's eyes on him, Winslow touched the sore spot, laughed and said, "No, it was another critter who did this, Laurie." She begged him to tell her everything, but he teased her out of it, insisting that a ring-tail gouger had done it.

After the meal, Laurie showed him what she had done at school.

"Did you like it, Laurie, the school?" he asked.

"Oh, it's not bad," she shrugged. "The teacher is Mr. Dutton. He's old and a grouch. He must be at least thirty!"

"Mighty old," Winslow agreed, catching a smile from Eileen, who was washing dishes across the room. After she finished she came over and sat across from the two and began knitting on a pair of wool socks.

As she watched Winslow and Laurie, Eileen was struck with the thought, *We're like a family!* Startled at the idea, she dropped her head to hide her confusion. She remembered hearing of a woman who had lost her fifteen-year-old son and had kept his room for years exactly as it was the day he died. Eileen had found that morbid, but she realized now that she had done that very thing too! *I've made this place a memorial to my dead husband!* To cover her agitation, she went to the counter and made some juice for her guests.

"Warm, but wet," she smiled, handing them the glasses. She got the third one for herself, then sat down and asked, "Will you be going out soon, Tom?"

"Not for a few days. I'm going to do a lot of talking to the tame Indians around the fort and in Bismarck."

"Will they be able to tell you much about the hostile tribes?"

Winslow leaned back, and Laurie, swift to note that it was

now time for the grown-ups to talk, moved to the table and began writing on her tablet. "Not a great deal, as a rule. But if I can get close to them, their attitude and words will be another way of reading the situation."

As he spoke there was something in his face that told her he was thinking of other things. She looked across the room at Laurie, busily working on her lesson. Not wanting to disturb her, she said to Tom, "Let's go out on the porch. It's a little warm in here."

When they were seated on the porch, she asked, "Do you think there'll be trouble?"

"Yes. Sooner or later it will come." He turned to face her and asked, "Eileen, what will you do?"

She knew he was asking what was on his mind—and on the minds of many people. "I don't know, Tom. I don't have any family to speak of. If Frank had lived, we'd have gone East, I think."

"Not much in the East for a career soldier, anyway. The army's small now, after the war. The quickest way to get promoted is to get a good combat record—and the only combat now is the Indian war."

"Frank wasn't really a fighting man," Eileen said. "He was more of an executive. I never would have married him if we hadn't agreed on this—going to the East. He had a good friend in Sherman's command, a colonel who was working on getting Frank a place in the War Department. But my husband was killed before he had a chance for that position."

"I'm sorry," Winslow said quietly. He wanted to ask her why she stayed at the fort, living with memories, but was not a man to pry. He let the silence run on, then said, "I don't know what to do about thanking you, Eileen, except to keep on saying it. But I'd like to pay you to keep Laurie."

"Oh no!" she exclaimed. "Please don't do that." She rose and went to stand at the edge of the porch. He joined her, and she turned to face him. "If I took a salary, it would change what Laurie feels for me. Now we're friends, but then I'd be a paid keeper of some sort. I'm not rich, but Frank had some money when we married, and I get a check every month—enough to get by on. Please don't ask me to do that."

Pleased by her words, he saw the wisdom of them. "Seems as if you do all the giving and I do all the taking, Eileen. A little hard on my pride, I guess."

"No, Tom, that's wrong," she murmured. "It's been good, taking care of Laurie. I—get so lonesome—!"

Then the tears she'd kept back rose to her eyes, and she trembled, fighting to gain control. As Tom watched, the tears spilled over and rolled down her cheeks. She was not a crying woman, Winslow knew, and without thinking, he reached out and pulled her into his arms. It was a gesture totally unplanned, something he had pushed out of his life. Nor was she a woman to respond to them, but her defenses were down, and she leaned against his chest, and despite herself, began to sob. He held her, conscious that this was something she'd not been able to do; and even as he held her, he was aware of her soft figure pressed against him—a desirable woman, one who was no longer loved.

Finally she pulled back, brushed her hands against her face, and said wryly, "Just what you needed, Tom. A weeping woman!"

He didn't even answer, but stood there, his eyes on her. "We all do our crying, Eileen. Nothing wrong with that."

"Even you, Tom?"

"Yes, even me."

They stood there quietly, thinking their own thoughts. Finally Tom said, "It's late. I'd better get Laurie home."

Before they left, Laurie hugged Eileen and asked, "Will you teach me how to make the dress, like we talked about?"

"Yes. The next time your father lets you come. Good-night, both of you." Gone was the grief she had let him see. Instead, her tone carried a warmth that had not been there earlier.

On the way to their cabin, Laurie asked, "Daddy, do you like Miss Eileen?"

There was a cautious quality in her voice, and Winslow replied, "Sure do. Why do you ask, Laurie?"

"Oh, I don't know, Daddy," she said with a sigh.

Later when he came to tuck her in, he looked into those enormous eyes and was reminded again how much she resembled Marlene. And as always, this brought pain to his heart. He drew the covers around her and under her chin, then kissed her good-night.

"Daddy," she said again, "you know . . . what I said about Eileen . . . it's like having a mother. It really is!"

Her words rang in his ears as he left the room. *She's missed having a mother,* he thought. Winslow had long suspected this. Now he knew for a certainty: His daughter had needs he could never meet alone.

CHAPTER TWELVE

AT THE CUSTERS'

★ ★ ★ ★

The lights from the large house in the center of the line were bright yellow, spilling over into the darkness when Faith pulled up at the guard post of Fort Lincoln.

"Yes, ma'am?" the smartly dressed trooper inquired.

"I'm to be at General Custer's house, Corporal," she said. "For the reception."

"Yes, ma'am. It's the house over there, the one all lit up."

"Thank you." Faith gave the horses a slap with the reins, and was proud of the way she'd handled the team all the way from the mission. There had been an afternoon meeting of the mission board at church, and Reverend Crenshaw had drawn her aside to say, "There's a small social affair at the home of General Custer tonight. A reception for new officers, I believe. Mrs. Custer attends our church at times, and I've told her about your work. She sent a special invitation for you to come."

The invitation pleased Faith, and she eagerly accepted. She had one problem—no proper dress. But Nick Owens' wife, Elaine, was about the same size as Faith; and when Elaine was told of the situation, she decided to offer one of her own gowns and immediately fitted Faith into a beautiful gray and red.

When Faith drove up to the house, a private stepped forward

and helped her down. Taking the lines he said, "I'll take care of the wagon, ma'am."

Feeling a little out of place, Faith ascended the stairs; but as soon as she entered the house, she was met by Mrs. Custer, who extended her hands cheerfully. "And this must be our missionary friend!" Libby Custer was a tiny woman with a pretty, animated face. She was the most social being around, filling her home and her life with a constant stream of guests. Now she put her arm around Faith informally and walked with her into a large high-ceilinged room. Her voice carried above the chatter, drawing everyone's attention as she introduced Faith. "This is Miss Faith Jamison, everybody! I haven't had a chance to warn her of our romantic young bachelors, but she'll find you all out soon enough!"

General Custer was the first to greet her. "Delighted to have you, Miss Jamison," he said. "I understand you're a missionary?"

"Yes, General."

"Well, that's just what we need in the Seventh." He glanced around with mischief in his blue eyes, a smile lurking behind the drooping mustache. "I hope you can enlighten some of these young lieutenants. They're a pagan crew!"

Captain Weir of D Company took the cue and hurried over. "I think I'm the logical man for you, Miss Jamison," he said. He assumed a pious look as he added, "My father was a deacon in the Baptist church."

A hoot of laughter went up, for everyone knew Weir was a woman chaser. "Miss Jamison, trust none of them," Custer said with a grin. "Come along, Weir. Let's join that group of senior officers."

"Now, Miss Jamison," Mrs. Custer said as her husband walked away, "I want you to meet some of our other guests." As the guests arrived, among them the officers' wives, Faith noticed that most of the them showed signs of the harsh weather they had been subject to in the West, but she was warmed by their friendliness and undaunted by the fact that in years to come she herself would show the same wear and tear. But she was here on God's business, and nothing would keep her from carrying that out, a commitment that would be tested in many ways.

When Faith had entered the room earlier, Lieutenant Grayson

straightened at once, giving her his full attention. At the time, he was speaking to Eileen Jennings. Grayson's avid interest in Faith was evident. As Eileen watched him, she could clearly see his hunting instinct for women, which he usually concealed. He had pursued her since her husband died, not in an obvious way, but nevertheless in a fashion no sensitive woman could miss.

"She's quite pretty, isn't she, Lieutenant? Shall I introduce you?"

"You know her, Eileen?"

"We've met. Come along and perhaps you can get ahead of some of the others."

He gave her a quick glance, wondering if she had classified him as a womanizer. It was no secret that he liked women and cared what they thought—at least until they surrendered to his advances. He'd been chagrined over his failure with Eileen Jennings, but now put her out of his thoughts as they approached Faith.

"This is Lieutenant Grayson, Miss Jamison," Eileen said. "After the general's warning, I will say no more."

After the introduction, Eileen left and the lieutenant wasted no time in maneuvering her toward the refreshment table where he could have her to himself. She really didn't mind because she had been curious about him ever since Laurie had mentioned her father's reaction to the man and then Tom's own response to Faith's questions concerning the situation. Now she had an opportunity to form her own judgment in the matter.

Grayson said, "Blast the general for giving us a bad reputation. I hope you'll pay no attention to it."

"I like to make up my own mind, Lieutenant." The dress Faith wore was a beautiful gray silk, with rich crimson trim along the bodice and sleeves. There was a fullness to her that was pleasing to the eye, and her auburn hair lay darkly back on her head, exposing the small and dainty ears with pearl pendants—also belonging to Elaine Owens. There was a reserve in her eyes and a strength in her features that pleased Grayson.

He drew her out easily, seeking a weakness in her—his usual tactic with the women he met. It was his theory that there were no "good" women, only careful ones who kept their vulnerability well armored. His tactics on women were exactly the same as he used on a military adversary—find a weakness and throw all your strength against it.

After fifteen minutes of probing without discovering any weakness, he excused himself and moved over to listen to the talk swirling around General Custer, but his mind kept reverting back to Faith. The fact that she was a missionary meant nothing to Grayson, for he had seen more than one woman violate her religious code for a man.

Faith did not remain alone. She was soon cornered by Benny Hodgson and a tall lieutenant named Edgerly, the latter as handsome a man as she had ever seen, with a delightful sunny disposition. Other officers pressed in for their share of attention, too. Overwhelmed by the attention, she was relieved when a superior officer walked over and shooed them off. "I'm Captain Algernon Smith. These men can be a little too much sometimes. How are you doing? My sergeant has told me about you."

"Sergeant Winslow?"

"Yes." Smith studied her thoughtfully, then remarked, "You've not known him long, I think he said."

"We met on the trip from the East." She liked the captain and felt comfortable with him. "Is he going to be successful in his new life?" she asked.

"Coming back into uniform? I don't see why not. He's one who's born to be a soldier."

They spoke of her work with the Indians but were soon interrupted by Grayson, who approached them with Mrs. Smith in tow. His smooth handsome face was alive with humor as he said, "Now, Mrs. Smith, tell your husband to let his poor subordinates entertain the young lady!"

Mrs. Smith, an attractive blue-eyed blonde, nodded. "I always have to drag him away from the young women," she said, taking his arm.

"Emily—" Captain Smith protested. "You know that's not true!"

Mrs. Smith smiled at Faith, the smile of a woman secure in herself and in her husband, and said, "No, it's not. But these young officers are all waiting to make fools of themselves, so we'll give them a chance."

As she pulled her husband away, Faith smiled at Grayson,

amused at his tactics. "You're very resourceful, Lieutenant."

"Tell me about yourself," he said. "Or shall I tell you about *myself*?" When she chose the latter, he immediately related several stories concerning his career. He made light of himself, revealing little vanity, though she was certain he had plenty of that quality.

They strolled around the room as they talked, and finally she spoke of her trip from St. Louis, and added, "I would have been in great difficulties if a gentleman hadn't come to my aid. He had his daughter with him. I didn't know it at the time, but he was on his way to Fort Lincoln to enlist in the Seventh. His name is Tom Winslow. Have you met him, Lieutenant?"

She didn't miss the slight hesitation before he nodded. "Oh, he's the new scout. He's assigned to A Company, I believe."

Faith did not pursue the subject any further, for she sensed Grayson's reluctance in speaking about his past experience, just as Tom had. She soon discovered that Grayson was a polished man with women, probably as a result of much practice—and that he was not truthful at all times, for he had concealed the fact that he and Winslow were old acquaintances.

Faith was ready to leave the party early, but was detained by Lieutenant Grayson. "I'd like to see your school, Miss Jamison. May I come for a visit?"

"I'm going back in the morning, Lieutenant. Come any time."

Grayson's interest in her was more than his usual desire for conquest. He had not felt this way for many years, and so asked impulsively, "May I ride out with you? I'm off duty tomorrow."

Faith nodded. "I'll be leaving with a wagonload of supplies about nine o'clock. If you're at Owens' Hardware Store, I'll be glad to take you for a guided tour of my school."

"I'll be there!"

★ ★ ★ ★

Lieutenant Grayson had tied his horse to the back of the wagon and insisted on driving. The air was crisp and the sun just rising as they moved down the road on the way to the mission. Faith had wondered if she had done the right thing in inviting him to accompany her, but as the morning wore on, she grew more relaxed.

"I enjoyed the evening at the Custers' last night," she remarked. "He's been a celebrity for some time."

Lieutenant Grayson nodded. "And wants to be an even bigger one," he said.

"Really?"

"Oh yes. Most men are a little hesitant to draw attention to themselves, but Custer is so hungry for fame, he'll do anything to get a headline."

"That's not good for a soldier, is it?"

"Doesn't seem to matter much," Grayson said. "Some humble men make rotten commanders, and some—like Custer—advance with one eye on their own press clippings."

"Who was the officer with the snow-white hair?"

"That's Captain Frederick Benteen." He gave her a thoughtful look. "What made you notice him?"

"Well, I'd guess he's no admirer of General Custer."

"You guessed right." Grayson shook his head emphatically. "Hates the ground Custer walks on!"

"Why?"

"Custer led the Seventh into a battle on the Washita about seven years ago. It was the dead of winter, and in the fight an officer named Elliot, with a few men, got separated from the main body. Custer knew it, but didn't do a thing to help them. A few days later Elliot was found with his nineteen men, all dead. Benteen holds Custer responsible."

"Was the general really so callous?"

"Can't say," Grayson shrugged. "He thought he was in a tight fix, and it's hard to make decisions in a close fight." He smiled at her, adding, "Not too long ago an officer wrote a letter to a St. Louis newspaper, blaming Custer for Elliot's death. Custer called all his officers together and informed them he was going to pistolwhip the author of that letter. Benteen went and got his revolver, and when he came back, he said, 'You can begin the whipping anytime, General. I wrote that letter!' "

"What did Custer do?"

"Just turned red and said, 'I'll see you later, Captain!' It was a pretty close thing, for Benteen's a tough fellow. And that's why Custer's assigned him to Fort Rice, to keep him out of his hair."

The sun grew warm, and Faith removed her coat, her mind

still on what Grayson had just related. "It sounds more like a bunch of jealous boys than professional soldiers," she commented.

Grayson laughed with delight. "Exactly right!" he nodded. "But men will do anything to gain their ends—and the one goal of an officer is promotion."

"Not all men are like that."

He saw that he had gone too far. "No, not all. Captain Smith, he's a fine officer. But he'll never go higher because he's too good a man to get into the political side of soldiering."

They reached the mission and Faith proudly showed him around. The barn had been made into two smaller rooms, leaving one a little larger. The lumber was still fresh, giving off the smell of pine rosin. Faith liked it. As she moved around, making expressive gestures with her hands, Grayson watched her, admiring her graceful figure and bright eyes.

"Where are the students?" he asked.

"They only come in the afternoon," Faith said. "That's what they want, so I let them pick the time."

"Gives you lots of free time," he suggested. "Don't you get lonesome?"

"I haven't yet, Lieutenant." She thought of this, and shook her head. "No, I won't get lonesome. Sooner or later the school will grow. Until then I love the privacy."

He asked her bluntly, "Why haven't you married, Faith?"

Taken off guard, she flushed, but turned to face him. "I was engaged, but he called it off."

"He walked out on you?" Grayson was astonished and exclaimed, "What a blind fool!"

"No, he's not a fool, Lieutenant. And it wasn't I he walked out on. It was—all this." She motioned to the school and the horizon. "He couldn't face being just a small unimportant missionary."

She turned and they walked to the house. When he'd seen it all, they went outside, and he drew water from her well. As he was engaged in that, a rider appeared suddenly. He'd come from the south, on the other side of the barn, so they hadn't seen him.

Faith felt a sense of shock as she saw it was Tom Winslow,

and she turned to see that Lieutenant Grayson's eyes were riveted on the approaching rider.

Winslow had recognized Grayson instantly, but did not slacken his pace. He was covered with dust, and his face showed several days' growth of whiskers. His eyes and slumped shoulders showed extreme weariness.

"Hello, Sergeant," Faith said as soon as he pulled to a stop. "Get down and water your horse."

Winslow nodded and slid to the ground. He let the black he was riding drink for a while, then pulled him away.

"Let me get you a glass," Faith offered.

"No, this is fine." Winslow tied the horse to the rail, pumped with one hand, and drank the water as it flowed from the lip of the pump. He straightened up, wiped his mouth with his sleeve, and for the first time, acknowledged the presence of Grayson by saluting. He waited until Grayson returned it, then moved back to his horse.

"Tom, you're not going?" Faith asked.

He considered her, letting his eyes convey an unspoken thought, then glanced at the lieutenant; and as clearly as a man could make it, he let his displeasure be felt. "I'm in a hurry to get back to the fort," he said coldly. "Thanks for the water."

He swung into the saddle and without another word spurred the horse into a fast trot.

Anger and humiliation rose in Faith, for she knew in his mind he had judged her and found her wanting.

He has no right to think I'm wrong! she fumed, letting it show on her face so clearly that Grayson said, "He's a surly, bitter man, Faith."

She turned, and the bitterness in her grew. "He hates you, Spence. Why?"

"It's all ancient history," Grayson shrugged. "He's cold and bitter. I wish he hadn't come here." He hesitated, then said, "He spoiled our afternoon."

"That's not your fault, Spence."

Her words encouraged him and he asked eagerly, "May I come again?"

She hesitated, finally saying, "Yes—but you and I are not alike."

He smiled at her, easing over the hard moment. "No, but there's always a chance a man can change. You believe that, don't you, Faith?"

She looked at the dust raised by Winslow's horse, and then back toward Spence Grayson. Her eyes still bore the hurt from Winslow's unjust perception, but she nodded and said softly, "Yes, Spence, anyone can change."

He nodded, jumped on his horse, and shouted as he rode away, "I'll see you again—very soon!"

She stood there watching the two dust trails while trying to deal with the humiliation Tom Winslow had given her.

Finally she softened her attitude. "He's been hurt so badly, he doesn't even know when he's doing it to somebody else!"

PART THREE

WAR PAINT

★ ★ ★ ★

CHAPTER THIRTEEN

AN APOLOGY

★　★　★　★

The winter of 1875 would be remembered as one of the worst Dakota ever suffered. It began mildly enough. The sultry days of summer lingered through August and most of September. But when October arrived, it hit with a vengeance, and the winter that had crouched silently entered swiftly—in one night—to touch the land, turning it black and bitter, shriveling every living thing exposed to it.

Laurie Winslow awoke to find the glass on her windows etched with frost, and when her father called from the kitchen: "Laurie—pile out!" she threw back the covers and dressed. She still wore boy's clothing—trousers and shirt and boots—though the schoolmaster, Mr. Dutton, had suggested she wear dresses. That was one thing she *didn't* want to do, so she persuaded her father to buy her a pony, which could not be ridden in skirts, of course!

He had agreed easily, taking pleasure in giving her the horse—a well-shaped bay mare with a gentle temperament. He had long ago taught her to ride, but this was the first horse she could call her own. Winslow had been aware that he could not ignore Mr. Dutton's rules, but in this case, the teacher made an exception. Apart from this one regulation, Laurie would observe all the other requirements.

Laurie had spoken of Laurence Dutton as being "crabby," but Winslow had discovered differently. The schoolmaster was serious enough, but a spark of humor often glinted in his gray eyes, and the two men got on well. At the age of twenty-six, Dutton was the younger of the two. Of average height, slender build, with coppery red hair and a round boyish face, his youthful looks frequently deceived people, for beneath the innocent exterior lurked a sharp mind.

Winslow discovered on their second meeting that Dutton was a schoolmaster only by default. Laurie had brought word to Winslow that Dutton wanted to see him, and he had gone the next day just as school let out. He was somewhat apprehensive, thinking that Laurie was in some sort of difficulty; but as soon as Dutton had sent the children out for the day, he said, "Let's have some coffee."

They had gone to a small cafe and talked over peach pie and strong black coffee. Tom broached the subject first. "Is there some problem with Laurie?" he asked.

"No, none at all," Dutton said. "She's a very bright girl." Seeing the look of relief on Winslow's face, he laughed. "Always a shock to get called in to talk to the teacher, isn't it?"

Winslow grinned. "I guess I remember my own days in school too well. The teacher never called on my folks with good news."

"Well, there is a problem, but it's mine more than Laurie's." Dutton frowned, seeming to have difficulty knowing how to say what was on his heart. Then he shrugged. "You see, Mr. Winslow—"

"Just call me Tom."

"All right—Tom. What I want to say is that I try to make people believe I know how to teach school, but I'm really a fraud."

Intrigued by the schoolmaster's confession, Tom attempted to put the man at ease. "I guess we all put on a front sometimes."

"I suppose so. Well, I'm not really a schoolteacher, Tom. Or at least, not for longer than I have to be. I'm about half a lawyer. As soon as I get a little more cash, I'll become the other half. Another year here and Travis Long will take me into his office to study with him." Dutton smiled, adding, "He's a pettifogging old fellow, but sharp as a needle."

"I hear he's the best trial lawyer in the state," Winslow nodded. "He got those Catlin brothers off with a prison term."

"Didn't he, though?" Dutton sighed with admiration. "And they were caught red-handed and would have been hanged if it hadn't been for Long."

"A lawyer's the last thing in the world I'd want to be," Winslow said. "But I wish you luck if that's the way your stick floats."

"Well, it's hard to make it without financial backing, but my mind's made up."

At that moment, Eileen Jennings entered the cafe, and Winslow called, "Eileen—come and join a lonesome pair." When she came over, he said, "I suppose you two have met?" nodding to Dutton.

"Not really," Eileen smiled. "I know you by reputation, Mr. Dutton. All the children from the fort come to tell me what a horrible ogre you are—especially Laurie." She put out her hand, adding, "I'm Eileen Jennings."

Dutton took her hand. "Sometimes I think *they're* the ogres!"

Winslow waved the waitress over, and Eileen ordered tea. "Is Laurie in trouble?" she asked, and was surprised when both men laughed. When Winslow explained that he had mistakenly thought the same when he received the summons to meet with Laurie's teacher, she said, "Well, that's a relief."

"Laurie's fine," Dutton said. "I was just about to tell Tom that I can't do much for her in the one area she likes the best—which is literature. I can handle the other subjects, math and history—but literature's always been my Achilles' heel."

"I'm not much along those lines myself," Winslow admitted. "Maybe we can order some more books?"

Eileen sipped her tea as she listened to the two men discuss the problem; then when they seemed to have reached an impasse, she said, "Well, I could never get my arithmetic problems to come out right—and my teachers all agreed it was because I read too much poetry and fiction. If you would like, Mr. Dutton, I'd be willing to help Laurie."

Dutton's face lit up, "Why, that would be excellent, Mrs. Jennings!"

"Hate to put you out, Eileen," Winslow said. He shook his

head, adding, "I've just dumped Laurie on you as it is—maybe too much."

"She's a sweet girl, Tom. I enjoy having her with me." Turning to Dutton she asked, "Would you want me to make a list of books I have? Perhaps with some sort of schedule and even some quizzes?"

"Could you do that? I'd be glad to stop by and pick them up."

"Why don't you come with me now?" Eileen got to her feet and both men rose. "Some are just romantic novels, but we can sort them out and use what's workable."

"That would be great," Dutton replied quickly. Like most of the other single men in Bismarck, he was starved for feminine companionship, and he had been covertly studying Eileen, appreciating her attractiveness.

"Can you come for supper, Tom?"

"Thanks, Eileen, but I promised to take Laurie out for a little hunting trip. We may even camp out all night. Could you extend that offer for another time?"

"Of course."

When they left the cafe, Winslow went to locate Laurie, while the other two walked toward Eileen's wagon, where Dutton tied his horse to the back for his return trip, then joined her in the wagon. Their ride to the fort was pleasant, and she discovered that he was a witty man, but rather shy, despite his profession. She thoroughly enjoyed his stories of disasters in the classroom; and when they reached her house, they spent so much time going over the books that she said, "It's too late to cook a big meal, but if you'd like to stay, Mr. Dutton, I'll fix some bacon and eggs."

"Sounds good to me, but please call me Larry," he said. After the meal, he insisted on helping with the dishes. When he was ready to leave, he lingered at the door, wanting to say something, but his wit seemed to have failed. Finally he said, "It's been a fine evening for me. Thanks for the meal."

"It was fun, Larry," she responded, then hesitated. "I . . . get lonely sometimes."

"So do I," Dutton replied, feeling awkward. "Well," he said, "thanks again. I'll get at the books right away."

When he was gone, Eileen thought of the help she could be to Laurie, pleased to have some work to do. The evening had been enjoyable. The supper with the schoolmaster had been pleasant, and she found herself marveling at the ease she felt with the young man. She had not missed the admiration in his eyes, but she was accustomed to that. Unlike others, however, he had not pushed his advantage, and it had been good to discover that there were still men like him in the world.

★　★　★　★

When Winslow told Laurie what her teacher had said, she was relieved. "I'm so glad!" she exclaimed as the two of them rode out of Bismarck. "I was afraid it was because I had a fight with Tommy Clarenton."

"You didn't tell me about that."

"Oh, he was teasing me, so I got mad."

"What was he teasing you about?"

She seemed embarrassed by his question, but finally said, "He likes me, I guess."

Winslow glanced at her, caught off guard by her statement. She was boyish looking enough in her trousers and shirt, but he could see she was changing. She was growing into a real beauty, and in a few years she would pass out of childhood into that mysterious zone between child and woman. He hated to think of it, but was realistic enough to understand that it was inevitable. His mother had told him once as he had held Laurie in his arms, just a squirming red-faced baby: *Tom, enjoy this time. It will be the easiest of all. The older children get, the more pain they can bring you. Right now you can do what you will with Laurie—but as she grows older, she'll move away from you. You'll want to stop her from making bad decisions, to shield her from the hurts she's headed toward, but you won't be able to.*

Now he felt the power of his mother's words, and it brought a sadness. To cover it, he asked, "Did you have a real fight?"

"Oh no. He pulled my hair and I slapped him." She grinned, looking at that moment very much like her mother. "Mr. Dutton paddled us both—but not very hard." Then like the very young, she jumped to the next subject. "Are you going to take me camping, Daddy?"

"Yes. Maybe we can shoot something to take to Miss Eileen."

When they arrived at the fort, he was greeted by Captain Algernon Smith and immediately saluted.

Smith returned the salute, then smiled at the girl. "Hello, Laurie."

"Hello," Laurie said. "My daddy's going to take me camping, Captain, so please don't make him go with you."

"Laurie!" Winslow shook his head at the child. "You can't say that to Captain Smith!"

"Oh, I guess she can, Sergeant," Smith grinned. "I've had worse said to me. This camping trip, it's just for tonight?"

"Yes, sir." Winslow realized it wasn't a routine question. "Something up, Captain?"

"Might be. Some miners got jumped this morning. Captain Moylan took some men out to check on it. He sent word that three men were killed and that he'd try to follow the Indians who did it. I'd like to take a squad in a couple days and relieve him. We'll leave at first light. Like to have you come along."

"Yes, sir. I'll be ready." When the officer walked away, he and Laurie rode to the house. It was growing dark, and after they finished supper, Winslow listened as Laurie read from one of the books Faith had given her. He sat there, sipping coffee and enjoying the dramatic flair with which she read. Finally he tucked her in bed, saying, "Sleep tight. It'll be a tough day tomorrow."

They rose the next morning just before dawn and fixed a big breakfast of bacon and eggs. Winslow had persuaded the sergeant in charge of the mounts for the Seventh to lend him a mule for the trip, and he had packed blankets and food on the animal. He saddled the two horses; then they mounted and rode out of the fort. He skirted the river and headed toward the low-lying hills, the beginning of the plateau. By the middle of the morning, they came upon little hills and bluffs bordering the winding course of Heart River. By noon they were fifteen miles from the fort and stopped to eat the lunch they had packed.

Sitting on a fallen tree beside the river that purled at their feet, they devoured sandwiches and the remnants of a caramel cake Eileen had provided for the trip. Afterward they drank from the cold waters of the river, then sat leisurely, enjoying the warmth of the sun. A small furry animal swam into view, his sleek head making a V-shaped ripple. "Look!" Tom whispered, "but be very quiet." They watched the furry animal scramble out of the water. He was eight inches long and another six in the tail. The tail itself was black and scaled, and was flattened vertically, like a belt stood on edge, not horizontally like beavers. They could see his water-slick coat that emphasized the smooth contours of his body, and the pale soft hair underneath, almost like rabbit fur.

He began chomping on a ten-inch weed, pushing it into his mouth steadily with both forepaws as a child feeds candy into his mouth. For at least five minutes, he moved among the weeds, totally unaware of being watched.

Then he stopped abruptly, his body quivering, and with a flash of movement dived toward the river and disappeared into the water.

Winslow looked up and motioned toward a red-tailed hawk sailing overhead. "That bird just missed his lunch," he commented.

"What was it, Daddy?"

"Muskrat."

"And the bird would have eaten him?"

"Sure would. Hawks and owls—and minks and otters, too. But I guess men are their worst enemy. I had a friend in Virginia, years ago, who trapped muskrats. He told me that in ten years he killed 30,000 muskrats."

Laurie's lips grew firm. "I think that's just awful, Daddy! They're so adorable!"

"So is a young calf," Winslow shrugged, "but both of us ate those steaks last week." He saw that the concept bothered her but knew of no other way to introduce her to that grim aspect of the world. "Well, let's get moving," he said, and they mounted and moved toward the ridge, where they would camp.

He shot two rabbits later that afternoon, adding them to the pack on the mule. Later he downed an antelope and dressed it. "This will make a good meal for Miss Eileen," he said, noting that Laurie had looked at the beautiful animal with some degree of sadness. He made a try at modifying this, by saying, "God made all the animals for man's use. Pretty nice of Him to watch out for us."

That thought pleased her, and by the time they reached a clump of timber, she was excited about making camp. He let her do as much as she was capable of—helping gather wood, putting the blankets down for their beds, getting out the food. He hobbled the horses, and by the time the sun fell, the cheerful fire drove the falling darkness back. He cut sharp sticks with his knife and let her roast one of the rabbits. When they were eating, he said, "Food always tastes better outside, doesn't it? No matter how bad it's cooked, I always gobble it down. But you did a real good job of cooking, Laurie."

After supper they sat and watched the fire, adding branches from time to time. The firelight reflected the glow of pleasure in Laurie's eyes, and she talked excitedly about the day's events. Once after a pause she asked, "What did my mother look like, Daddy?"

She had asked him this many times. "She was very beautiful, Laurie. When you're a few years older, you'll see her every time you look in the mirror."

She thought about that when she drifted off to sleep later, wondering what it would have been like having a mother.

As they slept, the fire snapped and popped, and the logs settled with a sigh from time to time. A heavy silence muffled the land, broken occasionally by the cries of a timber wolf that floated on the night air.

At dawn they awakened and fixed a quick breakfast of eggs and bacon, saddled up, and moved away from the camp. This was not hostile Indian territory, but Winslow kept a sharp watch, for the Sioux were not shut in by boundaries. All morning they roamed the low hills, exploring small creeks and stands of timber. Often they saw deer, but Winslow took no shots, content to let Laurie enjoy their floating gait as they fled away.

At noon when they crested a hill, Laurie saw something on the horizon and asked, "What's that, Daddy?"

"That's the school, the one Miss Faith teaches in."

"Oh, let's go see her!"

Winslow agreed, but as they rode toward the buildings, he felt distinctly uncomfortable. He had seen Faith only twice since

his encounter with her and Spence Grayson, both times chance
occurrences in Bismarck. She had been civil enough, yet he had
not missed the restraint in her manner—and could not blame
her for it. When he had left her place that day, the anger the
sight of Grayson always triggered had slowly faded, and it was
then he realized he had been unfair to the woman. But there had
been no way to speak of it to her; even now when the opportunity was before him he felt uncomfortable and wished he'd
taken another route.

Faith had been reading a story to her pupils—twelve of them,
ranging from the ages of ten to fifteen. It was an awkward situation, for she read in English, and Gray Dove, the oldest girl,
translated into the Sioux language for the others. At the sound
of horses, Faith had gone to look out the window. "I'll be right
back," she said. "Why don't you draw a picture of a buffalo on
your tablets?"

Stepping outside, she greeted them with a smile. "Hello, Laurie—Tom. Nice to see you."

Laurie slid off her horse and ran to Faith, beginning at once
to tell of the camping trip. Winslow removed the antelope from
the mule and held it up. "Brought your dinner."

"Oh, that will be good," Faith said. "Let me put it in the
larder." She waited until he halved the antelope, then led the
way to the back of the house where a shed had recently been
added. "The men thought this would be handy," she said, opening the door.

He entered and hung the half from a nail in a rafter. "You
might want me to salt that down for you. It'll keep better that
way."

"I don't know how to do that. I'll get the salt." She watched
as he began to treat the meat. "I really appreciate that, Tom.
Now, I'd better get back to my classroom. Come meet my pupils,
Laurie."

When Winslow finished salting the meat, he washed his
hands and went to the schoolhouse. The Indians looked at him
questioningly, and Faith said, "Say something to them in their
language, Tom."

He said a few words, which pleased them. Seeing their
smiles, Faith asked, "What did you say?"

"That they are a fine-looking group, and that they have a fine teacher."

Faith flushed and shook her head. "Gray Dove there is trying to teach me the language. She's a good teacher—but I'm so slow."

"Takes time," Tom said. "But it'll mean a lot to these people." He moved toward a chair, nodding to Laurie. "Come over here and let's listen. Maybe we'll learn something."

Their presence flustered Faith for a time; then she got caught up in her work. She was trying to teach them the letters of the alphabet, and not doing very well. She drew the first three letters on a piece of slate fastened to the wall, pointed at them, and tried to get the students to repeat the sound. They responded poorly, so she said to Winslow, "They just don't seem to see any sense in learning."

"I guess that's about my story when I was their age," Winslow replied. He told her about his experience at teaching the Apaches in Arizona in a school the government had started for them. "It seems they learn in spurts—or it did there. No progress at all; then all of a sudden they catch on."

He paused for a moment. "Well, that's about all I can tell you," he said and he stood up. "We'd better be riding on, Laurie." He walked to the door and Faith came out to stand beside the two as they prepared to mount. "Thanks again for the meat," she said. She was unaware of how lovely she looked in her long-sleeved blue woolen dress, with the sunshine highlighting her auburn hair as she stood there.

Winslow hesitated, then noting that Laurie had gone to get one last drink of water from the well, he said quickly, "Last time I was here, Faith, I was pretty surly. Sorry about that."

His confession surprised her, for it was her impression that he was not a man who could apologize easily. And now as she looked up at him, some of her surprise mirrored in her eyes, she knew she'd been right. But she was pleased at the character trait that enabled him to admit his wrong.

She said simply, "I was hurt, Tom—but now it's all right."

He looked down at the ground, a tall man suddenly made taciturn by his admission. Then he looked up and saw the joy in her eyes. "Well," he said with a deep sigh, "I've been rehearsing that speech for days. Don't know why it's so hard for a man to say he's been a fool."

"Let's forget it," Faith said. "I've missed you and Laurie. Will you let her come and spend weekends sometimes?"

"She'd sure like that." Laurie ran up, and the two swung into their saddles. "Maybe I'll come and hear you preach," he grinned, feeling greatly relieved. The incident had burdened him heavily, but now it was as if a dark cloud had passed away. He took off his hat and slapped the flank of his horse, sending him out of the yard, dragging the mule with his neck outstretched.

Startled by his actions, Laurie stared after him, then cried, "Goodbye, Miss Faith!" Digging her heels into the sides of her mare, she turned around and shouted, "I'll make him come to church!"

Then they were gone. As she turned to go back into the building, Faith felt strangely lighter, and the dark eyes of the Indian children watched her carefully, wondering why she was so much happier than before.

CHAPTER FOURTEEN

DEATH ON PATROL

★ ★ ★ ★

"Prepare to mount. Mount!"

Twenty bodies hit the McClellan saddles, accompanied by the grunt of horses and the clack of carbines and canteens and belted trenching tools.

"Right by twos, march!"

The line moved, gray and indistinct; saddle leather against the ruffled beat of the walking horses sang a rhythmic melody as Captain Algernon Smith led the men of A Company past the guard post. They were joined by twenty more troopers commanded by Second Lieutenant Spence Grayson of E Company. They moved out at a fast trot two by two, up the slope of the ridge east of the fort, the line evening out as they headed away from the river.

Captain Smith rode beside Sergeant Hines, with Winslow off to one side. The long double rank of troopers was silent at that hour but gradually took on life as the sun rose higher and the warm rays and ride loosened their muscles. Most of the troopers were Irish, their faces mustached, burned and weather-beatened. Some of the countenances of the group reflected a mixture of good values, hardness, or wildness; others, young, untested innocence.

Winslow sat easy in the saddle, conscious of the sounds

around him, the squeezing sibilance of leather, the clinking of metal gear, the slap of canteens, and the talk among the men as the hour moved on. He turned and looked down the line, pleased with the sight of the column, the men so dark of face that their eyes seemed to glitter. It was a tough line, like a sinuous whip being dragged across the country. He saw Babe O'Hara grin at him, and grinned back, glad for a new rapport between them.

They paused for a rest two hours out of the fort, then again at noon. The air was brisk, but not as cold as it would be in a month. Today the breeze was fresh, clean, and so sharp it went to the bottom of a man's lungs. About one in the afternoon, they found Captain Moylan and his men waiting for them at the foot of a long, broken butte that lay along the west. Moylan and his men were worn thin, eyes bleary with fatigue. Lieutenant Grayson came forward to listen as Moylan gave the details of his scout. Grayson didn't look at Winslow, but kept his eyes on Moylan who said, "We've stayed pretty close to them, Smith. Too close, maybe."

"How's that, Captain?" Smith inquired.

"They could have broken up into twos and threes and faded away," Moylan went on, scratching his chin. "That's what they usually do." He cautioned Smith, advising, "Be careful, Captain." Finishing his report, he motioned his command forward and as they passed, the waiting troopers and officers saw that some of Moylan's men were so weary they could hardly sit in their saddles.

"Sounds encouraging, Smith," Lieutenant Grayson said, his eyes keen with excitement. "We're fresh and they've been on the run for a long time." He waited for Smith to respond, then urged, "Let's head out after them as fast as we can."

"No," Captain Smith said, "I think we'll be a little cautious. If these are some of Gall's warriors, they're tough." He turned to Winslow. "Sergeant, ride out and see if you can get a reading on this bunch."

"Yes, sir."

As Winslow left, along with Yellow Face, who had kept well off to himself, a frown creased Grayson's brow, and he said, "I don't trust these agency bucks. He could lead us right into an ambush."

"I doubt that," Smith said briefly. "And we've got Winslow along to check his findings."

"He's brand new at this."

"Charlie Reynolds says he's all right—and Charlie's a hard man to please."

Smith kept the troop at an even pace, and at four o'clock Winslow and Yellow Face returned at a fast gallop. Pulling his horse to a halt, Winslow said, "They're still bunched up, Captain."

"How far ahead?"

"Maybe five miles."

"You sure, Sergeant?"

"Sure enough, sir," Winslow said emphatically. "We got a glimpse of them from the top of a rise."

"Let's hit them now!" Grayson said.

The inclination to attack was clearly in Captain Smith, Winslow saw, for the stocky officer was a pugnacious man. But now as he looked toward the low-lying hills settling into the fast falling shadows, he hesitated, finding something not to his liking. Finally he shook his head, saying, "No, I think not. By the time we caught up with them, it'd be dusk at least—or maybe dark. Better to get an early start and try to make contact as soon as possible."

Grayson was disappointed, but when he tried to protest, Smith shook his head, saying in a clipped tone, "That's it, Grayson." Then he turned to Winslow. "Sergeant, is there a spot to camp with water?"

"Yes, sir. A small creek in the timberline—about two miles."

The troop advanced to a scattered fringe of trees that marked a creek flowing from the northwest. Darkness closed in, and the men removed their blankets and started small fires. As the guards took the horses away from the camp, the smell of bacon and coffee laced the cold air, and soon Winslow was sitting in front of one of the fires, eating hungrily. Babe O'Hara and Leo Dempsey, another Irishman, were swapping stories concerning their success with women. Billy Satterfield, at eighteen, the youngest recruit of A Company, listened avidly. He was a thin towheaded boy, just off the family farm in Ohio, and was gullible to a fault. Ace Guidry, a dark-skinned Cajun from New Orleans, grinned at the boy. "Boy, don't believe all you hear from them two."

Dempsey, a tough one who didn't like to be challenged, said, "Keep your mouth shut, Guidry, or I'll shut it for you!"

A long, thin-bladed knife magically appeared in Guidry's hand, and he said softly, "Come on to me, boy. I'll beat the Indians to your scalp."

Dempsey half rose to his feet, but O'Hara broke in. "Cut it out, you two. Ace, put that pig-sticker away before I take it away from you."

There was a moment's tension, but then Ace laughed and put the knife away. "I don't think I'll try your mettle tonight."

Corporal Nathan Zeiss, a sober German, changed the subject. "You think we'll have a fight tomorrow, Sergeant?" Zeiss had a worried look on his blunt face, for he was married, with a child on the way. His hitch was up in four months and he was anxious to be out of the army and with his family in Kansas.

"Looks like it, Nathan," Winslow said. He took a bite of bacon and chewed it thoughtfully. He was aware that most of the Seventh had not seen action, and this small group was typical. Only O'Hara and Dempsey had been in action; the others were green and nervous. He had seen this often during the war, had been green himself before Bull Run. There was something mystic about war, he thought, looking at the faces of the men. As terrible as it was, men were drawn to it, hypnotized, it seemed, by its very violence. He remembered his brother Mark relating what he had heard Lee say about it. Mark had been a courier at the time, and had carried a message to Lee. The general had been looking down on the Union troops who had crossed the Rappahannock River. The Confederate Army was entrenched along the top of a hill in an impregnable position, but the Union General Burnside sent the troops against it. The Federals had moved across the field in perfect parade-ground order, lines straight and in step with the music of a band. They had marched straight into the mouths of the Confederate guns time and time again, falling like rows of wheat cut with a scythe as the muskets and artillery of Lee's men shot them down.

Mark had overheard Lee say to his adjutant: "It's well that war is so terrible, or we would become too fond of it!"

Now, sitting in front of the fire and watching the faces of the young soldiers, Winslow saw fear and apprehension, yet it was mixed with anticipation of the battle. He sipped his coffee, wondering which of them would not be around a campfire after this one. But realizing such thoughts were not for him to express, he spoke up cheerfully, "It's a small bunch, boys, and they usually break up as soon as they get hit."

Monte Simms, a tall, lanky Texan, agreed. "That's right, Tom. I been on three chases after the Sioux, and they none of them ever stuck together like these."

"I hope we get 'em surrounded!" The speaker was an undersized redhead, the truculence emanating from his thin face. He bore the unlikely name of Jeff Davis, suffering countless fights over this. He looked at Winslow, adding, "I expect they're plain yellow, Sarge. Ain't that right?"

Winslow grinned at him. He liked the young man, for he had a cheerful disposition and was always ready to tackle any chore handed him. "Well, Jeff, if Sitting Bull and Roman Nose and Gall are cowards—I guess nobody ever found out about it."

"Why don't they fight, then?" Davis demanded.

"They do fight, Jeff," Winslow answered. "Matter of fact, aside from hunting, that's about all an Indian does. The squaws do most of the hard work. The braves just lie around and tell lies to each other except when they're hunting. But fighting's what they like best. There's been war between the tribes since Columbus's men stepped off the boat. An Indian boy goes through basic training before he loses his baby teeth and continues on as he grows up, learning how to use a bow, a knife, and a lance. By the time he's in his teens, he can put an arrow through a man's eye from fifty yards away—and enjoy it."

But Winslow's answer didn't satisfy the young soldier. "Well, gosh, Tom, why don't they stand still and *fight* if they're so tough?"

"Not their style," Winslow shrugged. "We fight like the Europeans do, which is pretty dumb. But it's a tradition and men love tradition."

"Like the Europeans?" Zeiss asked. "How is that, Sergeant?"

"In Europe there's lots of flat country. The generals would line their armies up across from each other, and they'd advance.

Each man had one shot in his musket, so the army that had the most men would usually win. That worked in Europe, but it won't work in America."

"Why won't it work?" Billy Satterfield asked. He was sitting cross-legged, his eyes shining in the firelight. He appeared to be about fifteen years old.

"Because the country is full of hills and woods. When Braddock came over and tried to fight the French and Indians like that, they hid in the woods at the Monongahela and destroyed him. George Washington was Braddock's aide, and he learned a lesson from that. But men learn hard, and time after time in the Civil War, even the best commanders threw huge armies against men who were entrenched and some who had repeating rifles."

"That's right," Babe O'Hara nodded. "Even Lee tried it at Malvern Hill during the Seven Days. Got chopped to bits!"

"What's all that got to do with why Indians won't fight?" Jeff Davis demanded.

Winslow stretched, then turned to look at Davis. "Well, Jeff, why should they fight by our rules? They'll hit and run, nibble away at us any way they can. But you'll likely see them fight a little different sooner or later. They've been pushed off their land, and this country you see right here is the last chance they've got. They know that, so you'll likely find what you're asking for—a big old-fashioned battle."

The talk died down then, and soon they all wrapped up in their blankets and went to sleep. The next morning they moved out after breakfast, with Winslow riding ahead with Yellow Face to ascertain the position of the Indians. By nine o'clock Smith halted his line of blue-clad troopers as Winslow came racing back.

"Right up ahead, Captain," Winslow said, pointing at a group of rising hills flanked by timber. "Rough country up there. Be hard to keep a tight formation."

"Are they moving on, Winslow?"

"Don't seem to be in a hurry."

Smith nodded and made his decision. Lifting his hand, he threw it forward and the troop broke into a gallop. Winslow rode beside him, not liking the terrain, but there was no other way. It was a raw and primitive spot, cut with deep gullies and broken with sharp rising cliffs covered with scrub oak and brush. It was not a good spot for a formation of cavalry, and he suspected that the Indians they were after were as aware of that as he was.

When they had covered three miles, Winslow moved ahead to study the ground. Coming back he reported, "Lots of tracks, but the country is pretty wild."

Grayson had come up to hear his report. He suddenly tilted his head back and stared into the distance. "I see somebody moving up there!" he exclaimed.

Winslow and Smith turned to look. Presently they made out several moving figures. Captain Smith said thoughtfully. "They want us to know they're there."

"That's right," Winslow said dryly. "If an Indian doesn't want to be seen, you wouldn't see him."

"Pretty certain of themselves," Smith commented. He studied the gray-brown slope that lay under the pale glare of the sun. "That slope will be a pretty hard climb," he murmured. The troop sat quietly, and both Grayson and Winslow waited, knowing that it was a difficult decision for Smith.

"We'll move in," Smith said firmly.

Double file, the detail took to the slope and started the long climb, carbines canted forward. A defined trail ran irregularly through the rock scatter. High up, to the extreme left of the summit, an Indian on a horse moved into sight and cut a distinct circle on the slope, waving his lance and moving out of sight again. When the troop had advanced another four hundred yards, Smith said, "Skirmishers," and watched his column break into a single line abreast of him. "If we run into more trouble than we can handle," he said to Grayson, "we'll fort up in these rocks."

As they moved forward, Winslow saw the blur of Indians in motion. The line of skirmishers dismounted, passing reins over to the horse-holders. The rest spread out and began the last climb on foot, bending in and around the trees and outcroppings of earth. When they were within two hundred yards from the top of the rise, a dozen Sioux leaped over the rim as a burst of gunshot from the top of the ridge covered them.

Winslow yelled, "Here they come!"

"Fire!" Smith yelled, and the troopers opened fire. A volley smashed out, hard on the heels of the captain's command, sprouting the dirt up where the bullets struck around the racing Sioux. One of them fell, rolling in a ball, but the rest seemed to fade into the earth. The firing grew more intense, and Hines yelled, "Come along now—waste no shots, boys!"

Winslow braced himself against a tree, firing when he saw a target. He saw some of his shots hit, but a slug smashed into the tree beside his head, throwing him off balance. He moved forward when Smith called out, "Forward!"

A pair of Sioux sprang up from a depression in the ground, both of them firing at the troopers. A soldier in front of Winslow gave a surprised grunt, dropped his carbine, and fell to the ground, writhing like a cut worm. Winslow took careful aim and hit one of the Indians in the throat, driving him backward when he tried to get off another shot, but Jeff Davis finished him off with a bullet to his brain.

The other Sioux shot at Davis, his bullet hitting the young man in the thigh. As he fell, the Sioux took dead aim, but Winslow shot him twice in the chest and he fell limply to the earth. "Thanks—Sarge—!" Davis gasped.

Winslow laid his carbine down and quickly put a tourniquet on the leg, then rose, saying, "Be still, Jeff. You'll be all right."

He raced forward and pulled Billy Satterfield behind a tree, for the boy was standing straight as a ramrod as he fired. "Stay behind some cover!" Winslow shouted, then moved ahead to join Captain Smith, who said calmly, "Winslow, take ten men and try to flank them on the right. Lieutenant Grayson, you take ten and try the left."

The two men called the names of the men they saw, then split off. Winslow led his group in a wild scramble through the bushes and trees, dodging bullets. Ace Guidry gasped, "What we doin' now?"

"Got to break them up," Winslow answered. The steep rise was taking his wind, and he said no more. When they got a hundred yards to the right, he said, "Up we go—and watch yourselves!" He led them up the slope, his eyes moving constantly over the terrain, but they had not been seen. Turning left, he moved at once toward the sound of the firing, and with his small force came onto a group of Sioux who were caught off guard. "Let them have it!" he cried, and they moved forward, shooting as they went. He could sense that the group led by Spence Grayson was coming from the opposite direction, and thought, *We've got them caught in a squeeze!*

But the Indians faded back into the thick brush, and the troopers were too winded to follow. When the detail gathered at the top of the rise, they were just in time to see the band of Sioux sink out of sight into a canyon flanked by two sharp hills.

"Go signal the horses up," Smith ordered. By the time they were mounted, most of the men were over the exertion of the climb. Smith led them forward in time to see part of the band file down the narrow mountain trail into the canyon.

"They're right ahead, Smith!" Grayson said, excitement burning in his eyes. "We've got them!"

Even as he spoke, other Indians appeared from the trees and entered the canyon. Some of them stopped and took a drink at the small creek that flowed along the edge of the canyon.

"They're not in a hurry, are they?" Sergeant Hines said. His anger flared, for he had lost some good men in the fight.

But Smith was studying the area ahead. He ran his gaze over the rising country to the right and left of the canyon, noting that it would be difficult to take the troop up such a steep grade, then stared at the canyon itself.

Impatiently Grayson exclaimed, "They're getting away from us, Smith! Let's get after them!"

But Smith replied, "I think that's what they want us to do, Spence."

"You're right about that, sir," Winslow said. "They didn't all go down that canyon. Some of them are still in the timber, I think."

Grayson glared at Winslow, but spoke to Smith. "We're as close as we'll ever be. We can't let them get away."

But Smith disagreed. "No, that canyon would be a bad place for us to get caught." He was disappointed, for it would look good on his record to wipe out the entire band, but he was a cautious man. He would risk his men when necessary, but this was too great for the gains involved.

"We'll take care of the wounded and then head back to the fort."

"I hate to see them get away." Grayson's voice was hard.

"We'll have to wait for a better chance," Smith said.

"Not very spectacular campaigning!"

"No, but twenty dead cavalrymen at the bottom of that canyon would be."

They took care of the wounded, and tied the three dead men on their horses. The air grew colder, and when they camped that night the temperature dropped. As they huddled around the campfire, the men were somber, saying little.

"I lost a good friend today," Corporal Nathan Zeiss said slowly. "George Simmons. He was a good young man. I will have to write to his people."

The crackling of the fire made a cheerful sound, and Winslow said, "Well, you boys have seen the elephant, and you did fine. I heard Captain Smith say that if the rest of the Seventh has the grit you do, we'll be all right."

"Did he say that, Sarge?" Billy Satterfield looked across the fire, his eyes lightening at Winslow's words.

"He sure did." Winslow got some hot coffee and brought it to Jeff Davis, all wrapped in his blankets. "Drink this, Jeff," he said. He helped the boy sit up, and after Davis had downed the coffee and lay down, Tom put the blankets around him. "Good thing that bullet went right through. It hurts worse to have a doctor digging it out than getting the shot in the first place."

Jeff said, "Yeah, I'll be all right." He was groggy from the laudanum Winslow had given him, and muttered, "Thanks, Tom—" then was asleep at once.

Winslow rolled in his blanket and fell asleep with the effortlessness of a natural man sleeping beneath the brilliant stars. His last thought was of the three dead troopers, and as always, he wondered, *Why was it them—and not me?*

★　★　★　★

When Eileen heard the knock on her door from where she sat, she looked up with a quick stab of anxiety. She jumped to her feet and rushed to the door, hesitated, then opened it.

"Tom!" she cried, reaching out and pulling him inside. "You're all right!"

"Sure," he nodded, surprised at her concern. The detail had

gotten back at dusk, and he had accompanied the two officers to report to Custer. The general had listened, then nodded. "You did well. We'll have to push them hard. The press is down on us, you know, and both Sheridan and Sherman want to squelch the Indians."

Winslow had left the meeting depressed, going immediately to Eileen's house. Now as he stood there, worn and tired to the bone, he was surprised that Eileen had been worried about him. The discovery broke through his fatigue and he smiled.

"Was it bad, Tom?"

"We lost three men. That's always bad, I guess."

Eileen was shocked by the rush of emotion she felt and tried to cover it with a smile. "I'm glad you're all right. Laurie's next door, spending the night with the Moylan girl. They've become great friends. I hope you don't mind."

"No. I hope she'll make many friends."

She said carefully, "I've worried about you. It's like when I sat up waiting for my husband when he was on patrol." She looked small and vulnerable, feminine and very attractive. Her eyes were large and her lips softly curved in the lamplight. Suddenly she said, "I wish you didn't have to go out to fight."

"My job, Eileen."

"I know—but it's so hard on those of us who wait." She gave her shoulders a shake, then added, "I sound like a nagging wife, don't I, Tom?"

"Been a long time since I had anybody worry about me," Winslow said quietly. "I'd almost forgotten how good it feels."

She was standing close to him, the look in her dark eyes drawing him like a magnet, and he bent closer. Then he felt the stirrings a man feels for a woman and would have drawn back had she not whispered, "I *do* worry about you, Tom!" The softness of her voice, the gentleness of her lips moved him, and he put his arms around her—waiting to see if she would resist.

But she didn't, and he lowered his lips and kissed her with a sudden rush of fervor. She was a soft warmth against him, and he felt her respond, her hands reaching up behind his head. He held her tightly, conscious of the richness of her embrace, forgetting everything for that one blinding moment except the soft response of her lips under his.

Then she moved, and he dropped his arms. "I didn't mean to do that, Eileen—but you're so beautiful. And you've been so kind to Laurie and me."

Eileen had been shaken by his caress and said a little breathlessly, "Good-night, Tom. I'm glad you're safe!"

When she closed the door, she leaned against it, closed her eyes, and let the moment linger. *I've been alone too much*, she thought. *Am I too easy? What will he think of me?*

But no answer came. She was a woman who needed to love and to be loved, and Tom Winslow had awakened the knowledge in her. He was a man she could admire; and as she thought of his caress, she mused, *He won't forget that kiss!*

CHAPTER FIFTEEN

YE MUST BE BORN AGAIN!

★ ★ ★ ★

The weather turned colder, ice forming on water buckets and frost turning the dead, brown earth a glistening white early in the mornings. Fur overcoats and hats were issued to the men of the Seventh, and graze for the horses became a problem.

Sickness came in the form of colds, which turned into more serious illnesses, and one of the first casualties was Laurence Dutton. He got soaked in a sudden rainstorm, neglected to change his clothing, and the next day developed a hacking cough that grew worse until he finally gave up and took to his bed.

His students were mildly sorry for their teacher, but enjoyed their unscheduled holiday. Laurie rode her mare—whom she had named Lady—back from Bismarck, and went by to tell her father the news. Winslow had been planning to ride out to make contacts with some of the more peaceful Indians, but was forced to call off his trip. He spent the next two days with Laurie, though Eileen had offered to keep her. "Let her stay with me, Tom," she had urged. "She's no trouble at all."

But Winslow felt a constraint and had answered, "Nothing real pressing right now for me to do. Indians won't be moving around much during the winter. It'll give me a chance to work on the house some."

For two days he tightened up the boards on the shack, sealing the inside with old lumber to cut out the icy fingers of wind that seeped through. He took Laurie out to cut wood, and tried his hand at cooking some dishes more sophisticated than bacon and eggs—with only a minimum of success. At nights he and Laurie read the books that Eileen and Faith had put together. Laurie could read very well, but she liked to hear her father read to her, so they took turns.

As the wind crept around the tiny cabin, the fire in the stove cracked and popped and the green wood cried as the sap ran out. The yellow light of the coal-oil lamp lit up their kitchen, and Laurie said, "I wish we'd get snowed in, Daddy. This is nice!"

"We'd get pretty hungry," he smiled. "I got snowed in once on a hunting trip to Colorado. It was all right for a week, but my partner was an old mountain man who was pretty rough. We got so touchy we wouldn't even speak for days." A smile curved his lips at the memory, and he added, "If we hadn't gotten out when we did, I think one of us would have shot the other."

"But we're not like that, are we?" Laurie demanded.

"No. We get along better than anybody."

His answer satisfied her, and he thought, *I need to tell her things like that more often.* He sat there listening as she read him a story from a dog-eared book. When she finished, he said, "Know what I've been thinking? We ought to drive out to Miss Faith's mission. I'll bet she's getting lonesome out there all alone."

"Oh, Daddy, can we?"

"Sure. Tell you what, we'll pick up some goodies in town for her and the students. Be a nice surprise for them."

"Can we stay for church? I promised her I'd bring you."

"This is Friday, isn't it? I guess it'll work out. We'll go tomorrow and come back after the service Sunday."

Laurie was up early the next morning anxious to start, and when they went to the general store in Bismarck, she scurried around bright-eyed with excitement, picking out some cans of food and some sweets for the Indian youngsters.

He finally had to say, "Whoa, now, Laurie. You'll make them sick with all this rich stuff!"

When Winslow went by the fort to tell Sergeant Hines of the outing, Hines looked at the sky's dull lead color and said doubtfully, "Don't like the looks of that sky, Tom. Don't fool around.

Could turn into something bad."

"I'll hole up if it gets rough," Winslow nodded. He left the office and climbed up on the seat of the wagon next to Laurie, who was bundled up to her eyes. "All right?" he asked, and when she nodded, he flicked the reins and the horses started forward. The river they had to cross was swollen from the late rains. They drove their wagon onto the ancient ferry, not certain of its safety. The ferry skewed across the current, then fell five hundred yards downriver as the power of the water took it. Winslow hung on to the wagon and Laurie, worried about the danger, but then the engines revved up and the ferry slowly worked its way upstream and nosed into the slip. Relieved, Winslow picked up the reins and drove the wagon ashore.

They saw almost no one on the road, and the cold seemed to have brought a silence on the land. As they rocked along the rutted tracks of the road, their voices sounded loud as they talked and Laurie sang some of the songs she'd learned from Eileen. Her flute-like young voice rang out in the clear air. Once she stopped and said, "It's a lonesome time, winter is. I like summer better."

They arrived at the mission at noon. Faith grabbed Laurie and hugged her. "What a nice surprise!" she cried, then turned to Tom. "Nice to see you." She was wearing a heavy black wool skirt, a checkered blouse, thick-soled boots, and a short fur jacket, which made her seem bulky. Instead of a braid, her thick auburn hair hung loose down her back, almost to her waist.

Laurie tugged Faith's hand, pulling her to the back of the wagon bed. "Look—we brought some good stuff to eat!"

"Bless you both!" Faith said, looking at the wooden box filled with canned goods. "I'm so hungry for something different I could eat anything!" She hovered close as Winslow brought the box, her eyes sparkling with excitement as she pulled out each can, reading the labels. "Smoked oysters!" she exclaimed. "I've never tasted them, but I'll bet they're better than the tough old ham I've been living on."

Nothing would do but that she fix a dinner right then, and Winslow noticed how she drew Laurie in, letting her help with every aspect of the meal. "I'll have a go at that woodpile, Faith," he announced. "You're going to need a big stack if that storm hits."

He found two short lengths of an oak trunk, and for the next hour he sawed lengths of the oak, split it into wedges, and stacked it against the side of the house, handy to the door. When Laurie stuck her head out the door, calling, "Daddy—come and eat," he put the axe down and went into the house.

Faith said, "This may not be the best meal you ever had, Tom, but I'll bet it's different!"

They sat down, and Faith bowed her head, saying, "Thank you, Lord, for this food and for those who brought it. Thank you for giving us to each other. In Jesus' name. Amen."

Tom lifted the cloth covering a platter and stared at the food. "What in the world is this?" he demanded.

"Don't ask," Faith suggested. "Just eat!"

The supper consisted of potted ham, smoked oysters, canned salmon, candied yams, spiced peaches, and one item on Tom's plate that Faith wouldn't identify until Tom urged her.

"The can said it was calf brains," Faith said demurely, a glint of humor in her eyes. "Laurie and I decided to let you have all of it."

Winslow gave her a suspicious look, then took a small portion of the food on his fork. When he put it in his mouth and tasted it, Laurie piped up, "What does it taste like, Daddy?"

Winslow chewed thoughtfully, then said evenly, "Taste like? Oh, kind of like pig's lips, I guess."

"Tom!" Faith cried out. "You never ate such a thing!"

"Sure did! Last year of the war, down in Georgia. We'd been living on handfuls of parched corn for a week, and one of our fellows liberated a shoat. Small one, no more than thirty pounds. But when we dressed him out and started cooking, I guess every soldier in our company got a whiff of that pork and came around hoping for a taste." He looked down at the table as the memory of that time swept over him, thinking of the wolfish faces of his friends, all of them skinny as rails and dressed in rags. Then he shook his head, forcing the memory away. "We ate that sucker, all except the hide, I guess. My share was three ribs and the lips. It was good, too, much better than mule, I always thought."

"Daddy, not *mule*!" Laurie protested. "I don't think it's nice to talk about eating mule at the table."

Winslow grinned, enjoying the discomfort of the two. "If

you're going to feed a man calf brains, you've got to take the consequences," he said firmly.

After the more exotic elements of the meal, Faith removed a pie from the oven and set it on the table. Slicing it into wedge-shaped sections, she passed two of them to her guests, then took one for herself. Taking a bite of his portion, Winslow exclaimed with a note of surprise in his voice, "Why, this tastes like fresh apple pie!"

"Just dried apples, Tom, but I guess if you get hungry enough anything tastes good."

After the meal Winslow said, "You don't have enough wood, Faith. I'll go drag in a couple of logs." He sharpened the axe and rode out to a stand of hardwood two miles from the mission, cut three of them, and snaked them back one at a time. Afterward, he put in another hour cutting one of them into lengths. After he split them, he went inside and found Faith and Laurie working on a dress with needle and thread.

"Oh, Daddy, Miss Faith's going to teach me to sew! And I'm going to make me a Sunday dress!" Laurie exclaimed. "Look what I've got done."

Winslow walked over, took the cloth, and studied it. "Well, now, that's good-looking work, Laurie. Maybe you can sew up some of my shirts now that you're a seamstress."

"Sit down, Tom, and let me get you some coffee and maybe a small piece of pie to hold you until supper." She got up and Winslow sat back, talking with Laurie as he ate the snack. Then he grew sleepy from the warmth of the stove. Closing his eyes, he put his head back on the chair and listened to Faith and Laurie chatter. He awoke with a start when Laurie touched his shoulder, shaking him slightly.

"What was that, Laurie?" he asked, looking at her grinning face at his side.

"I said, supper's ready."

Winslow became aware of the smell of freshly baked bread and said, "I must have dozed off."

Faith was putting plates on the table. "For nearly two hours," she said. "I've never seen anyone who could sleep like that. Just like a cat."

Winslow got up, stretched, and made his way to the table.

"I learned that in the army, I guess. How to sleep in little naps—whenever and however you could. Once when Stonewall Jackson was flanking three different armies in the Valley, we marched three hundred miles or more, I guess, in a few days. It rained one night, a real toad-strangler." The memory made him squint his eyes, and he smiled wryly. "I'd just dropped to the ground, in a little depression. When I woke up, just my face was above water! And I was too tired to move! I remember thinking, *Well, if it gets another two inches higher, I'll drown. But then I won't have to march anymore.* But I didn't drown, so I had to get up and march when the order came."

"Was Jackson a good general?" Faith asked.

"The hardest man I ever knew," Tom shrugged. "If a man fell out from exhaustion, Stonewall had no thought of him. He'd give some impossible task to his officers and men; then, if it didn't get done, he'd be angry. If it did, the most he'd ever say was 'Good.' "

"Did you ever see General Lee?"

"Oh, sure, many a time—"

Winslow rarely talked about the war, but he did that evening. Faith and Laurie sat together on a battered overstuffed chair, listening to every word, their eyes seldom leaving him. Outside the wind rose, a low keening, with an occasional roar that struck the cabin like a blow. The stove glowed, radiating a pleasant warmth—a welcome contrast to the barren cold just outside the thin walls of the house.

Laurie leaned against Faith, who had let her arm fall around the girl. She grew sleepy, but she had never heard her father say so much about the war, and she wished he would never stop. There was a curious feeling about being held by Faith, and she sat there quietly savoring it.

Finally Winslow started and gave an embarrassed laugh. "I'm getting to be an old bore! Next thing I'll be sitting around the courthouse with all the other old vets telling how I showed Bobby Lee how to fight a war!"

Faith shook her head. "It was a terrible time, wasn't it? I'm glad it's over."

"So am I. I left a lot of good friends on those fields in Virginia." Then, wanting to change the subject, he asked, "How's the school going?"

"Not too well, I'm afraid."

Winslow gave her a quick glance, noting that her face was somewhat drawn, with a few lines etched around her eyes. "You mustn't be discouraged, Faith," he said quickly. "It takes a long time to get to know these people. They've been shoved around for so long by white people, it's a wonder they don't hate us all." Then he added, "Some of them do, of course. Geronimo and Roman Nose and Victorio—the real fire eaters. I don't think they'll ever become tame Indians. They're just too wild to become farmers."

"All the papers from the East are talking about the Indian problem. And they don't agree with each other." Faith got up and brought a few newspapers from a table. "This is from the *Boston Post*." She read the item to him aloud. " 'The history of relations between the white man and red has been an unbroken story of rapacity, cruelty and of complete lack of feeling on the part of the white. Nothing has been constant with him except his sacred right to seize whatever land he wished from whatever Indian tribe he wished. We have no reason to be proud of our dealings with the weaker savage race. We have no right to call ourselves a civilized or cultured people with that record against us.' "

Winslow listened carefully, then said, "I wish more people felt like that."

"So do I! But here's an editorial from my own hometown paper, the *St. Louis Globe*." She began to read, the anger noticeable in her face as she read:

" 'There is no use entering into a discussion of the morals of the white man versus the red man. All the debate in Christendom cannot blink the fact that the white man is a surging tide of conquest, of settlement and progress, whereas the Indian is content to roam nomadically across the land as he has done for tens of thousands of years, ignoring an earth which could provide him riches were he industrious enough to cultivate it. Primitive indolence and barbaric narrowness is his character, nor does he wish for anything we call civilization. Let us not shed tears over the ills done poor Lo. Poor Lo has been at the business of killing and raiding and stealing for many centuries—before the white man came. It is his one great objective in life. It is his

198

profession and his pastime. Whereas, a white boy is taught to believe that the purpose of man is scientific and literary and social advancement, the one and only training an Indian boy ever receives is to go out and kill his enemy, thereby becoming great in his own tribe. Were the race of the Indian to die off tomorrow, there would be no permanent handiwork behind him, no inventions, no scholarship except a few primitive daubs on this or that rock, no system of ethics at all, not one worthy thing to justify his tenure upon the fairest of all continents. By contrast look upon the white man's record in a brief 250 years here. That should be answer enough to all the silly sentimentality current in the East. It is time now to end the endless marching and countermarching of skeleton cavalry columns commanded by officers who know nothing of savage warfare. It is time now to send in one large and determined expedition to crush savage resistance permanently and to confine the red man to the reservation, so that at least the white race may get on with its appointed destiny, which is to harness the continent and to build civilization's network across it.' "

Faith abruptly walked over to the stove, opened the door, and with an angry gesture threw the paper into the glowing fire. Her face was flushed with more than the heat of the stove, her wide, expressive lips were drawn tightly together, and her gray eyes glinted with agitation. "I wonder what that editor would think if someone moved in and took his home away from him as he says we ought to do with the Indians!"

Winslow had not seen her like this, and the outburst of fiery temper pleased him for some reason. "You look like a Sioux on the warpath," he grinned at her. "Would you scalp that newspaperman if you got a chance?"

Faith stopped her pacing, gave Winslow a startled glance; then a rueful smile tugged at her lips. "Well, maybe not—but I'd like to yank some of his hate-filled hair out by the roots!"

"Gosh!" Laurie's eyes were wide and her mouth open with surprise. "I didn't know preachers ever got mad!"

Her remark tickled Faith, and she ran over and gave the girl a hug, laughing as she did so. "Now you know better," she said, then straightened up and gave a slight shrug of her shoulders. "I guess you're shocked at my fit, aren't you, Tom?"

"No. You look very attractive when you're mad. Makes your eyes sparkle."

His remark took her off guard, and she studied him to see if he was serious. When he smiled, she asked him, "Tom, will it happen like he says? Will there be a big battle?"

"Yes, it's coming. That editor could have said it all a lot quicker, like, 'You Indians have the land and we want it, so we're going to get it if we have to kill every last one of you.' "

"And we call ourselves *civilized*!" Faith exploded. "How can I preach the love of God to them when every day they see we don't mean it?"

"*You* mean it, Faith. Some of them will see that." He hesitated, then added, "I don't think people find God in big groups, do they? It's always one at a time. And you're here to do that, I take it."

"But . . . it's so *slow*, Tom!" Faith said, her tone sad. "I'm only one person and there are so many of them!"

"Well, Jesus was just one person, wasn't He?"

His question caught at her, turning her silent. She stood there, her hands behind her back, clenched together, and finally she nodded, "That's right, He was. And He spent most of His time with just twelve men. Oh, He preached to large crowds, of course, but it was those twelve He really gave himself to."

"That's what you'll have to do, isn't it?" Winslow asked. "Get just a handful to believe you've got the right way for them. Then those few will have to go out and convince others." He stopped. "Listen to me," he said, "telling you how to do your job!"

"Don't say that, Tom!" Faith protested. "Because you're right. I can't be grieving because I can't do it all. But I *can* reach a few!"

"Are you going to preach in the morning?"

Faith glanced at Laurie, smiled, and nodded. "I'm going to try. Will you interpret for me, Tom?"

"If you trust me."

"I trust you," she said quietly. "There's nobody I trust more."

★　★　★　★

The congregation Winslow faced the next morning was predominantly women and children, with a sprinkling of older men. He had gone in and built a roaring fire in the large potbellied

200

stove, then after a good breakfast, had gone back to the larger building with Faith and Laurie for the service. Faith wore a light gray dress with dark maroon trim and a pair of high-topped black shoes that peeped in and out from beneath her skirt. Her hair was pinned up, piled in a rich gathering, and she looked very attractive as she stood up and said, "We are happy to have Mr. Winslow and his daughter Laurie with us this morning. Mr. Winslow has worked with your people for many years, and I have asked him to interpret for me. But as usual we'll have a song service first. Join with me as much as you can."

The hymns were all familiar to Winslow, and he sang along, though feeling a little uncomfortable. The Indians knew only a smattering of the words, but they enjoyed the singing, humming along and pronouncing such words as they did know.

When they had sung several numbers, Faith looked a little nervous, but said in a strong, halting voice, as simply as possible without interpretation, "I have a little surprise for you." Then she lifted her clear voice in a verse of "Amazing Grace"—in the Sioux language.

It was a poor translation and she made more than one error in pronunciation, but when she ended, a mutter of approval went over the congregation, and one old warrior smiled, saying, "Good!"

Faith sang the song several times, and by the time she had completed it three times, most of the congregation were singing along—especially the young people. "That's so very good!" Faith nodded, pleased with her effort. "Soon we'll have many songs in your language. And one day I'll be able to speak to you without an interpreter, but today Mr. Winslow will help."

Winslow stood next to Faith as he translated and found that she had mastered the art of using an interpreter well. She broke her thoughts and words up into small phrases, then waited until he had put them into the Sioux language. More than once he had trouble with some word or phrase, and the Indians liked that. This occurred early, for her text was from John, chapter three, and when she read the verse, " 'Except a man be born again, he cannot see the kingdom of God,' " Winslow hesitated. "I don't know just how to put that," he said to Faith.

"Just put it like it is," Faith insisted.

Winslow did, and immediately an old man lined by years and trouble spoke up. "Why would any man want to be born into the world twice? Once is trouble enough!"

A giggle swept over the small congregation, and when Winslow translated the old man's response to Faith, she said, "Yes, it is a hard world, and Jesus knew that. But there are two worlds, as you well know, Father," she said to the man. "One is dirt and water and sun and food. We all enter this world. But not all things are beneath a person's feet. Some things can be found only in his heart." She was encouraged when she saw heads nodding, and began to preach, stressing those two aspects of man: the physical and the spiritual.

Winslow did his best, struggling at times over the concepts, but anxious to get the clearest meaning across.

But he discovered that the task of giving the Gospel to the Sioux was not so difficult as another factor. The story of Jesus as Faith told it stirred old memories, flashing back to his earliest childhood. He remembered the first time he heard about Jesus with any sort of clarity—the first time he'd thought of that moment for years. He'd been about six or seven at the time, and when a visiting preacher had described the sufferings of Jesus on the cross, Tom had pulled at his mother's sleeve, asking when she bent down, "Why did they hurt Him, Mama?"

Even as Winslow was speaking, giving Faith's words to the Sioux, the memory welled up in him—of the tears that had stood in her eyes, the smell of lavender, the pressure of her arm hugging him, and the answer she gave: "He came to be hurt, Tom. He gave himself to be hurt—so that we wouldn't have to be hurt."

Winslow had understood almost nothing of his mother's words, but over the years the truth had kept coming back to him, and now the impact was so powerful, he suddenly faltered, his voice breaking.

Faith glanced at him quickly, noticing the hesitation in Winslow's delivery as she mentioned the cross and the death of Jesus.

Finally she concluded. "All of us have been born into the world of stones and trees and the earth. But Jesus says that is not enough. He came to help us enter that other world—the world of God himself. And He did it by the only way possible."

She paused. There was a stillness in the room. Everyone's eyes were focused on her. Then she went on. "God had said that sin must be paid for. Jesus said, 'I will pay it for them. I will become a man and go to the earth. There I will die—and then they can come to the Great Spirit freely.

"And how can a man or a woman or a child enter this other world—be born again?" Faith asked. "Jesus tells us how in this book that gives the words of the Great Spirit. It says, 'Jesus said, if any man thirst, let him come unto me and drink.' " Then she closed her Bible and looked out at them, her eyes glowing. "Jesus is the water of life. If you have no earthly water, your body dries up. You all know that. But we are thirsty for another kind of water. We long for God, for the Great Spirit. So Jesus says that He is *that* water!"

She stopped then and offered a simple prayer. As she prayed, Tom Winslow found himself greatly moved. He had grown up among Christians, but the war had hardened him. Now he felt some of the same urgency about God that he had as a very young man. Faith had made no appeal as he had heard countless evangelists do—yet now he felt as if God was speaking directly to him.

When she opened her eyes, Faith saw the struggle in his face. She wanted to go to him, but felt the Lord's restraint, so she prayed that this—the first vulnerable trait she'd seen in Winslow—would be an open door to God.

But even as she watched, she saw him pull himself straight, his lips drawing into a thin line. He had hardened himself. Why, she didn't know, but the evidence was clear.

Faith was right. Tom's realization of his need for God had been invaded by thoughts of Spence Grayson, and all at once his bitterness flooded back, drowning out the gentle urging of the Spirit.

Later as Tom and Laurie were leaving, Faith sensed his openness was gone, but she said only, "It was so good to see you. Will you come again, both of you?"

"Oh, I will!" Laurie cried.

"I can't promise, Faith," Tom said. Then seeing that he had hurt her, he added, "You're a fine preacher."

As they rode away, Faith's heart ached. *He came so close!*

CHAPTER SIXTEEN

OFFICERS' BALL

★ ★ ★ ★

The Officers' Ball for the Seventh Cavalry was held in the only structure suitable for such an event—the upper story of the Citizens' Bank, which was utilized for political meetings, lectures, and church meetings by groups having no buildings of their own.

Spence Grayson tucked his hand under Faith's arm and guided her up the wooden staircase attached to the outside frame, smiling wryly. *Never thought I'd be taking a lady preacher to a dance,* he thought. He had tried to convince himself that the scarcity of women had brought him to such a strange choice, but despite his flaws, he was always honest with himself.

When he had asked Faith to the ball, she had stared at him, surprise leaping into her eyes. "Why, Spence, you don't want to take me to an affair like that! You might as well ask your elderly aunt to go!"

He had liked her forthright manner, answering it honestly in a manner he would not have used with any other woman. "I don't think it's *quite* that bad, Faith, but you know me pretty well, I think, where women are concerned."

"They're a challenge to your ability, Spence."

Her directness surprised him. "Yes, I suppose so. They've used their wiles on men, and I've answered in kind."

"So now having tried your luck with all the available women, you'd like to see how well I can withstand your charm?" She had laughed outright at his embarrassment, but surprised him by saying, "I'll go with you, Spence. I think a woman needs to be tested by a good-looking rascal once in a while."

"Might get you in trouble with your deacons."

"They're not paying me, so I guess they can't fire me!"

Now as they walked up the steps, Faith's foot slipped on a board, slippery with ice. As she faltered, Spence put his arm around her and steadied her. Holding her he said, "Feeling properly tempted, Miss Jamison?"

"It's better than falling down the stairs, Lieutenant," she teased, aware of his powerful charm. He had the clearest blue eyes she'd ever seen in a man, and his intensely masculine features would attract any woman. She had accepted the invitation out of curiosity, prompted to a large degree by Tom's animosity toward Grayson and, she had to admit, out of a perverse determination to throw herself into the officer's company—to prove that she was immune to his charms. But as she entered the ballroom, she was uncomfortably aware that despite her frivolous teasing of Spence, she did sense an attraction to him that went beyond what she felt for most men.

She enjoyed the startled expression that swept across his face as he looked at her after slipping the coat from her shoulders. The dress was stunning. Elaine Owens had practically forced her to wear it, despite Faith's protests. It was a form-fitting gown of pale blue watered silk looped with blue ribbon and tiny blue flowers. Mischief danced in her eyes as she said to Grayson, "Just an old dress I salvaged, Spence."

His eyes glowed with admiration. "I've not seen anyone like you, Faith!"

His voice was quiet but resonant, and she understood at that moment how he could win a woman. A scoundrel he might be, but there was such intensity in his gaze that she knew she would be in danger if she didn't stay on her guard.

"They've done a marvelous job with the room, haven't they?" She swept the ballroom with an approving glance. The walls were decked with colorful bunting; the ceilings with long graceful festoons of brightly colored paper, catching and reflecting the myriad rays from the lamps. At the end of the room a band, composed of a piano, two guitars, a mandolin, and a violin, started to play. Immediately couples began to swirl around the room. The brass buttons on the officers' coats winked merrily, mingling and shifting like a kaleidoscope with the colors of the women's gowns—red, yellow, green, blue, white.

Grayson handed their coats to a corporal, turned to Faith, and put out his arms. "Come now, before those green young lieutenants carry you away!"

Faith smiled and the two swung into the waltz rhythm, sweeping across the floor. He was, as she had guessed, a fine dancer. "When I became a Christian, I cried because I thought the Lord would make me give up dancing."

"I'm glad to see that wasn't one of God's conditions!"

"Well, it was—for quite some time. But later I came to understand that it wasn't the *dancing* that God was displeased with; it was my unwillingness to give it up."

"That could be said of any pleasure, do you think?"

She laughed, tossing her head back, the bright amber beams of the chandeliers catching the golden highlights of her auburn hair. "Now, Lieutenant, *that* won't do!"

"I didn't think it would," he answered, pleased at her response. "But a fellow has to try, doesn't he?"

They danced for the next half hour until she was whisked away by other eager officers.

When his fellow officers razzed Grayson about bringing a preacher to a ball, he replied, "You're sore because I thought of it first!"

He poured himself a drink at the punch table, thinking how delightful Faith Jamison was. He had been totally surprised to encounter a girl as filled with joy as any he'd ever met, not the grim and sour woman he had expected.

The truth was that Spence Grayson was jaded with success. He had never met a woman who had been able to resist his charms—though in all honesty he admitted that he had turned from several, sensing pursuit was useless. Perhaps he was getting older—or wiser. For years he had played a game with women, but now he saw himself as a person with no substance— empty.

He watched Faith moving across the floor and knew that she was not the type to be interested in what he had offered other women. Suddenly he realized he had no desire to pursue this young woman as he had others. She struck a chord in his spirit he had thought long dead—and now he wondered what it would be like to have such a woman love him.

His reverie was interrupted by Lucy Darrow, the wife of Major Darrow now stationed at Fort Rice. "Why, Lucy," he said, hiding his impatience. A woman of thirty-five with traces of youthful beauty, she had been one of his conquests—so easy that he had lost interest in her after a brief romance. It had been an old story—an aging husband, a wife searching for romance, and a handsome young officer. She had fallen easily, and now seemed intent on picking up their affair.

He made light conversation, but her eyes grew bitter. "You don't like to be confronted with the foolish women you've tired of, do you, Spence?" Her words dripped with acid.

Grayson glanced around the room, noting that several people were watching them, including Lucy's husband. He forced a smile and said quietly, "Now, Lucy, this is no place for such talk."

With a curl of her lips she spat out, "You've found a new interest, very pretty. Shall I wish you good hunting?" Then she too became aware of those watching and forced herself to smile. "Goodbye, Lieutenant. I won't interfere with your fun!"

She crossed the room to her husband, a pleasant-looking man in his early fifties. Major Darrow turned and said, "Will you dance with me, Lucy? You're the finest-looking woman in the room."

"Why, Dan!" she said, surprise lighting her face. "You haven't said anything like that to me for so long!"

"Too long," he nodded. "But it's true. It's always been true for me." He took her in his arms and they moved out on the floor, unaware that Grayson had been watching them anxiously.

He thought of several confrontations he'd had—two involving bloodshed—with the husbands of women he'd pursued. The memories nagged at him. With disgust, he felt a sense of shame at the charade of his life. *I'm not a callow boy to be chasing after women*, he thought with a flash of bitterness. *A man's a fool to keep that up forever!*

He shrugged off the heaviness he felt and brought Faith to the table and poured her a glass of punch. She accepted it and said, "All the officers seem in good spirits. I suppose it's like a family, the Seventh?"

"Hardly!" Grayson returned quickly. "The Custers have no children, but they have pets."

"Pets?"

"Yes, pets—all the way from a mouse to a wolf. The general has about forty dogs, but not all his pets have four legs." A cold smile touched his fleshy lips. "There is an inner circle in the Seventh—the chosen ones of the regiment. Benteen calls it 'The Royal Family.' "

Faith glanced toward General Custer, surrounded by a small group of officers, all hanging on to his words. "I'm surprised," she murmured. "Which ones are in the circle?"

"Tom Custer, the general's brother. He's a hard-drinking man and a woman chaser, if rumor is to be believed. He's the only man alive to hold two congressional Medals of Honor, and Custer is livid with jealousy over it! There's Lieutenant James Calhoun, he got into the circle by marrying Custer's sister Margaret. And see that officer over there, with the yellow hair? That's Captain George Yates. He's on the inside, and so is the adjutant, William Cooke."

"Is that all?"

"Well, there's Captain Thomas Weir. There—the officer with the youthful face dancing with Mrs. Custer. And that's an item, too—Weir and Mrs. Custer." He shrugged at her puzzled look, adding, "There have been many rumors about them—but Benteen is the chief spreader of such."

"I don't believe it," Faith said. "She has such a sweet face!"

"Well, I think you're right. Benteen is the leader of the anti-Custer group. Come, let's see what the general has to say."

Custer was wearing the uniform he designed himself, a fancy coat with a sailor suit collar with a general's stars in each corner and a loose red silk neckerchief tied around his throat. He was speaking heatedly as the two approached, saying, ". . .has finally decided to settle this confounded Indian question, and we shall do it this spring!"

"The regiment is far below full strength, General," Captain

Moylan said. "I don't think we can take the field with more than eight hundred men. That's not enough."

Custer bridled at the officer and snapped angrily, "The Seventh can whip any collection of Indians on the plains, Captain!"

Major Reno spoke up. "This won't be an easy campaign. According to the scouts there are a formidable number of Indians gathering even now."

Custer gave him a scathing look. His lack of respect for the man was evident in his tone. "That's scare talk, Major!" He swept the room with a wide gesture, stating emphatically, "Our only problem will be catching up with the hostiles!"

Benteen, his eyes cold as polar ice, had stayed on the edge of the crowd. Now he said, "Did you know that traders have been freighting repeating rifles up the Missouri to trade for fur? The Indians we meet will be armed with Winchesters and Henrys—repeaters, some of them."

Custer said in a grating tone as he stared at Benteen, "Sir, we shall defeat them!"

Grayson touched Faith's arm and drew her away. "That's the way it goes, you see? Custer will pay no attention to counsel. All he knows how to do is get on a horse, pull his sabre, and go charging into the biggest crowd of Indians he can find."

Faith studied him. "That's hard on the rest of you, isn't it?"

"I know, but the War Department thinks Custer is the best Indian fighter we've got."

At the end of the evening Grayson and Faith said good-night to the general, who said to Grayson, "I'm happy you're keeping such good company, Lieutenant. I know you do it as an example for the other young officers."

Mrs. Custer gave Faith a warm hug, genuinely happy to have her there. "Thank you for coming, Miss Jamison. We must see more of you in the future."

When Grayson and Faith were settled in the buggy, Grayson asked, "Do you have to be in right away?"

"Not really. I told the Owens I'd be late."

"A ride by the river sound all right?"

"A short one, Lieutenant."

The air was sharp and clear, the moon full and bright. As they pulled up beside the river, they sat watching the black waters rolling in, the little waves making ringlets as the ripples touched the shore.

"My, it's quiet!" Grayson exclaimed. "I never realize it until I come here like this because I live in such a noisy world."

"Do you come often, Spence?"

"Sometimes. At night, most of the time. Just to think." He turned to her. "You probably don't believe I'm that kind of a fellow."

She studied him by the light of the moon, and her attention made him a little nervous. Finally she said, "Why, I suppose most of us do things like that. Why should you be different?"

"That's not what you think, Faith," he responded quickly. "You've pegged me as a rogue and a rascal." He thought of Tom Winslow and demanded, "Has someone told you about me?"

She perceived his thought. "You mean Sergeant Winslow?"

"Yes!"

"He won't say anything—though I tried to get it out of him." She grew very serious. "What's between you two, Spence? Why do you despise each other?"

Grayson's back was stiff, his eyes hard. After a moment he sighed. "Faith, it all happened a long time ago. We . . . cared for the same woman. An old story, I guess."

"Were you friends?"

"Good friends once." He fixed his eyes on the river, the slight gurgling of its waters a sibilant sound. "See the water?" he said quietly. "It's there only for a moment, then it's gone. It never comes back—that's the way life is. There's never any going back. Once a thing is done, it's written in a book, and nothing a man or a woman can do will change it."

She was moved by his words. "Are there things you'd like to change, Spence?"

He searched her face as she spoke, admiring the smoothness of her cheeks, soft even in the cold air. She seemed set apart from other women he knew.

"Yes, I'd change one thing," he said. "I wish I'd never told some of the women I've known how much I love them." He reached out and put his hand on her shoulder, pulling her around to face him. "Because now I'd like to say some things to

210

you, things I feel. I wish I could say those words to you for the first time."

Faith felt the impulses that ran through him, powerful and demanding. As he pulled her closer, she did not draw back—as one part of her knew she should—and when he kissed her, part of her responded.

But it was only part of her, and Grayson sensed her withdrawal. At once, he pulled away, something he would not have done with another woman. "You see?" he said, making a gesture with his hands. "You don't think of me as a man you might grow fond of."

"Spence, you wouldn't want me," Faith protested. "We're as far apart as any two people can be. We don't want the same things, not at all."

"I want love, Faith, and so do you. I could tell that much, even from one kiss. If I've learned anything from the life I've led, it's that hell is being alone."

"What a strange thing for you to say!"

"Because I'm outgoing, because I get along with people?" He shook his head. "A man or a woman can be alone in a crowd of a thousand people, Faith." He turned to her, and his smooth features were carved into sharp planes by the light of the moon. "But with just one person—if it's the right one—there's no need for anyone else. The whole world is right there—in that one woman."

His words disturbed Faith, and she knew it was because she had felt he was too proud to know a thing like that. It made her look at him differently, for she knew he spoke the truth. She took a deep breath, let it out, then said quietly, "Take me home, Spence."

"All right."

The hooves of the horses made a steady *plopping* sound as they drove back to town, and when he pulled up in front of the Owens' house, she got out at once. He followed her to the steps, pulled off his hat, and said, "Thanks for going with me to the ball."

"I enjoyed it, Spence."

"How about riding with me this week?"

Faith hesitated, then said, "I don't want to, Spence. We shouldn't see each other."

"Don't you think men can change, Faith?"

"Of course!"

"Then you must believe me when I say I'm changing. You've affected me as no other woman has. I've always had to conquer the woman I was attracted to, no matter what it took; but with you, it's not like that. Why, I don't understand, couldn't explain. It's . . . well, other women I wanted to *take* from—you, Faith, I want to *give* to. That's love, isn't it?"

Faith shook her head, and as soberly as she had ever spoken, said, "It can never be, Spence. I've given my life to God."

"Are all Christian women single? None of them have a husband?"

"Of course they do, but if I ever married, I'd want my husband to feel as I do about what's important in life."

When he didn't argue or beg, Faith appreciated that in him. "Good-night, Spence," she whispered. At the door, she turned and said, "I'll go riding with you—but that's all it is. Just a ride."

Grayson drove back to the fort, sobered by the way the evening had ended—especially by his own behavior. He knew he had little chance with Faith, but he was a man of great confidence and went to bed thinking of her promise. As he lay there, suddenly pictures of Marlene Signourey . . . Winslow flashed into his mind—and a spurt of fear shot through him. Not fear of the physical, for he was no coward, but he became keenly aware that the patterns of a man's life could haunt him. Would his? He had loved Marlene as he had loved no other woman—at least until now. His mind shifted to Faith, and for a long time he lay there thinking of her, of the moonlight on her face, the innocence in her.

I've got to have her! he thought, the desire consuming him with such restlessness his mind became a battleground against the shadows gathering around his bed.

CHAPTER SEVENTEEN

A BUGGY RIDE

★ ★ ★ ★

The flu that had hit Laurence Dutton proved to be more serious than anyone thought, progressing from a cough, to a high fever, to a state of almost complete helplessness. Double pneumonia, the doctor suspected, adding, "You can forget about teaching school, Dutton, for two or three weeks at least. We don't have a hospital, but you need some nursing care."

This latter proved to be more difficult than the doctor supposed, for other families were sick as well. For a while women divided their time caring for Dutton, though it was spasmodic at best.

Help came from a most surprising source as Eileen Jennings offered to nurse the schoolmaster; but when his condition worsened, she said as she looked at his feverish face, "This won't do. You must have better care."

Dutton's temperature had shot up, making him light-headed, his eyes glazed, his tongue parched. He licked his lips and whispered hoarsely, "Guess it's the best we can do—"

Fortunately he was mistaken, for later in the day Eileen returned with two privates from B Company. "Put him in the ambulance," she commanded with the authority of a sergeant. "Wrap him well in those blankets, and I'll get his things."

"What—?"

Eileen put her hand on Dutton's brow. "It's all right. I'm taking you to my house where I can care for you properly. The doctor says it'll be better."

The soldiers were rough but efficient, wrapping Dutton in blankets until he looked like a thick woolen cocoon, then putting him on a stretcher and carrying him out to place him in an army ambulance. The cold air revived the sick man enough to protest when Eileen came out with his suitcase. "Miss Jennings, I don't—"

"Don't talk," she interrupted firmly, tucking a corner of the blanket under him. He blinked like a sun-stricken owl, but obeyed, and soon the rocking of the ambulance lulled him to sleep.

Eileen sat between the two soldiers, both of them old acquaintances. They had been in her husband's company and had shown kindness to her after his death. One of them, Micah Singer, with a lantern jaw and tobacco-stained lips, said as they moved along at an easy gait, "Going to do a little nursin', Miz Jennings?"

"Yes, Micah. He needs good care. You know how dangerous pneumonia can be."

"Shore do. My little boy died of it," the trooper nodded. "I shore do miss the little feller." His black eyes shot a sharp look at her. "I guess you miss the lieutenant like that, ma'am."

"It gets easier," Eileen replied. "Losing someone is like losing an arm, I suppose. You're never whole again, even if the pain leaves. And you always live with the memories."

Singer nodded. "Yes, ma'am, that's the way of it."

The other soldier, a corporal named Al Canseco, shook his head in a doleful gesture. "Reckon there'll be more widows and orphans when we take off after the Sioux in the spring." He sighed heavily, shifted his feet on the floorboard, and went on. "We left some good men buried down on the Washita. Now we're gonna lose some more in them hills over thar."

"Oh, shet up!" Singer said, his voice edgy. "You're worse'n an undertaker, Al!"

"I suppose you're right, Al," Eileen said thoughtfully. "Everybody talks about the campaign that's coming." She swayed as the wheel of the ambulance hit a rut, looked back to see that

Dutton was all right, then turned back to the men. "You two be careful when it starts. Don't try to be heroes."

"Why, Miz Jennings," Singer grinned, "me and Al has already put in to be horse-holders. Let them other fellers win all the medals. I jest want to finish out this hitch and get home to my family." He grew morose then, adding, "Solgering ain't no job for a family man."

"No, it isn't!"

Both men looked at her, for her voice was sharp, almost terse. Singer shook his head slightly at Canseco, and the two began to talk about a riding contest that was going to take place in Bismarck in the spring. Later, Singer said to Canseco, "She looks all tensed up, don't she, Al? I reckon she needs to get away from the army. It don't help her none to be around soldiers—especially when the fightin's about to start up again."

"I reckon you're right, Micah," Al responded. "She ain't never got over losin' her man. Don't think she ever will."

When they pulled up in front of the house, Eileen led the way in, directing the men to the room she had prepared for Dutton. "Thank you both. Come by tomorrow and you'll get your reward—some of my cherry pie you like so much." She saw them out, then went back into the bedroom and began to unpack the suitcase.

Dutton was awake, but when he tried to speak, he went into a spasm of coughing that racked his body terribly. Eileen quickly brought a glass of water and helped him sit up. Holding him till the coughing subsided, she handed him the water. After he had drunk enough, he turned to face her, saying in a raspy voice, "Thanks." In spite of his critical condition, he was cognizant of the feminine surroundings and whispered, "Shouldn't . . . be taking your . . . room."

"Don't worry about that. Just work on getting well." She helped him lie down, spread the quilts around him, then said, "I've got to run an errand. You try to sleep."

Leaving the house she went at a fast walk to Suds Row, stopping at a shack in the middle of the line where the laundresses lived. When she knocked on the door, she heard a faint voice, and opened it. A Mexican woman was lying on a bed, her face wan. "Why, Delores," Eileen said, "you're sick!"

"Sí, señora. Since two days ago. I no can wash for you now."

Eileen hesitated, then said, "Don't worry about that. Do you need anything?"

"No, señora Jennings. Juanita—my sister—she take care of me ver' good."

Eileen left the shack, her mind on her own situation. It had been her intention to hire Delores to help with Dutton, not so much for the nursing care as for her presence. A widow with a young unmarried man in her house would be a prime target for gossip, she well knew—in spite of the illness. She had acted on impulse, and now the problem of making it look "respectable" became a factor.

"Hello, Eileen."

Eileen looked up to see Tom Winslow, who was leading a bay horse. "I hear you're going into the nursing business."

"Oh, who told you about it?"

"Canseco and Singer. I ran into them when they were returning the ambulance to the stables. How's Dutton?"

"Not very well." She bit her lip, obviously upset.

"What's wrong, Eileen?" he asked.

"Oh, I was counting on Delores coming to stay with me, but she's sick." She hesitated, then added, "I can't be alone with a man in my house, Tom."

"I guess not." He slapped the reins in his hands, gave her a thoughtful look. "What about if Laurie stayed with you?"

"Why, that would make it all right, I think."

He grinned. "Having a little girl for a chaperon makes a difference. People are that way, I guess."

"I know. Poor Larry can hardly lift his head, but you know how people talk."

"I'll send Laurie over. Later I'll come and sit with the patient myself."

That was his plan, but he came by later in the afternoon to say, "Eileen, I've got to go out on a patrol. Be gone for two days, maybe three. I hate to leave Laurie with you—"

"We'll make out fine, Tom," she said quickly. "Laurie can help me a great deal." She hesitated for a moment. "Is it dangerous . . . this trip?"

"Shouldn't be too bad. We're just going out to cut some sign.

Try to find out if there's been any of the southern tribes coming in." He looked at her more closely. "You shouldn't worry so much, Eileen."

"How can anyone manage that?" She was a little embarrassed at letting him see her concern. Always she tried to keep a neutral appearance, not letting people know about her fears. She had never kept it from her husband, and it had made him miserable. He had dreaded leaving her, for she had made him feel as if it were his fault, not the government's.

In reflection, she realized her attitude had made him feel inadequate—as a husband and a soldier, but he had to obey orders. When he had died, she had determined not to let anyone else get close enough to see her concerns—yet there was something about Winslow that renewed the old fears. She smiled. "I'm sorry to be such an old mope, Tom. You go on and don't worry about Laurie. When you get back we'll have a birthday party."

"Whose?"

"Yours. It's next Friday. Laurie told me. And she said chocolate is your favorite cake. We'll see you then."

★ ★ ★ ★

Having been reared in one of the more austere homes for orphans located in Chicago, Larry Dutton knew almost nothing of the gentle side of life. That he had survived the experience and gone on to educate himself was a tribute to his determination. He was, despite his youthful, almost boyish appearance, a man who possessed an inner tenacity, but the sickness had destroyed some of his self-confidence. He had never been seriously ill, and when pneumonia hit him, he realized for the first time how fragile life really is.

For several days he was too weak to do more than obey Eileen's simple commands. Yet during that time he was vaguely conscious of a missing element in his life—the woman's touch. As he gained strength, the fact became more clear.

Therefore, it wasn't strange that this experience would strongly influence him. He was basically a shy person in spite of his rough upbringing; but as Eileen cared for him, the intimacy of the sickroom destroyed the protective wall Dutton had built around himself—not one brick at a time, but the entire wall fell!

So a week after his arrival, he rebelled against having her help him with the breakfast. "I've been feeding myself for a long time," he complained when she sat down to assist him. "You can't feed me for the rest of my life."

Eileen's eyes sparkled with humor. "Well, you're feeling better, I see. All right, you can feed yourself. I'll just sit here in case you need something."

He found he was very hungry and quickly consumed the entire breakfast.

Eileen laughed as she watched him. "There's plenty more, Larry. And nobody's going to take it away from you."

Chagrined, he smiled shyly. "I guess my table manners aren't the best. But my appetite seems to be coming back."

"You look better." She touched his forehead. "No fever."

The touch of her hand had been gentle, and he said impulsively, "Why did you take all this trouble with me, Eileen?"

His question flustered her. "Oh, I don't know," she laughed. "Maybe I was just bored." Then she smiled wistfully. "I get lonely sometimes. And I've felt so useless since Frank died."

Her answer caught him off guard. She was one of the most attractive women he knew, and he had assumed she would be well supplied with suitors. Then he realized that would have been flaunting the custom since her husband had been dead less than a year. He looked at her, admiring the smooth skin, the clear blue eyes, and the trim figure. "I was in pretty bad shape, Eileen. If you hadn't taken me in, I might have died."

She wanted to avoid any overtures of gratitude, so she said lightly, "It was little enough. It gave me a chance to cook and Laurie an opportunity to learn how to do some nursing."

He wanted to thank her, but he sensed she wished to avoid that. So he said, "She's a beautiful child, isn't she? And I like her father."

"So do I."

Something in her voice caught at Dutton. He had heard someone say that the widow and Tom Winslow would make a fine couple, and he asked cautiously, "You've known him long—Tom, I mean?"

"No, only a short while. He's done a good job raising his

daughter." She smoothed her hair, adding, "But it'll be harder for him from now on. Laurie needs a mother." Suddenly her face reddened. "I . . . guess that sounds like a man-hungry woman, out to trap a man!"

"Why, a woman like you, Eileen, doesn't *have* to worry about that!"

She looked up at him, seeing the kindness in his eyes. He looked like a boy, with his red hair all awry and his round face. The long hours of nursing him had given her a motherly feeling, which had amused her at times, but now she saw this was no child. The honest admiration pleased her. It made her feel good. "Thank you, Larry. A woman needs to be complimented at least once a day."

"You deserve more than that, Eileen," he said. "I've never known a woman like you!"

"I'm nothing special," she protested.

From that moment she felt differently about Larry Dutton. As the days passed and he grew stronger, she saw not only his intelligence but the humor that lay just beneath the surface of his mind. He had a sly wit, and to her surprise she discovered she had some of the same qualities. Since there was little to do and he was awake for longer periods, they talked for hours. She learned of his harsh boyhood in the orphanage, and came to appreciate the drive that was in him, his determination to be a lawyer.

"You'll be a fine attorney, Larry," she told him. "You have a way of getting to know people."

"Well," he grinned, "I've gotten to know *you* pretty well, but I can't get pneumonia and go live with all my clients, can I, Eileen?"

He *had* gotten to know her well, she realized, for as he had shared the story of his life, she had told him more about herself than she had anyone else—even Frank.

"That depends on how many clients you have!" she joked. Then she went on. "When you become a lawyer, will you miss being a teacher?"

"I like the children, but I've always wanted to be a lawyer."

"I love children. That's why I've appreciated so much having Laurie."

220

"You'll miss her when Tom marries, won't you?" he said innocently. He saw the surprise on her face and said hurriedly, "No, I haven't heard he's getting married, but a handsome fellow like Winslow is sure to find a wife."

"He hasn't so far, Larry, and his wife's been dead for years." The subject seemed to disturb her, and she rose and left the room abruptly.

Dutton lay there thinking about her swift departure. *The big fellow—she's pretty gone on him, even if she won't admit it. Well, we'll see. I'm still in the game.* Seeing her attraction to Winslow was a challenge, and he was determined to find a way to get her to look at him with the same light in her eyes that she had for Winslow.

★　★　★　★

The wind was making such a shrill keening that Faith didn't hear the horse approaching. She had developed a sense of her surroundings, always alert to any sound out of the ordinary. But the rising wind had muffled it; so when she heard the knock at her door, she whirled to face it, her eyes wide with apprehension.

"Faith? Are you home?"

At the sound of Tom's voice, she touched her cheek with relief and ran to open the door. "Tom!" she cried, "come in." He moved past her into the warmth of the room. "What in the world are you doing here?"

He looked exhausted, but he said cheerfully, "Came to get you to go for a buggy ride."

She stared at him suspiciously. "You've been drinking!"

He laughed, his teeth white against the bronzed color of his face. His whiskers made fine points of light, for he had not shaved for three days. "Nope. Just getting back from a three-day patrol. I cut away from the others a few miles back."

"Here, have some coffee," she offered, and when he was drinking the bitter hot brew thirstily, she leaned against the wall and asked, "What's this about a buggy ride?"

He finished the coffee and handed her the cup. "That was fine!" Then he shrugged out of his coat. "You won't be having any school for a few days. I've come to take you home with me. Laurie and I need company."

She was pleased at his manner, but shook her head. "Why, I can't do that, Tom."

"Sure you can," he grinned. There was a wolfish air about him, his cheeks lean and his eyes bright. "Eileen's nursing that schoolmaster, Dutton, and you can give her a hand with that. And there's a new preacher coming to the church next Sunday. Owens told me to tell you to come. His name's Hunter, I think Nick said. Supposed to be a red-hot evangelist."

"Oh, I've heard of him!"

"Well, get ready, and you can hear him for yourself, Faith!"

She wasted no time, and half an hour later they were on their way to Bismarck. The wind cut across the land, swirled around them, biting at the exposed parts of their faces. "Tell me about the scouting trip," she said.

"We won't find much this winter—but all the signs are bad. There'll be trouble in the spring, I'm afraid."

As they drove along, she told him about the school and showed off her accomplishments with the Sioux language by speaking a few words. When she caught his grin, she demanded, "What are you laughing at?"

"Why, you just said, 'I hope a red bear eats your ugly baby.' "

"I did not—!" Faith gave him an indignant look, then saw that he was teasing her. "You're *awful*, Tom Winslow!"

"I always was," he nodded. "You're just noticing it. Tell me more about the school. You seem to be making progress." He listened as she spoke of her pupils, pleased with the happy expression that gave her face a piquant expression. He had missed her, he suddenly realized, and the thought surprised him. He had lived alone for so long—just he and Laurie—that he had assumed they would never need anyone else. Now he was beginning to feel a vacuum in his life, that he and Laurie were not enough.

Finally she finished telling about the school, then cautiously said, "I went to the Officers' Ball last week."

"Did you?"

"Yes. It was fun." She hesitated, not sure of herself. "Lieutenant Grayson took me." When he didn't say anything, she said, "I asked him about the trouble between you two."

Winslow shook his head stubbornly. "Faith, it's better not to go back to those things."

"*Back* to it!" she exclaimed. "Tom, you've never gotten *away* from it! You're letting that time control your life."

He sat loosely in the seat, but Faith knew he resented her intrusion. He turned to her and asked, "Do you poke into everyone's business—or am I somebody special?"

She flushed, knowing that she deserved the rebuke, but shook her head defiantly. "I know it's wrong of me, but it's such a *waste!*"

"What's a waste?" he asked.

"It always makes me sad when I see somebody who has such good things just throwing them away. And you have so much, Tom! Men respect you and trust you. You could be a wonderful officer."

He thought of that, then said, "Some pretty good officers I've known have had some pretty rough flaws—even as bad as mine."

"That's not the question and you know it!" Faith's voice was sharp, and in her eagerness to reach him, she put her hand on his arm, squeezing it. "Bitterness is like a terrible disease, Tom. Like poison in a fine, clear spring. You've done well with Laurie, but you could be so much more if you'd just let God help you with your struggles."

The outline of Bismarck was rising out of the flats, and as they rolled along over the rutted road, he thought about her words. Finally he said, "Part of me knows you're right. Did you ever hear of my sister, Belle Winslow?"

"The one they called The Dixie Widow? I didn't realize she was your sister, Tom."

"Belle married one of the officers in the Confederate Army. When he was killed at Sharpsburg, Belle swore she'd never love anyone again, not until all the Yankees were driven from southern soil. It was a hard thing to see, Faith. I loved her a lot. She was such a beautiful girl—a little thoughtless, maybe." His face hardened as he spoke, thinking of those times. Finally he shook his head, adding, "I saw what unforgiveness can do to a person. It nearly killed Belle."

"What happened to her, Tom?"

"She fell in love with a distant cousin—a Yankee officer named Davis Winslow. At first she hated him, as she did all Yankees, blaming him for killing her husband. But she got rid of all that hate at last. A fine woman, Belle. She and Davis have four children."

"How did she get rid of her unforgiveness?"

Tom Winslow studied the outline of the town for a moment, then said quietly, "She found God." He was silent for a while. Finally he spoke. "I've thought about that a lot, Faith. But it takes a strong person to forgive—maybe I'm not as strong as Belle."

"I think you've got it wrong, Tom," Faith said. "None of us is strong enough to live as we should before God. It's not strong people who make it. It's the weak." She read his puzzled stare. "Paul the apostle once said, 'When I am weak, then I am strong.' That never made much sense to me. But it does now."

"I don't see it."

"Neither did I, Tom. I was always a fairly resourceful person. I took care of my own problems. But when something came into my life that I wasn't strong enough to handle, I found the secret. God is looking for weak people so He can pour himself into them. Remember all the stories of Jesus, how people wanted to touch Him? Remember the woman who had an issue of blood and had spent all her money on doctors? She just went up and *touched* Him—and Jesus healed her instantly. Suppose she'd said, 'I'm strong enough to take care of my problem!' Why, she'd have died of her sickness!"

They entered the long street that led into Bismarck and then to the ferry that would take them across. Faith sat quietly beside him, and only when they were within sight of his house did he speak. "Maybe that's right, Faith. My mother says it is, and she's about the strongest Christian I know."

"You're a strong man, Tom," Faith replied. "But no man or woman is stronger than the bitterness that unforgiveness brings. I don't know what's between you and Spence, but I do know whatever it was—no matter how bad—it has to go or it'll destroy both of you."

He pulled up in front of Eileen's house. As he helped Faith down, he held on to her for one moment, looking into her face.

"I'd hate most people to speak to me about Grayson," he murmured. "You're a persuasive woman, Faith!"

Faith rested in his arms, and though he said no more, she realized that what had happened was a victory—a small opening. She knew the woman Tom and Spence had quarreled over was alive in Tom Winslow. *He's the prisoner of a dead woman*, she thought, and it grieved her. No man or woman could set him free from the prison he had built with his own hatred. She knew it, but he would have to realize that for himself.

CHAPTER EIGHTEEN

THE TRAP

★ ★ ★ ★

Winslow had been talking idly in the bunkhouse with Nathan Zeiss and Babe O'Hara when Sergeant Hines entered. "Tom, the general wants to see you—on the double." Hines frowned and added, "He's in a bad mood, so keep your voice down."

"I always speak softly around generals, Hines." Winslow winked at O'Hara, adding, "General Custer probably wants my expert advice on tactics."

"Yeah, Sarge," the big Irishman grinned. "Tell him the best thing would be to give us boys better morale. Maybe weekend passes and an issue of whiskey."

Winslow went directly to see General Custer. "Go on in, Sergeant," Corporal Devourney said sourly. "Glad you're going out in this mess instead of me."

"A patrol?" Winslow ventured.

"He'll tell you, I guess."

The general was standing in front of a map with Spence Grayson when Winslow entered. Grayson's face was expressionless, but he stared at Winslow steadily.

"Sergeant, you will accompany Lieutenant Grayson on a three-day patrol."

"Yes, sir."

Custer's bony face was drawn with irritation. His temper was evident as he struck the map with a wooden pointer. "We've got to know if the tribes are massing in this area. Charlie Reynolds thinks they are. I'd send him, but he's down with the flu or something."

Winslow was well aware that Custer put more confidence in Reynolds than any of the other scouts. The quiet little man was about as different in temperament from George Armstrong Custer as a man could get, but for some reason Custer had taken to him.

"What about the Ree scouts, General?" Winslow inquired. "Will they be going along?"

"No. I sent them with Lieutenant Hodgson to scout out the territory back of the Blue Hills."

"That may be best, sir," Grayson put in. "I've never put too much stock in the Ree reports. They're so afraid of the Sioux that they multiply their information. See one Sioux and report a dozen."

Custer made no answer, but scowled as he stared at the map. He was tense and restless from lack of activity. Built for action, he longed for spring when he could mount his stallion and lead the Seventh out into raw, violent confrontations. That is what had made him famous. But when he was confined, as he now was by the cold weather, he was crusty and irritable.

"I want to know what these Indians are doing!" he snapped, throwing the pointer on the desk. "When the fighting starts, we've got to have them pinpointed. Otherwise they'll slip through our fingers as they have before." He spoke rapidly, outlining the job he wanted done, and ended by saying, "Lieutenant, this is your first taste of this sort of scouting. I want the job done—but these Sioux can be tricky. They'll try to draw you into a trap, so don't allow yourself to be deceived. This is a scouting party to gather information. What we don't need is a story breaking in the eastern newspapers with the Indians winning a victory over us."

"Yes, sir, I understand."

"Listen to Sergeant Winslow," Custer said. "He knows these Indians. Come back in three days with the information. That's all."

"I'll do the best I can, General," Grayson said.

When they were outside the room, Winslow drew himself up, expecting anything. But Grayson just gave him a hard look and said, "Sergeant, pull ten men out of B Company. Have them issued fifty extra rounds of ammunition. Have them ready to leave at dawn."

"Yes, sir." Winslow saluted and returned to the barracks, where he conferred with Hines. The two of them chose ten men, including Babe O'Hara and Leo Dempsey.

"If you don't watch those two, they'll be having a little something to keep them warm," Hines warned, "but if you run into trouble, they're tough enough for it."

"Don't guess we'll be doing much in the way of fighting," Winslow responded. "Custer just wants to know where the Indians are bunching up." He left the barracks and made his way to Eileen's house.

Laurie opened the door, saying brightly, "Daddy, we're making popcorn balls!"

He picked her up and gave her a resounding kiss. "You smell sweet. Are you wearing perfume, young woman?"

"Yes! It's Miss Eileen's," Laurie beamed. "Ain't it sweet? She said I could use some of it." Then she squirmed and when he put her down, she said, "Come on to the kitchen. We're all in there."

Winslow followed her into the kitchen, where Eileen was at the stove and Faith at the table with Larry Dutton, sticking popcorn together with sticky-looking syrup. "Ah, more help has arrived!" Dutton said. "Join us, Tom. We need help with this stuff."

Winslow sat down and gingerly picked up one of the balls. He took a bite, chewed it, then nodded. "Good! Haven't had one of these since I left Virginia."

"We're going to make taffy tomorrow," Laurie said. She had on an apron and was standing beside Eileen stirring the syrup with a wooden spoon. "Will you come and help pull it, Daddy?"

"Not tomorrow. Got to go on patrol."

"In this weather?" Eileen asked, surprise on her face. "Why, the Indians won't be moving about in this cold."

"I don't think so either, but when the general says to go, we poor soldiers have to move." Winslow took another bite of the sticky ball, then looked at the man across the table. "Wish I could get sick, Larry. Must be nice to have all these women waiting on you, cooking all your favorite food."

"It's a nasty job, but someone has to do it," Dutton grinned. He was wearing a robe, but looking much better. "I'm really all well, but I practice on my cough at night so Eileen doesn't throw me out."

"You're not fooling anyone," Faith said. "You've just found a soft heart and you're exploiting it."

"What's 'exploiting'?" Laurie demanded.

"It means doing something to get your own way—like you do to me all the time," Winslow explained.

They sat in the warmth of the kitchen, chatting and nibbling on the popcorn. It was a fun evening, one of the best Tom could remember. He was persuaded to stay for supper, and the men were shooed into the living room until the meal was ready. Dutton pulled out a chessboard, asking, "Do you play the game, Tom?"

"I know the moves."

When they finished the first game, Dutton, who was an expert player, was shocked to lose. "You've just 'exploited' me, Tom," he said, then put his mind to the game. The next game was a long one, which Dutton finally won. "You ought to be a good officer, Tom. I imagine it takes the same kind of thinking to win in battle as it does to win at chess."

"Well, sometimes," Winslow nodded. "Lee had that sort of mind—which was why he could beat the Yankees. Seems like all the generals the Yankees sent to whip him could only think of one move at a time. They were all like that—McClellan, Burnside, Hooker. So Marse Robert and Stonewall would plan ahead for about six moves—and win."

"Didn't work with Grant, though," Dutton observed.

"No. Grant didn't need that kind of thinking. When he lost a pawn, he just reached back and got another one. But when Lee lost, there were no replacements for the men killed. Grant just wore the South out—and he slaughtered thousands of young men from the North to do it. 'Butcher' Grant, they called him."

"What about Custer? Can he think ahead enough to whip the Indians?"

Winslow frowned. "Well, the Indians don't think like us. They have little discipline, and they'll follow a war chief only as long as he's winning. That sort of force is bound to lose when it's faced with a trained army."

"So you'll win?"

"In the long run, Larry—but this campaign is going to be different."

"Different how?"

"More Indians than anyone has ever seen. And Custer has a poor opinion of them as a fighting force."

They spoke of the Indian problem until Laurie came in to say, "Supper's ready."

The table was set with a white cloth, sparkling china, and silver tableware. As Winslow sat down, he said, "Not sure I have the manners for this setup. Laurie, you keep an eye on me. Be sure I don't lick my knife."

"Faith, will you ask the blessing?" Eileen said, adding after the prayer, "Laurie made this special dish, so you all better enjoy it."

The dish was passed around and the contents tasted and praised lavishly, making Laurie's face glow with pride. The conversation was light and happy, interjected with lots of humor. "It's good to have people to do things for," Eileen said. "I've missed this so much!"

Dutton gave her a peculiar look, started to say something, then changed his mind. The expression on Dutton's face wasn't lost to Winslow, and he wondered if the red-haired teacher didn't have more than a casual interest in his hostess.

"How much longer will you be laid up, Larry?" Winslow asked.

"Oh, I'm checking out day after tomorrow," Dutton shrugged. "Going to spend a few days in the hospital here, but I'm over the hump." He looked toward Eileen and added, "If you get wounded, Tom, I recommend that you come here. It beats any hospital all hollow that I ever heard of."

"It was a little thing to do," Eileen protested, her face flushing.

"Not to me, Eileen," Dutton argued.

"I agree with Larry," Faith added. "He was a very sick man

and needed the special care." She glanced around and said, "Now that we've consumed your delicious meal, Eileen, I'd like to do the dishes, so the rest of you scoot out."

"I'll dry," Winslow offered.

After the others departed for the living room, Faith and Tom made a leisurely job of cleaning up. "I think Dutton's coming here saved his life," Winslow said. "I heard he was in a fair way of dying."

"That's true," Faith nodded. "He's a fine man, isn't he?"

"Sure. He's taken with Eileen, did you notice?"

"It's pretty plain," Faith nodded. "He hasn't had much to do with women, Tom. I'm afraid he's in for a disappointment."

"Why?" Winslow asked in surprise. "He'd be a good choice for Eileen. She needs a husband and he needs a wife."

Faith looked at him quizzically, then laughed. "That's very neat, Tom, but love doesn't work like that—all organized and orderly."

Winslow mused on that comment, his eyes half closed. He made a strange-looking figure standing there, the fragile dish in his large hands. "That's an odd thing to say," he remarked. "Are you saying that love is out of control? Like in the dime romances where a man and a woman gaze at each other for the first time and go into some sort of fit?"

"Oh, Tom, how awful!" Faith laughed. Her face was rosy from the hot water, her eyes sparkling. "Of course love's not like that—well, not exactly." She washed another dish, then said, "You were married once. Wasn't there something special between you two? Wasn't she somehow different from all other women?"

Winslow dropped his eyes, remembering those days. "Yes," he said quietly. "Yes, there was something special."

"Well, I'm not sure a person can *arrange* that. Larry may need a wife, and I know Eileen needs a companion. She's born to be a wife. But it takes more than that to make a marriage work, I think." She stopped, embarrassed by what she had said. "Listen to me—a spinster spouting off on courtship and marriage. And the only experience I ever had was getting jilted at the altar!"

The sadness in her voice touched him, and he turned her around with a firm hand. "Don't talk like that," he insisted.

"You've got *everything* a man needs—and wants, Faith." Then the memories of the past rose sharply. "Well," he said almost brusquely, "that's it with the dishes. Let's see what the others are doing."

Dutton and Eileen were listening to Laurie read a story she'd written. When she saw Tom and Faith, she stopped and said, "I'll start over."

When she finished, Winslow said, "That's very good, Laurie."

"Miss Eileen helped me with it a little," she confessed.

"Just a tiny bit, but it's your story," Eileen responded, patting Laurie's head.

Winslow picked up his coat, saying, "Got to be on the way before dawn." He halted, then looked toward Faith, adding, "Lieutenant Grayson wants to make an early start." He saw the startled look in her eyes, but she said nothing. He kissed Laurie firmly. "I'll see you in three days."

"Come and see me, Tom," Dutton said. "I'll be at the post hospital or back in my room."

Later when Faith and Laurie had gone to the kitchen for cocoa, Dutton said, "Tom's quite a fellow, Eileen." When she nodded, he continued. "You know, he's the kind of man I always dreamed about being—big, tough, and always doing something heroic." He smiled painfully, adding, "At the orphanage, when I was a kid, I made up stories with a man like that as the hero, then pretended to be him."

His confession touched her, and she smiled. "We all do that. I pretended to be the beautiful heroine I'd just read about in the romance novels."

Dutton dropped his eyes. "Well, *you* turned out to be beautiful, but *I* turned out to be just a runty schoolteacher."

"Why—Larry! What a terrible thing to say about yourself!" Eileen scolded. "You've gotten a fine education against all odds, and one day you'll be a successful attorney."

"Maybe," he shrugged, "but I'd rather put on a uniform and ride out with Tom in the morning."

"No! Don't ever say that!" Her sudden vehemence caught him off guard, and he was acutely conscious of her hand squeezing his arm. "It's no life for you, Larry. It's terrible!"

"Why, it's not that bad, Eileen." Dutton hesitated, then said daringly, "You wouldn't refuse to marry Tom because he's a soldier, would you?"

Agitated, she turned away. He had no way of knowing it was that very question that had plagued her for days. She had felt Winslow's gaze on her, had known that it was for Laurie's sake they had grown close. But she knew Tom was lonely and found her attractive. More than once she had felt that if she had chosen, she could have drawn him into a closer relationship, but she had not enticed him, though the thought was in her heart and mind.

"I don't know, Larry," she replied. "It's a hard life for a woman. She'd have to love an army man a lot to risk that."

Her answer depressed him, for he was perceptive enough to see that Eileen was thinking a great deal of Winslow. "Well," he said, "he's a fine man. I hope nothing happens to him on this scouting trip."

"If it doesn't, Larry," she said evenly, but with pain, "there'll be another scouting and another battle. That's the life of a soldier—and of the woman who marries him!"

★ ★ ★ ★

The first two days of the scouting were uncomfortable and unproductive. Snow threatened constantly, but on the afternoon of the third day the sun came out, shedding a welcome warmth, and Winslow found the trail of a large band of Indians.

When he brought back the news, Grayson's eyes glinted. He had said nothing to Winslow up until that time, but now his voice crackled as he shot back, "How many and how far?"

"I'd guess at least a hundred, Lieutenant. I cut their sign about five miles from here. I figure they passed through less than twenty-four hours ago."

Grayson looked up at the sky, calculating quickly. It was past two o'clock, but there was a chance they could catch up with the Indians before dark. He made his decision and called out "Mount!" and when the troop was in the saddle, he commanded, "Take us to the spot, Sergeant Winslow."

"Yes, sir."

Winslow led them at a fast trot to the sign he had cut, and pointed down at the trail. "Heads toward the foothills, sir."

"Go ahead," Grayson ordered. "We'll follow so we don't confuse the sign. I want to catch them, so make it as fast as you can." His eyes shone with excitement. "Let's go!" he said impatiently.

They followed the sign until almost dark, with Winslow ahead. Then he waited until the troop caught up with him. "Going to be too dark to follow the sign in another half hour, Lieutenant."

A gust of temper rose and Grayson spewed out an oath. He shook his head stubbornly. "We can't be too far behind. We'll leave at first light."

"Well, the general said to make it a three-day scout, for information," Winslow said.

"You do the tracking, Winslow! I'll give the orders."

Sergeant Jess Moody was close enough to hear this exchange, and later when they were hunched over small fires eating supper, he asked, "What's going on with the lieutenant, Tom?"

Winslow shook his head. "Can't say, Jess."

But Dempsey spoke up. "A glory hunter, that's what he is!" He tore hungrily at the food, adding glumly, "Winslow, don't you find them Indians tomorrow. If there's as many as you claim, they could wipe us out."

"Maybe I'm a glory hunter, too, Dempsey."

"Naw. You got sense," the burly soldier grinned. "You want to keep your hair just like the rest of us poor troopers. It's the officers who got to get a bunch killed to get their names in the papers."

The next day the sun rose brightly, and after a quick breakfast, Winslow rode ahead, following the sign, which was easy. At nine o'clock he halted to let the column catch up. "They camped here last night. Ashes still hot from the fires."

"How far ahead, do you think?" Grayson asked.

Winslow gave a dubious look toward the horizon where some low lying hills scored the sky. "Not far. And we're not going to sneak up on them."

"Call me *sir*!" Grayson yelled. He looked toward the hills, his face sharp with anticipation. "You go ahead. We'll follow. When you make contact, give me a signal."

Sergeant Moody spoke up. "Sir, he'll be a sittin' duck out there that far."

"Never mind!" Grayson snapped. "Get moving, Sergeant Winslow!"

"Yes, sir." Winslow galloped ahead, and when he was far enough away, Grayson waved the command forward. For the next hour they covered the ground at a fast gallop until they reached Winslow, who had pulled up his horse to wait.

"They're right ahead of us, just the other side of those hills, Lieutenant."

"How many?"

"Must be over a hundred. And these are braves—no women or children to hold them back."

"Have you actually *seen* any Indians?" Grayson demanded.

"No, sir. But they've seen us."

"You can't be sure of that! Let's push on."

Winslow looked up, his face bearing a trace of shock. "Through that gap, sir?"

"That's where they are, Sergeant."

The spot Grayson was looking at was a barrier of rock with a peak in the center. The rock was a six-foot breastwork heaved up by some ancient slipping of the earth's crust; it lay a quarter mile forward, and to either side the land rose in broken hummocks. "That's a bad place to be caught, sir," Winslow protested.

But Grayson was adamant. "Forward!" he called out, waving his hand in an imperious gesture. The column broke into a trot, aimed at the lowest section of the rock barrier. The steady run set up a clatter of iron hoofs on the solid ground, and suddenly what had appeared to be clumps of brush became round black heads. A shot broke the silence, its echo rocketing all up the hillsides.

"Skirmishers!" Grayson called.

Sergeant Moody's voice beat at the troopers as they rushed along a long, broken line abreast Grayson. Winslow flung his horse around and rushed to the right of the line. Rapid firing broke from the rocks, the smoke indicating the Indians to be scattered along the parapet. Grayson took a quick look toward an empty spot to the left and promptly rushed for it, signaling the men to follow. The move whirled the troopers into an irregular grouping, forcing them to cross the line of fire. Instantly a trooper dropped lifeless and his horse bolted.

When they halted, Winslow saw that a series of broken hummocks rose sharply before them. Grayson urged his horse toward the end of the rock parapet, his troops close behind. When they neared the hummocks, they were caught by the cross fire of lead as the bullets rained upon them. The Sioux showed themselves between the hummocks, and the troopers returned their fire. Winslow saw Dempsey shoot one of the Indians at point-blank range. Suddenly, Tom was caught between two mounted warriors armed with carbines. He lifted his revolver and shot one of them in the chest. The other Sioux was right on top of Tom, ready to fire when the warrior fell away, his face a bloody mask. Winslow looked up to see O'Hara grinning at him. He rode in, saying, "Let's git out of here, Sarge, this place is too hot!"

Firing as they rode, they caught up with the rest of the troop. It was a tight and wicked moment, the troopers caught by the fire of Indians stationed along the uplifting rock, well-hidden and safe from return fire. They kept fading and reappearing from spot to spot, giving ground stubbornly.

Grayson had charged straight at a small group, taking a few of the men with him. Winslow saw other Indians were heading for that spot. The lieutenant waved the men forward. "Come on! Stick close! They can't stand a charge!"

As Grayson got farther into the broken country, the Indians kept retreating, vague as shadows. He suddenly realized that he was cut off from the troop with only three men and that the Indians were closing in from three directions. There was no way to fight his way back, yet he knew no fear, so great was his battle fury.

As he prepared to sell his life dearly, he looked up to see the bulk of the troop appear from over a slight rise, firing as they came. With a bitter twinge, even at that moment, he saw that Tom Winslow was leading them.

The charge broke the back of the Indians' defense, and they faded away, like vanishing shadows, but not before shooting two of the troopers. Even Grayson knew that there was no use to pursue. The country was rough and the Sioux knew it well; to follow them would be to invite another trap.

As the last few shots rang out, troopers dismounted, going

to the fallen men, walking loose-jointedly along the uneven earth. Sergeant Moody came to stand before Grayson, his old soldier's eyes bitter as he asked, "What's the order, Lieutenant?"

Grayson was filled with acrid disappointment. He looked around at the men, feeling the judgment in their eyes. "We'll return to the fort."

"Tyson's dead, sir, and so are Given and Pearson."

"We'll take them back for burial."

He rode over to where the dead men lay, realizing that he had fallen into the Sioux's trap—like any raw beginner. He also knew what Custer, and his own fellow officers, would say. But the great rush of bitterness flooding him stemmed from the fact that Winslow had been right. That would be known, too. With a murderous look in his eyes he watched as Winslow lifted one of the fallen men. Memories of the past returned then. *I hate him worse than I've ever hated the Sioux!*

He sat there, enraged by the failure. It was an unreasoning anger, and he knew that nothing could erase it!

PART FOUR

THE FIERY TRIAL

★ ★ ★ ★

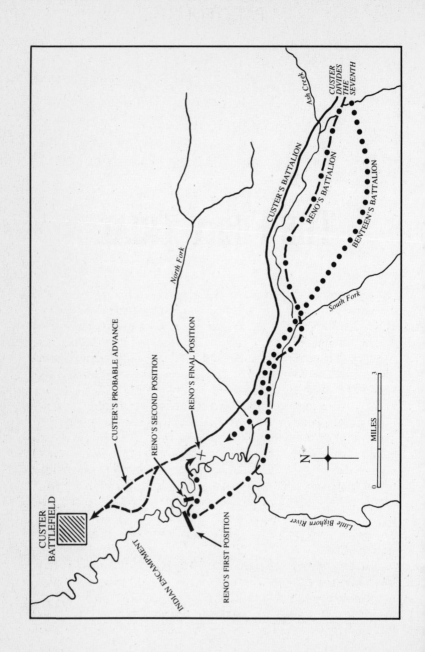

CHAPTER NINETEEN

BLIZZARD

★　★　★　★

Libby Custer was exhausted. It was two in the morning, and the general and his wife had just returned to their hotel rooms. The Custers had been to see *Julius Caesar*, in which one of their closest friends, Lawrence Barrett, had played the leading role. Afterward they had been invited to a mansion facing Central Park where, surrounded by money and power and considerable beauty, Custer had dominated the conversation with the guests both by his exuberance and because of his reputation.

They had been in the East for several weeks, leaving the regiment at Fort Abraham Lincoln; but Custer's driving energy was just as strong in the city as it had been at the fort. Even now as Libby sat slumped into a chair, so tired she couldn't bring herself to get ready for bed, her husband was pacing the room like a caged animal, speaking of the things they would do the next day.

"Autie," she broke in, "what is this trouble about the post traderships?"

Custer sat down beside her. They had a closer bond than most married couples. He was an incurable romantic, writing her love letters when out on a campaign, some of them running up to twenty pages. And Elizabeth Custer had one goal in life: to do what she could to advance her husband's career. Her ambition was less obvious than his, but no less powerful. In the peacetime army, there were few promotions, and both of them were determined that the top was the only goal worth striving for. She had learned the politics of the army, and was more tactful than Custer, so it had disturbed her to hear him speak so bluntly at the dinner. Not all of the men there, she understood, were friendly to the general, but he had paid no heed to that. When someone had mentioned the scandal over post trader-ships, Custer's eyes had flashed and swept the room with an impetuous gesture. "The system is corrupt to the core!" he had exploded. "The prices charged by the post trader on the frontier are three times what they should be. And what is their excuse? They have to pay such enormous fees—which is a way of saying 'bribes'—that they must recoup themselves!"

"How can such things go on, General?" someone had asked.

"Because there are gentlemen in Washington who sell these post traderships to the highest bidder! There is a corrupt ring in Washington so protected by high-placed officials that they can't be touched. In fact, one brother of the very highest public official of our land is deep into such dirty dealings!"

Thinking of that scene, Libby attempted to tone down her husband's volatile way of attack. "Autie, was it wise to speak of President Grant's brother so bluntly?"

Custer's face flushed, and he said impulsively, "I shall be in Washington soon, and I shall speak the truth about the matter." Then he looked at her quickly. "Libby, I'm caught in a trap. There's no way to go up! My enemies are in high places, and dull officers are promoted above me. There's no way to turn!"

"Why, Autie, you're a famous man! We're welcomed into the homes of some of the most powerful people in the country. I'm very proud of you. What more can you want?"

Custer didn't answer, but they both knew that nothing but being at the very top of his profession would satisfy him. This was not unusual, for ambition is a common enough element in military men. In George Armstrong Custer, however, ambition had grown into what the Greeks called *hubris*, the sort of "vault-ing ambition" Shakespeare dramatized in characters such as Macbeth and Henry the Fourth, men whose driving egos brought them to destruction.

Custer was a child of adventure. His fame had come from action, raw action, blind charges that ignored all odds. Routine was death to him, and now at the age of thirty-six he was less well known than he had been at twenty-five. And in the slow, ponderous turning of the machinery of the regular army his status was falling behind, so that in ten more years he would be just another middle-aged Civil War officer—his greatness forgotten.

Custer jumped up, grabbed a pen and began writing rapidly. "I shall offer my services as witness to Clymer. This corruption in high places must stop!" Congressman Clymer had begun an investigation of the Indian Bureau and the War Department, with Belknap, the secretary of war, as his target.

"Autie," Libby said, putting her hands on his shoulder, "are you sure that's wise?"

"Wise or not, I shall do it!" he said as he continued writing, using his words like a cavalry sabre, slashing at his enemies. He saw himself being forced out of action by his enemies in Washington, and he had to have action. It was his only gift, and without thought of defense or skill or retreat—the method which had made him a young general at the age of twenty-five—he drove at his foes with his pen.

* * * *

With Custer gone, the routine of the Seventh slowed. Early winter rains fell, and the Missouri rose five feet, transforming the current into a mud-greasy surface filled with driftwood. Sections of the bluffs collapsed, sending small tidal waves onward. Inside the fort, life went on. Two soldiers deserted, but were captured the next day and tried the following week. If Custer had been on the post, they would have been shot, but they escaped with a year's prison sentence.

Fifty recruits arrived to replenish the Seventh's thin ranks. In addition to rumors of a War Department scandal, the news filtered west of a plan being formed by Grant and Sherman to crush the Sioux. General Terry, the department commander at St. Paul, sent urgent orders for the Seventh to overhaul its equipment and to whip its recruits into shape as rapidly as possible. This meant that on the bitter cold mornings recruits went through their monotonous revolutions on the parade ground, marched outside the fort for rifle-range practice, and daily scouted westward. Freighters broke the first light snowfall with supplies for the quartermaster and commissary depots on the reservation. *The Far West,* a riverboat with Captain Grant Marsh commanding, came downriver and stopped briefly to report he had been fired on four times in four days along the upper stretches of the Missouri. On December 6 the telegraphy flashed news from the East that couriers would be sent out to instruct the recalcitrant Sioux to come into the reservations by January 31 or be treated as hostiles.

The absence of the commanding officer meant that Winslow and the scouts spent little time roaming the hills. As Mitch Bouyer put it to Winslow, "Them Sioux are holed up fer the winter, Tom, 'cept for huntin' parties. Don't see no sense wearing our backsides out in them hills."

Herendeen added, "They'll be out soon enough, come spring, like ants swarming outta an anthill."

Winslow agreed and was glad for the relief. He put in some time on the post, but the scouts needed no advice from him as to keeping their horses and equipment in good shape, so he was able to spend more time with Laurie than at any time in the past. They enjoyed being together, all the more because Tom knew that it was the peace before the storm that would break loose in the spring.

Eileen, of course, was with them a great deal those days, and somehow Larry Dutton was drawn into their circle, coming often for dinner at Eileen's. Occasionally the four would go to town for entertainment. It was on one of these trips one early Tuesday afternoon that they stopped outside a building to read a crude poster advertising a troop of traveling entertainers.

Laurie's lips moved as she read the huge block letters, then asked, "Daddy, what's an Ethiopian Eccentricity?"

"Nothing you should see, I'm sure." Winslow grinned over her head, winking at Eileen and Dutton. "Besides, it says 'Adults Only.' "

"Oh, Daddy!" Laurie pouted. "I'll bet it's nothing at all!"

Dutton patted her shoulder. "Don't worry, Laurie. There's a minstrel show coming in two weeks. I'll get us some tickets right up front for it."

His promise satisfied Laurie, and they moved down the street toward the restaurant. While they were eating, Eileen asked, "Do you know your part for the program, Laurie?"

"If she doesn't, I do," Winslow said emphatically. "I've listened to her say that poem so much, I've memorized it myself!" They were in town for a school function, with Dutton's prize scholars performing.

After the meal, as they were walking to the school, Winslow looked at the sky and commented, "Some bad weather coming at us. We'd better hole up like squirrels after the program."

The room was filled, parents talking loudly while waiting for the program to begin. Winslow looked around at the families gathered, most of them country people, awkward and gentle, from the outlying area. Their faces and hands looked leather-like as a result of rain, worry, and work. Most of them had few possessions; their struggles were occupied with keeping the roof dry and the stove warm. They were slow to speak and humble in their beliefs and a thousand miles away from the main stream of American life.

Dutton announced from the platform, "I guess we'll get under way. Will all the students please come forward."

Somebody played the piano while a group of first graders made a ring on the stage, singing as they turned a circle; others danced or recited. But it wasn't the first graders Winslow noticed. Across the aisle, a farmer's wife, the mother of one of the children performing that day, sat bent forward, her hands clutched on her lap, her eyes closed, her lips moving—every thought, every feeling seeming to flow on her face, softening and making it wistfully pretty. Later he would always remember that face, how she had savored that moment of pleasure out of a hard existence.

Winslow's thoughts were interrupted as Laurie came forward to the edge of the stage. He was surprised to discover he was nervous for her. In fact, he couldn't remember the first line of her poem. He didn't have to worry—Laurie did well and was applauded enthusiastically.

When the program was over, Laurie rushed up to Tom. "Did I do all right, Daddy?"

"You did fine, sweetheart. I was the one who was nervous.

I couldn't even remember how the poem went." He brushed his hand against her rosy cheek. It startled him to see how much she looked like Marlene. With a sudden force he realized she would soon pass into that mysterious realm of young womanhood—and he would not be able to go with her. A twinge of sadness rose in his heart.

Eileen sensed it. "She's growing up very fast, Tom," she said quietly.

He looked at her quickly, but before he could speak, Nick Owens approached him, a worried look on his face. "Tom, it's getting bad out there. Could be a blizzard moving in."

"Got the feel of it, Nick," Winslow nodded. "What's up?"

"Well, I'm worried about Faith," Owens said, rubbing his chin nervously. "She's out there all alone, and she don't know blizzards."

"Why, she's been in storms, I'm sure," Eileen assured.

"A blizzard is not a storm. It's the world turned upside down. It'll drive the breath from your lungs and the heat from your body—and kill you almost as quick as a bullet!" Owens corrected her. "She could get caught just going to the barn and wander off and die. And I feel responsible. I was out there two days ago, and she didn't have much wood. I was going to send Earl out to take care of that, but I forgot."

"Like me to run out there, Nick?"

"Hate to ask you, Tom, but I got a sick child, and—"

"No problem. Maybe we could put a load of split wood on your wagon."

"Say, that's a good idea! I'll run get some fellas to help me load the wagon—"

"Daddy, can I go with you?" Laurie asked as Owens hurried away.

"No, not this time." He picked her up and gave her a resounding kiss on the cheek, then put her down and turned to Eileen. "Can you keep her tonight?"

"Yes, Tom. Will you be back tonight?"

"Well, I doubt it. By the time I get there and have the wood unloaded, it'll be pretty late. I'll probably stay over and come back tomorrow."

Something in his reply seemed to disturb Eileen, Dutton noticed. He waited until Winslow was gone and Laurie moved away to talk to one of her schoolmates. "What's wrong, Eileen?"

She started at his abrupt question, then shrugged. "Well, it seems a little . . . imprudent. The two of them all alone out there."

Dutton studied Eileen so directly that she flushed. "I suppose I shouldn't think such things, should I?"

"You're jealous of the preacher lady."

Eileen blinked, and though she kept her voice down, there was anger in it. "Jealous! Don't be silly, Larry!"

Dutton shrugged, knowing that he was making her angry, but there was a streak of perversity in the red-haired school-master. He had watched Winslow and Eileen together ever since his recovery and had said nothing, but now he spoke out. "If you weren't jealous of her, Eileen, you wouldn't be so upset at the mention of it."

His logic caught her, and she dropped her eyes. Finally she lifted them and said quietly, "You have sharp eyes, Larry. I didn't think I was quite so transparent."

"Be strange if you weren't drawn to him," Dutton said. He made an unimpressive figure as he stood before her, his slight figure upright and his face almost boyish. "He's a man women admire—and you've been lonely."

Eileen looked at him with a new interest. "Well, what do you think, Mr. Lawyer? Do I have a chance with him?"

"Sure you do," Dutton nodded instantly. "The question is—do you really *want* him, Eileen?" His lips drew firm, and he shook his head, saying, "You get all tense every time he goes out on patrol. And you've told me what a misery it was for you when your husband went out. I admire Tom as much as I admire any man—but I don't think he can make you happy as long as he's in the army."

"He's a very talented man," Eileen answered quickly. "He could have a career outside the army."

"Maybe—but I don't think he wants that," Dutton said. "We've talked a lot, Tom and I, and from what I hear, he's got no plans to leave the army. He'll get a commission when the campaign is over. Custer's promised that to him."

Eileen was defensive and asked rather sharply, "I thought

Tom was your friend, Larry. Why are you talking against him?"

Dutton looked down, considered his reply, then made it, looking up to meet her gaze. "He's my friend, but I'm convinced he'd make you unhappy. You might talk him into leaving the army, but that would make him unhappy. But there's one more thing . . ."

"Yes? What is it?" Eileen asked when he hesitated.

He smiled crookedly at her, but said evenly, "He's not the only man in the world, Eileen. I'm here."

Eileen gave him a startled glance, taken off guard. But then she thought of his attention toward her since she'd nursed him and recalled that the possibility of his saying something like this had flashed through her mind more than once.

"Took you a little while to get around to that, didn't it, Larry?" she said gently. Then she added, "Come along, let's take Laurie and go home."

He took her arm and said, "Maybe we can talk later."

She smiled. "You lawyers . . . I'm afraid of you! You just come and make the popcorn for Laurie and me." They collected Laurie and left the building, each of them holding one of her small hands.

* * * *

The blizzard caught Winslow only a mile from the mission. At five he could see the building, but ten minutes later the light failed. A sound like the trembling echo of a distant train came to him, and he whipped up the horses in an attempt to outride the storm. But ten minutes later he knew he had lost the race, and pulled the team to a walk.

A gray wall moved toward him, awesome and frightening. Nothing could stand before it, and then he felt the first snowflakes. Almost at once the full pressure of the blizzard was on him, the winds tossing the wagon from side to side, howling like a demented spirit.

There was nothing to follow, for the snow blotted out the road instantly, and there were no telegraph poles or rails to follow. His only hope was to keep the team aimed as straight as possible toward the mission, for if he missed the buildings and headed into the rangeland, he would be dead before morning.

The wind rocked the wagon and the team fought him. There was no time in the midst of that vortex—just blind power of wind and cold. The horses stopped, and when he lashed out with the reins, he realized his movements were as slow as if he were under water. The bitter cold had begun to paralyze his mind, and a sense of danger shot through him. He stamped his feet on the floor of the wagon, but felt little. Then he yelled into the wind and stretched his arms, moving very slowly.

The team plodded ahead, shoved by the wind, and when Winslow realized that he was freezing, he stepped out of the wagon. There was only faint sensation in his feet as he walked to the head of the team to lead it. By now the sound seemed muffled and farther away.

Walking warmed him somewhat, but the cold was slowly sucking the vitality out of him. Once he thought of leaving the team, but shook that idea out of his mind. He pounded his face with his hands, and then stamped his feet. He was losing his senses, for the sound of the wind faded, though he knew from the whipping of the snow around him that it was as potent as ever.

It became a matter of putting one foot in front of the other, each step a conscious decision. An insidious warmth seeped through his legs, and he knew he had little time.

Ten more steps—and his head struck something unyielding, the force of it knocking him to the ground. Brilliant lights shot across his vision, and when he tried to get up, he failed. The wind seemed to die down to a muted moan, and the warmth began to flood his entire body.

With a start, he jerked himself to his knees, then struggled to his feet. He put his hand out, now almost numb, touched a post, then ran his hand up and felt a cross piece. His fuzzy brain barely comprehended the thought: *Why, this is the sign on the road in front of the mission!*

Turning at right angles, he drove himself forward, pulling the reins on the horses after him. Five minutes later he ran into the side of the barn. To his right, he saw a faint gleam and knew it came from Faith's house. Staggering like a drunken man, he made his way to the front of the barn, managed to unbolt the doors, and with what was left of his strength, pulled them open, led the team inside, then closed the doors.

His face was stiff with ice and his hands were numb, but he knew better than to rest. Unhitching the team took half an hour, but by that time the relative warmth of the barn had restored some of his sensations. He remained there, slapping his arms against his sides and stamping his feet until he could feel needles of pain, then opened the door and made for the house.

When he hit the porch, he fell, and the door swung open, shedding yellow light. "Tom!" a voice said, and he felt Faith's hands pulling at him. "Get up . . . help me. You can't stay out here!"

He pulled himself up with her help, and she half shoved him through the door, kicking it shut behind her. He heard the sound of the door slam, but it was muffled and faint. The warmth of the room was like a drug, and he shuffled toward a divan and fell sprawling into it, his feet on the floor.

He never knew when she picked them up and put them on the divan, for despite his determination to stay awake, he slipped into sleep, falling helplessly into the blackness as a man might plunge into a dark hole.

CHAPTER TWENTY

"HE'LL NEVER CHANGE!"

★   ★   ★   ★

A sharp stinging sensation in his feet awoke Winslow, and he opened his eyes to find Faith sitting in a chair beside him. He turned his head to look out the window and saw that the storm had spent itself, or so it seemed. It was quiet, the keening of the wind had ceased, and he could hear the faint crackling of wood burning in the potbellied stove across the room.

"How do you feel?" Faith leaned forward anxiously.

"Feet are tingling," Winslow said. He lifted himself, swung his feet to the floor, and flexed his hands, which were also prickling as if thousands of small insects were biting him. He tried to smile but his lips cracked. "A couple hours of sleep made a difference."

"Almost eight hours," she said. "It's six in the morning."

He stared at her, then shook his head. "Cut it pretty fine, I guess. Can I have some of that coffee?" He stood to his feet, feeling strangely light-headed, but was relieved that it was no worse. She brought him a mug of steaming black coffee, and he drank it slowly, savoring the sensation.

"What brought you out here, Tom?" she asked.

He drained the cup and handed it back to her. "Didn't like the thought of your being alone in the middle of a blizzard. If you don't know those storms, they're dangerous." He grimaced and flexed his fingers, adding, "Even if you do know them, they can get you."

"That was thoughtful of you," she said quietly. "I would have been all right, I think—but it was kind of you." She seemed strained and nervous. Something was on her mind, something she wanted to say but was holding back. He had never seen her like that. He waited for her to speak, but when she did, it was an abrupt, "I'll fix breakfast."

"Got a load of wood for you—from Nick Owens," he said. "I'll unload it after breakfast."

She suddenly lifted her head and turned toward the door, for the sound of steps on the porch came clearly.

"Somebody's out in bad weather," Winslow murmured in surprise. He thought perhaps one of the Indians might have dropped by, but the door swung open, and there stood Spence Grayson!

Grayson was wearing a pair of heavy mittens and a thick buffalo overcoat, and carried a load of wood in his arms. At the sight of Winslow, he shot a steely look at him before crossing the room to dump the wood into the woodbox beside the stove.

Instantly, tension filled the cabin like electricity, and Faith said quickly, "Tom, the storm caught Spence. He dropped by yesterday afternoon and by the time he was to start back, the blizzard hit."

A strange mixture of emotions surged through Winslow—his close brush with death, his struggle to stay alive, his intense hatred toward Grayson. Away from the routine responsibilities of life at the fort, yesterday's battle with death had brought to the surface feelings held in check for years. The raw wound lay exposed and demanded revenge.

Life as a soldier seemed a million miles away, and of no importance. The sight of Grayson's handsome face as he stood across the room unleashed the bitterness and a gush of black anger that Winslow could no more control than he could have controlled the storm that had almost killed him. Grayson was watching him with an alert expression, his eyes glinting with hatred.

"Up to your old tricks with women, Grayson?" Tom asked softly, deceptively.

"Tom—I told you how it was," Faith broke in. "He was caught in the storm just as you were."

"Sure. He's always got a reason for what he does to people."

Grayson glared at Winslow. Ever since Winslow had come to his rescue from the Sioux, the dislike in him had grown, and now he said, "Get out of here, Sergeant. You can make it back to the fort. The blizzard's over."

Winslow was poised to move toward the officer. Grayson knew it and pulled his revolver, warning, "Don't make that mistake, Winslow. You know I'd be justified by any court if you attacked me and I shot you. Get out!"

Winslow stared at him, then nodded. "I'll dump the wood," he said tonelessly.

When he left the room, Faith said, "I think both of you are fools!"

"You're probably right," Grayson nodded. He put his revolver away and went to the window to watch Winslow as he unloaded the wagon.

Faith was shaken by the confrontation and started making breakfast mostly to have something to do. When it was ready she put a plate on the table, saying, "Here's your breakfast, Spence. I'll take the sergeant's out to him." She was fixing a plate when the door opened and Winslow entered.

"I've got something cooked," she said, holding out the plate.

"Thanks." Winslow stepped forward to get it and moved slightly behind where the officer was sitting. Instead of taking the plate, he moved swiftly, throwing one arm around Grayson and plucking the revolver from his holster. Then he stepped back as Grayson scrambled to his feet.

Grayson's face was livid with anger. "I'll have you court-martialled for this, Winslow!" he cried out.

Winslow stared at him, then tossed the revolver across the room. It hit the wall, bounced to the floor, and Grayson dived for it. He fumbled at the weapon, got a grasp on it, then swung around, his eyes wild with hatred. Faith cried out, "Don't Spence—!" But just as the officer turned, Winslow—who had expected exactly this and had come closer—struck Grayson a sledging blow on the cheek.

Involuntarily, Grayson squeezed the trigger, the explosion

filled the room, the bullet smashing against the front wall of the kitchen. The force of the blow drove him backward, and Winslow followed at once, grabbing for the gun. He caught it, wrenched it away from Grayson and walked to the door. Opening it, he tossed it outside, then turned and advanced on the officer with his face cold, his eyes glittering.

"I'll have you shot!" Grayson yelled, fury welling up in him, and then he ran toward Winslow, striking out with a wild right hand. The blow caught Winslow on the chest, forcing him backward a step; but as Grayson lunged at him, he planted his feet and drove a powerful right hand into Grayson's face. The force snapped the head of the officer backward and dulled his senses. He fell forward, grappling with Winslow, and the two careened around the small kitchen, crashing the table to the floor. They rolled around, punching each other with short, vicious blows. Then Grayson pulled his feet up and drove Winslow away with a powerful kick that caught Winslow in the side.

The pain raked through Winslow and he got up slowly— enough time for Grayson to grab a chair and swing it at him. But he missed his target when Tom stepped back. Instead, the force of his swing threw him off balance. Instantly, Winslow jumped forward and began to drive long, looping blows into Spence's face and neck.

There was no mercy in Winslow, and he threw into the blows all the hatred that had lain in him for years. He thought of his wife dying, abandoned by this man, and the memory lent strength to his arms. He beat the man's arms down and drove him against the wall. Grayson's eyes glazed and he dropped his arms, helpless, unable to defend himself.

"Tom! Stop it!" Faith ran forward and thrust herself between the two men. Winslow shook his head, then stepped back and Grayson slumped to the floor, sprawling there, only half conscious.

Winslow stared down at him, the hatred that had risen in him still raw and raging. But he pulled himself up, turned and walked to the door. He paused to say, "Get the man out of here, Faith," he said, his voice grating with the hatred that was in him. "He's ruined everything he's ever touched. He'll do the same to you."

"Tom, he'll have you shot for this!"

"No, he won't. If he does, I'll tell the court how he ran away with my wife and then left her alone to die. I'll tell them about the other women he's ruined." Winslow let his hard eyes fall on Grayson, who was groping his way to his feet. "He won't expose himself, Faith. It might hurt his chances with some of the other women he's got on his string."

Faith stood there, humiliated by the scene, and angry, for she realized that no matter what Tom Winslow said about other women, it was she herself who was partly at the root of the antagonism of the two men. Lifting her chin, she said, "Tom, I've told you how it was. He was caught by the storm. What harm is in that?"

Winslow faced her, trying to make her understand. But the black thing that was in him was not something that could be explained, and finally he shook his head stubbornly, saying, "He's no good, Faith. He ruins everything he touches." Then he wheeled and left the room, slamming the door forcefully.

Faith turned to face Grayson, who was wiping the blood from his face with a trembling hand. "Is what he said true, Spence—about his wife?"

Grayson blinked at the bluntness of her question. He tried to find some way of putting the thing that would not make him appear so bad in her eyes, but finally he nodded, "Most of it—but it was a long time ago, Faith. We were all very young." His defense sounded false in his own ears, and he looked at her more closely. "It's all over, isn't it, Faith—between you and me?"

"Spence, there was *never* anything there. We're too different."

A sense of loss hit him at her words, yet he knew she was right. He had longed for something he saw in her, but now he realized that it was a dream that could never be. "I'll be getting back to the fort," he said.

"Spence, don't use this against him," she pleaded.

He gave her a calculating look, but said only, "No, of course not. But just one little warning, Faith. He's in love with you, but don't think it will come to anything."

"Why do you say that?"

He pulled his coat on, slipped into his mittens, then moved toward the door. He turned after opening it, his lips bruised and swollen and a sadness in his eyes.

"Winslow can never bring a woman anything, Faith. Whatever gentleness was in him once, he lost it all years ago. He'll never change. He can't change what he's become."

Faith watched him ride away, and in the distance she saw the outline of the wagon Winslow was driving. It was only a smudge on the white snow. Then even as she watched, it disappeared.

★ ★ ★ ★

In February, the Seventh received news that General Terry was to have full freedom of action in bringing the Indians to their knees. The General of the Army, Sherman, had dispatched a column under Crook north from Fetterman, with the intent that Crook and Terry would be able to catch the Indians in a nutcracker. But Crazy Horse, fighting in desperate recklessness, gathered his warriors and threw Crook's column into disorder and drove it away. Terry found his own plans for a winter attack wrecked by a series of blizzards that swept the land.

Custer expected to be in the thick of things as spring approached, but he had the misfortune to annoy Ulysses Grant. Early in March the long, simmering scandal concerning the War Department broke out. A broker in New York came forward with evidence implicating Secretary of War Belknap, or Belknap's wife, in taking bribes, and the secretary resigned on the eve of the investigation. And it was Custer's testimony against Belknap, plus his flaunted association with the leading Democrats, that had exasperated the President, whose dream of a third term collapsed because of the Belknap scandal.

Custer, anxious to get to his regiment, took the train west to St. Paul and reported to General Terry, where he was given his orders. Custer was to go on to Fort Abraham Lincoln immediately to put his regiment in readiness and to march out to meet the Sioux as soon as possible.

Custer and Libby left from St. Paul by train. When the general arrived at the fort, he threw himself into getting the Seventh into a state of readiness. He drove them hard, and soon three more companies were sent to him, which brought the Seventh to full strength for the first time in many years.

But on the eve of the campaign, a wire from Washington arrived, directing Custer to return to testify against Belknap. Custer was stunned, for his own indiscreet behavior had at last caught up with him.

He begged to be allowed to send his testimony by mail, but this was not acceptable to the committee, so near the end of March he returned.

"Maybe this will teach Custer to keep his mouth shut," Sergeant Hines said to Winslow.

Sherman attempted to persuade the President to allow Custer to return to his command, but with no success. No one available to General Terry had the rank and ability to take Custer's place, and Grant's action stunned Custer, who could not believe that the President would knowingly endanger the campaign out of political retaliation. It was a tragedy for Custer, for he foresaw his regiment marching without him.

Finally Custer traveled to the White House and handed in his card. He waited for hours in the President's outer office, conscious of his own helplessness as old officer friends paused to say hello.

At five in the afternoon, the secretary announced, "The President will not see you, sir."

Custer stood up, his face pale. He left the office and that night caught the train west. As he stepped from the train at Chicago to transfer to St. Paul, an aide of General Sheridan's met him with a telegram that had come from Sherman to Terry:

General: I am at this moment advised that General Custer started last night for St. Paul and Fort Abraham Lincoln. He was not justified in leaving without seeing the President or myself. Please intercept him at Chicago or St. Paul and order him to halt and wait for further orders. Meanwhile, let the expedition from Fort Lincoln proceed without him.

When Custer lifted his face to his wife after reading the telegram, shock had frozen his hawkish features.

"Libby, they've broken me!"

Then for the first time in his life, Custer was terrified—he who had feared nothing. In one moment all his audacity and flamboyance fled, leaving him utterly empty. He had flaunted regulations all his life, and now his future lay in the hands of Grant, who had no love for him.

He left for St. Paul and threw himself on General Terry's mercy. Terry was an able lawyer and a compassionate commander, and he wanted Custer in his command, having great confidence in the man as an Indian fighter.

"You have brought this on yourself, General," Terry rebuked Custer. "You know how unfitting it is for a soldier to publicly criticize his superiors."

"Can you do nothing for me, General?" Custer asked humbly.

Terry thought about it, then sat down and composed a letter and handed it to Custer.

I have no desire to question the orders of the President. Whether General Custer shall be permitted to accompany the column or not, I shall go in command of it. I do not know the reasons upon which the orders were given rest, but if these reasons do not forbid it, General Custer's services would be very valuable with his regiment.

Custer said, "I thank you with all my heart, General Terry!"

The letter was sent to General Sherman, who added his endorsement, then sent it to the White House. There was nothing further Custer could do but wait. He knew that Grant was not a man to forgive his enemies easily, but the answer came a few days later from General Sherman, who wired it to Terry:

The President sends me word that if you want General Custer along, he withdraws his objections. Advise Custer to be prudent, not to take any newspapermen, who always make mischief, and to abstain from personalities in the future.

As Terry read the letter to Custer, the black cloud that had plunged him into despair dissipated. Elated, he left department headquarters, meeting on the street Captain Ludlow, Terry's chief engineer.

"You look pretty well for a disgraced man," Ludlow commented.

"Oh, that was nothing, Ludlow!" Custer waved his hand freely, adding, "I'm taking the next train west to join my regiment."

"You'll do well on the campaign," Ludlow nodded. "Terry is an excellent officer. A little cautious for your taste, I suspect."

"Oh, once we're in the field I shall cut loose from Terry," Custer said airily.

In truth, Custer was intoxicated with his reprieve—yet determined to restore his reputation. He intended nothing less than to rush headlong into battle in order to win a great victory, and was equally determined that the other officers and units would not rob him of his triumph. It would be the Seventh who would sweep the field, and he meant to destroy the Sioux no matter what it took to get the job done.

CHAPTER TWENTY-ONE

WINSLOW MAKES AN OFFER

★ ★ ★ ★

The winter's ordeal had left Custer raw of nerve and pride. When spring came, he unleashed his animal energy, seized the regiment in his rough hands, and began shaking it into fervid activity. Officers' call was a repeated summons throughout the day, and the men worked late at their duties. Custer's sharp eyes were on everything as he whirled out of camp to the fort, the drill field or the rifle range, rushing at times across the prairie to find release for his energy.

The regiment was whole again, all twelve companies collected. Adjoining the cavalry troops were two companies of the Seventeenth Infantry and one of the Sixth Infantry, armed with three Gatling guns. One hundred fifty wagons were assembled in the nearby wagon park. The Ree scouts, Winslow's chief concern, were increased by Charlie Reynolds and two interpreters—Fred Girard and Isaiah Dorman, a black man.

Under the early May sunshine, the disorganized force continued training—the companies drilling, the horses wheeling and moving with the precision of long training. Men sweated off the fat of winter and refreshed their memories of duties grown vague by disuse. Equipment was overhauled and replaced, guns tested and clothing mended or newly issued.

Slowly the regiment, equipment, and plans were coming together. At night campfires blazed on the earth, yellow dots against the velvet shadowing of the land, and the men sang, or sat still, or wrote last letters home.

New faces appeared with the returning companies: Lieutenants Godfrey and Hare from K; Captain McDougal transferred from E to command B; Lieutenant McIntosh, with the strain of Indian blood in him, Benny Hodgson, a youngster loved by the command for a sunny disposition, Porter, and Captain Myles Keogh, a sharp-eyed, swarthy-skinned man with a pointed black mustache—all from I Company.

With spring came the arrival of General Terry, which alerted the regiment that the campaign was imminent. His presence meant that everything was accelerated even more. Long marches and sudden strains and unexpected shocks would come to the command.

The story of Custer's near dismissal was common knowledge throughout the camp. Winslow and several others of A Company discussed it one day as Corporal Zeiss related details of Custer's difficulty in Washington. "So he got himself in hot water, Custer did. Got Grant all stirred up—which was a fool thing to do! He should have known better."

Winslow agreed. "He's a hard one, Grant. Far as I know he's not noted for forgiving his enemies."

"Not him!" Babe O'Hara spit into the dust, then shook his head. "Way I heard it Grant and Sherman and Sheridan was all disgusted with him. You know how them big ones stick together. Custer stirred up a hornet's nest when he went against Grant's brother."

Zeiss looked worried, his stolid face revealing his fears. "Well, Terry got him out of the mess—but Custer was chastised before the whole country, and he knows it. He'll take it out on us, I think."

"You got that right, Nate," Hines nodded. "He'll be thinking of ways to make the ones who spanked him look foolish. And the only way he can do that is to whip the Sioux—come back a hero."

"And he'll ride this regiment into the whole Indian nation to do it," Zeiss said soberly. The others knew he was thinking of his wife and new baby.

"Don't worry, Nate," Winslow said. "Terry will hold him down."

"No, he'll promise to be good, like he's always done, and then he'll cut loose and do what he wants to do—just like he's always done."

The men continued to argue as Winslow left to report to Tom Custer. After seeing the captain, Tom walked slowly across the parade ground toward the officers' quarters. He had been thinking of the campaign a great deal—and the future. Ever since he had nearly died in the blizzard, the awareness of his own mortality had gripped him. He was not afraid of facing his own death; it was leaving Laurie alone that bothered him.

Night after night he had lain awake, searching for an answer, and out of his confusion, an answer had emerged. He was a man who hated indecision, and even though he still entertained doubts, there was a relief in the act of moving forward.

"Why, Tom—" Eileen said, surprised at his sudden appearance at her door. "I thought you'd be gone for a few days." She looked at him closely, noting the strain on his face. "Come inside. Is something wrong?"

He put his hands behind his back and nodded. "Yes, there is. I guess you know about it, Eileen." Winslow hesitated, struggling to get the words out. "You've been good for Laurie, Eileen," he said slowly. "She's needed a woman for a long time."

"I guess all little girls need a mother. Just as boys need a father."

That seemed to make things easier for Winslow. He lifted his head, his eyes fixed on her, and nodded. "Sure. If she were a boy, we'd make out fine, but as things are, I'm not able to handle some things."

Eileen was puzzled by his words and attitude. He was a man who had few doubts, yet now as he stood before her, there was a hesitation she'd never seen before.

"Eileen," he asked, "have you thought of me as a man you might marry?"

"Why—!" His question caught her off guard, and she blinked, trying to think of a suitable answer. He kept his eyes on her, watching carefully, and finally Eileen nodded. "Yes, Tom. I have."

He breathed a sigh of relief and shrugged. "You know what I am. You'll never be rich, but I don't think you'll ever know want. I'm a hard man to live with, I guess, in some ways—but you'll never know meanness from me."

Eileen was still unable to think clearly. "Tom, I don't know what to say. You're a strong man, and I'm lonely. And I love Laurie dearly—" She stopped a moment, then asked, "Do you love me, Tom?"

Winslow knew what his answer should be, the answer she deserved, but he had thought all this out. "Eileen, you're an attractive woman, and I've been alone a long time. I think about you a great deal, and I can't imagine anything better than coming home from a detail with you waiting for me." He saw something in her eyes, something he could not understand, and without thought, he put his arms around her and kissed her. She returned the pressure of his lips, and when he stepped back, he said, "If thinking you're a woman I'd like to share my life with and wanting you is love—then I love you. Maybe that's not enough for you, though. A woman wants romance, and I'm not much for that anymore."

"I'm not a green girl, Tom," Eileen said quietly. She stood there, examining him with care and a sort of wonder. "It's too soon for me to say, I think. It's too soon for you, too. We're very vulnerable, Tom. Both of us have big needs, but maybe that's not enough to build a marriage on."

"I don't want to rush you, Eileen," Winslow said. "The regiment will be leaving pretty soon. I wanted to say this to you before we left so you could be thinking about it. When I come back, we can talk again."

She frowned and shook her head. "Tom, I'm afraid! Everyone is saying this will be a hard fight."

"Probably will. But it'll be the last one, I think. I know you don't like the idea of a husband in a fighting outfit, but that's one of the things you can think about until I get back." He took a deep breath, then smiled. "Proposing is hard on a man. I'd rather dig a ditch."

Eileen laughed, the pressure of his offer fading. "I'll expect a *little* more in the way of courtship when you get back, Thomas Winslow!" She moved forward and kissed him on the lips lightly, then stepped back. "Don't say anything to Laurie."

"No, I won't. Well, let's go into town and have a celebration, you and Laurie and me."

"Celebrate what?"

"Celebrate that you didn't turn me down cold!"

The scene had left Eileen stunned, and for the rest of the afternoon she did her work mechanically, thinking of the strange proposal. There was something oddly unsatisfying about it, some element missing. Finally she put her apron aside and walked out of the house, anxious to get away. Borrowing a wagon from the quartermaster, she drove slowly toward the river and took the ferry across. For an hour she drove down the road leading east, barely aware of the signs of spring beginning to appear—the green shoots of grass, the fresh smell of warmed earth, and the golden tips of buds beginning to appear on the trees.

She stopped to let the horses drink in a small creek that ran across the road. As they nuzzled the water, she let her mind dwell on the scene again. What was it that was not *right* about Tom's proposal? The question nagged at her, making her half angry. *What did you expect him to do—take you out in the moonlight and get down on one knee quoting poetry?* She was a practical woman, accustomed to analyzing problems and meeting them in a workable fashion. This was ridiculous! Why was it so complicated? Yet she could not rid herself of the sense of something incomplete.

He'll make you a fine husband, she argued in her mind. *He's a strong man who would never let a woman down. Look how he's given his life to bringing Laurie up—that's enough loyalty for any woman to know. And when he kissed you, there was something there. He wanted you—and you wanted him, too! More than you'll admit—more than you wanted Frank, to be honest!*

That thought disturbed her, for she didn't want to think she was driven to marriage by that sort of hunger. She pulled the horses around and sent them back over the dusty road at a fast trot, trying to dismiss the matter, yet knowing she wouldn't be able to do so. After all, it was the most important decision facing her—one she'd have to make soon.

She passed by the school just as the children came running

264

out of the front door, with Larry right behind them.

"Eileen!" he called.

She swerved over and came to a stop. He grinned up at her, his youthful face smooth as he said, "What's your hurry? You're driving like a practice run for a chariot race!"

Eileen said quickly, "I thought I'd catch Laurie before she left."

"Faith came by and took her down to Beeker's Store. A new shipment of books came in, and they're looking them over. She'll be back in a few minutes, I think. Get down and have something to drink."

"No, I'll meet her there."

Dutton looked at her more closely. "Anything wrong, Eileen?"

She had learned that he was sensitive to her moods, that she hid little from him. "No, nothing's wrong—" Then she bit her lip, for she saw he wasn't convinced. "I think I will wait here for Laurie," she said, and when he had gotten her a drink of water, they sat down on two cane-bottomed chairs beside the well.

He spoke of Laurie's progress, but saw that she was only half listening. Finally he said, "The regiment will be going out soon, I hear. Laurie will be staying with you, I suppose."

"Yes, she will."

Her reply was short, and Dutton hesitated. Finally he said, "Are you worried about Tom?"

She swirled the water in her glass, then looked up at him. "Yes, I am, Larry."

He nodded, then asked abruptly, "You're very fond of Tom, aren't you? I guess I don't have much chance against a man like him."

Eileen knew then that she had to tell him what was happening. "Larry, Tom's asked me to marry him." His eyes looked stricken at her words, and pity ran through her. "I . . . I haven't said yes, but you have a right to know about it."

Dutton nodded briefly, trying not to show his disappointment. "You'll get a good man, Eileen," he said quietly.

"Oh, Larry, I don't *know* what to do!" she said, upset by the scene. "Tom needs somebody to take care of Laurie, and I need someone. I've not told anyone how lonely I get!"

"You're not a woman who goes around looking for sympathy, Eileen," Dutton said. "But I think I know."

"Yes, I really think you do, Larry. You're the most sensitive man I've ever known." She looked at him, surprise dawning in her eyes, for until she said the words aloud, she had not grasped that truth. He was not a dashing man, but there was a steadiness in him she liked. She had known for some time his feelings for her, and if Tom and Laurie had not come into her life, she would have fallen in love with Larry Dutton. The thought disturbed her for some reason, and she was glad to see Laurie and Faith approaching.

"Look at the books Miss Faith got for me!" Laurie cried as she held up a package for Eileen.

Eileen gave the books a cursory look, then said hurriedly, "We must be going, Laurie. Your father will be hungry, and I haven't even started cooking supper yet."

As they drove away with Laurie's mare tied to the back of the wagon, Faith said, "I've got to get home, Larry. Thanks for letting me take Laurie out early."

He seemed not to hear her words, but stood staring after the wagon. Then he turned to say, "What? Oh, that's okay, Faith." He left her abruptly and returned to the schoolroom, preoccupied and heavy of heart.

★　★　★　★

Time moved forward with the Seventh, and the plans made by Sherman and Sheridan in Washington were relayed to the officers in command. Keen with excitement, Tom Custer met with the sergeants of the regiment late one afternoon. "Gather around, men," he said, his high tenor voice crisp. "I want you all to know what the general idea is." He pointed at a large sheet of paper pinned to the wall, pointing out the areas as he spoke:

"Here's where we are—and here's where the Indians will be—right in this area in Montana territory. We've got to pen them up, so Sherman and Sheridan have come up with a three-pronged attack. We'll leave here with General Terry and General Custer, heading west. General Crook will leave Fort Fetterman, down here in Wyoming territory heading north. General Gibbon and his forces have already left Fort Ellis up the Yellowstone

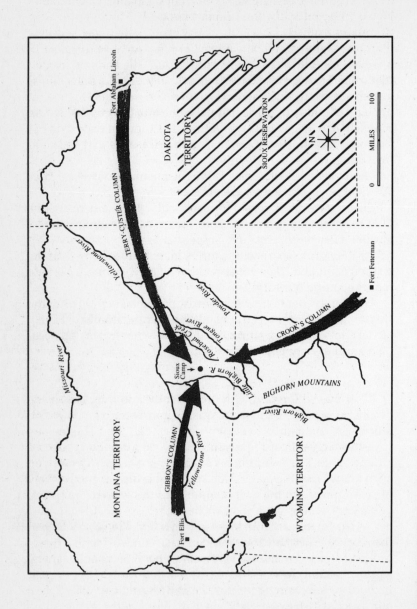

headed for the area." He looked up, eyes gleaming. "We'll have Sitting Bull and the rest of them caught in a vise—a vise with three jaws instead of two! Any questions?"

"How about supplies, Captain?" Winslow asked.

"No problem there. We've got a ship, *The Far West*, headed down the Missouri loaded to the deck. She'll go up the Yellowstone as far as Rosebud Creek. Any more questions?"

Sergeant Hines spoke up. "How many Sioux we going against, sir?"

"Oh, maybe a thousand at most," Custer said carelessly. "We'll take that many men into the field, and with Gibbon's and Crook's commands we'll have three thousand." He grinned boyishly, adding, "There won't be enough Indians to go around, I'm afraid."

Winslow made no comment, but after the meeting when Sergeant McDermont asked him about the numbers, he shook his head. "The Ree say there's more Indians in that area than we suppose. I'm glad Gibbons and Crook will be on hand. I'd hate to run up against Sitting Bull with no reinforcements."

"Well, I guess this is my last campaign," Hines said slowly. "My bones are achin' with twenty-eight years of campaigning. I want to go out with trumpets sounding and guidons flying, Tom. Like to see the Seventh cover itself with glory—not for Custer's sake but for fellows like me who've eaten dust and taken the bullets all down the line."

"You'll see it, Hines," Tom said, slapping him on the shoulder. "This one will be something we'll be telling our grandchildren about!"

When he got home that afternoon, he found Laurie primed for him. "Daddy!" she cried out, clutching his hand after he kissed her. "Guess what? Miss Faith sent word for me to come out and spend a week with her before school starts. Can I go, please!"

"Why, I don't see why not," Tom said, thinking rapidly. He had always been honest with her, and now said, "You know I'll be going out with the regiment pretty soon? Be gone for a few weeks, I guess. Tell you what, I'll take you out there and visit with Miss Faith; then if we leave before you get back, we'll have our goodbyes all said."

Her face grew still, and she thought hard. "I'd like to be here when you leave, Daddy."

"All right, I'll come and get you for that." It pleased him that she wanted to say goodbye to him, and he said, "We'll go tomorrow morning."

The next day he took her to the mission, much to Faith's delight; and after Tom had said goodbye to Laurie, Faith walked out with him.

"Laurie's excited about this," Winslow said. "Nice of you to think of it, Faith."

"It'll be good for me. She's such a sweet girl." Faith stood there, sober and attentive. "Will you leave soon—the regiment, I mean?"

"In a week or so, I'd guess. Always takes longer than you think to get this many men off."

"Be careful, Tom," Faith cautioned, her eyes soft as she looked up at him.

Winslow had thought about their last meeting, when he had come to the house and fought with Grayson. Now he said what he had planned. "I was wrong the last time I was here, Faith. Had no right to pick a fight with the lieutenant." He shrugged his shoulders and made what apology he could. "I think it did something to me, almost dying in that blizzard. I've thought about it a lot."

"What did it do, Tom?"

"Hard to describe. I've had some close calls in my time, in the war and after. But this was different. Always before I was right in the middle of a lot of noise and action. Could have been killed at any second, but there was no time to think about it. The blizzard wasn't like that. When I was freezing and fell to the ground, some things came to me, I haven't thought about in years." He shifted, his eyes half shut, and murmured in a thoughtful tone, "I thought about God mostly. All my people have been godly. You'd have liked them, especially my grandfather, Christmas Winslow. He was a rough mountain man, but after he was converted, he spent the rest of his life preaching to the Indians."

"He must have been a wonderful man, Tom."

"Yes. You'd have liked him," he said again, "and he'd have

liked you. When I was about to die in that storm, I had some sort of dream—a memory, I guess. I heard him preach once when he was very old, and I never forgot it. He was a big man, powerful in every way, but I remember how gentle he was when he spoke of Jesus. I couldn't have been very old when I heard him preach, but I recall him saying, 'Many things don't matter. How much money you have or if your name's in a newspaper. The one thing that matters to every man on this earth is *Jesus*. He's the answer to every need you'll ever have!' " He paused, looked up at her, then said, "While I was going under, I heard him say that. Maybe I was crazy—but anyway, it got me up and going."

"I think it was real, Tom," Faith responded, tears in her eyes.

"Well, I don't know what it means, but I do know I was wrong about the way I acted that day at your place."

Faith waited for him to go on, but when he didn't, she said, "Larry told me you and Eileen are going to be married."

"Why, we've not said so!" he said, startled at her words. When she looked surprised, he asked, "Did you tell Laurie?"

"No . . . but Larry didn't say it was a secret."

"It's just something we've talked about, Faith. I asked her to think about it, and she said she would."

"I see."

He saw that she didn't see at all.

She went on. "Larry is taking it hard. He's in love with her, you know."

His eyebrows shot up. "No, I didn't know it was that way with him!"

"He's not one to cry in public, Tom. But I could tell." She saw that her remark had disturbed him, so said quickly, "Goodbye. I'll be praying for you."

He got into the saddle, then took a long look at her. She had left her mark on his memory. He admired the full, firm lips and the clear shining eyes. There was something in this woman, he knew full well, that he would never find in another, and now he felt a faint regret as he said, "I'll come back to get Laurie in a few days."

She nodded, saying only, "All right, Tom."

He put his horse to a gallop, and when he was a hundred

yards away, he had to fight against the impulse that rose in him—to go back and try to explain how it was between him and Eileen. But he knew nothing he could say would make sense to her, so he clenched his teeth and rode at a dead run for the next mile, as if running away from something he could not bear to look upon.

CHAPTER TWENTY-TWO

CAPTIVES

★ ★ ★ ★

"Tom! Tom Winslow!"

The sound of someone calling his name so urgently stopped Winslow short as he came out of the mess hall. He looked up as Nick Owens came running across from the adjutant's office. Alarm hit him like lightning, and he cried, "Is it Laurie?"

"Yeah, Tom, it's her and Faith! They been carried off by the Indians!"

"When?" The question shot from Winslow's lips.

"Must have been last night, Tom. Zeno Bruton saw her last night, but when he went by this morning, she was gone and the mission was wrecked!"

"Where's Zeno now?"

"At my store." Stark fear emanated from his eyes. "Tom, we got to find them—!"

"I'll find them, Owens!" Winslow broke in.

"All right, but hurry! You know what them red devils are like!"

Winslow ignored this remark and ran for the adjutant's office. "Lieutenant Cooke," he said, finding the officer talking with his corporal. "My little girl and Faith Jamison have been taken by the Indians. I need to start after them right now."

"Good God, Winslow!" Cooke started. "Yes—we'll get a

troop mounted and on the way at once."

"Send them to the mission, will you, Lieutenant? I want to get there and see the ground before the trail gets obscured."

"You're not going alone?"

"I'll take Bloody Knife. He's the best tracker."

"I'll send B Company, Sergeant. They'll be at the mission as soon as they can make the ride."

Winslow saluted, then whirled and ran out of the office. He found the Ree scouts at the stable, and all of them wanted to go. "Just Bloody Knife," Winslow said. "It's going to be a stalking matter, and the fewer of us the better."

Ten minutes later he and Bloody Knife were pounding out of the fort. Each of them was mounted on a good horse and leading another. They crossed on the ferry, disembarked, and headed east at a dead gallop. When they were halfway to the mission, Bloody Knife called out, "Horses not last! Better slow down!"

But Winslow paid him no heed, and when they pulled into the mission, the horses they were riding were winded. "Change saddles to the other ones while I look around, Bloody Knife," Winslow snapped. He ran across the yard and into the house. Every room was in shambles. The curtains were ripped from the windows, food had been torn from the shelves and scattered over the kitchen floor. Then he ran for the barn. It, too, had been damaged. He found traces of a fire in one area where the Indians had started a fire with some of the books, but it had smoldered and gone out.

As he left the barn, he found Bloody Knife mounted and circling the grounds, his head down as he studied the earth. When Winslow jumped into the saddle and rode up to him, the Ree raised his head, his obsidian eyes gleaming. "Go that way," he said, pointing toward the low-lying hills to the west.

"How many?"

"Maybe six—seven. They take two shod ponies."

Winslow looked at the hills, thinking hard. "They've got a long start on us, Bloody Knife. The dark will catch us, and we won't be able to track them."

Bloody Knife nodded, but said, "We catch up tomorrow."

"They know they'll be followed, so they'll be moving pretty fast," Winslow said doubtfully.

"We get them Indians tomorrow," the Ree said. He hated the Sioux with a passion, and his lips turned cruel. "We kill them all, Winslow!"

"If they see us, they may kill the captives."

"They no see. Come!"

Tom Winslow was an adequate tracker, but not in Bloody Knife's class. He followed as the Ree pushed forward, his eyes fixed on the ground. As he rode, he found himself trembling, and tried to shake off the fear that came to him. He had seen women and children after the Sioux had finished with them on their raids, memories he wished he didn't have. Now as he followed Bloody Knife he found himself praying, "God—let us find them! I don't care about myself, but don't let Laurie and Faith be harmed!"

* * * *

The attack had come as Faith was making breakfast. She had awakened at dawn, gotten up and dressed, then built a fire in the cookstove. Laurie was sleeping soundly, and there was no reason to get her up. Faith smiled as she sliced the bacon, thinking of the past four days. The time had been enjoyable for both of them. Laurie had discovered that Faith had a playful side, and the two had played games, sometimes giggling as though they were both ten years old.

"You're more fun than anyone," Laurie had said sleepily as Faith had tucked her in the previous night. "I wish I could stay with you all the time!"

This had pleased Faith, but she had said, "This has been a special time, Laurie. A vacation. I have to work hard, and most of the time it's not nearly so much fun out here." She hesitated, then said, "You have a fine time with Miss Eileen, don't you?"

"Oh yes," Laurie nodded. "But she doesn't—" She couldn't find the expression she sought and reached up and pulled Faith's head down to kiss her. "Can I come and stay with you a lot more?"

"I'd love that. We'll see if it can be worked out," Faith had said.

As she put the bacon in the iron skillet and it began to sizzle and curl, she thought of that moment with a smile. Then she heard a sound and turned, thinking it was Laurie.

She gasped, the smile freezing on her lips! There before her stood two half-naked Indians, their faces streaked with paint! Her hand went limp and she dropped the skillet. Her heart raced with fear, for she knew why they were there. The rifles in their hands and the long knife half lifted told the story.

She had thought of such a thing happening, but there had been no way to prevent it, living alone out on the prairie. Now she forced the cold fear away and said, "You startled me. I didn't hear you ride up." She bent over and picked up the skillet and put it on the stove. Her mind raced for something to say and she asked, "Are you hungry?"

The taller one, with a lantern-like jaw, said, "Want whiskey!"

Faith shook her head. "I don't have any. But I have much food."

The tall one spoke a word to his companion, and the two moved to the cabinet, pulling canned goods out, dropping the cans on the floor with a clatter. When they found no whiskey, Faith tried again. "Let me fix you food."

Both of them glared at her, and at that moment two more Indians came in, both carrying guns. They fixed their eyes on the woman, grinned, and one of them said something to the tall Indian, who was evidently the leader. The others laughed, and the speaker came forward and grabbed Faith by the arm. She let no trace of fear show on her face, and the leader spoke sharply, at which the Indian dropped his hand at once.

"Fix food—quick!" the tall Indian said. "Where your man?"

"I have no man," Faith said quickly. "Just one little girl is here." His face was cruel as he looked toward the door that led to the bedroom. Moving quickly he opened it and stepped inside. Faith started to follow, but was grabbed immediately by the other Indian who had come with the leader. She heard a startled cry and then a muffled sound. Faith cried out, but then the leader appeared, grasping Laurie by one arm. The child's eyes were wide with terror, and she tried to escape. When the Indian released her, she flew to Faith.

"Don't be afraid," Faith said, holding her tightly. "God will take care of us."

The lantern-jawed warrior stared at her, then said, "God sometimes sleep."

Faith shook her head. "Not the true God. He sees us at all times. What is your name?"

"Ansito." He added with a gleam of humor in his eyes, "Means 'killer of men' in white man's tongue." When her expression didn't change, he asked curiously, "You no afraid?"

Faith breathed a quick prayer, then said, "I know that you may kill us, Ansito. But you may die, too. We live with death every day—all of us, red and white."

Her answer caught his attention. His face showed little, but he said, "Fix food."

"Help me, Laurie," she said quickly, and the two hurried to prepare the meal. One of the other Indians, a short, muscular warrior, said something, Ansito grunted an assent, and the Indians went through the house, whooping and destroying. Faith ignored them, giving her attention to keeping Laurie busy. She cooked huge piles of bacon and eggs, and when it was ready, she said, "Here's the food, Ansito." She put her arm around Laurie, holding her close while the Indians gobbled the food down, using their fingers. When they consumed that, she opened all the cans of fruit she had, and they devoured that as well.

Finally they finished and began arguing. Faith had learned just enough of their language to understand that two of the Indians wanted to burn the station and kill her and Laurie. She kept her face expressionless, knowing that to show fear would not help any more than begging for mercy.

She turned to Ansito and asked, "You have children, Ansito?"

He nodded. "Two boys, one girl."

Faith said, "I have a school here. I came to teach Indian boys and girls. If you will bring your children, I will teach them."

"What you teach?" he demanded. "White people take land from Indians. They make promises, then lie."

Faith said, "Some white men lie. Not all. Some Indians do bad things, yes? But some of us love the Indians. God is the same, and He loves the Indians."

"White man's god!"

"No, the God of all," Faith said. His face was sullen, but she spoke in a normal tone of voice, telling him of her desire to help. She was aware that there was little mercy in the man, but at that moment God gave her a peace in her heart.

When she ended her words, Ansito did a peculiar thing. He drew his long gleaming knife and came to stand before her. He held the tip of it to her breast, watching her face carefully. "I kill you, white squaw," he whispered, and his followers grunted assent.

Faith knew fear, but shook her head. "My life is in God's hands, Ansito. Be kind to the child. She has done no wrong."

Ansito pushed the knife until it touched her chest. She felt the tip of it penetrate her dress, then her skin, but said, "God loves you, Ansito. He is a good God."

Suddenly the warrior pulled the knife back and thrust it into his belt. An angry cry went up from one of the other Indians, but Ansito spoke sharply. "Take what you want. We will take woman and child. Sell them."

The Indians rushed through the house, taking everything they wanted, then moved outside. "You come," Ansito said, motioning to the door.

"Let me get clothes?" Faith asked, and when he nodded in a surly fashion, she and Laurie got what they could, then went outside. Ansito kept looking around, and finally said, "Saddle ponies."

Faith and Laurie quickly saddled their horses just in time, for Ansito cried out, and the band swept out of the yard, bearing plunder stuffed in sacks.

As they left the mission, Laurie turned, tears running down her cheeks. But she said, "Don't worry, Miss Faith. My daddy will come for us!"

"Yes, he will, Laurie," Faith nodded. "But don't say anything to the Indians."

All morning they rode at a fast pace, taking a break at noon. They made no fire but ate the canned goods they had brought from the mission. Faith and Laurie shared a can of beans, which they ate from the can; then all too soon Ansito called out, "We go!"

All day they rode, though the pace slowed, and that night the Indians made a fire, cooked up some of the quarter of beef they'd found in her larder, and ate the whole thing. Faith asked for some for Laurie, and one of the warriors threw her a chunk of half-cooked meat, which she and the girl ate. Afterwards she and Laurie slept under the single blanket Faith had managed to bring, clinging together for warmth, for it was very cold.

The next morning Faith heard them arguing back and forth, and again she sensed that only Ansito's curt orders kept the others from harming them. Later when they stopped for a rest and a drink at a small stream, she said, "Ansito, I thank you for being kind. God will reward you."

"What kindness?" he demanded abruptly.

"I understand some of your tongue," she said. "Enough to know that your word has kept us from harm."

He seemed embarrassed by her words. "I will sell you for money or trade for horses. You will both be slaves of Sioux people."

"That may be," Faith said. "But I know what your warriors want to do to us. You have kept us from harm."

He stared at her, but made no answer. She sensed the cruelty in the man and knew he would kill them with no remorse if the situation changed. She was convinced that God had worked a miracle, and she kept on praying for deliverance.

That afternoon the sky darkened, and a hard rain fell just at dusk. They stopped next to an overflowing creek and set up camp. Faith and Laurie were soaking wet and found a way to change into the relatively dry clothes they'd brought. There was no way to do this modestly, so the two knew they were being scorned and laughed at.

Darkness came quickly, and the Indians cooked a very small doe that one of them had brought in. As it was sizzling, Faith sat holding Laurie close to her. Ansito squatted across from her, staring into the fire, his face coppery in the flickering light. When the meat was done, the warriors gorged themselves, but did throw a small portion to her. It was half raw and had a strong taste. "Try to eat a little, Laurie," Faith encouraged.

After the band had eaten, Ansito said, "Little Wolf, go watch." The Indian rose and disappeared, and the other four began gambling, a game involving a wooden object. *They are just like unruly children*, Faith thought, watching them, *yelling with joy when they win and becoming sullen when they lose*.

Ansito took no interest in the game, but sat wrapped in silence, his gaze glued to the fire. Faith wanted to move over to speak to him, but Laurie, worn out from the hardships of the journey, had gone into a deep sleep.

Half an hour passed, and the gamblers began to get bored. Faith grew drowsy, her head bobbing with weariness. She was about to pull Laurie into the blanket and go to sleep when a voice cut across the silence.

"We have come for the woman and the child."

The warriors leaped for their guns, but the crack of a rifle sounded and one Indian fell, shot through the head.

"You will all die if you resist."

Now awake, Laurie whispered, "That's my daddy!"

Faith glanced across at Ansito, who was peering into the darkness for the man with the voice. The tall Indian had no weapon save the knife in his belt. "Who comes?" he asked, lifting his voice.

"I come for the woman and the child. Let them come to me and you will live. You are in my sights, Chief. If I pull the trigger you will die."

"A chief does not fear death!"

"I know that. But there is no need. If you had harmed the captives, I would have killed you all. Now I see they are all right. Let them go, and we will leave you in peace."

Ansito looked toward Faith, his eyes fixed on her. Faith said calmly, "God is giving you the gift of life, Ansito. He is rewarding you for protecting our lives."

Ansito stood motionless during the tense moment. Then he nodded. "Perhaps true. You go now."

Faith jumped up, took Laurie's hand, and ran toward the voice. She saw where the horses were tethered and rushed over to mount. When they were both in the saddles, they nudged their horses forward. They had not gone far when a shape appeared, and her heart leaped when she saw it was an Indian, but then recognized the Sioux lookout. He put his hand to his lips, cautioning her to be quiet as he guided her down the path.

As the two of them rode away, she heard Tom Winslow say, "Your life for theirs. Do not try to follow us."

Ansito said, "Take them. We will not come."

Faith and Laurie continued down the trail, peering into the

darkness. Soon they heard the sound of horses coming. Then Winslow appeared, his face tense in the faint moonlight. He halted his horse, reached over and pulled Laurie from her saddle. He held her without saying a word, and finally asked, "Are you all right?"

"Yes, Daddy! They didn't hurt us at all!"

"Thank God for that!" he said. He put Laurie back in her saddle and moved over to Faith. His eyes were filled with concern. "They didn't harm you?"

"No. I told the chief God would reward him for not harming us."

Bloody Knife came up, muttering, "Better go now!"

They rode away quickly, the Ree falling behind to be sure they were not followed. When they were five miles away, Winslow said, "I've been pretty scared."

"I knew you'd come for us," Laurie said proudly. "Didn't I tell you he would, Miss Faith?"

"Yes, you did, Laurie," Faith replied. She smiled warmly at Tom as she echoed Laurie's words, "I knew you'd come." The tension had eased, leaving her weak from the ordeal, but oh so grateful.

All the way back to Bismarck, Tom tried to define what was in his heart. He knew part of his fear had been for Laurie, of course, but not all of it. When they got to town, he took Faith to the Owens' house, at her request. After the excitement of their return was over, Tom had a few moments with Faith, but he tried not to show his feelings.

Then she looked up and said, "I'll never forget it, Tom, how you came out of the darkness to save us."

He stood there, looking down at her, and the confusion he'd felt over her seemed to fade. He said simply, "Faith, when I thought something might have happened to you, it was as if the sun went out."

"Why—Tom!" She was taken aback by his statement and impulsively put her hand on his chest. "What a nice thing to say!"

He reached out and wrapped his arms around her, holding his face against her hair, and was astonished to find he was trembling. He held her until it passed, then drew back, an odd look on his face. "You've got a way of making a place for yourself inside a man, Faith."

He released her and walked away quickly as though he were afraid to stay, afraid he'd say more than he should.

Faith watched him go, astonished by his act. *You have a way of your own, Tom Winslow—of getting inside a woman's heart!*

CHAPTER TWENTY-THREE

THE SEVENTH PULLS OUT

★ ★ ★ ★

On the sixteenth day of May a general order went out: The command would leave the following morning. On the eve of departure, the officers held a ball on the regimental street, and all the ladies from town attended. The couples danced to the music of the band, swinging around in the glow of the campfires.

Eileen joined the throng, looking at the fringes of the crowd to see if she could find Tom. At length, she saw him with Laurie, and waved to them. Since this was an officers' ball, he could not come to her, so she danced with Cooke, Moylan, and several other officers—and later, Spence Grayson. She listened while he told her about the campaign as he swung her in and out around the other couples, seemingly enjoying himself. Then his eyes turned cold. Quickly she followed his gaze: Faith Jamison had joined Tom and Laurie.

"You heard about Faith and Laurie?" she asked.

"Yes. They were very lucky."

His tone was so abrupt that she said, "You sound grim, Spence. What's the matter?"

"Nothing," he replied. "I'm just thinking of how short life is and how few times we get what we want." After a couple of turns around, he smiled down at her and said, "What am I doing? Here I am with a fine-looking woman and spouting grim philosophy!"

She accepted his apology, though not satisfied with his vain attempt at covering up.

Across the way, Faith had seen the look Grayson gave them, but said nothing to Winslow. Since he had rescued them from the Indians, she had seen him twice—once when he came out with Laurie to help repair the damage the Indians had done, and again in town just for a few minutes. She had known he'd be here at the ball, for Laurie had told her he'd promised to bring her so she could watch the celebration. This time Faith had sought him out, but he seemed tense, and she wondered if it was because of the emotion he'd shown when he'd left her at the Owens' house. She herself had thought of the hard embrace he'd given her and the choking sound in his voice. *Could it have meant nothing?* She'd asked herself that question often, and now she was almost certain it had not concerned her, but had been his way of unleashing his strain over Laurie's abduction and near disaster. Still, it was a precious moment to her, though she'd never speak of it to anyone.

How surprised Faith would have been had she been able to read his mind, for he was thinking of that moment with a sharp sense of regret, spinning his thoughts into a pool of confusion. He had made an offer to Eileen, yet he felt drawn to Faith. He remembered her firm body pressed against his, and how his whole spirit had reached out for her. He'd been more shaken by her captivity, by the possibility of her death, than he'd thought possible by any woman anymore.

Even now, standing beside her, feeling the pressure of her arm as it touched his, he was recalling the wild flavor of his youth when he had reached out for life with a gusto and a hunger that he could never satisfy. He'd been a man of hopes who believed in dreams, but somewhere along the way, he'd lost that zest for living. Disillusion had opened him up and drained out his faith—until now. Somehow this woman had brought back at least a memory of it.

His thoughts disturbed him, for in his last conversation with Eileen, she'd clung to him when he was leaving, saying breathlessly, "Oh, Tom! I hate it when you leave me!" There had been a keen hunger in her voice, and he'd left hurriedly, afraid of his own desires. She had said nothing about his offer of marriage, and he wondered if she would ever bring it up. He felt bound by it, and his thoughts of Faith seemed to be a violation of his proposition to the other woman.

Finally he said, "We've got to go, Faith. This is our last night together for a while, Laurie's and mine."

"I envy Eileen," Faith said, giving Laurie a hug. "I wish I could keep you!"

"Daddy, can I go out to the mission some while you're gone?"

Winslow hesitated, knowing Eileen had been strongly against letting her go because of the danger. "When I get back, we'll spend a lot of time visiting with Miss Faith." Then he raised his eyes to Faith. "I'll see you when we get back."

"Oh, I'll be here to see you off, Tom. I think the whole town will be on hand."

And she was correct, for despite the fact that the next morning fog rested on the Missouri bottoms, Custer, ever ready for pageantry, paraded through Fort Abraham Lincoln, where many of the townspeople had gathered. The blue and gold regimental standard flapped above the headquarters' group, together with Custer's personal pennant, the old Civil War design of red and blue with crossed white sabres. A company guidon, swallow-tailed stars and stripes, marked each of the twelve companies that trooped behind in columns of fours. Mounted on white horses, the band played "Garry Owen" as the companies marched on past the quarters of the Indian scouts, with keening women and impassive old men; past "Suds Row," with sobbing washerwomen and excited, playing children; past the length of officers' row, with families watching in grief from behind closed windows.

As A Company filed through the gate, Winslow spied Faith among the crowd. At the same moment, she spotted Tom and kept her eyes fixed on him as he rode forward. He saw her face grow tighter and her lips move. He felt the effect of her glance, lifted his hat in acknowledgment, and continued on.

Half a mile out of the fort the regiment halted to wait for the supply wagons to come forward; the ranks broke and the officers and married men rode back to say a final goodbye. Winslow dismounted, but could not get the picture of Faith out of his mind. Finally, he jumped on his horse and galloped back down the hill. The grounds were swarming with people, but he found Faith by the gate.

Dismounting, he said, "Pretty picture, isn't it?"

"Yes, Tom."

To him, she was a picture of beauty, but it was the strength in her that he admired more. Suddenly he said, "You did well—when the Indians took you and Laurie." She told him the whole story, and he commented, "If you'd shown fear, it would have been a different story—not so happy."

"It was the Lord, Tom."

"I think so." He stood there, reflecting on the whole event, then went on. "I never heard of anything like it. Captives have been rescued—but not before being abused." He shuffled his feet, not knowing exactly how to say what was on his heart. "Well. I guess I did some praying myself on that one—"

"Sergeant! Get back to your outfit!"

The curt command hit Winslow like a bullet as Grayson's voice broke. The lieutenant had approached on a bay and vented his hatred from his position of authority.

Winslow nodded at Faith, turned and mounted, then rode away without a glance at Grayson. Almost as soon as Tom got back to his place, Custer rushed by, and all down the line sergeants began calling out their orders.

The regiment moved out into a snake-like formation half a mile long, Winslow and Hines riding side by side. They both looked back at the fort. Would they see it again?

Hines voiced their thoughts. "Be glad when we get back to that old fort again, Tom."

The column moved down a ridge into the broken country, toward the spot that the whites called "Little Bighorn" but the Indians called "Greasy Grass."

Faith stood on the summit of the hill watching the regiment move away, and at that moment the sun brightened the haze and she noticed that a shadow was thrown upright by the column. The shadow lengthened into a mirage, so that she clearly saw the regiment marching through and slowly fading in the sky.

A man standing beside her muttered, "That's a bad sign. Glad I ain't with them fellers!"

Libby Custer saw it, too, and would write about it in a book in later years: "A mirage appeared, which took up about half of the line of cavalry, and thenceforth for a little distance it marched, equally plain to the sight on the earth and in the sky."

★   ★   ★   ★

The first day's march brought the Seventh to the Heart River, but the next day brought sharp showers. As they made their way forward it grew colder and snow fell three inches deep. They followed the Beaver into rising broken country and on June 8 camped on the Powder River. Now it became a game of hide-and-seek, and the awesome responsibility of making contact with the hostiles rested squarely on General Terry's shoulders.

On the tenth of June he dispatched Reno with six companies of cavalry and one Gatling gun to explore the upper part of the Powder. Reno left early in the afternoon with his force, A Company included. Winslow and his Ree scouts, led by Bloody Knife, scouted the area and brought back reports of large forces of Sioux. Reno had orders not to go beyond the Tongue, but the sign was so evident that he moved to the Rosebud and scouted that valley before rejoining Custer on the Yellowstone.

On June 21, Terry called Gibbon, Custer, and Brisbin to the cabin of the *Far West* anchored on the south bank of the Yellowstone at the mouth of the Rosebud. Around a map spread out on a table, they discussed the details of a strategy that Terry had worked out during the morning. Terry said, "The Sioux are somewhere between the Rosebud and the Bighorn. General Gibbon, you will go up the Bighorn. Custer, you will go up the Rosebud. We must catch the Sioux with a strong, swift-moving strike force—and that's you, Custer—and drive them against a less mobile blocking force, which you will be, General Gibbon. An anvil and a sledge, the two of you will be. General Gibbon, at what time can you be at the mouth of the Little Bighorn?"

Gibbon studied the map and made his calculations. "I will be at the Little Bighorn on the morning of the twenty-sixth."

"Very well. General Custer, that will be your time to strike. Take your force up the Rosebud. Explore right and left. *But do*

not permit yourself to engage the enemy before Gibbon comes up!" Terry
was a mild man, but his voice was emphatic as he stressed this
order.

Custer nodded casually, and Terry asked, "Do you need more
men? Gibbon could give you Brisbin's battalion of cavalry."

"No," Custer said shortly. "The Seventh can take care of anything we meet."

The other three officers eyed Custer carefully. He was not
himself, they thought. There was a sullen glumness in him that
was unusual.

Terry admired Custer, thinking him the best Indian fighter in
the army, while the other two were less enthusiastic. Terry said,
"Gibbon, give Custer part of your Crow scouts. They can assist
Winslow and Reynolds. Custer, you will leave in the morning. I
will go with Gibbon, and if all goes well, we will meet on the
twenty-sixth."

When the meeting adjourned, Custer went immediately to
his own headquarter tent and sent for his officers. They soon
assembled, twenty-eight of them, dirty and tired from the hard
march.

"We shall leave in the morning," Custer said. He was a lank
figure in buckskin with a scarlet flowing kerchief and a head of
hair grown ragged. The sun had scorched his face and there was
none of his usual electric energy visible as he outlined the plan.
"Gibbon marches up the Bighorn while we march up the Rosebud. We will not take the wagon train. Each troop will have
twelve mules. Are there any questions?"

"That's not enough mules to carry everything, General. We
need wagons, too," Algernon Smith said.

"Wagons will slow us down too much."

Custer answered a few questions curtly, then dismissed the
officers. When they were moving back to their companies, Lieutenant Weir asked Edgerly, "What's wrong with the general? I've
never seen him like this."

"He's still sore over the treatment he got in Washington,"
Edgerly answered. "He's out to prove them wrong, but he's very
depressed."

The regiment settled down to sleep on the eve of the march—
all except Winslow and Nate Zeiss. "Looks like we'll be into this

thing soon, Nate," Tom said. "How do you feel about it?"

Zeiss shook his head, doubt in his black eyes. "Going to be bad, Tom. I feel it in my bones."

Winslow knew Nate was thinking of his family, and said, "Well, we'll meet them with a strong force. Custer has about a thousand effectives. That's more than the Sioux will have. Gibbon will be coming with even more, and General Crook will throw his entire force against the hostiles."

But what none of them knew—what neither Custer nor Terry knew—was that Crook's command lay with double guards around it, licking their wounds after a sharp defeat inflicted by Crazy Horse four days earlier. Nor did they know that Crook would not move to help them. Worse still, Crazy Horse had joined Sitting Bull and now, swelled with triumph, was waiting for the army to arrive.

The next morning the Seventh Cavalry passed in review before Terry, Gibbon, and Custer. In the absence of the band, massed trumpets supplied the music. Officers saluted smartly, and the lean, bronzed troopers followed in every variety of costume. Slouch hats, gray or blue shirts, and the regulation sky-blue trousers predominated. To ease saddle wear, many had lined their trouser seats with canvas. Each man carried a Springfield single-shot carbine and a Colt revolver with one hundred rounds for the carbine and twenty-four for the pistol. The pack-train followed, the unruly mules bearing rations for fifteen days and more carbine ammunition. In all, the regiment counted 31 officers, 566 enlisted men, 35 Indian scouts, and about a dozen packers.

Terry watched with a thoughtful eye as they passed. "You have a good regiment, Custer. The best in the service, I do believe."

Custer showed a flash of his old spirit. "The Seventh has been the best in the army for ten years."

Brisbin, a member of the Third Cavalry and a truculent man, gave Custer a sharply irritated glance. From the first he had thought that Custer's regiment was not strong enough, had urged that four companies of his own be added to the Seventh and had asked Terry to go in command. When Terry had rejected the idea, saying that he had not had much experience fighting

Indians, Brisbin had said, "General, you have more sense in your little finger than Custer has in his whole body. You underrate your ability and overrate Custer's."

Terry had only laughed, but Brisbin had said seriously, "I do not want my battalion placed under Custer's command."

"You do not seem to have confidence in Custer."

"None in the world," Brisbin had responded.

The last file passed, and Terry handed Custer a folded paper. "This is the written statement of the instructions I gave you yesterday. I have left them purposely indefinite in certain things. I have too much faith in your judgment as a commander to impose fixed orders upon you."

Custer took the paper, gave it a cursory glance, and thrust it into his pocket. Terry went on. "I shall be with Gibbon on the Little Bighorn on the morning of the twenty-sixth. Be sure to send Herendeen back as soon as you reach Tullock's Creek. We must work together. The victory depends on both columns striking at the same time. I wish you luck."

Custer grasped Terry's hand, then whirled around. As he broke his horse into a gallop, Brisbin called after him, "Now, Custer, don't be greedy. Wait for us."

Custer looked back, flung up his arm, making a figure of dash and gallantry in the day's growing sunlight. "I won't," he answered, and with that enigmatic answer, he let his horse go and rushed away toward the column's head.

As the Seventh moved up the Rosebud, Winslow watched the broken country unroll before him. The Rosebud lay at the bottom of a shallow canyon, and the column followed the edge of the water, but sometimes rose to the top of the bluff. The entire area was a powder-gray, fine-grained land with grass and sage tufting it, scorched by summer's heat and scarred by harsh winters.

The column camped short of twilight, still on the Rosebud, and fires began to gleam along the earth. Winslow sent the Crow and Ree scouts away, and when Custer summoned the officers, Lieutenant Smith said to Winslow, "Sergeant, I want you to go with me."

Custer stood beside a large fire, his giant adjutant standing close.

"Gentlemen," Custer said, speaking in a suppressed manner, "I have complete faith in this regiment. I call on you now to give me the best you have in you."

He looked tired, a rare thing for this man. His bony face tipped down, his thin long lips half hidden behind his mustache, his face in a shadowed repose. All of the officers, Winslow saw, were studying the general carefully, not understanding his mood.

"We can expect to meet a thousand warriors or more. We came here to find Indians, and we shall find them—if I have to march this regiment down to Nebraska or back to the Agencies. I have too much pride in the Seventh to go back empty-handed, and I know you feel the same way. General Terry offered me Brisbin's battalion of cavalry, but I refused it. I want nothing to break the present knit spirit of our command." Then his face took on a flash of his old spirit as he said, "I am confident that the Seventh can handle whatever it faces. That is all I have to say tonight. Thank you, gentlemen."

As the group dissolved, Winslow overheard Lieutenant Wallace say to Lieutenant Godfrey, "You know, I think Custer is going to be killed."

"Why do you think that?"

"I've never seen him so depressed. There's a shadow over him."

When Winslow got back to where A Company was bedded down, he gave an account of what Custer had said. Hines looked at him, puzzled. "Did the general say he'd march us to Nebraska? I thought Terry had restricted us to a fifteen-day march."

Leo Dempsey grunted, "You know Custer. He'll do what he pleases now that we're cut off from Terry."

They ate their bacon and lay around the fire speaking of the action to come. The talk finally turned to religion, and Dempsey said truculently, "I ain't worried about gettin' killed. There ain't nothin' out there after a man dies."

"No heaven, no hell?" Hines demanded. "That's what you're hoping for, Dempsey? Not me!"

Dempsey glared at Hines, his chin stuck out pugnaciously. He was a man who had given rein to his appetites, and even now with death just over the way was not ready to give up. "You believe all that stuff about the streets of gold, Hines? I thought you was a smarter man than that!" He grinned at Winslow. "Tell Hines about it, Sarge. You ain't one of them Bible-thumpers, are you?"

Winslow was poking a stick into the fire, watching it burn slowly, and he looked toward Dempsey with a sober expression. "I went through all four years of the Civil War, Leo," he said, his voice soft. "And in every battle, I was afraid. Not of getting killed, but of what comes after that."

"Aw, Sarge, that's just preacher talk! They get paid for talking like that!"

Tom Winslow leaned back, his eyes thoughtful. "My grandfather didn't get paid. He was a tough fellow, a mountain man. Could have been just about anything, I guess, but he spent his life in a little Indian mission, not too far from here. He married an Indian girl, my grandmother."

"I didn't know that, Tom!" Hines said with surprise. "These may be some of your kinfolks we'll be shootin' at pretty soon."

"Maybe so," Winslow said. He was silent for a time, and finally said, "I guess I've seen too many real Christians to be a skeptic. Lots of phony ones, but that's true of any group. Plenty of phonies and cowards in the Confederate Army, but I stuck with it."

"You really worried about getting killed when we go against the Sioux?" Dempsey said. He admired Winslow, and his confidence seemed to ebb away. "Well, I done some bad things, I guess. Maybe I done enough good ones so I'll balance out."

"My grandfather always said a man would lose if he tried to make heaven like that," Winslow said. He was thinking of the giant old man who so filled his memory.

"Well, how else is a man to get in?" Dempsey complained.

"He said we were all in such bad shape that nothing we could do would get us in. And that's why Jesus Christ was his only hope. When he died, his last words were, 'The blood of Jesus— it's good enough for me!' "

Zeiss nodded. "That is good, Tom. I'm a Christian myself. I want to live for my wife and child, but if I die, I know I will be with God."

Dempsey ducked his head, saying no more, and the talk died

down. The fire settled with a sibilant hissing sound, and Winslow rolled into his blanket. The conversation had sobered him, and he realized how vulnerable he was. Sleep would not come, and as he listened to sounds of the camp, he thought of his grandfather and of his parents—and of Faith and her steadfast spirit.

Just about everybody I admire is a Christian. The thought touched his mind, and he grew restless. He had prayed when he pursued the Indians who had abducted Laurie and Faith, and now the urge to pray came again. But always he thought of Spence Grayson, and he knew enough of the Bible to understand that as long as he harbored bitterness and hatred, he could not call on God. Finally sleep came, but it was a tattered sleep that brought no relief.

CHAPTER TWENTY-FOUR

VALLEY OF DEATH

★ ★ ★ ★

At dusk on the twenty-fourth Custer led the regiment into a freshly deserted Indian camp. The tracks of lodgepole travois scratched the ground everywhere, skeleton frames of wickiups and a sun-dance lodge indicated where a camp had been. One of the officers entered the lodge and discovered a white man's scalp hanging from a pole. "It must have been one of Gibbon's troopers killed on the Yellowstone last month," Lieutenant Cooke said.

The location of Gibbon's regiment was welcome news to Custer, but disturbing to Herendeen, who wanted more specific orders. "This is where I'm supposed to go find Gibbon, General."

He waited for Custer's order to take a message back to Gibbon, but Custer only glanced at him without giving him a direct command. That made Herendeen angry and he wheeled away. It was a dangerous ride, one which he would be paid for, but he'd just as soon not risk his life unless Custer ordered it.

That night they made camp as a dry hard wind rolled the desert's smoke-fine dust over them. Benteen, his face stiff with dislike, sought out Custer to discuss their plan of attack. He stared at Custer's flag, which bore the two stars of a major general stitched on the pennant's field. Custer had been that once, but now he had no right to use the title, in Benteen's opinion.

"I propose to make a quick jump at them, to cut them off before they can run," Custer said.

"Are you sure they're running, General?" Benteen asked dryly. "They know where we are. I think they may be picking their own spot to attack us."

Custer shook his head, dismissing the idea. At that moment the pushing wind caught at the standard, knocking it over. Godfrey picked it up and stuck it in the ground, but it fell again. When he left, Benteen muttered, "That was a bad sign."

The next morning, the twenty-fifth, a heavy pall hung over the camp as the men awoke and began preparations for the day. The work details were carried out with bitter, disgruntled cursing. The day's unknown seeped into their bones. Whose scalp would hang in the Indian tepee tonight? Winslow himself couldn't escape the intruding omens that fought to invade his mind. Winslow boiled his coffee, fried his eggs, and put his hardtack in the bacon grease to soften it. Lieutenant Smith soon joined him and began discussing the portents of the day.

They stopped abruptly as Grayson walked by. Spence gave Winslow a cold look, then asked Smith, "Any orders come down yet?"

"Not yet. But it'll be today. I'd bet on it."

"No takers." Grayson shook his head and walked away.

In a short while the regiment mounted and moved forward. Just then Winslow saw Custer approach with Girard. Charlie Reynolds motioned to Winslow, who spurred his horse and galloped in their direction.

As Tom joined them, he heard Charlie say, "You're going to have a big fight, General." Charlie Reynolds was an extremely quiet, soft-spoken man. Now he was trying to convince Custer of the danger ahead.

"What makes you think so, Charlie?" asked Custer.

"On my medicine," Reynolds nodded. "That, and I've seen enough track and dust to be certain." He pointed west. "There are more Indians over there, General, than you ever saw in one place before—"

"Look there," Winslow broke in. He had spotted something, and when they all turned, they saw a party of Indians riding hard toward the Rosebud. The sight of them caused Custer to make a crucial decision. He had been grappling with the fear that he had ridden with the regiment all the way from Fort Lincoln for nothing—that the village would break up and flee in all directions. He had to prevent that!

"We will break the command into three wings. Reno, you take M, A, and G companies. Benteen, take your company and D and K. I will take C, E, F, I, and L. Benteen, take your command to the left. Make a reconnaissance to a high point, then rejoin the rest of the command at Ash Creek."

Benteen shook his head, saying, "Hadn't we better keep the regiment together, General? If this is as big a camp as the scouts say, we'll need every man we have."

"You have your orders!" Custer replied briefly.

Benteen moved away, and the rest of the regiment took up the march down Ash Creek—Custer and his two battalions on the right side, Reno with his one on the left. A Company was at the head of Reno's column. Winslow kept close to that company, with several of his Ree scouts, including Bloody Knife. Their job was to ascertain any danger signs. As they rode, the pitch of the hills steepened, and dust thickened. A strange foreboding filled Winslow, one he'd often had during the war, and his eyes swept the horizon constantly.

Suddenly Girard, who was up on the ridge, shouted, "Injuns! Runnin' down the valley like devils!"

Custer immediately cried, "Forward!" and started down the creek, with his two columns following. Reno kept pace on the other side of the creek, stopping when Cooke left Custer's band and rode across with an order.

"The Indians are across the Little Bighorn, about two miles ahead of us. The general directs that you charge them at once. He will support you with the other battalion."

As Cooke wheeled and returned to rejoin Custer, Reno gave the command to advance, and the Seventh headed for the Bighorn at once. They urged their horses across the creek and emerged into a broad valley, with a tall bluff on the right, crowned by round-topped peaks. On the left the valley was held in by a low slope.

The companies had lost their formation, and Reno yelled, "Form up! Form up!" They obeyed and moved into some sort of order; then the battalion charged toward the village some three miles away, riding at a faster pace than some of the men had ever done before.

Winslow had sent the scouts to the rear, but he himself rode beside Lieutenant Smith. The column broke like a fan, four slanting out into a broad troop front. The two advance companies formed a spaced skirmish line sweeping at a gallop down the valley, A to the left and M to the right, with G Company a second line in the rear.

"There come some braves out of the village, Lieutenant," Winslow called to Smith, who nodded. They did not appear anxious to close in, but they raised a great cloud of dust.

"Look!" Smith yelled. "There's Custer on the bluff!" Winslow turned and saw a lone horseman but could not be sure it was Custer. They skirted the timber, spotting a dust storm ahead of them about two hundred yards away, and in the dust were shadows of Sioux warriors wheeling and making for the left of their line.

Reno threw up his arm and shouted, "Prepare to fight on foot!"

"That's wrong!" Smith yelled, but had no choice but to obey. Troopers dropped from their saddles and in groups of threes flung their reins to a fourth trooper who wheeled and ran back with the mounts. One trooper lost control of his horse, which dragged him directly into the Indians, where he was killed instantly.

The soldiers knelt and fired as rapidly as they could at the Indians. Reno walked calmly forward, drew his revolver, took careful aim, and fired. He downed the Indian, but the Sioux shots hit the troopers like a steady rain. Down the line from Winslow a man screamed in agony, then fell on his face. The firing grew more fierce, and one of the men ran up to Reno, asking, "Can't we send back to Custer for support? We can't stand this much longer!"

"Too late," Winslow shouted, pointing toward his left. "They've cut us off!"

Winslow hurried down the line with Hines, calming the raw recruits. "Take your time—pick your targets!"

The line sagged, taking heavy losses, and finally Reno yelled, "Drop back to the timber!"

The retreat was a disaster, for men were out of their units. Some of the greener men broke rank and ran, halting only when the voices of the sergeants and officers caught them. Pace by pace the line gave way and presently got to the edge of the brush and timber and stepped inside it.

But Winslow knew they were practically helpless. "The Sioux will chop us up one at a time in here," he said to Hines.

"You're right—ahhh!"

Winslow whirled. A bullet had struck Hines in the temple, and he fell without a tremor, dead before he hit the ground. Dempsey, nearby, cried, "We gotta get him out of here, Sarge!"

"No! We can't help him now, Leo. We're in deep trouble ourselves."

The two scurried back and heard Moylan say to McIntosh, "We can't stay here, Tosh. We'll be out of ammunition in fifteen minutes."

"I'll tell Reno!"

Now that Hines was dead, Winslow knew he had to fill in. "Move back!" he called loudly. "The Sioux have fired the grass!" He moved down the line, then stopped when he came to where Dr. Porter was kneeling over Charlie Reynolds. "Doctor, we're falling back. You need a hand with Charlie?"

"No, never mind." He rose and as they moved back, Winslow saw the black interpreter Dorman dead with a ring of cartridges around him.

They came upon Reno, who was standing by his horse, confused, bewildered, and indecisive. At that moment Bloody Knife jumped on his pony, saying, "Better go!"

Reno stared at him, then got on his own horse. At that instant a Sioux bullet struck Bloody Knife in the head, showering blood on Reno. Frightened, the officer clawed at his face and lost control of his senses. He shouted, "Forward!" and set his horse at a gallop toward the river, leaving the men in disarray.

"We can't abandon the wounded!" Moylan yelled after him, but Reno never slowed. And his panic was contagious. The soldiers left their wounded and ran, which meant certain death for the stricken men. Reno made no attempt to conduct a retreat. In an orderly withdrawal, soldiers shoot as they move and keep the enemy busy. If they run, the enemy can pick them off like animals in a hunt.

Winslow had no choice, for staying was impossible. He retrieved and mounted his horse, using his revolver close range. To his left he saw Zeiss locked in an Indian's grasp, trying to drag him down. Winslow wheeled and blew a hole in the Sioux's flank, and Zeiss and Winslow raced on. Ahead of them Lieutenant McIntosh threw up his hands and fell to the ground beneath the hoofs of the oncoming Indians.

Reno's battalion was a mere skeleton by now as he swung toward the river, to a point where the banks ran sheerly up and down. Grayson, to the left, yelled, "Here's a ford!" and the battalion turned toward it. Carbine fire began to fell the troopers as they crossed. One bullet struck Winslow's horse in the head, and Tom hit the water, holding on to his revolver. He struggled to his feet and was rescued by Babe O'Hara, who wheeled as he saw Tom go down. "Jump on, Tom!" he yelled, and Winslow leaped up behind Babe and grasped the man as they zigzagged across.

Tom saw Lieutenant Benny Hodgson go down, then come to his feet and stagger forward. Hodgson made it to the shore where a second bullet dropped him. O'Hara guided his horse out of the water and scrambled up the slope to the safety of the crest. Some troopers crawled, others dropped like limp bundles. Halfway up the slope Dr. DeWolf died from a bullet in his spine.

O'Hara and Winslow fell off the winded horse at the top of the rise and began to strafe the Indians with ammunition as the Sioux were slaughtering the slower troopers. In the midst of the battle Reno stood hatless, with a dazed expression, watching the men come up. He kept saying over and over, "Keep firing, men!"

The pressure grew worse, with fire coming at them from oblique angles. Winslow ducked, threw a shell into the chamber of his carbine, then rose up and got his shot off as quickly as possible. They were hitting the Indians but were still taking losses. "Keep down, Zeiss!" he shouted. "Pick your target carefully."

Even as he shouted, he glanced to the right of the field below. A flash of movement caught his eye, and he saw an officer trying to crawl up the slope, moving painfully along on his hands and knees. Two of the Sioux had broken across the river on their ponies and were headed straight for him. Winslow slapped his carbine to his cheek and knocked one of them down with his first shot. He threw a shell into the chamber, but the Indian had slipped off his horse, almost on top of the officer. Winslow had no time to take a long sight, but fired off one shot that drove the sand into the face of the Sioux, then with the next one caught him in the throat. Even as the Indian fell to the ground, Winslow saw three other warriors heading for the river.

Then he looked at the wounded man again. His face turned toward Tom. *Spence Grayson!*

Time seemed to halt for Winslow. The Indians still charged across the shallow water, though in Winslow's mind, they moved very slowly, as if they were under water. One of the braves had a bloody scalp dangling about his neck—but to Tom at the moment it was, somehow, strangely impersonal.

The firing and the yells seemed muted, far away, instead of all around him as he stared at the scene. He had felt like this once before, when he'd been struck in the stomach and unable to breathe or move for an instant.

Grayson's face was ashen, tendons of his throat stretched to bands, and blind panic in his eyes. Bright crimson blood was splashed on the front of his tunic and on his right leg. With agonizing strain, he scrambled along the ground for safety.

As Winslow watched, images from the past flashed rapidly through his mind, sharp and clear: Grayson's rescue of Tom when he was being mauled to death by two men. Spence's young, bright, innocent eyes as he grinned, crying, "Hold them, Tom! They can't whip both of us!" Again, memories of their fun, carefree days, the close friendship. Then the image of Marlene's face as she had lain dying in the hospital, abandoned by Spence. But now the rage didn't rise and flood Tom as before. For the first time since his friend's betrayal, he could remember without hate. It was there, but not possessing him. As the images rose in his mind he saw his future as bitter, empty, and meaningless if he continued to hate. He thought of Laurie—and of Faith.

Suddenly he heard the guns cracking and he shouted, "A Company—cover me!"

"Sarge!" O'Hara yelled. "Don't go out there—!"

But Winslow had dropped his rifle and gone over the crest of the hill, half falling as he threw himself down the slope.

"Hey—cover Winslow!" O'Hara bellowed, and every gun down the line began blazing away at the Indians who were now charging in greater numbers across the river.

When Winslow was almost down to where the wounded officer was crawling, he saw the man look up—startled as he recognized Tom. His lips formed Winslow's name, and at that instant a Sioux emerged from the right and lunged at Winslow with a lance. There was no time to pull his revolver, but Tom managed to parry the lance with his left arm. The Sioux screamed at him, dropped the lance, and leaped forward with a knife. It happened so fast that Winslow felt the edge cut through his upper arm like a streak of fire. He kicked with all his might, catching the Indian in the groin; and when the Sioux fell back, Tom pulled his revolver and shot him through the body twice. Another Indian rose up ten feet away, his rifle up, but Winslow got off the first shot, hitting the Sioux's mouth, driving his head backward.

Trusting that his friends would keep the other Indians at bay, Winslow shoved the revolver into the holster and moved to where Grayson lay watching him. "Come on," Winslow gasped, his throat dry. He picked him up and pulled him across his shoulders. Grayson gasped, but said nothing, and Winslow lunged back up the slope.

As he struggled upward, he heard O'Hara and Dempsey yelling, and when he looked up, he saw them charging down the hill, firing as they ran. They got to him, and O'Hara gave him a hand. While Dempsey covered them, the two climbed the slope, falling on the ground exhausted as they reached the top.

Totally spent, Winslow lay on his back gasping for air. When he was able to breath, he rolled over and saw that Dr. Porter was working on Grayson. The firing was slackening off, and he got to his feet and looked over the rim in time to see the Indians withdraw.

"That was a real noble thing you did," O'Hara said. "Next time you want to be a hero, give me a little warning, will you? I'll try to be someplace else."

Winslow grinned, reached over and struck his shoulder with his fist. "Thanks, Babe—and you, too, Leo," he said. He turned and saw Grayson regarding him steadily, but the rescued man said nothing.

Just then Moylan and Major Reno came by. Reno nodded to Winslow. "That was a fine thing, Sergeant. I'll see it's written up."

Moylan looked at the river. "They'll be back," he said soberly.

Benteen rode up and jumped out of the saddle, asking, "Where's Custer?"

"I don't know!" Reno snapped. "He was supposed to support me and—"

"He's over there with his men, I think," Moylan broke in, peering into the distance. "They're in a real battle, I'd say. Do you think we'd better go help him?"

"We're in big trouble ourselves, Moylan," Reno said, clearly nettled. "Look around at what we have left. And the first thing in the morning, the hostiles will be coming at us with all they've got!"

Thirty minutes later, Lieutenant Weir asked permission to give Custer aid. Reno agreed, and Edgerly went along with his company in support. But Weir had gone only five hundred yards when he was savagely attacked and had to fight a retreat back to the crest.

"Now you see what it's like!" Reno taunted him.

The Indians kept slashing at them, raising the number of fallen men discouragingly high. The officers brought them back behind the lines and cared for the wounded as best they could. Benteen paced back and forth, dodging the bullets that whistled close to him. There was no letup while the light lasted, but at eight o'clock the shadows fell.

Winslow was exhausted, but he knew better than to rest. He moved down the line, forcing the men to dig in, and finally began digging a trench for himself. Dr. Porter came along, took a look at him, and said, "Let me see that wound."

"Just a nick," Winslow shrugged. In the heat of the action, he'd forgotten that he'd been slashed by a knife. He pulled off his shirt, and Porter bound the arm. "How's Grayson, Doctor?" he asked.

"He'll be all right, I think. Flesh wound in the leg, and the one in the body bounced off a rib. He said to tell you to come and see him." The doctor looked out over the dark parapet of the crest. "It's going to be a near thing, Sergeant. Lucky if any of us get out alive."

"Yes. Keep your head down, Doctor."

When Porter left, Winslow finished his trench, then went to the area where the wounded lay. The night was dark, and he didn't see Grayson at first; then he heard him say, "Over here, Winslow."

Stumbling over some loose rock, Winslow moved toward the sound and found Grayson with his back against a small sapling.

"Why'd you do it?" Grayson asked.

Winslow's legs were weak, and he sat down. "You want some water?" he asked, ignoring the question.

"Had some. There isn't much." Grayson's voice was thin and reedy. "Porter said I'd make it, but we're not out of this thing yet. I may die—or you may."

"They'll be here early, I guess."

"Where's Custer?"

"I think he's dead. I think those who were with him are all dead."

Grayson was silent for a while, then said, "Tell me why you came for me."

Winslow was so tired he could hardly speak. He looked at the man who had done him so much wrong, and was astounded to realize that none of the hate was left. He had lived with it so long, he felt incomplete in a way.

"I can't tell you, Spence," he replied. "But I know I can never hate a man who was with me today in this fight." He thought about it but could find no logical explanation for his change of heart. Finally he shrugged. "I guess I came for you because I couldn't stand the thought of carrying that load of hate I've had for another thirty or forty years."

Neither one said anything for a long time. Finally Grayson broke the silence. "I can't understand it, Tom."

"Well, I can't either, Spence." He got to his feet painfully.

"Good luck in the morning," Grayson said.

"We'll make it, both of us," Winslow replied, then returned to the battle line. He dropped down, expecting to fall asleep at once, but his body ached with fatigue, his mind was dazed and confused, and sleep eluded him. For twenty minutes he lay there thinking of the strangeness of it all—especially his behavior toward Spence Grayson.

All the hate was gone, he knew, and he marveled. He couldn't see how risking his life for Grayson could purge him of the bitterness that had controlled his life for ten years. He closed his eyes, and as he did, a thought came to him so unexpectedly and so powerfully that he could not sleep. *I've been afraid to call on God because I knew it was useless. But the hate for Spence is gone— there's nothing to prevent me from calling on God now.*

The idea surprised him, in a way. He thought of his past and his future—both grim and bleak. It wasn't enough for him to be free of his hatred of Grayson, he realized. *I've got to have something to tie to!*

For a long time he lay there wondering how to come to God. Finally a sense of desperation swept over him, and he whispered, "Oh, God, I need you! There's nothing I can do to wipe out all the bad years—nothing I can do to make myself better. So I'm doing what my mother asked me to do . . . and what Faith asked me to do. I'm asking you to forgive my sins . . . and to save me from the man I am . . . and I ask it in the name of Jesus!"

When he said this, he slumped down and his muscles relaxed. He kept repeating: "In the name of Jesus . . . in the name of Jesus." Then he fell fast asleep. There was no great explosion of feeling such as he'd observed in others at camp meetings.

For Tom Winslow, coming to God was like a child, exhausted and worn out, falling into the loving arms of a strong parent. And even as he dropped off he thought with surprise, *Why, this is what I've been longing for all my life!*

CHAPTER TWENTY-FIVE

AN END—AND A BEGINNING

★ ★ ★ ★

On the third day of July, the *Far West* blew its whistle for the landing at Fort Abraham Lincoln and, with its jack staff black-draped and its flag at half-mast, touched shore. A runner went out immediately with the news; and in the middle of the night, officers reluctantly walked toward Officers' Row to notify the wives of the dead. The wounded were carried to the post infirmary.

Two days earlier Faith Jamison had come in from the mission to buy supplies, but the Owens had persuaded her to stay over for a performance by a group of Shakespearian actors. Laurie had asked Faith to take her, and the two had enjoyed the play. It was nearly ten by the time they returned to Eileen's, and Faith was invited to stay for the night.

Laurie went to bed at once. Fifteen minutes later the blast of the steamer's whistle cut through the air. "That's not the ferry," Eileen commented. "I wonder if it's new troops coming in." Eileen and Faith were drinking hot tea in the kitchen as they discussed Laurie's progress with her books. Ten minutes later they heard the sound of activity, of horses moving down Officers' Row, and they hurried out to the porch. Through the dim light Eileen recognized the form of Major Bradford, who was in charge of the fort during Custer's absence.

"Major, what's happening?" she called out.

Bradford guided his horse closer and said in a muted voice, "It's the *Far West* bringing in the wounded."

The women stood with bated breath, hardly daring to speak. Faith finally broached the fearful question. "There's been a battle, Major?"

"I'm afraid so," Bradford replied, tempering his fidgety horse. "It's not good news, either. The Seventh took a terrible defeat." His voice carried the grief he felt. "I must go to Mrs. Custer."

"Is the general wounded?" Eileen asked in a tight voice.

"He's dead . . . and so are half his command!"

"No!" Eileen cried in horror, and rushed inside, her face in her hands.

Bradford said to Faith, "She's thinking of the time her husband was killed." Then he touched his hat and lifted the reins. "I must carry the news to Mrs. Custer."

As Major Bradford moved down the line of houses, Faith hurried in to Eileen.

"Oh, Faith!" she cried as she paced the floor. "They're all killed! Oh, my God—" She began to sway, and Faith caught her and helped her to the couch, where she slumped down and began to sob.

Faith held her, unable to find the right words to say. Finally when the sobs lessened, she asked, "Are you all right, Eileen?"

"All right! How can anybody be all right in this place?" Her eyes were stark with hopelessness. "I can't go through it again, Faith!"

Faith knew she was thinking of Winslow. "I'll go to the infirmary. Tom may be there."

"No, he's dead! I know he is!"

"You don't know," Faith said. "I'll be back shortly." She rose and headed for the hospital. Dr. Long was directing his orderlies as they prepared to receive the wounded. Long was a Christian who had often come to the mission to treat the Indians for various ailments. When he saw Faith he said, "What a terrible thing!"

"Have you heard any details, Doctor?"

"Just that the regiment was decimated—nearly four hundred

killed, including the general. Many wounded, of course."

"I'd like to help if I could."

"We will need all the nursing help we can get, Faith," Long said, his face showing the compassion he felt. "Let me show you where things are." He gave her a quick tour of the facility, and soon the first ambulance arrived. The orderlies carried the men in and laid them on the beds, and Dr. Long went to work.

Faith helped the orderlies get the bandages and drugs to the doctor. Dr. Porter arrived with the second group. Soon the two doctors were doing surgery that could not be attempted on the field. Time passed swiftly as they worked. The infirmary was receiving more patients than it could hold, so the less serious cases were taken to one of the barracks, temporarily utilized as a hospital.

As Faith passed down the line of bunks with fresh water for the men, she heard her name called. She turned to see Spence Grayson watching her from a lower bunk. "Spence! I didn't know you were here," she said, noting the bandages on his chest and leg. She filled the glass on the table beside him and sat down while he gulped the water down. "Tastes good," he said in a thin, raspy voice. "I don't think I'll ever take a drink of water for granted again."

"Are you badly hurt?"

"No. I was lucky." He was unshaved and gaunt, his eyes sunk back in his head. But he seemed alert, and when she put her hand on his forehead, there was no sign of fever.

"I've prayed for you," Faith said simply.

He gave her a sober glance, then nodded slowly. "I can believe that. I said I was lucky, but it was more than that, Faith."

"Do you feel like talking?"

"Sure," he said, dragging himself to a sitting position. "I'm sick of lying flat on my back." She helped him get comfortable. Then he continued. "It was bad, Faith. All those men dead!"

"How could it happen?"

He related some of the events, and although she didn't understand the technical aspects of the battle, she quickly grasped the source of the defeat and said, "Custer didn't obey his orders, to wait for General Gibbon?"

"That's right. And that was a mistake—a big one." He sipped

the water, then paused, his brow wrinkling. "He divided the regiment into three parts, and that was another mistake."

"If you'd waited for Gibbon and if Custer hadn't split the group, would it have been different?"

"No. I don't think so. There were just too many Indians."

Faith sat there, saddened by the catastrophe. Finally she asked, "Where were you when you were wounded, Spence?"

"I was with Reno. When we got swarmed by the Sioux and had to retreat. It was a rout! Lots of men were shot in that action. There was a hill to our right, and we crossed the river and started up the slope. I got hit in the side. The slug knocked me off my horse, and when I got up to try to run, I caught another one in my leg. I began to crawl as fast as I could."

"How awful!"

"It was pretty bad," Grayson admitted, reliving the moment. "Men were dropping all around me, and when I looked back and saw a lot of the Sioux coming across the river, I gave up."

"It must have been frightening!"

Grayson brushed his forehead with a shaky hand. "All my life I've heard that when a man comes to die, his whole life flashes before him." He pursed his lips. "Always believed that was just an old wives' tale. But I got a taste of it." His eyes were sober. "There I was, bleeding my life out with a crew of battle-crazed Sioux coming to finish me off—and I thought about the sorry mess I'd made of my life!"

From down the room a scream rent the air, cutting across the hum of conversation; and both of them glanced involuntarily to where Dr. Porter was bending over a young trooper with one leg gone at the knee. Porter called out sharply to an orderly, "Help me hold him down, Johnson!" The patient thrashed out in his delirium. Faith turned away, her eyes filled with pity.

Grayson looked at her, then went on speaking. "You might like to know, Faith, that I thought about God." His gaunt face was broken into sharp planes from the ordeal. "Haven't done that in years, but I did then."

"What did you think, Spence?"

"Why, I wanted to call out to Him for help, but I've always despised men who lived like the devil all their lives, then when they came to die, tried to make it up to God."

"I don't think that's quite right," Faith said thoughtfully. "People seek God out of desperation. Some of us get desperate enough in the ordinary times. Sometimes people become hard and shut God out. But if at the time of death a person finally knows that he needs God, I think God wants to listen to him, to help him."

Spence stared at her. "I'm glad you think that, Faith. I hope you always do." He hesitated, then said, "One more thing. Like I said, I'd given up. The Sioux were right on top of me, and the closest help was far off, way up on top of that hill. And I knew it would be close to suicide for any of the men to leave that spot and come to help me. But one did."

"How wonderful, Spence!"

He gave her a wry look. "Miraculous, I'd say—because it was Tom Winslow." He grinned at her expression, adding, "Yes, I know, Faith—you're shocked. Well, you can imagine how I felt! I looked up and there, coming right at the Sioux, was Winslow—the one man who hated me more than anybody ever had! He picked me up, put me on his shoulders, and started up the hill. A couple of his men came to help, and then what was left of the Company strafed the Sioux with a steady stream of fire so they wouldn't get us."

Grayson paused, his eyes looking troubled as he recalled the rescue. Finally he said, "He dumped me down on the ground when we got to the top, and the doctor took over. The Indians didn't give up, so Winslow and the survivors fought them off all that day until the next morning."

"Did you talk to Tom?"

"Yes." He shifted in the bed, moving his body carefully to avoid the pain. "I can't figure it out, Faith. We've hated each other for years. I'd have let him die in the dirt and laughed at him. I believed he'd do the same for me. Can't figure it out, not at all."

His eyes grew heavy, she saw. "You're tired, Spence. Try to sleep. I'll come back in the morning."

She helped him lie down, pulled a blanket up, then put her hand on his cheek. "Thank God you're safe."

He smiled. "I guess it was God," he said in a voice slurred with sleep. "God . . . and Winslow."

310

She left the barracks and went back to the house. Eileen was sitting at the table and seemed much calmer. "Come have some tea. I want to hear all about it, Faith," she said. Eileen listened carefully; then when Faith told her the strange circumstances surrounding Grayson's rescue, she exclaimed, "That's unbelievable! Is Tom back yet?"

"No. Spence said General Terry sent him off with the Ree scouts to keep track of the Sioux. Only the wounded returned on the *Far West*. The rest of the Seventh is on the way back now."

Eileen got up from the table, walked over to the window and peered outside. "It's almost dawn," she said tonelessly, then turned back to Faith. "I'm sorry I behaved so badly, Faith—but it was so much like when they came to tell me that Frank had been killed. That was at night, too. I was in my nightgown, ready to go to bed when Captain Moylan came and knocked on my door." Her lips grew thin, and a haunted look came into her eyes. "As soon as I heard the knock, I knew he was dead!"

Faith wanted to go to her, to comfort her, but somehow she knew that would not help. She said, "I'm sorry, Eileen. And I know that no matter what people say, or how sorry they are—none of us can know what that is like."

Surprise touched Eileen's eyes and she nodded. "I think that's true, Faith. People have their own little place inside for grief, and somehow nobody can get in there." She crossed the room and sat down again. "And some people can handle things like this better than others. They have an inner toughness that most of us don't. You have it, Faith," she added quietly.

"I . . . don't think it's being tough, Eileen," Faith responded. "I'm no stronger than anyone else. But I've discovered that there's a way to let God carry my burdens. I know it sounds like a religious platitude, but it's true. I've had the props knocked out from under me and wanted to just quit." She smiled, her lips soft and gentle. "Well, in a way, I *did* quit. That's what faith is, I think. You have to give up on what *you* can do and believe that *God* will do it for you."

"You mean—just do *nothing*?" Eileen asked, a bit perplexed.

"Yes. I used to take care of my niece quite a bit. When she was learning to walk, she became very independent. We'd go walking and she'd pull her little hand away from mine, wanting to do it all herself. Then she'd fall flat—and the first thing she'd do was to reach up for my hand and begin crying for me." Faith was thoughtful, and she added, "I think that's how I learned to know God, Eileen. I'd been in church all my life. And I was very self-sufficient. I guess I had a self-made sort of Christianity. But when I fell flat, I saw there was no way I could go on—so I had to learn to lean on God."

Eileen shook her head doubtfully. "I don't understand that, Faith. It sounds too easy."

"It's not easy. It's very hard," Faith replied. "The hardest thing in the world, I think, is to take your hands off your own life and let God do anything He wants with you."

They talked for a long time while Faith tried to share what it was to completely trust in Jesus. Finally Eileen said, "I'm glad for you, Faith, but I don't think I could ever live like that." She looked out the window as a clear, thin bugle call sounded. "I've lived by that bugle. It called my husband to his death!"

"Men who aren't in the army die, Eileen."

She shook her head. "It's not the same, Faith." With a sigh she rose and said, "I'll go help at the hospital. We can get Delores to take care of Laurie."

They left Laurie in the care of Sergeant Maxwell's wife and went to the infirmary. The doctors were glad to see them, and for the next few days, they spent much of their time nursing the men. Some of them were very young and needed much encouragement, which Faith and Eileen were able to give, often sitting at their bedside or writing letters for them.

On Friday afternoon, Major Bradford stopped to speak with Faith. "You and Mrs. Jennings have done a fine job with these men, Miss Jamison. I appreciate it, and the men are very grateful."

"It was little enough, Major."

"No," he replied, "it was not little," and added, "A courier from General Reno came this morning with a report that the rest of the regiment will be returning soon. "

"There'll be no more fighting?"

"Not now, anyway. It was the worst defeat the Army of the United States has ever suffered in the Indian wars. There's no force to fight with now." He bit his lip nervously. "We'll go after them again, of course." With a sigh he turned and left, speaking to the patients along the way.

Faith felt it was time to return to the mission, so she said goodbye to Eileen and Laurie and the men at the hospital, stopping to bid farewell to Grayson last. By now he was well enough to sit in a chair with his leg propped up.

When she told him she was leaving, he said, "Wish you didn't have to go back out there, Faith. It's dangerous."

Faith smiled. "Living is dangerous, Spence. You've discovered that. Come and see me when you're able."

He stared at her, but knew her offer was purely an invitation from a friend. "Well, I will!" he responded lightly. "Maybe I'll even let you pray for me to get converted."

"I haven't waited for permission," she said.

He watched her leave and said softly to himself, "She's a fine woman!"

★ ★ ★ ★

The attitude of the Indians had changed, Faith soon realized when she arrived at the mission. The news of the defeat of Custer and the destruction of the Seventh Cavalry had sent shock waves through the white world, but it had done something to the Sioux as well. None of them mentioned the battle to Faith, but she perceived their pride. They had been lied to and stripped of their lands so often by the white man that it was inevitable they should feel so.

Faith said nothing to them about the battle, but went about her work as before. For a week she kept to herself, not going to town even once. On Wednesday Nick Owens came out with supplies. When he left, he said, "The regiment came back this morning—what was left of them, anyway." He gave her a curious look, then asked, "You ever feel like giving up on this work, Faith?"

She perceived he was testing her in some way. "I'll give up when God gives up, Nick."

Owens grinned. "Yeah," he nodded. "Well, I'll see you Sunday."

Faith watched him go, wondering why she hadn't asked him about Winslow. She'd wanted to but hoped the merchant would bring up the subject. Irritated, she pushed the thought out of her mind—or tried to.

Saturday she worked hard all day and then sat down to a cold supper. In the evening she worked for two hours on her vocabulary list in the Sioux language. She was still struggling with the grammar and trying to make the spitting noises that were woven into the system. "Talk as if you've got your mouth full of mush," Winslow had advised her once. As she recalled his words, she wondered if she would see him and Laurie soon.

She grew so engrossed in her study that at the sound of a hard knock on the door, she leaped to her feet, a thread of fear cutting off her breath. She hadn't heard a horse approach and rushed to get the loaded pistol Owens had insisted she keep. "Just show it—or fire into the air. Sometimes that's all it takes," he'd said.

Holding the weapon awkwardly, she carefully opened the door a crack and stepped back, saying, "Who is it?"

Winslow poked his head around the door and grinned. "Don't shoot, lady. I'm not dangerous."

"Tom!" Faith cried, shocked at the emotion she felt as she looked at him. She had not known until that moment how much she'd missed him. To cover her feelings, she put an angry look on her face. "You're going to get shot if you don't call out when you ride up in the middle of the night."

Winslow was lean as a wolf, she saw as she replaced the revolver. His eyes, black against his tanned face, looked worn and tired. Fatigue and strain had taken its toll.

He was looking at her so intently she said nervously, "I've got coffee, Tom."

He shook his head. "I didn't ride all the way out here to drink coffee." He was smiling at her, and added, "I've missed you, Faith."

"When did you get in?"

"Just yesterday."

"It was a terrible thing, wasn't it?"

"War always is."

"Why did you risk your life to save Spence?" she blurted out. "He told me about it."

He shifted his weight. "Well, it's a long story. Maybe I will have that coffee." He sat down, not taking his eyes off her as she poured the coffee and took the chair across from him.

He recounted the battle and eventually the part where he'd seen Spence about to get killed. "When I saw him about to die, I guess I was glad. But then something happened." His voice was soft. "I finally saw what you've seen all the time, Faith— that for a man to spend his life hating someone is really sad." He took a few sips of coffee, then went on. "Going to help him wasn't a logical thing, though. I didn't even stop to think about it. Just went after him, and some of the boys helped me get him to the top of the hill."

"It was a wonderful thing you did, Tom," she said. "It would have been even if you'd liked the man—but to do it for someone you've hated, that's greater!"

He squirmed uneasily, and she knew he didn't like talking about it, but she could not help asking, "Did you go see him when you got back?"

"Yes. It was a peculiar thing, Faith," he said with amazement in his voice. "It was as if he was another man, somehow." He smiled then, the smile softening his expression. "Poor Grayson! He had a hard time when I stopped by. Tried to thank me, and I guess it was the hardest thing he ever did! But he did something I never thought Spence Grayson would do. He asked me to forgive him for what he'd done to me and my wife years ago."

"And what did you do, Tom?"

He shrugged. "I told him to forget it as far as I was concerned." He looked at her, adding, "Funny, it was at the center of my life for ten years—and now it's gone."

"I'm so glad, Tom!"

They talked so long that Faith got up to get some water to quench their thirst, and found the water pail empty. "I'll get some fresh water."

He followed her out to the well. "Let me do that," he offered and drew a bucket of fresh water. Looking at it, he said, "We needed this on the hill. Never was so thirsty in my life."

It was a clear night, the sky starry and the moon full. As silence fell, an awkwardness settled upon them.

Suddenly Winslow said, "I'm not taking the commission I came for, Faith."

"I thought it might be like that," she replied intuitively. She hesitated for a moment, weighing her next words, then said, "Eileen would never be happy married to an army officer."

"No, she wouldn't," Winslow agreed. He lifted his head, listening to the faint cry of a coyote. "That's why she's not going to marry one."

Faith felt a quick stab of loss, but kept her voice even. "I suppose you two have plans, then?"

Winslow shrugged. "Her plans are to marry Larry Dutton."

Faith thought she had misunderstood him. "What did you say, Tom?"

Winslow laughed, easily and without strain. "Larry came to me almost before I got out of the saddle. He's a small fellow, but I could see he was ready for trouble. He took me off to one side and said, 'Tom, you're my friend, but you probably won't be in two minutes.' He went on to tell me that I wasn't going to ruin Eileen's life, that he loved her and would marry her if he had to kidnap her!"

"Tom! He didn't say that!"

"Sure did, and when I went to Eileen, she said pretty much the same thing." He mused over the memory, then said, "Oh, she didn't even mention Larry. Just said that she could never marry me, that she wasn't cut out to be an officer's wife. Said, too, that I was just marrying her to get a baby-sitter for Laurie."

"I can't believe she said that," Faith murmured.

"Well, she was right, pretty much," Winslow said slowly. "Eileen's a fine woman, but she deserves a whole man, not just part of one."

Faith tried to grasp what he was saying. Finally she asked, "Was it really that way with you, Tom?"

"I haven't been a whole man for a long time, Faith. I would have brought Eileen very little love—and a lot of bitterness." He paused. "Faith," he said, "I found out something on that hill and—"

He stopped, then told her how he had called on God. "It's been different, Faith. I was like a stream all polluted and muddy. Now everything seems clear. I'm at peace for the first time in years."

"I'm so happy for you, Tom!" Tears had welled up in her

eyes, and she dashed them away. Then his comment about the commission popped into her mind, and she asked, "Did you say you weren't going to stay in the army?"

He nodded slowly. "It was the only thing I could think of to bring some kind of order into my life. I needed it for Laurie. But things are different now." Sadness edged his voice. "The Indians have had a hard time, Faith, but they're in for a worse one. The whole country is angry, and General Miles has been named to command. He's a hard man, and he'll hit the Indians with a huge force. I don't want any part of it. I've already talked to General Terry, and he gave me a discharge."

"But what will you do, Tom?"

Suddenly he grasped her arms firmly and said, "I have a plan."

His touch made her tremble and she cried, "Tom, let go of me!"

His grip tightened. "I can't do that, Faith," he murmured. "I'll *never* let go of you!"

"Tom—!" His lips muffled her words as he kissed her. She struggled, but he put his arms around her, pulling her against him. A turbulent eddy enveloped them as she yielded to his embrace. She had longed for love, but had kept that ache locked away. Now the pressure of his lips and the insistence of his kiss brought her needs to the surface. His embrace was demanding and strong, but there was a sweetness in her that returned his kiss willingly.

He finally released her, lifted her hand and kissed it, saying in wonder, "I'd forgotten what it was like—loving someone like this!"

"Tom—we've got to think—" Faith stammered. "We don't even know—"

"I know I love you," he broke in. "The short time I've known you, I've watched you, seen your strength, your love for God and people. I want to know Him like that." He paused, stroked her cheek lovingly, smiled, and said, "Maybe I'll be a missionary like you, and like my grandfather. You can be sure I don't want just a baby-sitter for Laurie!"

Faith looked up at him, her eyes bright. "I'm not sure—"

"You only have to be sure of one thing," he said. "The rest will be all right."

"What must I be sure of?" she whispered.

He reached out, kissed her lightly, then said quietly, "That you love me."

Faith stood there, loving the touch of his hand.

"Yes, Tom!" she said softly. "I'm very sure of that!"

She was happy, and with a sigh, snuggled into his chest as his arms closed around her. They stood there, holding each other, each taking and receiving. Then she lifted her lips to his again and said, "I thought we had lost each other." And she knew it would always be this way between them—this strength, this closeness . . . yet never enough of it.